DEMON WEATHER

DA SILVA TALES - #1

CHICO KIDD

Dragon Moon Press

Edited by Katie Flanagan

Print ISBN: 978-1-988256-53-5
Ebook ISBN: 978-1-988256-54-2

Library of Congress Control Number: 2012905188

www.dragonmoonpress.com

Dedication

As always, for my father
Kenneth Charles Kidd 1921-1994

Acknowledgments

A big thank you to the good folks at Booktrope who made this finally happen.
To all the Captain's fans- I hope it's been worth the wait!
And to Rosemary Pardoe for all her encouragement and support.

"The souls that shall be gathered are seven in number, because seven is a miraculous number. Seven has contained within it one, symbol of unity, and six, symbol of perfection. Seven is the number of life, containing the body's four elements, spirit, flesh, bone and humor; and the soul's three elements, passion, desire and reason.

"The soul of a venturer shall be gathered by the demon Mastiphal and stored in an amulet of agate. And the guardian of that soul shall be the armored one.

"The soul of a scholar shall be gathered by the demon Bifrons and stored in an amulet of chrysophase. And the guardian of that soul shall be the executioner.

"The soul of a lover shall be gathered by the demon Bitru and stored in an amulet of beryl. And the guardian of that soul shall be the castrator.

"The soul of an artist shall be gathered by the demon Belphegor and stored in an amulet of jasper. And the guardian of that soul shall be the destroyer.

"The soul of a child shall be gathered by the demon Gaziel and stored in an amulet of malachite. And the guardians of that soul shall be the corruptor.

"The soul of a hunter shall be gathered by the demon Malphas and stored in an amulet of jacinth. And the guardian of that soul shall be the night-hag.

"The soul of a warrior shall be gathered by the demon Alastor and stored in an amulet of sapphire. And the guardian of that soul shall be the terror that comes by night."

From the Book of Estêvão Gonçalves

Não se vence perigo sem perigo.
"Danger can't be overcome without danger."
--Portuguese saying

Quem tem cu tem medo.
"Anyone who has an asshole can be afraid."
--Portuguese saying

Prologue: House of the Four Winds

REVENGE IS A DISH BEST EATEN COLD.

"I still think you should just kill him," said Teresa Graça Batista, removing her mask and pushing damp hair from her forehead.

Her father, whom she had just comprehensively outfought, copied her example. "No, little one, my way is better. We've discussed it a thousand times."

Teresa scowled at being called *little one*, since she was nearly his height and scorned the epée in favor of the saber, which most women could not handle. She replaced her sword in the rack and followed him out of the salle. "How can you be sure this piece of...medieval magic will work?"

"It will work," replied her father patiently, recapping an argument they had gone through many times. "I have called all the seven demons successfully now. I have bound souls into amulets and released them, with no harm. Vicente's manuscript has proved its worth before, and I trust it on this."

"But you know you can't trust the *demons*," Teresa pointed out.

He laughed. "Teresa, every sorcerer who ever lived knew he couldn't trust demons. That's what *spells* are for."

She stared morosely out of the window. "I hate Lisbon. I wish we were home in Rio."

The leather-bound manuscript currently residing in Batista's study, which was part of the reason which had brought him to Lisbon, was written on vellum. Once, it had been the whitest, smoothest surface a pen could write upon. But now, some four hundred years later and worn by time as well as its two transatlantic voyages, the westward one in a caravel, it had aged to brown and its edges were fraying.

Hoping to preserve it, Batista had initially smoothed it between sheets of glass to use it. But whole sections of it had flaked away and were lost. Luckily, the passage which interested him was still intact.

Centuries ago, before it went to Brazil and was lost to European cataloguers, it had been known as the *Book of Souls*. Now many scholars dismissed it as legendary. Indeed, most discredited it altogether, with its fanciful recipes for making the perfect man.

Francisco Domingues Batista, late of the city of Rio de Janeiro, examined the manuscript once again, thinking: When Paracelsus and the alchemists of old manufactured homunculi out of their own bodily secretions; when the English *mandinguiero* Roger Bacon made his brazen speaking head and the Qabbalists activated their golems by a spell on a piece of paper; when St Thomas destroyed the automaton Albertus Magnus had made; and Victor Frankenstein stitched together a man from bodies of the dead; each of those manufactured men, every *androides*, was imperfect because it had no soul.

Which was why he intended building himself a construct of souls at the instruction of his forefather's book. Because when he collected all the souls he needed for *his* perfect man, he needed no artificial body, however formed. For they would combine and enter his own body.

Making him not only perfect, but invincible.

Because Batista had scores to settle.

1

EMILIA DA SILVA SAT PERFECTLY STILL BY A WINDOW THAT SHOWED A BRIGHT SCRAP OF LISBON behind her head, and felt guilty. She was here in this room with a man who was not her husband, and he was painting her.

What made it worse, perversely, was that it was all perfectly innocent. The artist who was capturing her on canvas was well over seventy, and he was her father-in-law.

Whom she had met for the first time less than a month ago, although Emilia had been married to his son for nineteen years.

They never spoke about what had estranged father and son, but the old man genuinely seemed to enjoy her company. And that of eight-year-old Caterina, who was crouched on the floor like a kitten, creating her own masterpiece with wax crayons on a piece of scrap paper, her tiny pink tongue protruding with either concentration or artistic inspiration. On their second meeting, he had asked Emilia diffidently if he could paint her portrait. Her eyes flickered to him, briefly. His eyes were the same incongruous blue as his son's.

She could not identify what had prompted her to contact her father-in-law after having lived in the city for four years, since her relationship with her own father had been ambivalent to say the least, but as an incurable optimist she hoped that everything would work out in the end.

Trying not to move her torso at all, she surreptitiously eased her right leg, crippled since childhood by infantile paralysis, into a more comfortable position, and sighed silently. *Isabella*, her husband's ship, was due in port the following morning.

And Emilia, for the first time since they had met, had no idea what she would say to him.

* * *

I know all the ghosts that loiter where *Isabella* has her berth by now. Know them intimately. Four and a half years of coming back to anything breeds familiarity. Meu Deus, is it really that long, I thought, appalled. Four and a half years since a demon took out my left eye and left me with the ability to see the dead. That's not something I consider a fair exchange, by the way. Seeing ghosts is far more trouble than it's worth. But you learn to live with it, just like you learn to cope with missing an eye. Or, I imagine, an arm, or a leg. Put that way I suppose I'm lucky, really. No essential bits missing. Hang on to that thought, da Silva.

The ghosts I see are simply shades, echoes of an existence. They drift around where they met their deaths, fading over the years. Shadows of men, women, children, phantoms of ships— every sailor knows that ships have spirits. Voiceless things, aimless, harmless, more like nickelodeon images than anything else. The only criterion seems to be that their deaths were untimely. Which means that there are a hell of a lot of them in Lisbon.

Some are very faint indeed, for if the stories are true the city was founded by Ulysses himself. And since then, of course, the place has been overrun by any invaders you care to mention, from Romans to Visigoths to Moors. And that's before we even mention the great earthquake. Sixty thousand dead, some say. The Convento do Carmo, open to the sky to this day, is almost too full of ghosts to bear. All those nuns, praying their socks off when the roof fell on them. Which doesn't say a great deal for the power of prayer, if you ask me.

They're no trouble at all, those ghosts. It's when you have to start summoning the real thing from the grave that life starts to get... interesting. And that's why I say that seeing them is, frankly, a pain in the backside. I do *not* like calling them up. Nor do I like being a necromancer, for that's what you are if you speak to the dead. It's too much like slavery for my taste. Because when you summon a ghost, you bind it. It has to do what you tell it. It has to answer your questions— those it can, that is. And I spent too many years having to do one man's bidding to like imposing my will on anyone else. Alive or dead.

But that's what I have to do, sometimes. Having been given a talent, I feel obliged to use it. Obliged, note, not bound—obliged, melodramatic though it sounds, to fight evil. And that's a thought too far for a sober man.

This morning, however, there was another phantom standing on the quayside, bareheaded in the bright sunlight. It made a halo out of his white hair. And if he wasn't, strictly speaking, a ghost, he still came out of a past I thought dead a long time ago. I should know by now, the past never dies. As soon as you start thinking like that, it rears up and bites you in the ankle.

It was my father. There was no mistaking him, even though I hadn't seen him for thirty years. Last century. When steamships were a rare and wondrous sight. My mind emptied of coherent thought. I couldn't even manage a curse. I simply stared at him for at least a minute without moving. Da Silva, struck dumb. Would you credit it. And then the moment turned, and volition came back, and with it the power of speech.

"Take over here, Mr Ashley," I said sharply to my first mate, and strode off without waiting for a reply. Though I could feel his shock as he stared after me. He is an Englishman, and rather a stickler for politeness. Or, if you care to put it another way, a stiff-necked *filho da puta*. But I normally try not to ruffle his feathers.

My father stared at me. I was fourteen years old when we saw each other last. He's seventy-six now. Thin, almost frail. Stooped, and walking with a cane. White-haired. Beard, neatly trimmed. Thick spectacles magnifying his eyes. He looked me up and down, taking me in. A man taller than he is, now. Graying, too. Clean-shaven. (If I let my beard grow now I'd look like a badger. Besides, they itch.) A patch over my left eye, not completely covering the three-inch scar running from eyebrow to cheekbone.

The differences are fewer than the similarities.

"Luís," he said. Not a question. He knows me as surely as I know him. Must be some kind of instinct, to recognize your kin no matter how many years have passed. His voice, though, was wary, almost tentative.

What could I say? It's been a long time? Too much between us to be that shallow. An abyss, and one not only made of time. "Papaí." I took a deep breath—unwise, that: being summer, the harbor was more than a bit ripe—a step forward, and put my arms round him. He returned the embrace stiffly, and drew back.

"You grew up."

"Grew up, got old," I said lightly. He snorted, not in amusement.

"I'm old," he said. "All *you've* lost is an eye."

Well, that's a point of view. I found my hand on its way to rub the scar, and went instead for the pocket where I keep the small black cheroots I like to smoke. Took one out, and lit it. Always find something to do with your hands when you're ill-at-ease. My palms were sweating, which irritated me. I wiped them on my pants.

Couldn't think of any indirect way to ask the question running round my brain. So I just said, bluntly, "What are you doing here?"

"You broke your mother's heart when you left, boy," he said.

"She never had a heart to break," I retorted.

He frowned. "That's rather harsh." I didn't reply. I wasn't going to take that back. Not being fourteen years old any more. "She's dead, Luís."

Silently, I stared at the screeching seagulls, wheeling and squabbling over detritus in the water, rubbish on the land. Watched the floating ghosts, things of air and mist. Drew in smoke. Felt nothing. Not even a distant emotion. All too long ago: I could barely remember what she looked like. "When?" I asked finally.

"February," he replied. He put his hands in his pockets and stared downriver. The sunlight broke on the water like gold shattering into straw, the fairy-tale in reverse. *O Mar da Palha,* they call it, the Sea of Straw. Almost made you forget the stink of the harbor. "It was her heart." So she must have had one, after all, I thought. There's a surprise. She never showed it.

Again, I had nothing to say. I'm sorry for your loss? Not such a hypocrite. "Do you miss her?" I asked instead. The sun was hot on the back of my neck. I felt moisture starting to gather under my arms.

My father shrugged. "To be honest, not really. She was fairly heavily involved with the church, the last few years."

The last *few* years? "She was a religious nut thirty years ago," I pointed out, rubbing my cheekbone. Had him squandering his talent, wasting his life, on altarpieces and the like. Who in the world needs another picture of São António or John the Baptist or the Virgin, blackened by candle-smoke? And I spent *years* on my knees, thanks to her. At least, it felt like it. I took another mouthful of smoke, surprised to find that I was still resentful at the memory. As I hadn't even *thought* about my mother for months.

"Would you like to come aboard?" I asked, gesturing towards my beautiful barque *Isabella.* Yes, I'm proud of my ship. I suppose I wanted to show her off. Grow up, da Silva.

"You've forgotten, then," he said, a little sadly, patting his middle. "*Mareado.*" The sea was calm as a bowl on a table. But if it disagrees with you, it disagrees with you. And I *had* forgotten. How could I have a father who gets seasick?

"Sorry," I said, for some strange reason regretting it quite strongly. Odd thing, guilt. If that was what it was. I looked at him, feeling a mixture of emotions I couldn't untangle, let alone identify. When I left home he would have been two years older than I am now. Too complicated, I thought. I took refuge in smoking and watching the ghosts.

"Met your wife," my father remarked, unexpectedly. I lifted my eyebrows.

"Emilia?" I said stupidly. He shot me an odd look.

"Testing the water," he said. Was that a flash of humor? "How'd you get a pretty little thing like that to marry you?"

Killed the man who was going to rape her. What would he say, if I came out with that? Or how about another unpalatable truth: most men aren't interested in cripples. Think they're damaged goods. I smiled crookedly.

"Just lucky," was what I came up with, suddenly wanting very much to be with her, and changed the subject. "Would you like to meet your grandson?" Who would, like his father, have run away to sea, if I hadn't taken him as a 'prentice on my own ship. Who was now, I realized, the same age as I had been, the last time this man had seen me.

His face brightened. "José? Very much."

I turned *Isabella*-wards and yelled to the nearest crewman. It was Ortigão, the fellow they all call Don Giovanni, though personally I can't imagine what women see in him. There was a suspicious number of sailors loitering near the rail trying to look busy. I wondered if they knew, too, who it was I was talking to. If it was plain for everyone to see.

"Yes, *senhor capitão?*" he shouted back.

"Ask Zé to step ashore, will you?" I switched to English, the lingua franca of the *Isabella*. "And the rest of you, if you haven't got anything better to do I'm sure Mr Ashley can find you something! Now bugger off!"

My father was hiding a smile. I wondered what he was thinking. I learned English from him, partly. But mainly from his mother, my grandmother, who was born in London. That's where the blue eyes came from. Though as a child I had resented those, being teased for being different. Until I gave the bullies black eyes (and broken teeth to boot). I flung the butt of my cheroot into the water to join all the other rubbish floating there. It fell through the drifting ghost of a drowned woman.

"I'm painting her portrait," he said.

"What?"

"Your wife. I'm painting her portrait."

Zé's arrival saved me having to comment on this startling bit of information. He is nearly my height now, having shot up in the past six months. Not that I'm particularly tall, but Emilia's only just over five feet. He was looking a little annoyed, which made me smile. He's not like me to look at, but meu Deus, he's got the da Silva temperament.

"It's my *watch* in two minutes," he informed me.

"Five," I said. "Zé, this is your grandfather. Sebastião Fernandes da Silva."

His mouth dropped open. Boy was as speechless as I was. But he recovered more quickly than I had, and said with great politeness, "How do you do, sir?"

Stepping forward, my father embraced him with more warmth than he had me. Not surprising really. I didn't blame him. He looked at me over Zé's shoulder before releasing him and said, "Good thing the boy favors his mother." Which made me laugh. Though I don't think he meant only in looks. Then he ruffled Zé's hair, which made me peculiarly jealous, and said, "Do you like being a sailor, then, José?"

"Yes, sir," said Zé, smiling tentatively, but looking at me.

"You like these old sailing ships, then?" said my father.

"She's not *old*," Zé protested. "She's…she's *Isabella.*"

From the ship, eight bells sounded, and he grinned in relief. Saved by the bell, as the English say. I raised an eyebrow at him, hiding a smile. If I'd had two eyes I would have winked.

"Better run along and sail her, then," my father said indulgently, and Zé dashed off. *Então*, I thought, that'll be all over *Isabella* in five minutes now. If they hadn't already guessed, that is.

I lit another cheroot and said, "How is Emilia?" He blinked. Good. I could still wrong-foot him, then.

"She's very well. And your little girl." He put his hands back in his pockets. "How did you wind up marrying an *italiana*, then?"

You want the story of my life, do you? I said silently. You won't get it. "I worked for a Venetian ship-owner for nineteen years," I said, giving him the short version. The expurgated version. The version that didn't say, he saw me kill his brother, so he could get me to do just about anything. "Met Emilia there, got married. He left a pile of debts, and we bought *Isabella* off his creditors for next to nothing."

In my mind, very clear, the Venetian's dead face, mouth moving with words he couldn't say. His eyes sliding from yellow to brown as the demon that had animated him, possessed him, withdrew. His blood trickling slowly from his throat when I sliced into it, freeing me from my bondage. My own blood streaming down my face. And the memory of pain. I closed my eye for a second, drew in a deep breath. Let it out. Opened my eye to find my father looking curiously at me. Oh, nice work, da Silva.

"What is it?" he asked, sounding concerned.

"Getting old," I replied, inhaling smoke. I rubbed the scar on my cheekbone, and he stared at my hand.

"You do that a lot," he observed. "Is it painful?"

Not in the sense you mean. "No," I said, staring at phantoms. "Not any more."

"How did it happen? The eye?" I shook my head. Only one person knows what happened that rainy winter night in the Venetian's palazzo, and that's Emilia. And that's the way it stays. No arguments. Half of Venice thinks I murdered him anyway, despite the total lack of evidence. Of a body, to be precise. Which the demon destroyed, not me.

"A fight," I said, which is the only explanation I ever offer, when pressed. "What are you really doing here?"

He wouldn't let it go. "A *fight?*" he repeated.

"Old history," I said dismissively. "You should've seen the other fellow." Get it through your thick head, old man, I'm *not* going to tell you about it!

His shoulders sagged. "You're not an easy man to talk to."

Give me a chance, I thought, raising an eyebrow. I've only just met you for the first time in thirty years. It tends to limit the conversation. Aloud, I said, "You never used to talk to me very much anyway."

"No, I suppose not," he agreed. "Your mother made conversation difficult."

I took a final drag from my cheroot, contemplated it, and threw it after the first one. "That's the first time you've ever admitted that."

"Probably," he said, and looked down at his shoes, embarrassed. They were slightly scuffed, though his suit was neat—admit it, he's a lot better-groomed than you are, I thought. Dapper, that was the word. I tend to look a bit like a pirate at the best of times, and not only due to the eye-patch. I ran a hand through my hair. It needed cutting. Only I thought of Emilia's fingers in it, and decided not to bother right away. Unwise speculation, here on the quayside talking to your father. Get your mind due north, da Silva.

"Are you all right?" I asked, putting a hand on his arm. He looked up again, gave me a genuine smile. And answered the question I'd asked earlier, the one I thought I wasn't going to get a reply to.

"I suppose I came because I'd like to get to know you," said my father.

* * *

Another old man, in another city. Francisco Domingues Batista. Twenty years ago. An old man— or so I thought at the age of twenty-four— in a towering rage. Blocking my path. Wanting to beat me, by his expression, into a pulp.

Only the fact that we were in a church was preventing him. That, and the priest glowering at him, waiting to celebrate Mass. The Mass for the dead.

"How you have the nerve to come here—!" he snarled.

"Your brother was my employer's agent," I pointed out. "I was doing business with him."

"I hold you responsible for his death, da Silva. Don't think I won't forget this." His face was white with anger. I had never seen that particular phenomenon before. Although I once knew an English captain who used to go an interesting sort of puce color.

"I had nothing to do with it," I said. "Dona Elvira's brother killed him." Which he had. Shot him in the balls and the head and then put a bullet through his own brain. Because he had a mistress. Ironic, really.

He put his mouth next to my ear and hissed, "You put horns on him."

That, unfortunately, was true.

We all do stupid things at that age. Having an affair with this angry man's sister-in-law was one of the more idiotic things I've done in my time. Not that thinking with your groin is ever smart.

At twenty-four you also think you are immortal, so I brushed past him and went to find myself a seat.

Quia peccavi nimis cogitatione, verbo, et opere. As they say on occasions like these. See, I can quote scripture as well as anyone. Not that I'm ever going to use that particular bit of Latin in front of a priest, having sinned in thoughts, words and deeds most of my life.

* * *

Four hours ago I hadn't a care in the world. I'd sighted the Torre de Belém and known I was home. Strange how that little white knobbly tower makes your heart lift. Or maybe not so strange. Every Portuguese seafarer since Vasco da Gama has felt that, I suppose. It's a symbol of *saudade*, nostalgia, yearning— the spirit of fado. We've voyaged past it for centuries. Setting out for India, Brazil, Angola, Moçambique, the Indies, the world.

And now I suddenly have a father again. Whether that's a good or a bad thing remains to be seen. Although the simple fact that he's painting a *portrait* had to be a good sign. No more bloody simpering saints that nobody ever looks at. Not that I'm implying people don't go into churches. Plenty of people still do, much good it does them. But who notices the artwork? Unless a painting's by Tintoretto or someone, and even then the only people who come to see it are well-heeled philistines on their Grand Tour. And they cross it off in their Baedecker and move on to the next one. Cynical, da Silva? *Não me diga.*

"Will you walk a little way?" he said diffidently. I nodded. Lit up and fell into step on his left. Felt eyes boring into me from *Isabella*. I ignored them, as I ignored the shades teeming around me. Some places, it's like walking through a fog. A mist of ghosts.

The sun was warm on my back, but not uncomfortably hot. That was something to be thankful for, at least. Wearing an eye-patch in hot weather is having a little humid area of Purgatory all to yourself. And it can get pretty hot in Lisbon. Today, though, there was a breeze off the sea to temper it, and sweat was threatening rather than running.

"Where are you living?" I asked my father.

"Same old place," he said. "What are you seeing?"

That stopped me in my tracks. I stared at him, expelling a lungful of smoke abruptly. *"Desculpe?"*

He looked at me, rather too shrewdly, and said tartly, "I may not have seen you for thirty years, boy, but you've got my blood. I know you. You're seeing something I can't. Do you think I don't remember the story of Tiresias?"

The blind seer. Not the first time that sort of thing's been suggested. But I don't feel particularly oracular. "I can't see the future," I said, taking a drag on my cheroot. "If I could, I'd have known *you* were going to show up."

My father gave a short bark of laughter, but I hadn't deflected him. Yes, I'm his offspring, right enough. "So what is it, then?"

I shot him an irritated glance, and kicked at a seagull that had ventured unwisely close. It flapped up into the air, squawking crossly. Messy creatures. Shit-hawks, my third mate, Harris, calls them. An American with a nice turn of phrase. He is also, as it happens, a werewolf. But that's another story.

"Ghosts," I said. "I see ghosts." And started walking again. He kept pace. Didn't seem surprised to learn his son was seeing phantoms. I gave my scar a scratch. Stopped when I caught him watching me.

"There'll be a good reason for that, I imagine," he observed dispassionately. "Does your wife know?"

"I've no secrets from Emilia," I said, knowing it wasn't quite true. But I hadn't ever thought she'd even want to know the details of who I might have slept with before she married me.

The old man had antennae like a bloody great fly, however. He raised a sardonic eyebrow at me like my aged mirror-image, and I thought, is that how I'll look in thirty years? But he made no comment. I dropped the butt of my cheroot, and stepped on it.

Abruptly, he said, "I shouldn't take up any more of your time. If it's all right with you, I'll get on with Emilia's portrait tomorrow." I nodded, a little bemused, and he walked away.

Ghosts surged round me. I've never been quite sure whether these faint memories of the living have anything resembling consciousness. Sometimes one will do something that seems to imply intelligence. But it may be just a reflex. Like severed heads. Which should be avoided for some minutes after decapitation. They bite.

But something seemed to've agitated the shades this morning. They were like a crowd an elephant has charged through. Milling, regrouping, startled out of normality. And yes, I've seen a crowd after an elephant has done that. It does more damage to flesh and blood than its — psychic equivalent could to something so insubstantial.

Now why did I come up with that image, I asked myself. My back prickled, and I looked around. Come on, nothing's going to happen in broad daylight. But I stayed wary. I've learnt not to ignore feelings like that. Wish I'd brought the knife that usually travels with me, concealed down my back. It's fourteen inches long and contains enough silver to do serious damage to anything uncanny. On the other hand, fourteen inches of razor-sharp steel without any silver content would see off just about anything short of a knight in armor. And you don't see too many of those, these days.

However, when I'm on board ship it usually lives in my cabin. And even if I'd been capable of thought when I saw my father, I hardly think he posed that much of a threat.

I don't, personally, know any of the quayside shades. One of my crew was killed by a kind of vampire-ghost in Lisbon four years ago, but he actually met his death up by the castle of São Jorge. Yet I know how they usually appear.

Something's definitely put the wind up them. I know I'll find out what soon enough. Depend on it, da Silva.

* * *

About nineteen miles away, a retired sea-captain by the name of Henriques Verdinho was smoking a thoughtful cigarette, recovering from an argument with his wife Paciência. As usual, he had lost. He often thought her parents had been tempting fate by naming her that, for she had never given him any indication of having any patience at all. Her voice had the power and projection of a Galli-Curci, more suited to the operatic stage than the placid home of an ex-sailor. She was also, he knew, rumored to be a witch, though he had no idea how she had acquired that reputation. That it was because it was true had never occurred to him.

Verdinho, an unusually tall man who looked a little bit like a stork, put his cigarette carefully on the rim of a marble ashtray and sipped at his tea pensively. His bald scalp gave the impression that it was breaking through his thin salt-and-pepper hair in the manner of a mountain peak clearing the clouds surrounding it. He was deeply fond of his wife, but oh dear, she could be vexing.

Never an enthusiastic ship's master, but always a lucky one, he had retired from the sea on his marriage. He was now seventy-three, having fallen for Paciência twenty years before, and the father of nineteen-year-old Luzia. And she was the reason for the fight. The age-old reason of a child romantically involved with someone wildly unsuitable.

Now he sat in his sloping garden above Sintra, looking out towards the sea. Tall aloe spikes, like giant stalks of upturned hairbrushes, silhouetted architecturally against the sky. Acanthus leaves, huge, glossy, and convoluted enough to send William Morris into ecstasy lined the pavement, their own flower-spikes no slouch in the sculptural stakes, counterpointed by the jagged blood-red constructions of castor-oil plants. Light relief was provided by bushy mirabilis, blooms spattered as by an artist's brush with pink and white and yellow, by multi-colored paper-chains of bougainvillaea trailing everywhere in extravagant garlands, and swathes of morning-glory, its impossibly blue flowers like drops fallen from the sky.

He sat under the shade of a paper mulberry tree and contemplated the unsuitability, in every possible way, of young Pedro Ortigão for his daughter. Who, to be fair, like all parents, he still thought of as about nine years of age.

That was when he became aware of a curious disturbance out to sea. Or, to be more precise, above it. He narrowed his eyes—his sight was still good enough not to wear spectacles—and peered at it with curiosity.

Concentrated on one spot over the glinting steel-blue waves, the sky appeared to be *boiling*. It also seemed to be oddly viscous, as if the disturbance were somehow thicker than the surrounding air. Verdinho frowned and got to his feet, wanting to call for Paciência but reluctant to disturb her after their recent battle. In all his years at sea he had seen nothing like it.

And then the air burst open, and a knight in full armor mounted on a charger burst through with a roar like an immense engine. The noise was so overwhelming and so unnatural that it even overcame the patent impossibility of what he was seeing. He clapped his hands over his ears, dizzy and bewildered, but it did no good at all.

The knight galloped through the air towards Verdinho faster than anything he had ever seen and halted, steed snorting, above him. The old sailor staggered back, legs weak with a withering terror, and fell to his knees, shaking. His mouth opened and closed, but no words came out.

He could see, closest of all, the horse's hooves. Except that they weren't, precisely, hooves. At least, not any natural horse's: they looked razor-sharp. And they were cloven.

Verdinho, bowels clenching with dread, looked up. If the hooves were frightful, the horse's head was that of a nightmare. Its eyes were blazing red, and its lips were drawn back from teeth that no horse ever had. They were the fangs of a tiger, sharp as pikes, longer than his hand.

It snorted at him, and charnel breath bloomed from its nostrils. Nausea climbed up his throat. The roaring in his head continued. He tried to close his eyes, but found his trembling terrified gaze drawn higher, to the armored rider. Who was worse.

Who sat astride the nightmare, arrogant as a prince, beautiful as a woman, crueler than death. The nails on his long hands were talons, the red of clotted blood. His lips were the same color. His crowned helmet framed a face of frightening perfection, but the pupils of his eyes were black, and when he opened his crimson lips in a smile, his teeth were the same as his steed's. That smile was one to make the soul shrivel.

Leaning over in the saddle, he caught Verdinho's eyes with his own. The captain, all volition gone, staggered to his feet, and the rider seized his chin in an iron grip. Brought their mouths together, and sucked.

In his head, the vicious roaring seemed to burst his brain. Henriques Verdinho's last thought was the shameful realisation that he'd pissed himself.

* * *

I want to talk to Harris. Granted, he can't see ghosts. But he has a wolf's instincts, even in his human shape. And this close to the full moon, they get even stronger.

Won't find him in his cabin. I don't think he's very fond of confined spaces at the best of times. After a short search I found him by the charthouse, leaning on the rail and smoking a cigarette. Looking pretty dour, but that's his habitual expression. Never seen him smile. But then, turning into a wolf every month can't be a whole lot of fun. Mind you, at his age I'd already been married some years, but Harris doesn't stand much chance of that. Unless there's some amenable lady werewolf to be found somewhere. I joined him by the rail, and lit up too. The wind had freshened again and was blowing strongly, dispersing the harbor stink.

"Everything all right, skipper?" he asked, idly.

"I'm not sure," I replied.

Harris looked at me, startled. I gave him a lopsided grin. Da Silva admitting he's in need of help? Must be a first.

"What's happening?" He narrowed his eyes. "Ghosts playing up?"

"Something like that," I said. "Something's got 'em in a lather, anyway."

Above, I heard Zé call out, and someone replied; Benjamin, it sounded like. Their voices sounded distant, like something from another life. The Portuguese flag snapped in the freshening breeze. Still can't get used to it in red and green. Harris grew very still. He seemed, all of a sudden, to blend into the background. Like a wolf, I suppose. But how a man over six feet tall with a thatch of flaming red hair can suddenly become unnoticeable is beyond me. Time slowed. Smoking silently, I watched him.

Abruptly, he gave a growl, and shook himself. A palimpsest of something lupine overlaid his features for a second, and then he reverted to Harris once more. It was a reminder he was, after all, only passing for human. But I trust him. Somehow, part of his mind remains Harris when the rest of him is all wolf. I get the impression that's unusual in a werewolf. Not that I'm an expert, having only met the two. Although when one is trying to eat you and another one barges in and spoils its supper, I know which one I'm going to go with.

"There is something there," he said slowly, licking his lips as if something tasted bad. "Jesus, skipper— makes my skin crawl." He turned to face me, and his expression was bleaker than I've ever seen it.

"What is it?" I asked. But he shrugged.

"Hell, I dunno," he said. "Feels like— the way something dead smells. You know, when it's been dead for a while. Starting to rot."

Contemplating this unpleasant image, I drew in smoke, then exhaled slowly. "Near? Far?" He shook his head, frustrated.

"Can't tell. Might not even be there now. Just, it's left this stink-feeling behind. Like…I dunno, skipper…the way animals piss to mark their territory, seems to me. Can't explain it any clearer than that."

So the ghosts had felt something, in their pallid half-life. Something powerful enough to disturb things that are only a little bit more aware than a photograph.

The thought came back to bother me all afternoon. And the vague sense of unease never went away.

Ship's business took far longer than I liked. It always does. By the time I finally got away, all I wanted was a large brandy, a hot bath, and to go to bed with my wife. Well, to tell the truth I'd like those things every evening. But most of the time it's not exactly a practicable wish. Live with it, da Silva.

And when I did get home, it was obvious I wasn't going to get any of my wishes any time soon. Damn it.

For one thing, Emilia was still in her workshop. My wife works as a jeweler as well as handling the ship's business on shore, paperwork not being one of my strong points. Her father, who died five years ago, was a silversmith. Since he never remarried after Emilia's mother died, she became his 'prentice as well as his heir. She is more talented than he was, but they don't let women join the silversmiths' guild. Or any other guild, come to that. Their loss.

With Emilia I found Paciência Verdinho, who had been her friend ever since I brought her home to Lisbon. To my home, I should say. Emilia was born and raised in Venice. And I uprooted her as soon as I was able, fleeing that watery, decaying city, never wanting to see it ever again. But even that proved a futile wish.

Emilia's friend, who now lives in Sintra with her husband, is married to a man who was the captain of a vessel on which I was the third mate. Not the Venetian's. Before that. His name is Henriques. Known, inevitably, as The Navigator. But then I went off and got myself entrapped by the Venetian. Had to spend nineteen years with the old bastard. And incidentally, Paciência is a sorceress.

As I entered, their heads, both dark, one curly—I think Paciência's ancestors were likely Jews forced to convert—were bent over a tray of polished gemstones. The gas, not long lit, caught highlights off them, hair and jewels. Emilia looked up at me with a tired smile and put her finger to her lips. I was instantly captivated by the curve of her cheek. The swell of her lip. The hollow of her throat. Coming home.

Then Paciência raised her face too. Her eyes were puffed almost shut from tears. That was a shock. You don't think of witches as being that vulnerable. At least, I don't. Having met several, none of whom showed any sign at all of weakness.

"Meu Deus," I said involuntarily, "what's happened?"

"Henriques has had a catalepsy," Emilia explained. "He's in a coma."

"It's no catalepsy," Paciência said fiercely. "His soul's been stolen."

My heart thumped. So now it starts, I thought resignedly. "Who stole it?" I asked, patting pockets in search of a smoke. I was out of them, it seemed. Paciência stared at me, startled. She doesn't know about my odd abilities. She doesn't know how well-acquainted I am with the night. I've encountered creatures that *devour* souls, never mind steal them.

But she was too weary with grief to dissemble. "A demon," she said. And I sighed. Because I've met them, too. I scratched at the scar one had dealt me, absently, and went to stand behind Emilia's chair. Whether for her reassurance or mine, I'm not sure.

"Why?" I asked bluntly. "Who summoned it?" Since they don't come unless they're called. We can be thankful for that, at least. I placed my hands on my wife's shoulders. Felt the fine cotton of her blouse, the tension in her muscles. She leaned her head against my arm, then put her right hand over my left. Her palm was hot.

Paciência glanced at Emilia, then back to me. "What do you know about such things?" Her gaze was fierce. There was a challenge in her voice.

"More than I want to," I replied, raising an eyebrow.

"I don't understand," she said. "Emilia, what—?"

"Dona Paciência," I interrupted. She raised her eyes to me. I tapped my eye-patch. "A demon did this."

She crossed herself. There's no conflict of interest in witches being

Christians. At least nominally. Hell, I'm only nominally one myself. I certainly don't believe in ritual. Or prayer. Look where that got those poor bloody Carmelites when the earthquake collapsed their church in on them in mid-prayer.

"Virgin's bones," she breathed. Closed her eyes with a sigh, then opened them again. They glittered in the gaslight. "You can stand against them, capitão?"

I nodded, suddenly uncomfortable at her scrutiny. Emilia squeezed my hand. I looked down at the top of her head. Controlled an urge to bury my face in her hair. Time and a place for everything, da Silva. "Can Henriques's soul be recovered?"

If she thought I was taking liberties calling her husband by his Christian name, she didn't show it. "While his body lives," she replied bleakly. "But as to how—I don't know. I came to look for an amulet. I find—" her voice faltered "—I am afraid."

All the hairs on the base of my neck prickled. My hands tightened on Emilia's shoulders. "Have you found an amulet?"

"No," she whispered, staring down at the tray of gems. "No stone has enough power. No charm. My power is leaching away."

"That's just fear and grief talking," said my wife consolingly to her, leaning forward slightly. Though she didn't sound convinced. Paciência's words, on the other hand, had the certainty of augury. Ice trickled down my spine.

"All I can think of," the sorceress said, "is a line from a lost book. I don't even know what it means, or what it may be part of."

"What is it?" I asked. Even the gathering shadows in the room's corners, now, seemed to harbor portents. Emilia captured my other hand, crossing her arms over her breast.

"It says, *The first soul shall be that of a venturer, and it shall be gathered by the demon Mastiphal.*" I felt Emilia shiver. The *first* soul. How many more would there be?

"And the demon?"

"Mastiphal? A prince of hell. That's all I know of him."

"What is this book?" Emilia enquired.

"It was called *The Book of Souls*. It was last heard of in Lisbon in about 1500. Over four hundred years ago. I've seen it quoted, but I don't recall where." Her face, stripped by emotion, looked as it would look in twenty years, lined, all hollows and shadows. "I may not know why his soul was taken, but I know two things. The demon must have been bound by someone, otherwise it would have devoured it. And the soul must be stored somewhere."

Emilia released my hands and leaned her head back so it rested against my chest. It was a weary gesture. "Luís, would Father Pereira know about this book?" I stroked her hair. Wishing Paciência would leave. Not much chance of that any time soon, unfortunately.

"He might," I said thoughtfully.

"A priest?" said Paciência.

"An...unusual priest," I told her. Who knows, among other things, that holy water has more uses than you might think. And why I carry the kind of knife I do. I sighed inwardly. Domesticity will have to wait a bit longer, it seems. Outside, it was full dark now. But I didn't think Fr Pereira would refuse to see me at any time. Given what he has witnessed.

Paciência was looking down at the gemstones again. Idly stirring her hand in the box. After a while she picked one up, a banded oval stone that gleamed dully in the warm light. "Agate," she said thoughtfully, caressing it with her thumb. "Soothes the mind, so they say. And brings victory." But victory over whom, I wondered. Or what.

"I sold one like that a couple of weeks ago," said Emilia. "Take it, Paciência, if you like. If you think you can use it."

"Sold one?" the sorceress repeated. "For what?"

"Oh, you'd make a brooch out of it, I suppose," my wife said. "She bought seven stones, so I assumed she was a jeweler herself."

"Or a witch," I said before I could stop myself, dropping my hand to her shoulder again. Paciência's head snapped up, her eyes blazing. The air in the room suddenly seemed charged with her intensity. Whoa! I thought. Back off, da Silva. But it wasn't my foot-in-mouth that had roused her, apparently. Good. Getting on the wrong side of a sorceress is never a good idea.

"What were the other stones, Emilia?" she asked urgently.

"Oh—let me see." She stroked my fingers in an absent-minded kind of way. "A sapphire, that was the most expensive. Very dark blue, from Ceylon. Chrysophase. Black jasper. Green beryl, from Brazil, that was. Jacinth, a nice red. And Siberian malachite." We both looked at Paciência expectantly. But she shook her head, frowning.

"They could all make strong amulets," she said. "Individually. But I don't know why anyone would use that combination, particularly. They're not especially...complementary." Holding the stone, she pressed it to her brow and closed her eyes. After a moment she gave a weak smile. "I must go. Afonso will be thinking I've been kidnapped. Unless he's given me up and gone to get drunk in some bar. Did you know Henriques bought a motor-car?" Emilia shook her head. "Of course the thing is totally impracticable. It doesn't even *fit* in the streets up here."

I offered her my arm. "Let me walk you to it, Dona Paciência."

* * *

Father Carlos Pereira makes me feel tall. There aren't that many men who do. In Lisbon, anyway, I seem to be about the same height as nearly everyone I meet. Well, yes, that's what *average* means, da Silva. He would also make the *average* hippopotamus look quite slender. However, appearances are deceptive. As I well know. With me, people don't look past the eye-patch. And, I suppose, the scar. Which is not nice to look at, even partly covered. But if people take you for dangerous, they're also likely to take you for stupid. That can be a distinct advantage, sometimes.

Anyway, Fr Pereira's one of the most intelligent men I've ever met. And, by some freak of nature, he has a completely open mind, which for a priest is almost bizarre. Mind you, given what was happening when I first met him, he needed one. Either that, or ignore the evidence in front of him. The people with their throats ripped out, in that case.

I found him on his knees having a pray, oblivious to the world. Stood to one side, arms folded, to let him finish. Just because I don't believe in prayer doesn't mean it might not work for someone more devout. I wouldn't be surprised if Fr Pereira does talk directly to God. Me, I haven't even been to confession for twenty-four years.

Having finished his little chat with the Almighty, he crossed himself and got slowly to his feet, massaging the small of his back as he did so. Obviously he knew someone was there, because he turned immediately. And smiled. He always looks genuinely pleased to see me. And, of course, I have to believe he is. It'd be churlish not to.

"Well, look what the cat dragged in," he exclaimed, and shook my hand vigorously. I don't mind this at all. I think he's entitled. The second time I met him, I passed out in front of him and he had to douse me with holy water. You get injured by anything supernatural and it festers within minutes. Hurts like the devil, too. As if human flesh literally can't bear their touch. Holy water, however, at least the stuff that Fr Pereira has blessed, gets rid of the infection almost instantly. Unfortunately I didn't know this when the demon took out my eye. I was delirious for days.

"It's good to see you, too," I said, scratching my cheekbone.

"I suppose it's too much to hope that you've come to confession?" he suggested, mischievously.

I snorted. Stuck my hands in my pockets. "You know me better than that. Anyway, I don't suppose you've got a week to spare."

"If you ever feel you can, my son, I'll put aside a week specially for you," he said seriously. Making me suddenly uncomfortable. He sensed it, and patted my arm. "You know I'll never press you on that. What can I do for you, my gladiator?" This referring to my knife, which he insists in calling a *gladius* after the Roman short sword.

"I came to pick your brains, Father," I said, suddenly wondering whether any of my father's work hung in here. I pushed the irrelevant thought aside. Time enough for that later. "In your scholarly capacity."

His ears pricked up. "Ah?"

"Have you ever heard of a manuscript called *The Book of Souls?*"

Fr Pereira looked startled. I suppose any other priest would have blanched, crossed himself ostentatiously and staggered back in horror. "It's a grimoire," he said.

"Yes, I thought it might be," I remarked, raising an eyebrow. "Do you know anything else about it?" He looked closely at me.

"Yes, surprisingly," he replied, "since it's not been seen for half a millennium, and a lot of people think it never existed at all. Let me see now. It was supposedly written by a monk named Estêvão Gonçalves, which was almost certainly a pseudonym, around 1490. Yes, my child, what can I do for you?" This to a tall veiled woman, who shook her head slightly and knelt to pray. Fr Pereira watched her for a minute, a curious look on his face.

"What is it?" I asked quietly. He shook his head.

"Nothing...I don't recognize the lady, that's all. Come outside, Luís. It's too stuffy in here tonight." Which was true. The candles were radiating banks of heat like small furnaces. But it was pretty obvious what his real reason was. I agreed, of course. So I followed him down the nave. Our steps echoed hollowly.

Outside, the moonlight was very bright, painting everything uncompromisingly in black and white. The front of the church was covered in precarious-looking scaffolding. Builders' debris lay in an untidy heap, and a tarp had been carelessly draped over a small pile of bricks. Above, the moon's round face made me think, momentarily, of Harris. I took a deep breath, enjoying the air. You wouldn't call it fresh. Not if you spend most of your time at sea. But it's better than breathing incense and candle smoke and the memory of sweating congregations that seem to soak into the walls. I sat down on the wall and lit a cheroot. Why stand when you can take the weight off your feet? Getting old, that's what it is.

"Go on," I said to Fr Pereira. He put his hands behind his back, which made him look like a plump old crow. His beak of a nose reinforced the resemblance.

"Yes. The story goes that Gonçalves was excommunicated and all copies of the book ordered destroyed, but that one, or more than one, actually survived. There's a very strong tradition that one copy went to Brazil with a member of Cabral's crew. Though I don't suppose it survived very long in that climate, if that's the case." He frowned. "Why do you want to know about this?"

"You know me, Father," I said, taking a long breath of smoke and expelling it with enjoyment. "I'm just a superstitious sailor."

"Don't you be disingenuous with me," he said sternly, but he was smiling.

"Well, it's like this," I began, and told him about Henriques Verdinho. And what his wife remembered.

"The soul of a venturer," Fr Pereira repeated, thoughtfully. "Is he a venturer?"

"All sailors are," I said, shrugging my shoulders.

"It rings a bell, Luís. It definitely rings a bell." He paced along the stair, then back again. "I'm going to need to consult my library. Can you bear with me for a few minutes?"

"Of course," I said. I was quite happy perched on the wall. Small pleasures.

"I'll be back in a moment," he said, and bustled back through the black rectangle of the postern door.

Left to myself—a luxury I rarely enjoy—I stared idly across the narrow square. It was thick, of course, with ghosts. But these days I almost don't notice them. Strange, when I think how distracting I found them at first. Just proves you can get used to anything, given time. I lifted my eye-patch and let the cool air circulate. A welcome relief.

I had finished one cheroot, and was contemplating lighting a second, when Fr Pereira reappeared.

"Everything all right, Father?" I asked. He had a small frown on his face.

"Oh yes," he said. "Did you see that young woman come out?" I shook my head. "Well, never mind. Come along, come along!"

Smiling to myself, I let him hurry me down the steps and presently turned into a narrow alleyway that suddenly opened into a tiny courtyard. It was so crammed with plants in pots that negotiating a passage through without leaving a trail of broken earthenware in my wake was quite difficult. A large black cat, however, was accomplishing it effortlessly, so a da Silva ought to be able to manage.

Having steered my way successfully through the shoals, he ushered me through a venerable-looking door. To my eye it looked far older than the buildings around it. Not that I'm an expert. My knowledge of timber is purely nautical.

Once inside the door, I stopped, amazed. The tall interior was illuminated, to my astonishment, by electricity. Three stories above my head I saw the beams of a roof. The bright light turned shuttered windows on three levels into flat black mirrors. All that remained of the building's floors were three balconies encircling the central space. A system of long wheeled ladders allowed access to them. The four walls were entirely lined with books. It was, I admit, impressive.

"Meu Deus," I said at last.

"Welcome to the library of São Rafael," said Fr Pereira. With an understandable flourish. "One of the city's better-kept secrets."

"São Rafael?"

"The church which had that name was destroyed in the earthquake," he explained. "But this collection was begun in the fifteenth century."

"How in God's name do you know where anything is?" I wondered.

"Seek and ye shall find," said Fr Pereira gnomically. ""Knock, and it shall be opened unto you. I put my trust in God, who tells me that the volume I want is—" He stared around, like a dog casting for a scent, then pointed at one of the ladders. "Up there."

I raised my eyebrows. The left one pulled on the scar that cuts through it. Very well-organized, I thought, amused. Ladders need to be scaled, and here's a *marinheiro* at hand to do it for you. Oh well. I won't see forty again, but I can still climb a mast. So a little wooden ladder? *Canja.* Or, as the English say, piece of cake. "Right," I said. "Where?"

"Go up to the second story," he directed. Still a little bemused by the sheer scale of the library, I did as I was told.

"Now what?" I called down.

"Get off the ladder. Third shelf up to your left, look for a book with a red and tan leather spine." I stepped onto the balcony, seeing my reflection for an instant in one of the windows, a bit like a ghost itself. Unexpectedly unsettling. I turned to the shelves.

Sure enough, there was the volume he described. I pulled it from the shelf suspiciously, and opened it at random, expecting some dense indecipherable Latin text. But it was in Portuguese. Still pretty dense and indecipherable, however. The title page bore a Latin name, though. I raised my voice. "It says *Mappa Mundi.*"

"It's a metaphor," he called back. "That's the book." I tucked it under my arm and climbed back down. It was warm and stuffy in the library, though less so than in the church, and I was sweating lightly.

Fr Pereira took the book from me and put it carefully on the table in the center of the room. A faint ghost sat there, some forgotten scholar who had died at his work.

"What do you mean, it's a metaphor?" I asked.

Opening it with rather more care than I had employed, he explained, "A map of the world, in other words, the human spirit and the quest for understanding. This was published in 1572 —same year as the Lusíadas, incidentally. So while Camões was writing the story of the explorers, this author was summarizing the state of our knowledge. Of course this isn't literature, but it doesn't pretend to be."

It was more than I wanted to know, frankly. I don't want literary criticism at ten o'clock at night. Fr Pereira leafed gently through the closely-printed pages. They made a noise like leaves in the wind. "And you think there's material from the *Book of Souls* in there?"

"I'm sure of it," he said. "Yes, here we are. Ah, they quote the original. How's your medieval Latin?"

"Medieval," I said gravely. He laughed.

"I'll read it to you, then. Here's the author: *Another recipe for perfection, from the* Book of Souls, *stated that the souls of a venturer, a scholar, a lover, an artist, a child, a hunter and a warrior, needed to be stored in amulets of, respectively, agate, chrysophase, beryl, jasper, malachite, jacinth and sapphire. Magical formulæ for achieving this begin, 'The first soul shall be the soul of a venturer. It shall be gathered by the demon Mastiphal and stored in an amulet of agate. And that shall be a noble soul. And the guardian of that soul shall be the armored one. And the soul of a venturer may only be...'* And now a page is missing!" he exclaimed in outrage.

But I was hearing only the litany of stones. Agate, chrysophase, beryl, jasper, malachite, jacinth and sapphire. Those were the same that Emilia had sold two weeks before. Seven stones, seven souls.

"What does it mean, a recipe for perfection?" I asked. It made little sense to me. But then magic rarely does. Even when people point out I'm doing it myself. Or perhaps especially then.

Fr Pereira looked solemn. "If it weren't for these rather specific instructions, we might take it for another metaphor, that the perfect man should embody characteristics of all of those. But sending demons to *gather* the souls—and you say Sr Verdinho is in a coma—?" I nodded, but he wasn't looking at me. I'm not sure where he was looking, what he saw. After a moment he shook himself, and smiled. "Ah, wool-gathering," he said apologetically. Which I doubted.

I scratched my scar, more because I wanted a smoke than because it was itching. "Can the souls be freed?"

"Everything bound can be released," said Fr Pereira, with reassuring certainty. And I knew it for truth. Knew it, because I've achieved it. From both sides. "Go home, Luís. I need to look further. You need to go home to your wife."

A sudden pang reminded me that I did. I was still reluctant to leave him. But what could I do? I speak a number of languages well. Read some of them a little less well. Of Latin, though, despite my mother's efforts and schemes, I don't have a priest's knowledge. And, frankly, I haven't the patience to pore over musty old tomes.

Surprised by a sudden yawn, I patted his shoulder, said, "You're right, Father," and left the tall, strange, book-inhabited building.

His voice drifted after me: "I'll speak to you tomorrow."

Once outside, I negotiated the flowerpots before pausing to light a cheroot. And all of a sudden, crawling along my spine, a sense of danger.

Missing an eye is a distinct disadvantage when you need all-round vision. I turned my head from side to side, increasing my pace along the alley. Came out into the small square in front of the church. The steps leading to its big studded doors swept up to my left. Everything was very quiet. Not even a dog barking, not a cat stirring. Jumping at shadows, da Silva? I don't think so. The shadows are minding their own business.

The sense of menace increased, and I unsheathed the knife from down my back. Its solid weight in my left hand was reassuring. It hadn't taken me long to learn how a left-handed man can compensate for lacking his left eye. Basically, you attack first.

But there was still no sign of anything to attack. Yet the threat I felt was almost palpable. My shoulders felt tight with its potential, and the hairs at the back of my neck were prickling. There was *something* there. I was sure of it.

I stood in the center of the square like a gladiator in the arena awaiting his opponent. Heard my heart pounding as if I'd been running. Wiped a trickle of sweat from my face. Looked all round, turning in a slow circle. Still nothing.

And then the church's postern door opened, and an armored figure came charging down the steps. I thought, bemusedly...from the church? What would come clattering down a stone stair to kill me? Which was obviously what it had in mind.

There was little time to take it in. The figure was taller than me—no surprise there, then—armored partly in plate, partly in mail. The helmet it wore was closed, barring the eyes. Which gave it about as much peripheral vision as I have. That was a plus. Though why it would disadvantage itself I had no idea.

The strange knight's sword was raised over its head. As it flashed down, moonlight caught it. I realized it was the real Roman gladius, twenty-two inches long, three pounds in weight. It would shatter my knife if I tried to parry with it. And I would probably break my knuckles if I attempted to hit the armored figure. That would be the reason for the helmet, then.

I dodged its first slashing blow quite easily, skipping out of the way, but I couldn't fight this thing with my knife. It was too well-armored. And it knew exactly what it was doing with that sword, as well. The next stroke it aimed nearly parted my hair as I ducked away from it. My foot slipped on something and I fell to one knee, banging it painfully. Had to roll away quickly from another blow which smashed a burst of sparks from the pavement.

Cursing at the pain shooting from my knee, I bounced back upright, still clutching my knife uselessly. I wondered if I could trip my opponent, but its footwork looked a bit too fancy. It moved like a matador.

And that gave me an idea. Backing rapidly to avoid a punching stroke that would have spitted me, I raced up the steps in front of the church. Towards the builders' gear and the pile of bricks draped in tarpaulin. The armored figure followed me warily, obviously not liking the idea that I'd gone to higher ground. I could hear its panting breath. It breathes, then. I hadn't been sure.

I gave an experimental slash with my knife, and my opponent stopped just out of reach. Which gave me time to whip the tarp off the bricks and fling it over my antagonist's head and shoulders. Followed that with a solid sole of the boot in the middle of the breastplate. It overbalanced and tumbled down the steps with a clatter like a pile of scrap metal toppling over. But never let go of the sword. Damnation.

My knee protested as I gave chase. It felt as if I'd broken it. I jumped the last three steps, making sure I landed on the other foot, and trod hard on its sword-hand. Still swathed in the tarpaulin, it lashed at me with its foot. I wanted to give it a good kicking myself, but didn't fancy fractured toes. Instead I bent and wrenched the sword out of its hand with the sincere hope that a hundred and sixty pounds of da Silva stamping on it had done some lasting damage.

It rolled over, grabbed my ankle with its other hand. I went down on my bruised knee, swearing. The armored figure scrambled to its feet, flung the tarp at me, and took off. Showing an impressive turn of speed for something carrying that much metal. I thought about pursuing it but decided not to bother. I might have caught it, and I'm not that much of an idiot.

I sat on the bottom step to catch my breath, my knife across my lap. Rubbed my knee. Lit a cheroot and drew the smoke in gratefully. Eased my eye-patch away from the humidity beneath it. On second thought, there was no one to see, so I pushed it up to my forehead temporarily and examined the blade I had wrenched from my attacker. A formidable thing. Ancient design, modern steel, and sharp as blazes. I could have shaved with it.

Questions seethed in my mind. Why the Roman *gladius?* How had it come out of the church, if it was evil? And if it wasn't, why attack me?

Deciding I was too tired to think about any of these things, I wrapped the sword in a piece cut from the tarp and walked—or rather limped—wearily home.

2

FATHER CARLOS PEREIRA, IN THE TALL LIBRARY OF SÃO RAFAEL WHICH WAS ONE OF THE CITY'S TRUE ROOTS, burned the midnight oil. Or, in this case, the midnight electricity, a rare and strange thing. Not in the city's commercial center, true; here, though, an odd extravagance. But a sensible one, given the flammable contents of the building.

Searching a mental catalog, his mind was in a semi-trance. Drifting. Seek and ye shall find, as he had said to Luís da Silva. Who did not yet understand, as Fr Pereira did, that Lisbon is a city of many layers. As indeed are all cities. The present reality lies lightly over many other layers, or perhaps it is the other way round. Layers, not only of history, but of legend: Ulysses' city of Olisippi is, in that sense, as real as the Romans' Felicitas Julia. And they may leak into each other. Thin veils may rise, but they may also be penetrated.

Yet in every city there are a few constants that stay the same through all the layers. Not always the obvious ones. The Torre de Belém anchors Lisbon in time, as does the castle of São Jorge. But churches rarely perform this function. As with a human fanatic, an excess of belief weakens stability, destroys balance. Knowledge, however, strengthens them, which is why this library is such a potent place. And why the world faltered when the great library of Alexandria was burned by the Christians, and plunged into the Dark Ages.

Some people, too, as he knew well, are strong in this way. Just as some seem fated to destabilise the world. Again, many of these are neither great leaders nor famous men. However, Fr Pereira—along with a great number of others—believed the German Kaiser to be one of the great disruptors.

He was also almost convinced that Luís da Silva was one of their counterparts.

Although he really knew very little about the one-eyed captain, his instincts were rarely wrong. Da Silva's persistent avoidance of the confessional notwithstanding, Fr Pereira believed him to be a man of the light. Whatever lay in his past. However much he even doubted God. Why else would he feel he had a duty to fight evil?

And that was one of the reasons Fr Pereira was worried by the *Book of*

Souls's spell. For how could you create a perfect man from nothing—from souls who might be young, old, good, evil; disruptors or stabilizers? Saints—or monsters?

We men can never leave anything alone, he mused. We always have to meddle. He leafed through the book in front of him, concern making him absent-minded, and frowned as he recognized a passage he had already read.

Something else had disturbed him. The air felt tight, as if a thunderstorm loomed. He could almost feel it crackling around him. Pressure mounted in his ears, and he swallowed, bursting the bubbles. His face was damp with sweat.

Then there came a knock at the door, and he nearly jumped out of his skin. "You silly old fool," he admonished himself, and heaved his tired body to his feet. It was late, but scholars and antiquarians often kept odd hours.

He did not recognize the man outside the door, but that was not unusual, either. His visitor was a tall man, with Castilian features and the lean look of an ascetic. Grey hair tapered to a widow's peak on his furrowed brow, and old-fashioned eyeglasses hung on a ribbon round his neck. But there was, on a second glance, something sensual about his patrician face, as if he were really less of a scholar than a voluptuary. But of what kind was unguessable.

"Good evening," said this visitor, urbanely. There was something strange about his voice. It was resonant, but in some indefinable way almost *too* resonant. As though it echoed through more than one of the layers of time.

Fr Pereira was visited by an almost overwhelming urge to deny the man entry. There was nothing of logic in it. It was pure primal instinct that came surging up, all the way from a race-memory when his forefathers were peasants, huddling together for comfort in the dark which terrified them. He touched his crucifix surreptitiously for reassurance. Did his visitor flinch? Fr Pereira couldn't be sure.

"Please forgive me," he said to the stranger, covering a feigned yawn with his hand and too aware that he was absolutely no good at dissembling, "I'm dreadfully tired. Could you possibly come back in the morning?"

"I'm afraid that would not be convenient," said his visitor, implacably, and this time there was definitely something in his voice that put the priest in mind of hollow echoing pits. Fr Pereira found his knees were trembling and clutched at the doorframe to steady himself. This is a demon, he thought. Real. Here. Now.

"Then I'm sorry," he said, keeping his own voice level with an effort, "but I can't invite you in just now." He met the other's gaze, and wished he hadn't. His pupils were black, the shiny black of space, with the same sense of void in them. Legions whirled within their depths, like a universe of spinning stars.

The stranger's plump lips thinned into the beginning of a smile, then stretched further open. And further. And, impossibly, further still, revealing a mouthful of teeth like broken bottles. At the same time his face moved, distorting, as if its very bones were changing shape under the skin, beneath the flesh, and its color mottled, darkened.

Fr Pereira, appalled, crossed himself. *"Dominus illuminata mea,"* he said, *"et salus mea, quiem timebo?"* The Lord is the source of my light and my safety, so whom shall I fear? "Who are you?" he demanded.

There was nothing remotely human about the visitor's head, now. It reminded him of nothing so much as a beast's that had been roasted on the fire. The terrible eyes were lidless, the lips blackened and cracked. *Auto-da-fé*, he thought. But the voice was the same. "That which you must fear," it said. "But a name you cannot know." Since names are powerful beyond measure.

"And you cannot pass this threshold without an invitation," he countered. His voice was still steady, though he was shaking as with an ague.

It mocked him. "But you must leave, sooner or later. At the very least, you must sleep, and your little soul will lie naked and open. Even if you lurk within these walls, your weak old body will tire and wear out." Laughter, high and hateful, echoed in his head.

He found he was clutching his crucifix so hard it had left an imprint on his palm. Knowing its words for truth, nonetheless he pushed himself away from the doorframe and slammed the door in the demon's face.

But he could still hear it laughing.

Knowing, then, that he did not have much time, he sat down once more at the table and began to write in hurried but neat script.

"There may be another copy of the *Mappa Mundi*, but I have no knowledge of it; other scholars might. The missing pages are the best hope. There may be a way of using the incomplete book to locate them, if the metaphysicists are right when they say that incomplete things strive to be whole again.

"I may not be able to speak to you again. I have faced down a demon once tonight, but I suspect I will not be able to do so a second time. If this gatherer of souls wants a priest's soul next, in the end I cannot prevent it.

"Dominus vobiscum. May God be with you."

Folding the paper, he wrote da Silva's name on it and, as an afterthought, added the captain's address.

Then he knelt and started to pray.

* * *

I woke late the following morning. Beside me, a warm, Emilia-shaped hollow, full of the scent of her. Nothing to linger for, then. Although I moved into the space she'd occupied. Just because it was there.

And then, of course, it all came back to me.

Muttering a curse, I pushed the bedcovers off and admired the bruise on my right knee. Colorful. Strange how I hadn't noticed it last night. My head felt muzzy, as if I'd slept too long. Get yourself moving, da Silva.

The morning was bright and clear. The sky, the washed high blue that heralds a hot day. Shaving, I suddenly remembered the sword I had brought home with me. To tell the truth, I half-expected it to have vanished. But, when I went to look, it was still there.

This was puzzling. In fact, the whole episode was puzzling. Having slept on the problem, though, the conclusion was inescapable. No harm had come to me from touching the sword. It hadn't disappeared with the morning sun. Its owner had come out of the church. Therefore my attacker hadn't been supernatural at all, but human. Or at least partly.

Which raised, of course, a whole new series of questions. I hefted the gladius thoughtfully. It was a butcher's weapon. No finesse about it. Apart from being razor-sharp, it was a pretty weighty thing. Three pounds doesn't sound like a lot, but it's not like picking up a bag of potatoes. The weight distribution makes it seem a lot heavier. Although the thing was extremely well-balanced. I had to admit I liked the way it fit my hand.

"Damn it," I said softly. Dangerous thoughts. I don't go armed because I want to but because I have to. Ha. I don't see ghosts because I want to, either, but there's not a lot I can do about that. I wrapped the blade back in the tarpaulin and put it in the bottom of the wardrobe.

I needed to go back to the library again. Needed to know what, if anything, Fr Pereira had found out. Because there was more to this than met the eye, so to speak. I don't believe in coincidences.

But first things first. And since Emilia was already up, that meant coffee. Black. And strong enough to stand your spoon up in.

Emilia, however, was trying to coax Caterina to eat her breakfast. With little success, and that little turned to none when I turned up. Caterina launched herself at me like a small cannonball, crying "Papa!" and grabbed me round the middle. I picked her up.

"Ouf, you're heavy. Your mother's been feeding you on stones," I said. She giggled.

"Has not," she said, burying her head in my neck. Emilia, trying to look exasperated, sighed. Rolled her eyes heavenwards.

"Stones," she muttered. "Can't even get the child to eat fruit." I sat down, wriggling child on my lap. Felt like a sackful of puppies.

"Coffee?" I asked plaintively.

Some time later, Emilia said to me, "Are you going back?"

"Yes," I said, a little absently. The room was quiet now, bereft of Caterina. I had finished my coffee and was having a smoke. And looking at a half-completed portrait of my wife.

It really was remarkably good. I hadn't realized the old man was that talented. It made me regret the waste of his gift even more.

"He usually comes round at about ten, if you want to wait."

Too much ambivalence. I'm still not sure how to feel about my father. I shook my head.

"I think I need to talk to Fr Pereira as soon as I can," I said. "I need to find out what's going on."

She looked at me thoughtfully. He had caught the look in her eyes exactly. That grave contemplative expression, and the slight smile that curved her lips. I was hit by a sudden pang of envy that he was able to sit and look at her for hours at a time. Grow up, da Silva.

"What *is* going on?" she asked. "This...collecting of souls."

"I don't know." I stubbed out my cheroot. Looked at her again, reluctant to leave. Got to my feet. "But it's not a coincidence. I don't—"

"—believe in coincidences," she finished for me. I grinned. She knows me very well, that's for sure.

"I won't be long. I hope."

"Luís," said my wife. "Be careful."

"I'm always careful," I said, and kissed her. She kissed back. Soft mouth, soft lips. Usual reaction. I went on kissing her. But I had to leave. Ah well.

The sky hadn't lied. It's going to be hot later. Already uncomfortably warm. We wear far too many clothes, and why? What's the purpose of a tie, or a vest? Not that I was wearing a vest. And I refuse to put on a stiff collar unless meeting clients. Who probably aren't fooled anyway, so I don't know why I bother.

My knee hurt, but not too much. All in all, I suppose I got off lightly from my nocturnal encounter. Unfortunately the first thing I had to do was climb a flight of steep steps. Lisbon is built on hills. Seven hills, like Rome, they say. If you ask me it's more like seventy. Or so it seems, sometimes. Today was one of those occasions.

When I finally arrived at the church, though—I wasn't hurrying—Fr Pereira was nowhere to be found. Instead a nervous young priest who barely looked old enough to shave was apparently in charge. If he calls me "my son", I thought, I'll burst out laughing.

"Where's Fr Pereira?" I asked him. I must have been looking exceptionally villainous, because he flinched back from me. That's right, da Silva, put the wind up the curate. Nice work. Ha. At least the boy didn't cross himself.

"I don't know, senhor," he said, staring at me worriedly, as if he thought I might bite. "No one's seen him since last night."

Last night. My heart gave a sudden jump. I had left him alone in the library. Unprotected. Though of course he would have sworn he had God's protection. I wasn't sure how much that was worth, now. Good and evil seem more evenly matched than scripture would have us believe. Sometimes, the devil prevails.

I was pretty sure I could find the alley that led to the library. Damn it, I can navigate a ship across an ocean. But after a quarter of an hour I was beginning to have doubts. I might have expected a place like that to have some kind of mechanism to keep unwanted visitors away. But not to the extent of excluding me. That's downright insulting.

Eventually I found it, by the simple trick of not looking too closely. I'd returned to the church once more, feeling hot and cross and sweaty. Stopped to light a cheroot, and began to walk aimlessly in the first direction that took my fancy.

And then I saw the ghost of a bearded man in a turban loitering in the air, and headed purposefully for it. I followed him because he had the look of a scholar, and I had a hunch that the library of São Rafael had never been open only to seekers after Christian truths.

Ghosts don't stray very far from the place where they died, however, and scholars don't often die on their way to and from the library. But as I had half-suspected, there were more. All with something about them that made me think of academics. Or maybe that's the wrong word. Magi, perhaps: wise men.

And there was the alley I remembered from the night before. I grinned in relief and blew out a satisfied mouthful of smoke. And this time I took care to fix the way in my memory before turning into its narrow mouth. Instantly the heat of the sun faded, and I was enveloped by a sort of cool almost-dusk, roofed above by a ribbon of blue sky. The sun would never reach into it. Not wide enough. The chill of stone was a welcome relief, drying the sweat on my face. I pushed the eye-patch up to my forehead, not anticipating meeting anyone. Because even as I had turned into it, I had a strong urge not to notice it, to think of it as of no consequence. And I was looking for it. I knew it was there.

Torn between the urge to hurry and the urge to be careful, I walked quickly along the narrow way. Last night's black cat, a real monster of a beast, a demi-puma, barred the alley at its far end. It meowed at me loudly, twining itself round my ankles as I stepped over it, but didn't seem motivated to stop me.

In daylight the small courtyard and the secret library seemed much as they had by night. Well, apart from its not being dark, of course. Deceptive is what I mean. It looked like any tall, old building that had managed to survive the earthquake. You couldn't tell from the shuttered windows that the inside was any different from any of its neighbors. Which towered mute, enclosed, with that indefinable air of vacancy that uninhabited buildings have. I didn't have to knock at their faded doors or peer in between their peeling shutters to know that they had stood empty for a long time. The only bright colors in the tiny square were the potted geraniums, the exact colors of the new flag. Their musty, slightly cat-piss scent the only smell.

Repositioning my eye-patch, I deposited the butt of my cheroot in one of the flower-pots and turned the handle of the library's ancient oaken door. It moved smoothly on its hinges, admitting me willingly enough. Apparently I was still welcome here. Inside, the harsh electric lighting still shone, starker than the summer sun. Papers lay scattered on the floor round the table. And Fr Pereira was slumped over a book, breathing in a high harsh rattle.

For one relieved moment I thought, he's asleep. But I knew it was a false hope. Who do you think you're fooling, da Silva? His mouth was slack and open, a small puddle of saliva on the table. I felt his forehead, his pulse. I shook his shoulder. Couldn't wake him. As with Paciência's husband, so with the priest.

I sighed, looking at his bulk. Thinking of the heat of the day. He must weigh close on two hundred and fifty pounds, I thought sourly. Thanks a lot. All right, I could lift him, but he was entirely the wrong shape to carry easily. Why not call for help? Because I wasn't entirely sure I could find the place again.

Or that I would be allowed in.

If he was the second victim of the soul collector—and the second *was* a scholar's soul, according to the *Mappa Mundi* book—I really needed to find out what he had discovered. If anything. I gathered up his notes, scanning them rapidly for any clue he might have left.

One of the papers was addressed to me. A chill washed over me, and I glanced round quickly. Nothing. I picked up the *Mappa Mundi* volume. It just fit in my pocket. Fr Pereira's notes went into another. Then I looked at the priest's squat unconscious form, rather wanting to spit in disgust. I could have lifted his skinny young curate in one hand. But what I was going to have to carry was Fr Pereira.

Well, da Silva, nobody ever promised things were going to be easy.

As I suspected, the most awkward part was getting him balanced. I got him over my shoulder without much difficulty, having lifted dead weights before. But it was like carrying a sack of meal. My knee protested as I straightened. The first few steps were the worst, and then I got the hang of it.

As soon as I got outside with my burden, I heard the door close softly behind me with a snick! as of a lock engaging. Wondered briefly if I'd ever be admitted again. I'm going to bring the book back, damn it, I said silently.

The things you get yourself into, da Silva, I thought with a sigh. Fighting demons, raising the dead, shooting werewolves. And now carting a comatose priest the size of a hippopotamus about as the mercury climbed to eighty-five degrees. Even in the cool confined alley the sweat was pouring off me.

Despite the heat, people came running the minute I emerged from the mouth of the alleyway, sensing excitement. A talent humans have. I eased Fr Pereira's unconscious bulk carefully to the ground and stood up, wiping my hot perspiring face with my sleeve. And was instantly surrounded by a crowd, all clamoring at the tops of their voices.

"What happened?" "Is he dead?" "Where did you find him?" "What's the matter with him?" "Someone's murdered the priest!"

"Nobody's murdered anyone," I yelled at this last. They'll be on to the apocalypse next. "Somebody fetch a doctor."

Now the crowd parted to allow Fr Pereira's young deputy through. He crossed himself, knelt swiftly beside the older priest, and started to pray. A fat lot of good that is, I thought in disgust. I wiped sweat away again, and lit a cheroot.

And found myself face-to-face with a gape-mouthed Zé. "What happened to the priest?" he asked.

"Catalepsy," I said, falling back on Henriques Verdinho's physician's explanation. Stuck a finger under my eye-patch in a vain attempt to wipe away the accumulated moisture there. "What are you doing here, Zézinho?"

Fr Pereira, meanwhile, was carefully rolled onto a makeshift stretcher. Two men grumbled at his weight. I looked at them sourly.

"Mama sent me," said Zé, staring at his feet in embarrassment. "She said you'd been gone for too long, and she was worried."

I combed my fingers through my damp hair. That's not like Emilia. Does she worry about me when I'm thousands of miles from home, from land? I suppose she must, at that. I thought of a lot of things to say. None suitable to air in front of my son. In the end I just squeezed his shoulder. "Well, I'd better come and reassure her."

We walked in companionable silence for a while. Then Zé said, "Sr Harris told me to tell you something."

Harris. I trusted his instincts. What was wrong? "What?" I asked, trying to sound unconcerned. Not sure I succeeded.

"It doesn't make much sense. It's full moon, remember." Yes, he knows about Harris. Is as grateful to Harris as I am. It's a long story.

"Zé, he turns into a wolf. Not an idiot."

He scratched his cheekbone in unconscious imitation of my habit and said, "He said to tell you, he smelt the same smell last night."

"Ah." I breathed out slowly and bared my teeth. So Harris was sensing the soul-collection, was he? That could prove useful. You need all the help you can get when you're dealing with this sort of thing.

I touched the book in my pocket and hoped that Paciência knew enough to help, because she was the only witch I knew. Apart from Tatiana Dimitrova, of course, but she was in London. And there I hoped she would stay.

Emilia, however, had to disappoint me about her friend. She looked up from a design she was sketching, a tendril of hair falling over her brow. I pushed it back with one finger, tucking it behind her ear, but it fell forward again.

"She's only a hedge-witch, Luís. Potions and simples. She may not know how to do it." Well, I might have known, I thought. Although it'd be nice, just once in a while, to find a straightforward solution to a problem. She squeezed my hand. "I'll ask her, though," she went on. "Perhaps it's only a simple charm."

"Ask her?" I said absently, transfixed by the tiny laughter lines she was getting at the corners of her eyes.

"You know what her husband's like," she reminded me. "He likes to be modern. A twentieth-century man. They have a telephone."

Ten minutes later, she reported that Paciência was on her way. By motor-car. A little amused, I thanked Henriques Verdinho's passion for the new-fangled. He may dismiss me as hopelessly old-fashioned, still sailing with wind and tide, but his own brand of stubbornness was helping now. Helping him, I hoped. Because I needed all the help I can get. I may feel a duty to fight evil, but I never claimed I could do it all on my own. It comes down to that often enough, anyway. And isn't *that* a surprise.

"What did she say?" I asked.

"She sounded relieved," Emilia said. "I think she *can* do it."

Paciência, when she turned up, might have been an entirely different woman from yesterday's tearful frightened visitor. Bright-eyed and animated. She read Fr Pereira's letter carefully, nodding her head. Kept shooting me curious glances, though.

At last she asked, "Did you kill it, the demon that took your eye?" I nodded. Though it wasn't strictly true. I *had* defeated it, though.

Emilia looked at me, perhaps remembering, as I was, that night. The teeming rain sluicing the blood from my face. Hearing my footsteps outside. A sudden jolt of alarm—there's something wrong, what's happened? I shook myself, putting the thought away. The memory of pain. Silence stretched between the three of us.

Then Emilia said, "Can you do this…spell?" snapping the tension, and I exhaled sharply. Hadn't known I was holding my breath. I lit a cheroot without really thinking about it and breathed in the smoke gratefully.

"Yes, of course," said the witch impatiently. "It's only a simple finding charm. People want me to find things all the time. If it's not lost earrings, it's lost bags and lost walking-sticks. It's a pity there isn't one for lost virginity," she added tartly, and I gave a surprised bark of laughter. "May I see the book?"

I pointed to it. She picked it up, leafed through it curiously.

"Who tore the pages out?" Emilia wondered.

"We'll find out," said Paciência, confidently, putting her fingers to her throat and pulling something on a chain from round her neck. It had been concealed beneath her high-necked blouse. The pendant was a white milky stone.

Eyeing it curiously, Emilia asked,"What is that stone? It's not a moonstone or an opal. I don't recognize it at all."

"It's called galactides, milkstone," the witch said. "Please, don't smoke," she went on. I stubbed the cheroot out obediently. "And don't speak, or you'll distract the spirit."

"Spirit?" I repeated, more sharply than I'd intended. As in ghost?

Because I don't need you to talk to them. I can do it myself, thank you very much.

"The spirit of the stone." She dangled the pendant above the book and closed her eyes. I exchanged a glance with Emilia, who looked quizzical. I don't know what I looked like. Irritated, probably. For God's sake, I was thinking, she'll whip out a ouija board next. Paciência's lips began to move in silent recitation. And the pendant began to swing in a circle. Then, in a perfectly conversational tone, she said, "The mender of time." And then, "The rock of ages." Then she was silent for a while, though the stone continued to spin. It made a very slight whirring sound, like a clock preparing to strike. "A scent of poppies," said the witch. "A dog in a manger." The pendant stopped dead. Paciência opened her eyes, then blinked.

"What does all that mean?" I asked, somewhat peremptorily. Gnomic utterances are all very well. But when I want answers, they're no bloody good at all. I prefer a more direct route, preferably without the classical riddle-game. All right, I'm impatient. I admit it.

"May I have a glass of water?" Paciência asked, and I stood up to fetch her one. Had one myself while I was at it. When I returned, Emilia had written down the four phrases, and the witch was looking relieved.

"Good," she said. "That's simple enough. Oh, *obrigada.*" She drained the glass in one draught, put it down on the table.

"Simple," I repeated.

"Oh yes." She tapped the paper with her forefinger. And proceeded to explain. "It always does this. The mender of time, that'll be a clock repairer. The rock of ages, somewhere near the castle. A scent of poppies, an opium smoker. And a dog in a manger, someone who doesn't know what he has but wants to hang onto it."

If the Sphinx had tried its blasted riddles out on me, I would have beaten the hell out of it. At least ghosts give straightforward answers, however distasteful I find summoning the damn things. But this?

"A clock repairer somewhere near the castle?" I repeated. "Can you be a bit more specific?" Since the castle covers rather a lot of ground. Every defender since the Romans has dug in enthusiastically up there, extending fortifications in all directions. Not that there's much left standing now. And somewhere near, to me, doesn't mean right on top of. It could mean, say, a quarter-mile or so in any direction.

Paciência smiled and held her pendant out to me. "It'll lead you." I raised an eyebrow at her, sceptical, but took the chain from her hand. Immediately I felt a tug, not from the thing directly but in my mind. Well I'm damned, I thought. It does work. I made to slip the pendant in my pocket, but she stopped me. "You need to keep it in contact with your skin," she said. "Putting it round your neck is easiest."

I had shed my jacket on my return, having already dispensed with the tyranny of collar and tie. Feeling some kind of dim disloyalty to Emilia, I slipped the chain over my head and let the milky-white stone hang inside my shirt. Its unaccustomed weight felt strange. I looked towards Emilia, who gave me an encouraging smile. That same strand of hair had fallen across her brow again. I wished I had the leisure to push it back.

The tugging was quite insistent. I had to fight it just to pause to get my knife and resume my jacket. As I came downstairs Zé, who had apparently decided to spend his shore leave harassing me, popped out looking hopeful.

"Where are you going?" he asked curiously. I stopped, lit a cheroot.

"Haven't you got anything better to do?" I enquired. Zé shook his head, unrepentant. "Then go and ask your mother to find you something." He shot me a mutinous look. I recognized the expression, hid a smile. In my mind, the tugging grew more insistent.

"But I—"

"No, you can't come with me," I said. He looked mulishly at me for a moment, then finally realized arguing wouldn't get him anywhere and stomped off. I love my son, but sometimes he's so like me that it puts the fear of God into me, so to speak. Trouble is, the only way he's *not* like me is that he still expects the world to be nice. Despite all the evidence to the contrary. *Então*, I expect that's my fault too— if I'd brought the boy up a good little Catholic he's at least have some idea of original sin, no? Ha. Alternatively, I could've introduced him to his grandmother. Not that I'd ever inflict *that* on anyone. I sighed, and went out once more into the heat of the day.

Except that it wasn't. How did that happen? I looked at the sky, startled to find the sun gone behind long streaks of red cloud to the west. How long had we sat while Paciência worked her spell? That's one of the reasons I don't trust magic. No. Its practitioners are the reason. But I need *this* witch. Live with it, da Silva.

There was bustle in the streets and alleys now, as people who preferred to hide from the afternoon heat woke up and resumed their business. Dark interiors yawned behind newly-opened doorways. Cooking aromas began to drift on the air, more substantial than the floating ghosts. I wished I'd thought to have a drink before leaving. Thought of stopping briefly at a bar. But the spell still led me on. I heard a snatch of fado from somewhere, a woman's voice almost harsh with saudade: *Meu amor é marinheiro, e mora no alto mar...My lover is a sailor, he dwells on the open sea...*

Perhaps twenty-five minutes later, I found what I was looking for. In that it was a shop with a window full of dusty clocks and it was near the castle. Could hardly have been closer, in fact: Looking straight up, ruined battlements loomed. However, the sleek young Chinaman seated outside on a wicker chair smoking a cigarette didn't look in the least fuddled by opium. So maybe the scent of poppies was as metaphorical as the *Mappa Mundi* volume. Damnation.

Paciência's pendant, having done its work, was utterly quiet now. I pretended an interest in the clocks in the window. When I figured I had stood there long enough to make him vaguely curious, I said casually in the Mandarin dialect, "I hear you are a collector of documents as well as a mender of clocks."

My accent is bad. I sound like what I am, a Portuguese speaking Mandarin. But that's usually enough to catch the most complacent Chinese off-guard. Although after that they find it highly amusing.

"What kind of documents are you interested in?" he asked. His accent came from Hong Kong. Not, as you might expect, Macau.

Still contemplating the clocks, I lit a cheroot. Blew smoke out. "That depends on what kind you have," I said.

"Pages from many books," he replied in an undertone. "For a price."

I scratched my cheekbone. Stayed where I was. Didn't look at him. "Is it possible to see these...pages?"

He was standing beside me, now. I could see both our reflections in the glass. "In what year were you born?" he asked.

"In the year of the dragon," I replied, exhaling smoke. Which made me, I suppose, a fire-breathing dragon.

"Come inside," said the Chinaman. "I am called the Faithful Dog by some people." The dog in the manger? I wondered. "Though my name is John Yeoh." The English name, John. Hong Kong, for sure.

Standing by the door, he gestured for me to precede him into the dim sandalwood-scented interior. I heard the door close behind me. Fools rush in, I thought, with a grin to myself that was more than a little forced.

Because I hadn't the remotest idea what the hell I was doing. But then, that goes for most ventures of this sort. I went nearly forty years of my life before I started seeing ghosts. Twenty-five of them on ships. I know the ways of the ocean better than I could ever hope to navigate in this world of shadows. And frankly I'd rather be battling a hundred-foot sea or a force ten gale. Or both. Unfortunately, I don't have much of a choice.

John Yeoh lit the gas, then took his place, like a shopkeeper, behind the counter. Stared at me. I returned his gaze. Heard a drawer open. And then there was a gun in his hand.

Oh *merda*, I thought. And to think I nearly brought Zé. I held my hands out in front of me, palms forward.

"Who the hell are you?" he demanded.

"Just a...ship's captain," I said. "My name's da Silva." I weighed up the distance between us. Too far.

"Don't try anything," he warned. Ah well, it was worth the thought. "How did you hear about me?"

Now that was a tricky one to answer. I ran through several replies in my mind. Discarded them all. Eventually decided on the truth. If he didn't believe me, he didn't believe me. I just hoped he wouldn't shoot me.

"A witch told me," I said. Take it or leave it.

He frowned. But not, I thought, in disbelief. Or was that wishful thinking? A trickle of sweat ran down from my temple. Time crawled by.

"What do you know of witches?" he asked at last. The gun still pointed at me, unwavering. It was difficult to look away from that round black hole. I kept very still. Don't want him to get nervous. *Get* nervous, da Silva?

"Quite a lot." I took a deep breath. "Can you point that somewhere else?"

His eyes never left me. "I don't think so. Why have you come?"

There's nothing like someone pointing a gun at you to get at the truth. "I'm looking for some pages from a book called the *Mappa Mundi.*"

"Why?"

I wanted to shout with frustration. Kept my voice level with an effort. "To learn how to retrieve stolen souls, Sr Yeoh. My friends' souls."

"Stolen souls," he repeated, staring hard at me. What was he seeing? Or trying to see? After another couple of centuries, he replaced the gun in its drawer. I breathed out silently, badly in need of a smoke. Wanting, as well, to get the sweat out from under my eye-patch. I settled for wiping a hand over my face. It was better than nothing. "Would you recognize this...manuscript, if you saw it?"

Though I wasn't at all sure, I said "Yes." Wondering why he had suddenly decided to trust me. If he had.

"I will show you the documents," he said slowly. "I do not guarantee that I'll sell any of them to you."

"Very well," I said, wiping the sweat off my face. Having no other choice. Wishing, to make things easier for a change, that the next soul to be gathered was the soul of a thief. Why else would he be so suspicious?

"Are you armed?" he asked.

"Of course I am," I retorted. "But if you want me to trust you, you'll have to trust me." He smiled slightly. Which I took for agreement.

"You are a very strange man, Captain," he said. Yes, and he could talk. "But yes, I believe I *can* trust you." Well, thank you, I thought, grinning mirthlessly. Or nearly. It was almost funny. The guardian of secrets even Fr Pereira didn't know, a nervous Chinaman who had no idea what he had stolen.

Yeoh reached under the counter again, and I heard a click. What he had released was a tall display cabinet which swung out from the wall, revealing a flight of steps leading downwards. He stooped, picked up an oil-lamp, lit it. Reminded me I wanted a smoke. Better not. No sudden movements, da Silva.

Musty air flowed up from the depths. I descended the steep stair carefully. I'm not fond of enclosed underground spaces. Being the exact opposite of a sailor's preferred environment. And also, of course, in my experience, usually housing something unpleasant.

This cellar, however, was roomy, dry and clean. Dozens of box files stood on shelves. Mother of God, I thought, how long has he been collecting this stuff? He *looks* younger than me. I stared at him, scratched my eyebrow.

"What language is your book?" he asked.

"Portuguese," I replied, still transfixed by the sheer size of the collection. He indicated one section with a wave of his hand, for all the world like a librarian. Three boxes with "português" written on their sides.

"Go ahead," said Yeoh.

Of course, the pages were in the third box, by which time I was sure that Paciência's spell was a worthless piece of mumbo-jumbo. And then I recognized the passage.

"*...released by a venturer. Against the armored one, only the invulnerable may stand.*" The armored one? I thought suddenly, remembering my antagonist of the previous night. "*The second soul shall be the soul of a scholar. It shall be gathered by the demon Bifrons and stored in an amulet of chrysophase. And that shall be a noble soul. And the guardian of that soul shall be the executioner. And the soul of a scholar may only be released by a scholar. Against the executioner, only the dead may stand...*"

"You have found what you seek?"

"Yes," I replied. "May I buy it from you?"

He looked at me expressionlessly. "What if I said no?"

Oh, God, I thought, he wants to play games. My heart sank. Heaven preserve us from people who want to play games. The Venetian was a great one for that. Drawing things out until I wanted to beat him senseless. Baiting me. Enjoying the fact that I knew very well that *any* reaction from me would land me in the cozy confines of an Italian gaol. Or worse. But then, there *are* worse things to lose than your life, although I didn't know it at the time.

But Yeoh wasn't the Venetian. Hadn't had anything like that amount of practice. I could cope with him.

"Then I'd go," I said blandly. He held up one hand.

"Captain, I'll give you the pages you want on one condition."

"What condition?"

"You tell me what your demon's mark means."

"My—" I touched a finger to my cheekbone. "You mean this?"

"Of course, what else?"

What it means. Entirely too much. I sighed. Gave him the short answer. "It means I see ghosts, Mr Yeoh."

"And what else?" he demanded. A peculiar intensity had crept into his voice. "Can you raise the dead? Are you a necromancer, Captain da Silva?"

I did not like the way this conversation was going. "I can speak to the dead," I said harshly. "When necessary. And then I let them return to their graves."

"Oh, take the pages and go, Captain," he cried out, and I almost flinched at the anguish in his tone.

"What is it?" I asked. He had closed his eyes. His shoulders drooped.

"Not one of you can help me," he muttered. "You come, you find your precious pages, you tell me you can do nothing. And then you go. What use is western magic?"

Go, da Silva. Do as he says. But I couldn't. I have grown, it seems, altruism. Who'd have thought it.

"Tell me what you want." I'm going to regret this, I know. He raised his eyes.

"I was a sailor, like you," he said softly. "I had been married only two years when I left Hong Kong for good. I told my wife I would wait for her here. She was bringing my son to join me. Their ship went down off Ceylon. And I wait. And wait. And wait."

A chill went down my spine. "How long have you waited?" I asked.

"A hundred and fifty-nine years," said John Yeoh, and something clenched at my heart. Dear God.

Complications. Oh, that's all I want. "Listen to me," I said. "I can only raise the dead where their bodies lie. Have you tried to sail to the place where the ship went down?"

"I can't travel. I can't leave this city," he muttered. "I'm more than half a ghost myself. Except that I don't remember dying."

I put my hand out and grasped his wrist. Hoping that he'd realize that if he *had* been a ghost, I wouldn't have been able to do that. "You're not a ghost," I told him. "You put a geas on yourself when you promised to wait for your wife." He had bound himself. Meu Deus, I realized I'd do it myself. I *would* do it. The thought of losing Emilia...couldn't be borne. "Listen," I said again, "if I get through this, if I free my friends' souls, I'll think of a way to help you." Don't make promises you can't keep, da Silva. But I would keep this one.

"Captain, I believe you," said John Yeoh. "Now, take your manuscript."

Any satisfaction I might have felt at recovering the missing pages turned to dust and ashes at the thought of Yeoh's lonely vigil. I understood it. Married two years. Apart for an eternity. Every time I part from Emilia is a little death. But I've always come back to her, so far. We both know the risks. We live with them. John Yeoh's wife, though—and a baby—would not. And they were the ones drowned. The same could happen to me. Any voyage could be my last, and I would never return to Emilia. I suddenly appreciated the possibility of her anxiety and regretted my impatient thoughts earlier in the day.

And now I had put a geas on myself, as well. I needed a drink, but passed by the first bar because I heard a woman singing fado inside. Songs of love and loss were not what I wanted to hear at that moment.

In fact what I really felt like doing was getting drunk. But in the end all I had were two glasses of rather rough aguardente that I could have used to strip paint with. Smoked until my mouth felt like the bottom of *Isabella*'s hold. And then I went home.

Nothing's ever simple. Damn it.

To my relief, Paciência had taken her leave. *Família* da Silva had its supper together, the first time for months. Although Caterina, allowed to stay up, spent more time pushing her food round her plate than eating it.

"Don't you want that?" asked Zé at last. She shook her head, and he swapped plates with her and demolished her supper on top of his own. "Is there any more?"

"Were you that hungry at his age?" Emilia asked me.

"Yes," I said, "and I didn't have a little sister to give me extras."

By the time Emilia and I had a chance to talk, I'd rather have forgotten the whole thing until the morning. But that wasn't really an option.

Unfortunately.

I thought she looked tired, so I carried her to the settee and found her a footstool. Then I sat down next to her and put my arm round her. Told her the story of John Yeoh's endless wait.

"The poor man," she said, resting her head into my shoulder and closing her eyes. I pushed straying strands of hair off her face. "Perhaps the book will have something helpful."

"Maybe." I wasn't particularly keen on the idea of consulting it any further than I had to. It might not, itself, have been a grimoire, but it certainly quoted from the damned things. That felt like a step I didn't want to take. A boundary I didn't want to cross. As if I haven't already crossed enough. Who are you trying to fool, da Silva? I picked up the missing pages and flipped through them. Then put them back in the *Mappa Mundi*.

Emilia took the book off my lap and turned it round so she could read the completed passage. I took the opportunity of having a free hand to light a cheroot. Eye-patch off, arm around my wife, a smoke and a glass of good *vinho tinto*. Would have been perfect except for the small matter of people having their souls stolen. And holding Emilia was entirely too distracting to concentrate on things like that. I brought my mind back to the book, sternly.

'*The first soul shall be the soul of a venturer. It shall be gathered by the demon Mastiphal and stored in an amulet of agate. And that shall be a noble soul. And the guardian of that soul shall be the armored one. And the soul of a venturer may only be released by a venturer. Against the armored one, only the invulnerable may stand.*'

So far, so cryptic. But how could the soul be released? I scanned the page and then the rest of the restored ones. Nothing. The book, damn it, told us everything but that. No, I realized. It didn't include any instructions about the gathering or the storing, either. Maybe the *Book of Souls* did. But the *Mappa Mundi* didn't.

"So now what?" Emilia asked. Well, right now I wanted to kiss her neck. And maybe unbutton her blouse a little. You don't always get what you want, though.

"The woman who bought the jewels," I said determinedly, stubbing out my cheroot in the ashtray. "Did you get an address?"

"No, she paid in cash and took the stones with her."

"What did she look like?"

"Oh, very striking," said Emilia. "Tall, maybe five-ten. Expensive clothes, from Paris if I'm any judge. Too...strong-featured to be pretty. And Brazilian, I'm almost sure."

That surprised me, though I don't know why it should. "Well, a giantess from Brazil should be easy to find," I said.

"Do you think she's the one? Collecting souls?"

"She bought the stones. So she must have a copy of this *Book of Souls*. All I have to do is find a way to get hold of it."

"And find her," she pointed out.

"Yes. That first."

Emilia reached up and put a hand against my face. "I know you say you always are. But be especially careful. She steals souls."

I covered her hand with mine. "I know," I said. "If I promise to be careful, will you promise not to worry?"

"Not in this lifetime," she said softly.

* * *

"You see that girl?" The other two men, an Italian called Angelotti and a tall African who went by the name of Benjamin—although that was mainly because he claimed most of the crew couldn't pronounce his real name—obediently looked in the direction indicated. More to ogle the girl than to do what Ortigão said, true. She was worth looking at, though. Tall and slender with a mass of curly black hair. "She's waiting for me."

"Not a chance," said Angelotti. Benjamin merely laughed derisively.

Ortigão treated his crewmates to a rude gesture, and flashed his teeth at them. "And that's all you know," he said. Raising his voice, he called, "Luzia." She turned. A brilliant smile lit up her face, and she waved to him.

"Poor girl," said Benjamin, judiciously. "And she so pretty, too."

"What do you mean, poor girl?" Ortigão demanded, in an indignant tone.

Deadpan, Benjamin said, "Man, she obviously insane." Angelotti snorted with laughter.

"Oh, you can take the piss all you like," said Ortigão smugly, smoothing his hair. "But I don't see anyone waiting for either of you." And he sauntered off.

"There goes a man with a girl in every port," Angelotti said ruefully. "Do *you* know what they see in him?"

Benjamin shrugged. "No, on account of I ain't got tits."

Angelotti spat into the water and leaned on the rail, glumly contemplating the unfathomability of women, until Harris came and told them in conversational tones to shift their asses before he put a bomb under them.

"Miserable bastard," muttered Angelotti, mutinously. "Don't he ever smile?"

"It his time of the month," Benjamin said, earning another cackle from the Italian. It was commonly, if tacitly, acknowledged that Harris turned into a wolf at the full moon. Mostly, the crew was perversely proud of this fact.

"Hush up," Angelotti hissed, knowing how acute the third mate's hearing was, "he'll hear you." But Harris's attention, he saw, had gone into a kind of *listening* pose, For just a minute, he thought the American was, literally, miles away.

Harris, however, was staring closely at the woman, who was now embracing Ortigão with singular enthusiasm.

Something's wrong.

He shook his head. Still the strangeness persisted. A pretty girl one minute. The next, something rotten. He could smell something foul, down deep inside his soul. *If*, he thought morosely, and not for the first time, *I have a soul anymore.*

That was three times now. *I gotta talk to the skipper.* He sighed. *But now I gotta get below, before that goddamn sun goes all the way down.*

Or perhaps I oughta follow them.

Warning pain lanced through him, catching him off-guard as it always did. Harris winced and trotted to his cabin. But this time he did not, as was his usual habit, fasten the restraining collar round his neck. Nor did he lock the door.

Then the agonizing change began, like having all his bones shattered with sledgehammers. Something that was neither Harris nor wolf writhed on the cabin floor for an indeterminable time and then coalesced into lupine form.

He never knew how long the process took, was always surprised that his wolf-self comprehended the concept of time at all. But he thought Ortigão and his girl — or the thing that purported to be his girl — would not have gone far.

Sensory overload, as always, disoriented him for a good few seconds, the sense of sight now negligible but hearing and scent bursting with the brightness and clamor of the sun. Panting, he waited for things to steady and then loped off in pursuit of the lovers.

It didn't take him long to find them, since they had merely gravitated to the nearest secluded spot they could find. Harris, as wolf, observed them dispassionately through the scent of arousal, wet noises of lips and tongues, and harsh breathing, but Ed Harris would probably have been a little shocked. This was, supposedly, a young lady of good family whom Ortigão was pawing, and more than pawing.

For a few moments he was inclined to doubt his earlier ideas, sensing nothing of the rottenness which had alerted him. But then he caught it, masked by other odors but unmistakable: a scent like old blood, of rotting flesh. A smell which was also, in some indefinable way, unclean. It made him feel soiled.

Harris-wolf let his perceptions expand, not an ability he could ever explain either in lupine or in human form. His hackles rose, and a growl formed in his throat; he bared his teeth, the wolf's reaction to danger. He skulked back into the shadows that hid him from human eyes, disbelieving what his senses showed him.

The woman's real shape wasn't remotely human. He could feel it, as an aura: something monstrous, something predatory. Now it seemed feline, pard-like; now winged like an eagle. The beating of those wings would raise gales in the great void, the unfathomable abyss that lies behind all human fears. Would make a wind blow to strike terror into the heart of any sailor. It was the trade which drove Vanderdecken's haunted ship, the storm that sent vessels out beyond the winds of the world into unknown seas, never to return.

How could Ortigão not sense it? How could any man be sunk so far in lust as to ignore the fact that his soul was in peril?

Snarling a threat, Harris-wolf tried to move closer. And found himself quite unable to move. It was not fear that transfixed him, but some kind of terrible paralysis that rooted him to the spot as the aura of the thing that wore Luzia Verdinho's image *swelled* like the huge slow building of a monstrous wave. With a growl, he strained against the force in desperation, but it was too strong. The wolf was helpless in front of a predator far greater than himself.

He did not need sight to perceive it. It bruised his senses like a buffeting wind, growing brutally huge, bulging and pulsating. Somewhere in its center, a thing that was neither woman in form, nor leopard, nor eagle, put out from its maw a long thin spike and thrust it through Pedro Ortigão's chest. The point emerged from his back with a wet sucking sound, and his body convulsed once. Harris-wolf smelt the stink of voided bowels. It was such a human odor that it served to anchor him somehow, as the force which had held the young man upright dissipated, letting its victim fall to the ground.

Sure that Ortigão was dead, Harris cautiously tried to move. Found he could. He approached the body and sniffed it; then sneezed in perplexity. Not only was the sailor still alive and breathing, if stertoriously, but there was no scent of blood anywhere on him. Puzzled, he backed away.

As wolf, Harris did not entertain vocalized thoughts in his mind, but an impression of his captain was urgently there. He knew, though, that he would have to wait until he regained human shape before acting on that. For now, he could at least drag the unfortunate Ortigão's unconscious body back to *Isabella*. If the doctor was sober the boy might even get some medical treatment. On the other hand, O'Rourke would probably attempt to treat him anyway, not a hopeful prospect.

Seizing Ortigão's collar between his teeth, he began to pull him across the cobblestones.

The sailor's collar felt dry and nasty in his mouth, making him salivate in reaction. There was also the memory of a taint about him, the spoor of the thing that had attacked him. The echo of its foulness drifted on the air, unseen, unsensed by people with only normal perceptions. And pulling the dead weight was awkward. He had to stop twice and rest, panting, crouching nervously in the moonlight, wary of being seen. Humans, he knew from having been one—and still, of course, passing for one most of the time—tended to shoot first and ask questions later. If at all. The fact that any bullet he took was unlikely to be a silver one was not any great comfort. The lead kind still hurt like the devil.

On the other hand, as da Silva had observed, he knew how to make himself difficult to notice, and anyone glancing in his direction might only see shadows and moonlight. He made *Isabella*'s mooring without incident, then barked gruffly (feeling this rather beneath his lupine dignity) to attract the attention of a seaman who was smoking by the rail and singing quietly to himself. He did not need his expanded senses to identify the sailor as Benjamin, because the latter's curiously sweet tenor voice was unmistakable.

"What's up?" called the tall crewman softly.

"Or'iga'." Harris's wolf-mouth and throat were not designed for human speech. "Si-*ch*," he added by way of explanation.

"Right," Benjamin's voice floated back.

Satisfied, Harris-wolf padded off into the night, the urge to hunt upon him. Even if all he found was the odd rat, which he would regret when he regained his human form. It was better than chaining himself in his cabin.

Benjamin could have lifted Ortigão with ease, but declined to soil his clothes. Instead he enlisted the aid of a crewmate, a lanky Liverpudlian known as Tiny Jim for some unknown reason (since he was neither tiny, nor had he been christened James). Together they rigged up a canvas stretcher and lugged the unconscious man to the doctor's cabin.

O'Rourke was already very redolent of alcohol, but his hands were steady. No one aboard, including the captain, had ever seen him *appear* at all drunk. But Benjamin reckoned he was about ninety per cent proof.

He was not pleased at the intrusion.

"Jaysus, what's the stink?" he demanded in the stage-Irish accent he sometimes affected. "Who's been taking a bath in the bloody bilges?" He looked at his patient more closely. "Mary, mother o' God, could ye not have cleaned him up, now?"

"It ain't my job," said Tiny Jim succinctly, then jerked his head at Benjamin and added, "and it ain't his watch."

"Well, get one o' the bloody 'prentices to do it!" O'Rourke snapped, rather hoping that Zé would get landed with this unpleasant duty. Something deep down in his republican soul resented the captain's having employed his son on board, though nobody could ever have accused da Silva of nepotism. Wanting to keep an eye on the boy, yes. Favoritism, no.

It fell to Felipe, *Isabella*'s other 'prentice, therefore, who chalked up another reason for disliking the ship's doctor. But even clean and laid on the doctor's bunk, Ortigão defied all O'Rourke's attempts to rouse him and lay there snoring like a hog, his face the color of ash.

In the morning, Harris woke in his cabin, lying naked on the floor, with a foul taste in his mouth. *Goddamn rats.* He lit a cigarette to take the taint away, then struggled into his clothes. The world's worst hangover hammered in his head. *And I didn't even take a drink.* All his muscles felt stretched, and his joints ached. Hips, knees, neck, clicked as he dressed, painfully. *Wonder if werewolves get arthritis? Don't suppose one's ever lived long enough to find out.* He peered at his face in the mirror and grimaced at his reflection, seeing as usual after a wolf-night, about three days' growth of beard. At other times it was slow to appear.

He went to beg hot water from João, *Isabella*'s cook, and bumped into Benjamin, who was lurking outside his cabin.

"The doctor, he say Pedro have a seizure," the African said, stepping back from the mate's glowering expression. It was common knowledge among the crew that Harris was always like a bear with a sore head on his mornings-after. Or, of course, in his case, a wolf with a sore head. Either way, not to be messed with.

Does he think I'm gonna bite him? Yeah, probably. I might, at that.

"That's just doctor-talk for 'I don't know squat'," growled Harris. *Makes two of us. What the hell was that thing that attacked him? Come to that, what the hell did it do to him? What did it want? Will it come back for someone else?* Benjamin flinched away from the memory in his eyes, looking warily at him.

"We need to tell the captain," he suggested.

"Yeah, I know. I'm on it," Harris reassured him.

* * *

Harris at my door. Something's wrong. Oh yes, as if you didn't know that already, da Silva. Moreover, Harris, the morning after a night spent *changed:* shaved, neat, alert. Serious, even. But then he always looks serious. Me, I look debauched. I know, because I'd just been about to have a shave myself. Hadn't got as far as lather when he arrived. Hadn't even, to be honest, got around to brushing my increasingly annoying hair. I rubbed my chin, pointlessly. Lit a cheroot, and stuffed my hands in my pockets.

"What's happened?" I asked, a bit grimly. And the minute he said Ortigão's name, I knew.

The third soul shall be the soul of a lover. God. The collector had three, already. I sighed, scratched at my eyebrow in frustration. And I've still got no idea how to free them. Or even, come to that, how to *find* them.

3

HARRIS LOOMED IN THE PARLOR. HE'S GOOD AT THAT, BEING ABOUT THE SIZE OF A YOUNG BEAR. He's as ill-at-ease as a wild animal, too, twisting his cap in his hands. I think I make him slightly nervous, which is odd if you look at the size of him compared to me. But then, he has seen me blow a werewolf's brains out. One which he'd knocked off me himself. I made him sit down so he didn't dwarf the room quite so much.

"You saw what happened?" I asked him.

"Saw, ain't quite the right word," he said. "Witnessed it, yeah. It...sucked something right outa him. Then just left him lying there. Like it ate the fruit and left the peel behind, I guess." He looked down at his hands. "It was the same kind of dirty stink as the other times. You reckon it's done it before? 'Cause I do."

I looked at him thoughtfully. Knew I could trust him. Didn't know whether it was fair to involve him. Or, on the other hand, whether it was fair not to. Since I've known all three victims so far. "It's not the same thing, Harris," I told him. "It's been a different one each time. And they're stealing souls."

"Stealing," he repeated. "You mean, they can be gotten back?"

"In theory."

"What's stealing 'em?"

"Demons," I said. He grimaced, obviously not liking the idea. Então, neither do I.

"What's going on, skipper?" he asked. As if I'm some kind of an oracle. Of course, I could tell him about the gatherer of souls, but not the how or the why. Why would someone want to manufacture a perfect man? I thought uncomfortably of the Russian witch, Tatiana Dimitrova, who had made herself a golem for a servant. And, I suspected, more than a servant. But that wasn't a thought I wanted to pursue.

It *had* been a woman who bought the stones, though. Another witch? Meu Deus, I thought, how many of them are there in Lisbon?

"Someone," I said slowly, after taking a final drag from my cheroot and grinding the end out in an ashtray, "someone wants to collect seven souls."

"For Godsakes, why?" he demanded. I sighed. I was going to have to tell him. So what? You knew that all along, da Silva.

"Give me five minutes, Harris," I said. Had to shave, at least. "I'll come back to *Isabella* with you." Without breakfast. Ah well. I can pick up a *bica* on the way. An injection of caffeine always helps.

Emilia looked round in alarm, hairbrush stilled in her hand, as I interrupted her toilette. "What is it?" Catching my reflection in her mirror, I realized why she looked concerned. Attempted to look less forbidding.

"Don't worry," I said, trying for a reassuring tone. Perched beside her on the long padded seat. She put out her forefinger and touched the scar on my cheekbone. Somehow, when she does that, it's pleasant. I put my hand over hers.

"It's happened again, hasn't it?"

"Yes. One of the crew."

"I'm sorry."

I moved her hand so I could kiss her fingers. "I have to go."

"Who was it?" she asked.

"A lad called Ortigão." Emilia grew still. "What?"

"Is his Christian name Pedro?"

"Yes, why?"

"He's Paciência's daughter's beau."

Damn. Should I tell her? I squeezed her hand. "Then Paciência should put her foot down," I said. "Because he really does have a girl in every port."

She seemed unsurprised. "I'll tell her." Her other hand went into my hair. "Did you have a girl in every port, Luís?"

"No," I said. It was only ever Emilia. Mostly.

"Really?" she said with a smile, tugging my hair. "I thought you had one in Rio, before we got married."

Rio, I thought. A chill went through me. And not at Emilia's intuition, either. At the thought of a Brazilian woman, buying gems for amulets. Collecting souls?

"How old was the woman who bought the stones from you?" Yet Tatiana Dimitrova had said three years ago: All your other lovers are dead...was Dona Elvira dead?

"Twenty-eight, thirty, maybe— What, Luís?"

The past. Like I said, it doesn't die. Just when you think you've caulked and sealed against it, back it comes, seeping through the cracks you didn't know you'd left. And then you start to go down. This woman was too young, thank God. But I knew, with a sinking certainty, that the past has come back to haunt me. Again.

A bit distractedly, I said, "Revenge." Her brother had said it himself. *Don't think I'll forget, da Silva.* How old would he be, now? Seventy, seventy-five? The woman could be his daughter, then: Elvira's niece. I hadn't known she had one. Hell, I hadn't known until the day of the funeral that her husband had a brother. Let alone one who would let his grievance stew for twenty years.

"What are you talking about?" Emilia said. I looked at her a little ruefully. A little shamefacedly. Bite the bullet, da Silva.

"I did have an affair in Rio," I said. "And now I think her brother's come after me."

"After all this time?" Bless you, Emilia. No recriminations. She didn't even let go of my hand. "Do you think he'd go to so much trouble?"

I thought about Francisco Domingues Batista, the last time I had seen him. The only time I had seen him. "Yes," I said slowly. "I think he would."

Emilia put her arms round me. I reciprocated. Then she said, "So don't ever think I'm worrying too much again."

We sat without speaking for a moment. Until I couldn't put it off any longer. I disengaged reluctantly, then stood up. "Harris will think I've run away."

In fact, Harris was entertaining Zé. Well, *entertaining* is stretching it a bit, perhaps. I don't know what they were talking about. Zé's grin was a little too fixed, and he leapt to his feet like a stag when I came through the door. I raised an eyebrow at him.

"Ready, Harris?" I enquired.

"Sure, skipper," he said, lumbering out of his chair.

Zé was hovering by the door. Obviously torn between the instinct of civility and the desire to make himself scarce. He looked from me to Harris and back again.

"Go on, then, before I cancel your shore leave," I told him, trying not to smile. He didn't need telling twice, although he remembered to be polite. Just about.

"*Adeus,* Sr Harris," he said, smartly, and was gone.

Harris listened to my narrative without comment. Even when I was done, he only remarked, "Things sure do happen around you, skipper."

I didn't reply. It's usually the English who think that a conversation can usefully consist of stating the blindingly obvious. Which is not to say that I never do it myself, of course. Just not all the time. I went on smoking, watching the quick and the dead we passed on the narrow ways. A few hovering ghosts. Women hanging out their washing, like an arcane signalling system. Cats and dogs, the former searching for spots in the sun as it rose high enough, and haughtily ignoring the latter. Children running here and there, lost in their own worlds. Some of them were ghosts, too.

Things, as Harris called them, that have happened to me before were different. They weren't instigated by someone who had a personal grudge against me. Apart from the Venetian, of course, and he was dead by then. On the whole they haven't required me to think very much, either. Not like this, which was turning into a kind of odyssey. Hunt the grimoire. Find the grimoire, to be more precise. Not that I even knew where to start. Ah well. At least I admit my shortcomings.

"The first thing to do is find that woman," I said.

"I guess I could track her," Harris offered. I looked at him, startled, furious at myself for not thinking of it. Meu Deus, of course he could. Anything else under your nose that you've managed to miss, da Silva?

"Don't you need her scent?"

"She's been in your wife's workroom," he said. "I can pick her out. That is, if your good lady don't mind having a...wolf in there."

"She knows about you," I pointed out.

"Yeah, maybe, but she ain't never seen me changed." He had a point. Two hundred-plus pounds of werewolf is rather a shock the first time you see it. And the second. And—well, you get the idea. You don't, precisely, ever get used to it.

"Well, let's say she knows you won't bite her," I said.

"Hah," said Harris. I think it was a laugh. It was difficult to tell, because it didn't sound very amused and he didn't smile. But then he never does. So that might have been the Harrisian equivalent of hilarity, for all I knew.

"Y'know, skipper," he went on thoughtfully, as if an idea had just struck him, "I kinda think I might have seen her already."

"You do?" I asked, giving my eyebrow a scratch and watching the ghost of an enormously fat man who had probably died from the heat on a day like today. It was barely ten in the morning but I was already starting to sweat.

"Tall, dark...yeah, I know. Not much to go on. But now I think about it, I reckon she was watching *Isabella.*"

"When was this?"

"Yesterday," Harris said. "I guess I didn't really take a lot of notice, but I musta seen her half a dozen times during the day."

Who was she? I was only guessing at Dona Elvira's niece. Batista was probably fifty back then, maybe more. Plenty of men become fathers at fifty. On the other hand, perhaps the woman was his wife. Women of thirty have been known to marry men of seventy. Though in those cases, she's probably more interested in the size of his wallet. And if he thinks anything else, he's deluding himself. Which men do, all of the time.

My rather fruitless speculations were interrupted by someone calling my name. I turned to see, without much surprise—more with resignation—another old acquaintance from Rio. Bring them all on, I thought. The more the merrier.

This man had nothing to do with Batista, though. As far as I knew. He brought back other memories, for I had met him on the Venetian's business. He was an antiquarian, a book collector with a reputation for being able to find rare volumes. An Englishman, long resident in Brazil, by the name of Montague Pierce. The Venetian had sent me to his shop while I was in Rio on other business. To ask whether Pierce had, or could get, certain books. Books which I now know were grimoires. In those days, however, I didn't know much about magic. Not that I do now, really. But it hadn't taken me long to guess that was how the Venetian saw me kill his brother.

Twenty years on, Pierce's fair hair and beard showed little gray. So there is an advantage. Put up with sunburn all your life and you can go gray without anyone noticing. But for a few more lines in his face, a little extra gauntness, he still looked like a bleached grandee. And he still spoke Portuguese like an Englishman.

"It is you, da Silva. I wasn't sure." He extended a hand, and I shook it. "And a captain now. Been in the wars, I see."

"Sr Pierce," I said. I introduced Harris (in English), who nodded politely enough. I lit a cheroot and looked curiously at the antiquarian. A living ghost among all the dead around him. Which he couldn't see, of course.

"What brings you to Lisbon?" I asked.

"Oh, it's a long story," he said dismissively. Then smiled. "But an interesting one, if you have half an hour."

Of course it was no coincidence. "As a matter of fact, Sr Pierce, I could use the services of an antiquarian," I said, pulling out my watch. "I have some ship's business to attend to, but let's meet later. One o'clock?"

"By all means," he said, looking rather startled. Perhaps he hadn't expected me to take his bait. If that's what it was. "Ah... where's a good place to meet? Or even eat?"

There's a place called Salvador's that I tend to patronize. I told him how to find it.

"I'll see you later, then," he said, and we shook hands again.

What the hell was he doing here? I wondered. I'd find out soon enough.

But it's too damned convenient, and I don't like it. I don't like the feeling that events were being manipulated. That I was being manipulated. I shrugged. Ah well. Nothing I could do about it now. Play the cards you're dealt, da Silva. Pierce might be able to help. Might even be willing to help. I wiped sweat off my face.

"Skipper," said Harris suddenly, and I whirled round at the urgency in his voice, hand automatically reaching towards my knife.

"What?"

"That woman, I've just seen her."

"Where?" I snapped. He started to run. I swore, then followed. He's got longer legs than me. But he's also carrying a lot more weight, so I kept up well enough. We rounded a corner a minute later and I saw, just slipping out of sight, not the woman I had expected, but something that moved very much like the armored figure I fought two nights ago. I put on a spurt of speed I didn't know I had and gave chase, but it was no good.

Harris caught me up a moment later as I stood trying to get my breath back. Sailors don't do a lot of running. Well, there isn't much call for it on board ship. Not to mention no room for it, either. So I was pretty much puffed, red-faced and sweating like a stevedore. Swearing like one, too. I'd have liked to get some answers out of that character.

"Athletic kinda female," panted Harris, coming to a halt like a steam-engine.

I nodded, then lit a cheroot, wishing I could continue in pursuit. But right now I had other matters to attend to. Getting Ortigão somewhere he could be looked after. Finding out if anyone else had seen—or felt—anything. And so on.

Of course, it all took much longer than I anticipated. Doesn't everything? Consequently it was twenty past one when I finally managed to get to my rendezvous with Pierce. Half-expecting to find he'd become fed up with waiting and disappeared. But no, there he was, keeping a bottle of wine warm. With two glasses. Seated at a table jammed into a corner under a huge tiled *azulejo* mural of a caravel in blue and white. I fought my way to join him. The place was noisy, hot, smoke-filled. Smelled of garlic, fish frying, tobacco. It was, in a word, alive. I slid into the chair next to Pierce and lit up. Poured myself a glass of wine. He followed suit.

"So, what are you doing in Lisbon?" I asked him again. A waiter put a plate of *amêijoas* in front of him, and I interrupted myself to order some octopus. They cut the tentacles to order and grill them till they're sweet and tender as lobster.

"Well," said Pierce when the waiter had gone, sampling a clam, "you remember back in ninety-two when your boss wanted to know if I could get some books for him?" I nodded. Thinking ruefully of myself at twenty-four. When you think you're going to live forever. I shook the uneasy memories away and took a mouthful of wine. Pierce wrinkled his nose, as if he'd found something bad. Saw my quizzical look and smiled briefly. "No, there's nothing wrong with the food! I was remembering some of the books he wanted. Nasty books. Not the sort of thing I'd normally want to touch, you know."

"Grimoires," I supplied, and he looked up from his plate, surprised. I raised an eyebrow at him. Enigmatic, da Silva. Yes, well. Got to maintain appearances.

"Yes," he agreed. "Fairly obscure, some of them. And one I had never even heard of, which intrigued me."

All of a sudden I wanted to laugh. I drank some more wine instead. Then I pointed my cheroot at him and said, "Don't tell me. Something called the *Book of Souls*. By a monk whose name I can't remember."

Pierce's mouth dropped open, and he closed it quickly. Followed up by stuffing some more clams into it. "How on earth did you hear about the *Book of Souls?*"

"That's also a long story," I said, scratching thoughtfully at my cheekbone. "You tell me yours, and I'll tell you mine."

He laughed shortly. "I spent the next twenty years looking for it," he said. "Della Quercia offered me a fortune for it, if I could find a copy."

"He's dead," I pointed out, watching him eat. Thinking about demons. Then, and now.

"I know," Pierce said. "But I thought that if he was willing to pay that much for it, someone else would. And I was right."

"You have a buyer?" The waiter brought my *polvo*. I pointed at the wine bottle, and he nodded before bustling off. "How much did he offer?" I asked Pierce, draining my glass.

"Two and a half thousand American dollars," he replied, downing half his own wine in one swallow. "Nearly a thousand guineas in English money. And that's twice as much as Della Quercia offered me."

"Mother of God!" I exclaimed, staring at him.

"Yes," said the Englishman, with a thin smile, and returned his attention to his plate. I did likewise, stunned by the amount of money. After a moment, he went on. "I eventually managed to discover that the tradition that brought the book to Brazil with a member of Cabral's crew was correct. The man's name was Vicente Batista."

Batista. Now why am I not surprised?

Pierce divided the remains of the wine between our glasses. The waiter brought a replacement bottle and removed the empty one. I stubbed out my cheroot in the ashtray.

"So it did survive," I remarked, slicing off a piece of tender tentacle and putting it my mouth.

"Only partially," Pierce said. "The general opinion seems to be that it's been quite badly damaged. Which would push the price down, of course." Was his motive purely monetary, I wondered. Or did he want the book, as I did, for another reason?

"And you think the book's in Lisbon?" I asked.

"Yes. As soon as I realized Sr Domingues Batista must have it, I tried to contact him. Only to find that he'd left for Lisbon two days earlier."

"What makes you think he has it with him?"

The Englishman finished his plateful and looked at me, eyebrows elevated. "Because it's worth a lot of money," he said. "Now all I have to do is find him."

I know a wolf that can do that for you, I thought, hiding a smile and taking another mouthful of wine. "And what makes you think that Batista can be persuaded to part with this book? If he knows how much it's worth."

"Oh, I'm not too concerned about that. Not when my—customer is willing to pay that much. Every man has his price," he added, resorting to cliché. I wondered if that was really true. I had paid mine, but that hadn't been in money.

"You haven't told me why this book is worth so much. Or why some people think it is." Which is the same thing, really.

"For its spells, of course," said Pierce. "If you believe that sort of thing."

"Do you?" I asked. He laughed, self-consciously.

"Yes, I suppose so. They're supposed to be more powerful than any 'that was or will be'. For instance, some people believe that if anyone succeeded in working a spell called 'the perfect man' could quite literally have the power to rule the world."

Fork halfway to my mouth, I said, idiotically, "What?"

Pierce grimaced. "Of course," he said, "there's a drawback. You understand all this is purely theoretical?" I nodded, since he seemed to expect some kind of response and I had my mouth full. "There's a school of thought which believes a spell that powerful would upset the equilibrium. That it would be an act so unnatural it could destroy the world's balance."

Despite the heat, I felt as if someone had tipped ice water down my back. "Meaning what, precisely?"

"Well, chaos, you know. I mean, I'm guessing—but I suppose, earthquakes. Tidal waves. War, famine. Unprecedented destruction."

"And after that?"

"There is no after that."

Apocalypse.

Finding my mouth was dry, I finished the wine in my glass. Refilled it. Refilled Pierce's too. He watched me, a slight frown on his face. He didn't know, of course. I had to tell him.

"Pierce, he's working the spell. He's already gathered three of the souls."

The antiquarian's pale face turned even whiter. When he reached for his glass, his hand was shaking. "He has to be stopped."

And there you have it: the Englishman at moments of crisis. Reverting to type, and stating the bloody obvious.

* * *

Leaving the skinny tall tilted house with its mismatched windows and tile-patched facade which he was beginning, despite himself, to think of as a second home, Sebastião Fernandes da Silva returned Emilia's wave and set off into the maze that was the Alfama. He walked with a spring in his step despite seventy-six years and intermittent sciatica: he was almost happy. He had suddenly acquired a family. Painting Emilia made him happy. Entertaining Caterina made him happy, if a little exhausted. José—Zé—confused him a little, but then the boy was fourteen years old, and so that was only to be expected.

Thinking of his son, though, dredged up such a mixture of emotions that he almost wished he hadn't gone down to the quayside to meet *Isabella*. Try as he might, he couldn't feel any connection to the stranger Luís da Silva now was. Could those thirty years ever be bridged? He didn't know. Wasn't even sure his son wanted to try. Though he himself regretted those lost years with a bitter, nostalgic ache.

What made it worse, not better, was that he knew and understood why Luís had run away to sea.

María. His wife. His late wife. Now with God, where he presumed she wanted to be. Whom he had jokingly called Santa María when they were much younger, before the joke became too painfully real. Who had never in her entire life taken pleasure in anything, her Christianity being more of the mortification-of-the-flesh variety than the praise-God-for-all-our-blessings kind. She was a penniless aristocrat's daughter who had married an up-and-coming artist and turned him into a kind of ecclesiastical interior decorator.

And his son saw ghosts: what was he to make of that?

Sunk in his thoughts, old regrets, new faint growths of hope, the old man failed to notice his follower.

It looked like a young girl, fifteen or sixteen perhaps. You wouldn't have taken her for a whore: she was too modestly dressed, though her clothes appeared old and much-mended. Her bare feet were dirty, but her plain peasant face was clean. She didn't have the look of a beggar or — quite — of a gypsy. Her neat movements were like those of a dancer, graceful, precise. Perhaps, seeing her stealthy pursuit of the old man, you might have thought her a pickpocket. But she was not seeking to steal from him. At least, not at that moment. And not anything so mundane as money.

Skipping nimbly past him, she slipped a coin into his jacket pocket and tripped off without his even having noticed her. He was too lost inside himself.

Marked, the old man continued on his way home.

All of a sudden, he felt uneasy, and glanced around, but saw nothing that might have triggered an awareness of danger. But it was as if, between one heartbeat and the next, the world had changed. From something familiar into something threatening. A drop of sweat trickled down his temple: he mopped it absently with his handkerchief.

The sense of being watched, when he was no longer being watched — at least, not by anything he was capable of seeing — stayed with him all the way home like the heat of the sun beating on his head even through his hat, souring the day for him.

As he put his key in the front door, he saw the corner of a paper poking out from the letterbox. Some kind of handbill, he supposed. Probably political. He opened the door and pulled the leaflet out, leaving a corner of the page stuck in the flap, caught by the spring.

Shutting the door behind him, he stared at the paper in perplexity. It seemed to have been torn out of a book, and showed — inexplicably — a crude woodcut of a man trudging along a road by the light of the moon. This walker was being pursued by a demonic figure, depicted in unusually foul detail. Under the picture were the words, in English, "And turns no more his head."

Offended as much by the draughtsmanship as by the subject matter, he crumpled the page in his hand and threw it into the wastepaper bin.

Behind him in the empty hall, something laughed.

He whirled round. Nothing. Of course, nothing. The palms of his hands were wet. Sweat crawled in his hair. Angrily, he called his housekeeper's name, though fully aware that she would not be there at this time of day. His voice seemed to echo strangely in the hallway.

And then, again, the laughter. This time, he thought it came from upstairs. He felt his heart pounding, his breath coming short. Though he had no history of heart disease, the idea crossed his mind. He was, after all, seventy-six years old. So, too old to be starting at shadows. Of which there were none. It was broad daylight.

Deliberately, he calmed his breathing. Did not mount the stairs, but walked, instead, into what had once been the parlor but was now inhabited by canvases and was sweet with the redolence of linseed oil, the sharpness of turpentine: the scent of a painterly vinaigrette.

This was his home ground. Here, he had the advantage.

Or so he told himself.

Shutting the door, he turned round slowly. In the center of the room stood a young girl with a strangely sweet smile, a street-urchin by the look of her, holding a device — was it clockwork? he wondered. It looked a bit like the orrery in his studio.

Disarmed, he forgot to be scared for a moment. Until he looked into her eyes. "Who are you?" he asked, shuddering at what he saw there.

"My name is not important," she replied, in a hollow reverberating voice which struck a chill into him. It held the stench of the tomb and the dread of dying inherent in its timbre. "But it is written on the coin in your pocket."

But there was no coin—oh. He drew it out, but could not read the strange script. Tried to put it down, but it adhered to his hand in some foul sticky way. He found his knees were shaking.

"What is that you're holding?" he whispered.

She moved a small lever on the side of the device, and the thing that was not an orrery began to rotate. It made a strange low whirring sound with echoes so deep that he felt a jarring deep down in his bones.

"A machine for gathering souls," said the demon.

And gathered his, into the maelstrom it produced.

* * *

As wolf, I have to admit Harris is impressive. He makes a *lot* of wolf. In my house he was even more ill-at-ease than in his human shape. I watched him snuffling at Emilia's workbench and wondered whether this would work. And what the hell I was going to do if it did. His eyes gleamed yellow in the gaslight, almost like gemstones themselves.

Then he stopped his restless padding and grew still. I felt my scalp prickle with anticipation and stuck a finger under my eye-patch to clear out some of the moisture. It had been a sweltering day, and now it was a hot night.

"Go' i', ski'er," he said indistinctly.

"You're sure?" Stupid question. He jerked his head. A nod, I presumed. "All right, let's go."

The moon rode above us, huge. Everything was black and white. I followed the werewolf through the narrow sloping alleys, and not a soul we passed took a blind bit of notice. Perhaps we looked like a man taking his dog for a walk. Yes, sure, and I'm the President of Portugal. Harris-wolf stands as high as my waist.

And he had felt another demon, that day. Has Batista got four now?

He loped down a flight of steps, trailing ghosts like smoke, leaving me behind. Now, of course, he doesn't have longer legs than me. Just twice as many. "Slow down," I called urgently. He stopped at the bottom, impatient. Looked up at me with his big yellow eyes. Blinked once.

Two men came out of an opening in the wall and walked straight past him. Came up the steps, talking in undertones, and walked straight past me. I gaped. Harris's wolf-jaws seemed to grin, and I shut my mouth with a snap and ran down the rest of the steps, understanding at last that we were both hidden from casual sight by whatever "don't-look-at-me" power he possessed. Ghosts drifted past, unconcerned, but then I'm not sure most of them are aware enough to see the living anyway. The recent dead sometimes react to people they know, but that's usually it. Though they have proved useful, in the past.

Leaving the Alfama, we passed into the Baixa, which they say was rebuilt to be earthquake-proof. I'd rather not have had that thought. It reminded me a little too much of Montague Pierce's terrifying words.

I hadn't told Pierce about the mystery woman. Nor that I intended to track her with the aid of a werewolf. There are times when it's better to keep your mouth shut. However, I *had* told him that I thought I could locate Batista. Just not how.

There were more people around here, out in search of food or drink or less innocent things. But all of them passed by without a second glance. A useful talent, this. Especially so close to the Rossio. Which is always crowded.

The wolf-Harris moved through the night as if it was his element, and it parted like the Red Sea for Moses. I merely followed in his wake, thinking about how most werewolf folklore was just plain wrong. Apart from his size and reddish fur, Harris looks just like a normal wolf, not some kind of human-lupine blend. And no, you can't identify one in human form by the eyebrows.

The unfortunate Ortigão's eyebrows meet in the middle, and he's certainly not a werewolf. A wolf, yes, granted. Just ask any woman he's met.

Most important of all—at least to me—you don't change into a werewolf if all one of them does is bite you. I know, because I've been bitten by one. Admittedly I did wash the bite with holy water a few minutes later. But I was more worried about getting rabies from it. Anyway, I don't turn furry at full moon. I think Emilia would've noticed.

We started going uphill again. I guessed we were heading for the Bairro Alto and wondered to myself whether anyone would notice a werewolf on the funicular. Though I imagined we wouldn't actually be taking the funicular this evening. Great news, another hill to climb.

Cities at night are quite different from their daytime counterpart. They shed their facades and fill up with different crowds. Their noises are different, their smells. Their sights, too, but after dark you have to rely more on your other senses. Much as Harris, as wolf, has to. You have to adapt. Because if you can't, you're done for. Night-time makes were-creatures of us all.

We came to the earthquake-ruined Convento do Carmo and its thronging phantoms. Harris stopped, so suddenly I almost ran into him. "What is it?" I asked softly.

He rolled his eyes at me. If I can give a wolf a human expression, he looked frustrated. Then he blew out a breath: *fff!* and said "'oro'd."

"Followed?" I interpreted. He nodded, grimly. The Largo do Carmo was empty. I took out my knife anyway. Nervous, da Silva? Well, yes, but it's always better to be prepared. Harris started to walk again, a little more slowly this time. I kept pace with him, nerves tingling.

And then there was a gunshot. I ducked instinctively, heard the whine of the bullet, heard it smack into the wall beside me. It had damn nearly taken off my ear. "Run!" I barked at Harris, taking to my heels. The shot was followed by a second, and the wolf gave a yelping scream and I actually saw a spray of blood fly up from his haunch as he staggered to one side with the force of it. I swore in alarm, but he scrambled up and limped after me as I slid round a corner. Put my knife away and took out my own gun. Where had the shots come from?

I knelt beside Harris, who had collapsed. Put my hand on the wolf's heaving side. We were in deep shadow, apparently out of sight of the sniper. Since he wasn't shooting any more. Well observed, da Silva. "Can you walk?" I whispered.

The wolf grunted in pain. "D'n-no."

Oh, thank you very much, I thought. Now I'm going to have to carry the werewolf. As if it's not bad enough toting heavyweight priests about. Harris turned his wolf-head and snapped at the wound. Narrowly missing my hand, which I had just moved to wipe sweat off my face. "Hey!" I said, indignantly.

But we can't sit here till the sniper comes to find us. I got cautiously to my feet. My knee was beginning to protest. I paid it the compliment of a wince, then ignored it. I inched to the corner and peered cautiously round. Nothing. Good. I peered at the wall until I spotted the mark the first bullet had made, then looked up at the building it must have come from. Its name, by the door on painted tiles, was *Casa dos Quatro Ventos*, House of the Four Winds. All its windows shuttered, now. No way of telling whether they have been all along. I moved back round the corner, out of sight. Just in case.

There's nothing like being shot at to heighten your senses. I could hear Harris breathing. Hell, I could hear my heart beating. And then I could hear footsteps. I backed to the wall and raised my gun. My hand was slippery with sweat. "Play dead," I said to Harris.

The footsteps turned themselves into a stealthy shadow, and the shadow became John Yeoh. "Don't shoot, senhor capitão," he said, in Portuguese.

"Why not?" I snapped back. "Someone's shooting at me."

"I think they've stopped," he said drily.

"For now." I squatted beside Harris and switched to English. "Harris, I'm going to get you on your feet. You have to try and walk, d'you hear me?" He growled and swished his tail. I took that for a yes. All right, I would have to trust John Yeoh. I put my gun back in my pocket and hoisted the wounded werewolf to his feet.

"If you can get your...friend to walk," said Yeoh, also in English, "I know someone nearby who can treat his wound for him."

"I'll take you up on that," I said grimly. The werewolf limped a couple of steps. I pulled out a cheroot, much-needed, and lit it gratefully. I hadn't wanted to mess up the trail Harris was following with the smell of smoke. "Let's go, people."

Nothing stirred as we passed by the House of the Four Winds, not even one wind. Harris hobbled rapidly enough on three legs, but kept bumping into me. Being bumped into by over two hundred pounds of werewolf, not an enjoyable experience.

"Down here," said Yeoh presently, and turned left. Trailing creepers almost obscured the door he stopped at. They made a whispering sound, although there was no hint of a breeze. He knocked, a complicated pattern like a signal. The door opened quietly. Apparently of its own accord. No light spilled out. "Go in," he said. I felt a curious little shiver as I passed the threshold. But nothing yelled *Danger!* at me. There was a soft click as the door closed, and the air took on a curious, almost chill, dead quality.

As my sight grew used to the dimness, I realized that there was something insubstantial about the room behind the door. As if it was made out of dust or moonlight: something that may strike you as ephemeral, but is, in fact, eternal. But still no sense of unease. Whatever it was, was—neutral. And welcomingly cool on that hot night. Harris growled, a basso rumbling deep in his chest. I rubbed my eyebrow.

"Where are we?" I asked. Yeoh looked at me curiously. As if he was surprised I noticed anything out of the ordinary. But he gave me a straightforward answer. Well, sort of.

"In a pocket of time," he said. I raised an eyebrow at him, but made no further comment. I thought I almost understood what he meant. Time was, after all, his trade. Even if it had also become, somewhere along the line, his curse.

There was a ghost seated at the table, I now saw. Whether it had been there all along, I had no idea. But it was not the voiceless shade that would be hovering where it met its death. It was a summoned ghost, in appearance as solid as flesh.

It was the old scholar whose shade I had seen outside the library of São Rafael. Meu Deus, I thought, it's like a web. Intersecting lines. Are all the people I know, all the people I meet, all the ghosts I see, connected to each other? I looked round at Harris and found he had flopped down on the floor. A long pink tongue lolled out of the wolf's mouth, and he was panting harshly. Dried blood matted his fur, but the bullet-wound was still leaking.

"You said you could do something to help him," I said to Yeoh. But it was the old man's ghost who answered.

"And so we can, with your help, senhor capitão," he answered. Though how he knew how to call me that I had no idea. I was wearing a plain dark jacket and pants. Nothing to identify me. "Allow me to introduce myself. My name is…Isaiah. I was—I am—an apothecary, a surgeon. I was murdered by a mob in the year fifteen hundred and six. A Christian mob," he added, unnecessarily. "They burned my body in the Rossio."

Don't look at me like that, I thought. I'm not even sure I *am* a Christian any more, except nominally. If I ever really was one. "Is that your real name?" I asked.

"No, of course not," he replied with a smile. But who had summoned him? Whoever it was would have had to know his name. "Now if you could lift your wolf onto the table, we'll see what we can do for him."

All very well for him to say. He didn't have to do the lifting. I squatted down. "Harris," I said, "we need to get you onto the table."

He struggled to his feet, but it was obviously hurting him quite a lot. I sighed, got my arms round the wolf's body, and heaved him up with an effort. The old scholar peered at the wound, and I saw him flinch.

"The ball is silver," he said, and for a moment I didn't know what he was talking about. And then it stuck me. It was fairly obvious when you thought about it. Of course, I realized, flintlocks or whatever they had in his time didn't fire bullets. "You will have to help me extract it before I can treat the wound."

"Me?" I exclaimed, and simultaneously the werewolf gave a growl that said quite plainly, I'm not having you poking round in there. And that went for both of us.

Isaiah, amusement showing on his long face, said, "Tell your wolf not to worry. I am going to use a charm, not surgery." I relayed this. Harris looked, I thought, unconvinced. "Listen," the old man went on, "all of us here, save you, capitão, live a half-life. We cannot touch silver. You will have to do it. It is quite simple. All you need to do is place your hand over the wound, but be careful not to touch the wolf's flesh."

I did as he said, feeling heat radiate off the werewolf's body. Isaiah began to chant his charm in a language I didn't know. Hebrew, I presumed. After a moment there was an implosion, like a powerful inhalation of air, and I felt something violently *sucked* out of the wound. It hit my palm hard enough to sting, and I instinctively closed my hand around it and jerked it away. Opened my fingers to see a silver bullet, streaked with blood. Who had known enough to be prepared with silver ammunition?

The werewolf's blood would give me a rash until I got the chance to wash my hand with holy water. But for now I merely wrapped the bullet in my handkerchief and stuffed it in my pocket. Yawned, abruptly tired. Scratched my suddenly itching scar as I watched Isaiah sewing up the wound.

"How is it you can do that?" I asked, curiously. "I've never encountered a ghost with...solidity before."

"Ah, you forget the nature of your wolf," Isaiah replied. I wished he'd stop calling Harris "my wolf". I don't own him. Don't want to. "Since he is of the shadows, as I am, I can touch him if my intentions are benign. As with Sr Yeoh there." I looked briefly at Yeoh. The candles cast strange shadows on his face. "You, I cannot touch. Although other creatures of the night have done so, a mere ghost cannot do you harm."

He was doing it again. I frowned. "What do you know about me?" He looked up at me briefly, his eyes shadowed.

"You are known," said the old scholar. "I recognized you." And my mind flipped back two years or more to the ancient guru, Mohan Das, not long before Harris had knocked another werewolf away from me. *They know you now*, he had said. *Your sight, and your actions, mark you, and they will recognize you.*

"Who summoned you?" I asked him, but he merely smiled and made no reply. For all I knew, he had summoned himself. But I got the strong idea that he was afraid of me. He wouldn't tell me his real name. Was it because he knew who I was? That's a good one. Da Silva, the phantoms' bogeyman.

Not wanting to go any further down that road, I turned to Yeoh. "And just what were *you* doing?" I asked him. "Following us?"

"I came to your home," he said, "but you had just set out, you and the werewolf. I could see you were on the trail of something: I didn't want to intrude. So I followed you."

"Why?"

"I had been thinking about what you said," he replied. "And it occurred to me that if it's true, that I put myself under a geas, then I'm bound in a way like the souls of your friends. So if you were to find a way to free them, you may also discover how to release me. So…I decided to offer you my help."

The old surgeon finished his suturing, then dusted the wound with what looked like perfectly mundane sulphur.

"In doing what?" I asked Yeoh.

"Finding whatever you were looking for in the House of the Four Winds, capitão. How do you think I acquired my collection of manuscripts?"

I stared at him and then began to laugh. Though it wasn't really that funny. "Very well, Sr Yeoh. I'll pay you a visit and we can discuss the matter."

Isaiah cleared his throat, to attract my attention. Or, I should say, he made a throat-clearing noise. Since he didn't have a physical throat to clear. I turned to him.

"You should treat the wound as a normal injury when he regains his human shape," he instructed. "It should heal quickly."

"He can slap a bandage on his own backside," I said, and the wolf thumped his tail on the table. "Can you get down off there?"

Harris got stiffly to his feet and looked round the small cluttered chamber. Evaluating a spring, I supposed. Then he shook his head, slowly and emphatically, a human gesture that suited a wolf not at all. I sighed, then lifted him down again. He gets heavier every time. Still, with a bit of luck that'll be the last time I'll have to do that. Shut up, da Silva. Tempting providence is never a smart move.

We made our way slowly back to my house. Harris's "we're-not-here" power still seemed to be working, for which I was grateful. Although any interested party could probably have tracked me without any trouble by the trail of smoke.

I gave him a blanket in the parlor, and he collapsed like the world's biggest wolfskin rug in front of the settee. He'd begun to snore before I even shut the door on him.

* * *

"Sr Pierce," said Francisco Domingues Batista, looking at the Englishman's business card with arched nostrils and a faintly puzzled air. "I know you by more than reputation, of course." Although he had done business with the Englishman in the past, his tone managed to suggest that that reputation was not entirely savory. He put the card down on a table so highly polished that it reflected both his foreshortened form and the chandelier which hung precisely above its own center.

Pierce looked round the room a little surreptitiously, although there was nothing to detect. It was a very overt room, not like, say, a library, which can itself take on the nature of an abditory. Even if it does not house such artefacts, and who can tell that at a first glance, or even a second? But this, which Batista appeared to be using as a study—despite a conspicuous lack of any kind of paperwork—had evidently been intended as a breakfast room.

It held only the polished table, two chairs with barley-sugar legs which matched it, and a small sideboard. Its walls were white, very plain save for four *azulejos* depicting personifications of the four continents, Europe, Africa, India, Asia. Tall windows opened onto a narrow wrought-iron balcony enlivened by a terracotta trough of canna lilies and salvia and a view worthy of a *miradouro* clear across to the ruined castle. The room was cool and pleasant.

Batista was also cool, but there was a rather unpleasant undercurrent to his haughty politeness. Pierce, however, took it as merely the familiar disdain endemic to Rio's upper classes, and let it run off his back.

"I was rather hoping you could help me," he said blandly, his English accent harshening the softer sounds of the tongue he had not been brought up to speak, the language of the navigators. Batista noticed this in passing as only one more reason for contempt.

"And in what way would that be?" he inquired in his chill aristocratic tones, though he had no actual title.

"You may not care to acknowledge it at this moment, but you know very well that I am a...collector," Pierce said. The other man's expression remained unchanged, and Pierce sighed. Of course the damned Brazilian was going to make this as difficult as possible. "Of books, for the most part. And manuscripts." Batista inclined his head slightly, as if to imply that yes, he was aware of the fact as one is aware that tradesmen called at one's house, but did not require acknowledgement.

"*I* am not a collector of books," he pointed out.

"No, sir, of course I am aware of that fact," Pierce said hurriedly, all too aware of sweat running down his sides. He took off his spectacles and polished them, a diversion which is perhaps the only advantage of needing to wear glasses. "But, ah, I am reliably informed that you do have one extremely scarce volume in your possession." He could hardly believe that he was actually bearding the Brazilian in his den. Because if the man really was trying to work a spell from the *Book of Souls*, something only a tremendously powerful magus should be able to attempt...Well, it would be worth it to find out.

Before Batista could make any kind of reply, the door opened to admit his daughter. Pierce tried not to stare at her, although his glance naturally gravitated to the tall woman. If rumor was correct she might well have run him through with a fencing saber, if she suspected any impertinence. He'd seen the result of one of her bouts of annoyance. Mind you, rumor also had it that she had challenged an army officer to a duel over a supposed insult, *and* fought him, *and* won. And come close to castrating him with her blade. Pierce crossed his legs nervously and tried to focus on something harmless. Not her haughty face. Certainly not the fine banded agate which hung on her breast.

He stood up and bowed politely to hide his confusion.

"Oh, you have a visitor," she said. "I'll come back later."

Her father, pointedly neglecting to introduce Pierce to her, said "Later," and she withdrew, closing the door softly behind her. A moment later he turned to face Pierce again. "And what book might this be, Sr Pierce?"

Pierce, thoroughly intimidated, kept his voice level with an effort. "The book your ancestor, Vicente Batista, brought to Brazil in his sea-chest in the year 1500. The *Book of Souls*, by Estêvão Gonçalves."

Batista began to laugh. Pierce felt his face growing red. After a moment he turned on his heel and headed for the door.

"My dear Sr Pierce," Batista called him back between guffaws, "please accept my apologies. I'm truly sorry you've come all this way on a wild-goose chase. But really—! That rumor has been around for centuries. I had no idea anyone would take it seriously in this day and age. We are, after all, in the twentieth century now. A century, it is to be hoped, of rationalism." He wiped the corners of his eyes with a silk handkerchief and resumed his decidedly unamused expression. "No, Sr Pierce, I don't have the Book of Souls. And if I did, I doubt if you could afford it." He rang the bell. "Eduardo will show you out."

The manservant's curly hair and coffee-colored complexion implied he had accompanied Batista from Brazil, so Pierce saw no point in attempting to suborn him on the way out. He managed to recover sufficient composure to turn at the door and say to Batista, "Thank you for your time, sir."

"Sr Pierce," the other man said. The Englishman met his eyes, and rather wished he hadn't. There was something implacable in them that made him shiver through his nervous perspiration. "Who told you my address?"

"Ah, I don't remember offhand," Pierce lied, and knew that Batista knew he lied.

"Very well," he said coldly. "Good day."

"Good—good day, sir," stuttered Pierce, and scuttled off in Eduardo's wake.

The door in the high wall clanged shut behind him, and he found he was drenched in sweat. He felt like a mouse that has inexplicably been released by a cat after a session of play. Pierce shuddered. He would not have been surprised to see blood on his clothes.

Oh, the man had power, that was for sure.

* * *

Lisbon has twenty miles of seafront. So I consider myself lucky to have secured a berth for *Isabella* within walking distance of home. I suppose Harris was glad of it too on this occasion. When I asked him how he was he scowled blackly and growled, "Sore ass." His air of wounded pride made me bite my lip to stop a smile that wanted to come.

Now he was gone, limping but otherwise none the worse for his wound. I'd despatched a grumbling Zé to the *pensão* where Montague Pierce was staying, with the address of the House of the Four Winds. *Isabella* had a new cargo to load when she was ready to receive it, but Harris and Ashley and Costa, the Second, were more than capable of seeing to that. Delegation. That's what being the skipper is all about. It's taken me years to perfect the art, mind you. But I expect my crew appreciate not having the Old Man breathing down their necks all the time.

And I—I wouldn't say I had nothing to do. I had more than enough to occupy my mind. The trouble is, that's not what I need. Which is a course of action. Since I've never been able to sit around and do nothing. But I couldn't even make a plan until I heard from Pierce. Patience is a virtue: try and cultivate a bit, da Silva.

Emilia, unused to having me cluttering up the house, did her own delegating. She sent Caterina to entertain me until it was time for her lessons. Which is, in its way, more tiring than rushing round the midnight streets of Lisbon trying to keep up with a werewolf. Someone—I suspected Zé—had taught her to say "goddamn" in English. I tried, without much success, to persuade her not to air it in front of her mother. I say *without much success* because when Emilia returned to relieve me of my command, Caterina was bouncing up and down on the settee and singing it to a nursery-rhyme tune. The cause of maternal (and paternal) discipline was not advanced at this point. Emilia dissolved into laughter at the sight. And so, of course, did I.

You want a patriarch? Don't look at me.

Half past ten, and no sign of Pierce.

One of the nicest things about the house is its little brick-paved terrace on top of the flat roof of the scullery. Emilia's furnished it with a wooden bench and a lemon tree in a pot, and there's one of those climbing vines with the magenta flowers crawling about it. It's a pleasant place to sit, with the clutter of mismatched buildings rising all around. The backs of houses, shuttered against the sun. Strings of washing: Lisbon bunting. Whitewashed walls, most peeling. A fig tree—I've never managed to find out exactly where that has its roots. And I can sit there in shirtsleeves and not bother with my eye-patch. A rare luxury. Already the morning was hot, but direct sun only touches the terrace in late afternoon.

I lit a cheroot and opened the *Mappa Mundi* volume at the pages that referred to the *Book of Souls*. Hoping, perhaps, that inspiration would strike.

"*The souls that shall be gathered are seven, because seven is a miraculous number...*"

And this was the spell that could unseat the world. Because it was against nature? Or was it because, working it, a sorcerer was creating something... taking on the power of a god? But that wasn't true. Whoever embarked on this spell was simply following a recipe, like a cook. Picturing that arrogant old man as a red-faced blaspheming toiler in a galley like João, *Isabella*'s cook, diminished his threat considerably. Worked for me.

The small print was giving me a headache, though. I sighed. Somewhere, a clock struck eleven. A couple of sparrows arrived and started pecking at the crumbs of the pastry I'd just eaten.

"*The soul of a venturer may only be released by a venturer. Against the armored one, only the invulnerable may stand.*"

It occurred to me then that these injunctions were quite specific. They were instructions as well as warnings. "*Against the armored one, only the invulnerable may stand."*

Which meant I couldn't fight it. As I had no way of defeating the armored figure the other night. Which may, or may not, have been the same thing. The venturer who could release Henriques Verdinho's soul would have to be some other voyager. But who could be invulnerable to something so solidly armored? Who could not be injured? A ghost? But how could a ghost prevail, if it came to a fight? I lit another cheroot and stared at the smoke.

John Yeoh, I thought abruptly. He existed in two worlds, but in neither. Half-living, half-dead. His strange self-inflicted limbo meant he was more real to a ghost like Isaiah than to an armored guardian. I had been able to touch him, true, but then I have...odd talents.

Or if that failed, I thought mordantly, he could always shoot it.

I took the silver bullet, still wrapped in my handkerchief, out of my pocket and stared at it. Could that be the means to defeat the first guardian?

Now all I had to do was find the amulet. Oh, and persuade John Yeoh to go up against the armored one. That would be fun.

Of course, I still had no idea how to release the souls from the amulets. And there was still no sign of Pierce. Frustrated, I picked up the book again.

"The soul of a scholar may only be released by a scholar. Against the executioner, only the dead may stand."

Well, I thought, raising my eyebrow, last night I met a dead scholar. Who had even already been executed, to all intents and purposes. And Yeoh knew how to find him, too.

There are no such things as coincidences.

I sensed Emilia before I heard the tap of her stick on the bricks. Looked round with a smile that died when I saw her expression.

The *Mappa Mundi* slid to the ground as I jumped to my feet. "What is it? What's the matter?" I asked, starting towards her.

She said worriedly, "Luís, your father should have telephoned by now," and even through the stab of concern I thought, how strange, my father. "He's never forgotten before. Do you think he's all right?"

The fourth soul shall be the soul of an artist. Oh, God.

I put my arms around her, and she felt as frail as a bird. Her blouse couldn't conceal the slenderness of her arms and shoulders. I felt her heart beating, the softness of her breasts, and the heat of her hands on my back.

"I'll go and find out," I said into her hair.

The home of my childhood. When I wore a map of Lisbon on the inside of my head. I've forgotten a lot, but more has come back to me since I returned to my native city. And I could never forget the way to this house. Although I hadn't seen it for thirty years. My feet found it by entering an ancient groove, a tram-track of buried memory.

A squat house, with almost Manueline embellishments. Even the front door evokes memories. I rang the bell, not expecting a reply. But a trim little woman with a red nose and puffy eyes opened the door. Housekeeper, evidently.

"I'm sorry, Sr da Silva has been taken ill," she snuffled, and a cold fist squeezed my heart. "The doctor is with him now."

"He's my father," I blurted out, though I hadn't meant to say it. I don't know why. The small woman's mouth dropped open.

"Oh, blessed Virgin, come in, senhor capitão," she said, and I thought: he even told his housekeeper about me. "I'm so sorry."

The house was smaller than I remembered, and its smell was different: linseed oil rather than the odor of sanctity. I paused in the hallway, overwhelmed by memory and other things. Confused by familiarity. Even though I hadn't thought of going there for thirty years.

But now it no longer housed my mother. Although her pale smoky ghost would be in her bedroom. Nor, at the moment, I thought bleakly, did the house hold my father. My father's *body* didn't hold my father. And the only ghost I saw was a fourteen-year-old Luís da Silva.

The housekeeper was staring at me. "Ah, excuse me," I said. "Did you...find him, senhora? I don't know your name."

"Sra Reinaldo—yes, I found him, in his painting room." She gulped. "Cold as a fish, he was, poor man." I saw a tear leak from her eye. He can still inspire affection in others. Meu Deus, she cares for him more than I do. Should that make me feel guilty? I don't feel guilty. At least, I don't think so. To be honest, I don't know what I do feel. "The doctor's in his room, if you want to go up," she went on, and sniffed.

"Yes, thank you," I said, a little distractedly. The fourth stair still creaked. So did the eleventh, dipping under my foot in a way it hadn't when I was fourteen. Would he still use the same room? Of course. They'd slept in separate rooms all the time I could remember. What a terrible cold place their marriage had been, I thought. And how lucky I am. I couldn't recall him ever touching my mother, let alone kiss her, heaven forbid. What would she be doing if she were still alive? Praying. Not a tear on her cold face. But his housekeeper could cry for him.

Shaking my head to try and clear it of memory's oppression, I opened the door. The doctor looked up, startled. He was a slight bald man of about my own age. His head gleamed as if just buffed. I felt alarmingly hirsute, conscious that my hair needed cutting. He stared at me, frowning. Well, I have that effect on some people.

"Er—" he cleared his throat, but it didn't deepen his voice at all. "Who are you?"

"I'm his son," I said. "What's the matter with him?" Thinking, let it be something mundane. Praying, da Silva?

"I wish I could tell you, senhor," he replied, candidly. Good God, an honest doctor. "He's had a seizure of some sort. He's unconscious, as you see. Can't be woken. I hope that's simply a sign that his body is healing itself. But I'm sorry, I can't even guarantee that."

My father lay still in the bed, breathing noisily, almost aggressively. His chest rose and fell. But his soul was gone, imprisoned somewhere in jasper like a fly suspended in amber. There was nobody home.

4

A FOREST OF MASTS. ALL THE OLD-FASHIONED SAILING SHIPS SEEMED to have congregated together in one stretch of sea-front, like a gaggle of elderly ladies outside a church on a Sunday. The vessels creaked and muttered, as in some dying barquentine tongue understood by a decreasing few while the world changed around them. Seagulls whirled, screeching and brawling. Sailors chased them away, cursing, when they flew too close. Guano splattered the stones of the quay. Purposeful crowds went about their maritime business, taking no notice of landlubbers, shouting in a babel of languages from all the corners of the world.

Out in the broad Tagus, the *Mar da Palha* glittered sunlight back to the sun. Closer to land, the Sea of Straw became the sea of garbage and detritus, and the gulls squabbled over fish-guts and scraps thrown overboard. As the sun rose, the water's stink grew riper. An inshore breeze picked the smell up and dispersed it democratically to sailor and landsman alike.

Half-running, drenched with sweat and desperation, Montague Pierce scanned the ships' names. He had only a vague idea where the one he wanted might be, for he had crossed the Atlantic on a steamship which berthed elsewhere. Fear lent his legs speed but could do nothing about the condition of his sedentary body. Gasping for breath, he stopped momentarily, but even exhaustion could not hold him still for very long. He looked nervously back over his shoulder; his neck ached from doing this.

At last, there was the ship he sought. Pierce breathed a prayer of thanks. And hoped it was true that what pursued him could not cross water without being invited.

"Ahoy the *Isabella*," he called, his voice cracking with strain.

A face appeared at the rail. "Yes?"

"Is Captain da Silva there?"

"No," said the crewman—boy, he realized a moment later. "Sorry."

"How about Sr Harris?" suggested Pierce in increasing desperation, glancing nervously behind himself again.

"I'll get him."

"May I come aboard?" Pierce implored.

"Come along," the boy said, and disappeared. Pierce wasted no time trotting up the gangplank, and breathed a sigh of relief as he set foot on deck. A couple of sailors eyed him curiously, but he was too far from regaining his composure to manage any greeting.

The boy reappeared, leading a limping Harris. "Right, Fil', thanks," said the red-haired American, and turned to Pierce. "The skipper ain't here, but I guess Felipe just told you that. What can we do for you, Mister Pierce?"

"I'm sorry to impose on you," the antiquarian said, taking off his spectacles and mopping his crimson face, "but I—I'm being followed."

"What by?" asked Harris, and Pierce thought: why didn't he say *who*?

"Nothing good," he replied, in the same vein. He eyed the mate narrowly, wondering how much he knew. There was no reason to suppose he would be privy to da Silva's private business, other than the fact that the pair of them had seemed somehow conspiratorial the previous day when he had bumped into the captain. "Did—did the captain mention a book to you at all?"

Harris laughed grimly, at least Pierce assumed it was a laugh. The tall American did not look amused. "Yeah, you could say that," he said. He leaned against the rail with a wince, then lit a cigarette. "Old tome called the *Book of Souls*, you talking about?"

"Yes," said Pierce, relieved, and put his glasses back on. They immediately steamed up again. "Well, I paid a call on its owner this morning."

"Did you, by God?" exclaimed Harris, eyebrows lifting. "Did he happen to take a pot-shot at you?" he added, sourly. Pierce shook his head, puzzled by the question. "Never mind. You reckon he sicced something onto you?"

"Something, yes," Pierce agreed. "He swore he didn't have the book, but I'm convinced he does. And when I left his house, something was…watching me. Not—it feels not human. I haven't seen anything. But since then, I've had this, this huge, *over-reaching* feeling of being followed." He looked down at his hands. "Call me crazy if you like, but I thought I'd feel safer on a ship—over water."

"And do you?" The antiquarian nodded. "Fil'," Harris said to the loitering boy, "you know the way to the skipper's house?"

"Yes, sir, I do," replied the youngster smartly, looking eager at the prospect of an unexpected trip ashore.

The mate waved vaguely in the direction of the castle. "Need you to run there, and I mean run! Fetch the skipper here, soon as you can."

"*Claro*," said Felipe, and took off at speed.

Pierce watched him go with an inordinate feeling of relief. "Thank you," he said.

"Don't thank me," retorted Harris, blowing a smoke-ring and regarding it with an air of satisfaction. "I ain't done nothing."

"On the contrary." Pierce looked out to sea. "You believed me."

* * *

I should've seen it coming. Harris *told* me he'd sensed another demon, and I hadn't thought to ask him if he knew where it had appeared. Next time, da Silva, listen to the werewolf. And don't go charging off at half-cock.

Right now I've got something else to worry about. It's personal now. Well—more personal. Batista has taken my father, and he *will* answer for it. Sooner or later.

But now I was horribly conscious what the next soul on the list was. *The fifth soul shall be the soul of a child...*

How can I protect Zé and Cat?

Emilia found me sitting on the bed and contemplating the short sword I'd taken from the mysterious fighter outside the church. She looked at it with distaste, then lowered herself to sit beside me. I turned to look at her. Something I never tire of.

"What is it, Luís?" she asked, pushing hair off my brow. Reminding me I still hadn't got round to visiting a barber.

"The soul of a child," I replied. Her hand stilled.

"I was thinking that, too," she said softly. "What can we do?"

"All I can ever do," I said. "Fight back."

She leaned her head into my shoulder, and I slipped my arm round her. "Yes," she agreed, very quietly.

"Where's Zé?" I asked.

"In his room." That was a relief. "Studying."

Meu Deus, a miracle. "How did you manage that?"

"Oh, I have my methods," Emilia said.

Abruptly, I came to a decision. I'd had enough of Batista calling the shots. I wasn't going to skulk behind walls like a man in a besieged city. "Get hold of Paciência for me, will you?" All I know about tactics can be summed up in two words: Attack first. "Ask her if she knows how to bind a demon."

"Are you sure?"

Bless her for not questioning it. "I'm sure," I told her. But it still felt like an irrevocable step. To go from summoning ghosts to summoning demons. That's not necromancy, it's black magic of the darkest sort. Never swear you won't do something. You'll only have to break your oath.

And now here I am, emulating the Venetian five years ago. Drawing a pentagram on the floor of Emilia's workroom. Irresistibly reminded, too, of the English shipping agent Arkright, trying to confine the sorcerer's box. Only to have it slide clear out of the pentagram when the ship rolled. Well, short of another earthquake—bite your tongue, da Silva!—nothing's going to be doing any moving today.

"Blood," Paciência had said, succinctly, in answer to my question. "Blood to call, and blood to bind. Blood and iron."

In the still, stuffy room I was sweating heavily. Drops fell on the floor. I didn't know if they would have any effect on a conjuration. They were, after all, salt water. But I kept them well clear of the figure I was inscribing. All I'd ever seen told me you don't mess with demons. You want to take every advantage you can get.

This is your fault, I said to myself. This is all happening because twenty years ago you couldn't keep your mind out of your pants. But at twenty-four your mind is pretty much resident there. At twenty-four looking at the *sea* can get you aroused. If it hadn't been Dona Elvira it would've been someone else. Maybe, though, a woman with a brother who wasn't completely crazed.

Self-flagellation, da Silva, that's productive. Your mother would've approved. So consider—Batista would've done this anyway. Only with some other victim. One who might not have been able to fight back. So, perversely, I *am* in the right place at the right time. Ha. Work that one out.

At last I was done, and it was ready. No. Too soon. I think I was afraid. I know I was apprehensive. Which in itself is a feeble word. My hands were shaking slightly, my gut churning. If I could've thought of any alternative—any alternative at all—I would've taken it. But I couldn't. That's the problem.

Blood and iron. Get on with it, da Silva. I picked up the gladius. Not quite sure why I'd opted for that over my own knife, except that it was what it was. Cold iron, a butcher's blade. It felt heavy, but balanced, in my hand. I rested the edge on my right wrist. Clenched my fist and looked at the blue lines the veins made.

Drew the blade swiftly across one of them before I could change my mind, sucked in a breath sharply at the pain. Let blood drip into the saucer I'd borrowed for the purpose. Well, borrowed is the wrong word too. I don't think Emilia will want to use it again, after this. Then I held the cut closed until it stopped bleeding, then bandaged it tightly.

After that I had to clean the sword, something which made me uncomfortable out of all proportion. To prevent blood being left outside the pentagram, Paciência told me, I had to lick the blade clean. Blood and iron taste the same, I found.

I placed the saucer carefully inside the five-pointed star I'd drawn. Holding it in my left hand, at arm's length. As I stood up my right knee cracked like a pistol-shot. Reminding me that I was human, perhaps. Like a Roman conqueror's slave whispering in his ear. Well, we're all slaves to our bodies. Can't avoid that one. Not that I really need reminding.

Prevaricating, I thought. Wiped the sweat off my face. I wasn't wearing my eye-patch. My palms were damp too, so I dragged them down my thighs. Can't put it off any longer.

Very softly, I spoke the name of the demon. "Gaziel," I said. The one who shakes foundations, Paciência had said. Raises storms and spectres. Rings bells at midnight. Inspires terror. No argument on that last one.

Nothing happened, but the air in the room thickened slightly. I swallowed nausea.

The second time of calling. "Gaziel," I said again. Muted thunder growled, charging the air with electricity. I felt my hair prickle. My skin felt tight, as if it found me difficult to contain inside it. Mouth as dry as a desert. Sweat ran down my face, into my eye. I wiped it away.

Third time. Final time. "Gaziel."

Inside the pentagram, the blood in the saucer shivered, as if someone was shaking it with increasing violence. Thunder still muttered, somewhere. In the earth's core, perhaps.

Pressure pounded in my head, pulsing to my heartbeat. The shuddering of the blood took on the same rhythm, and a powerful ache ran down my arm. Curls of steam began to rise from the saucer, and the scent of a hot wind filled the room. The steam grew thicker, curled into a pillar of mist, whirling like a waterspout. My hand was slippery on the grip of the sword. My head felt as if it was about to burst.

Something beat at the air, blew my hair back from my face like a force ten gale, screamed like a hurricane in the rigging. Lashed at me like a scourge. Wanted to flay the skin from my body, the flesh from my bones. The thoughts from my mind. The soul from my body. Or wherever it resides.

And the mist began to take on a form. I clenched my teeth, swallowed on rising nausea. The form thickened, clotting, solidifying as I watched, and pressure battered and buffeted me like a vile stinking wind from all sides, through all my senses. There was a sandstorm whirling in my head, abrading the inside of my skull.

Raising a sorcerer is hard. They fight you. It's like trying to steer a ship under full sail in a hurricane, always supposing you could do such a thing without losing all the canvas. But this was worse. Much worse. Because what I was trying to control was so *other*, so completely alien, that I had no point of reference. Except one single, small piece of knowledge that kept the storm from overwhelming me entirely.

I knew its name. Something impelled me to say it again.

"Gaziel!" I shouted, and such was the storm-noise I could barely hear my voice. Again: "Gaziel!" That was five times. Five, Paciência said, the number of justice. Five senses. Five points of the pentagram.

The demon was imprisoned in the figure. Summoned by my blood. It was there for me to command. And I don't know which horrified me more, its presence or that other single fact.

Unlike the other demon I had encountered, it had no fixed form, was somehow plastic. Mostly, it was vaguely human in shape, if having two arms, two legs and a head are the criteria. But it also gave the impression of being winged without having visible wings. It ought to have had great spreading bat-wings, as it wore the face of a bat, splay-nosed and needle-fanged. Yet all this was for show, maybe only put on for my benefit. Masking some groin-shrinking foulness within that I was grateful I couldn't see and remember in nights to come. All my other senses were aware of it, though, and I had to fight myself to stand and face it when everything was yelling *run!* at me.

The demon lunged at me, face looming large, twice the size of a man's. I pointed the sword at it, and it flinched back.

"Human," it said, and the word screamed inside my skull and echoed off endless cliffs in my mind. I wouldn't have been surprised to feel blood running from my ears at that voice. "Why have you summoned me?"

"To do what I command," I shouted, near breathless with the impulse to flee, using Paciência's formula and hoping like hell that it would work. Well, quite literally.

Its face bulged and pulsated. "By what right?" it howled, and I wanted to stop my ears, but I had to keep holding the sword out in front of me. Wouldn't have done any good, anyway. I was sure of that. Because I wasn't hearing it with my ears.

"By blood and by iron." I steadied the sword with both hands, not quite managing to control their shaking. Sweat ran down my face. The demon thrashed to and fro in the pentagram, like a mastiff on a chain. Around me, the room shivered slightly, and a sprinkling of plaster fell from the ceiling. I thought of earthquakes. Some other time, I would speculate about that.

"Whence came the blood?" it screamed. "How came you by the cold iron?"

"The blood is mine," I said, words coming to me unbidden now, "the sword mine by right of combat."

Screeching, it slashed at me with taloned fingers, but was still confined.

As long as I held my ground, it couldn't escape. As long as I held my ground! Yes, that's the trick. I wanted to shrink into a corner and hide. I knew I couldn't. I concentrated on holding the sword as steady as I could. My arms were beginning to ache. I swallowed on nausea again.

"I am bound by your blood, human," the demon acknowledged, and I would have breathed a sigh of relief if I'd had any breath to spare. It stilled, apparently waiting.

This was the tricky bit. Well, relatively speaking. Calling it, binding it, holding it— took strength and nerve. Which were holding out. Just. Covering all the possibilities, though, took cunning. I had needed all the help Paciência could give me.

"You must swear," I said hoarsely, "to do no harm to any human of this blood, neither to body, nor to soul, neither to injure nor to steal. Nor initiate such harm by others. Nor aid others to inflict it. Not in the past, not in the present, not in the future."

The demon opened its reeking maw and hissed at me viciously. The stink made me wince. "You ask too much!" it roared. I almost gave back a pace, but instead gripped the sword harder. The cut in my wrist stung.

"You must swear," I insisted.

"And what will you give in exchange?" the demon bellowed in its clanging voice, enveloping me in a mephitic cloud. It's not real, I told myself, swallowing.

"Your release," I said tightly. The demon did not reply at once. It became still and then began to swell like a bladder inflating. It grew until it bulged against the confining pentagram. The pounding in my head grew worse. I wasn't sure how much longer I could deal with this.

And neither was the demon. Cunningly, it said, "All I have to do for that is wait, human. Until you tire. Until you drop your blade. Until your mortal body fails."

I advanced towards the pentagram with the sword extended. I could see my hands shaking. There was a sensation of flies walking all over my body. I felt sick to my stomach, my teeth wanted to chatter, and sweat poured off me in streams. I clenched my jaw.

"I don't think so," I forced out, and jabbed it with the point of the blade. It screeched like a train whistle magnified a thousand times and threshed about in its prison. Meu Deus, I thought, can it break out even now? "Swear it."

"I swear by the blood with which you summoned me," its voice hammered. "I swear it by the iron and the fire that shaped it. I swear by earth and air, earthquake and tempest. That I know and recognize this blood and will do no harm to its bearers, neither in the past, nor in the present, nor in the future."

Every word came out like a blow. It fought against speaking its oath, struggling against me until every muscle in my body was quivering with the strain. It was like trying to hold onto a sail full of storm-wind singlehanded. But I still controlled it. Barely. Commanded it. And it had no choice but to do what I told it. To swear the oath.

My knees wanted to give way from sheer exhaustion. Between sweat in my eye and tiredness flaring round my sight, I could barely see any more. But at last the demon spat out the final word and glared at me, its jaws snapping.

"Then go back to the place you came from," I said. All I could manage was a whisper.

It gave a shrieking roar that had to be the loudest noise I've ever heard, then disappeared. Air rushed in to fill up the space it had occupied with a rushing boom that knocked me off my feet, the aftershock of its shout still echoing in my head. For moments I was sure I'd been permanently deafened.

Rather unsteadily, I hauled myself to my feet, mopped my face with my sodden shirt, and lit a cheroot. Stretched a few overstressed muscles. After a minute, I knelt down and began to erase the pentagram from the floor with a shaking hand. The saucer's shattered remains lay confined in the central pentangle. No trace of blood, but I swept them up carefully all the same.

The room felt peculiarly empty now the demon was gone. I didn't know if Harris might have been able to sense anything, but I certainly couldn't detect any trace of its presence. Which I thought was odd. Something like that ought to leave a permanent taint.

I couldn't have fought that, I admit. It was the most powerful thing I'd ever encountered. The realization was more than sobering.

Feeling damp and sore and weary right down to my bones, I unlocked the door and walked unsteadily through. Back to reality. Leaned against the door and closed my eye, only to be interrupted by the noise of someone banging frenziedly on the front door. I was in no state to answer it, not wanting to alarm the neighbors, but Zé clattered past me, hardly sparing me a glance. Probably used to his father looking like someone who's just been keelhauled, I thought.

He flung the door open and dashed outside, and it was only then that I realized something was wrong. Really quick on the uptake there, da Silva. But binding demons slows you down a little. I sighed, pushed myself away from the wall, and followed in Zé's wake.

Saw him kneeling outside in the narrow street next to the still form of his fellow 'prentice and friend Felipe. Whose face was white as ash. Whose chest rose and fell regularly. But whose body, I could tell from there, no longer contained his soul.

The demon, deprived of Zé and Cat, had turned to the nearest child and stolen his soul instead.

Oh *merda*.

* * *

Father Ánibal Jerónimo was concerned. He had not known the priest he replaced very well. Fr Pereira now lay unconscious—his cold pallid body not even admitting to the possibility of consciousness—in the infirmary, where a tiny wizened nun patiently dripped water into his slack mouth, running a finger down his throat to make him swallow. The hospital smell, comprised in fairly equal parts of ether, blood, disease, carbolic and stale vomit, had soon driven Fr Jerónimo away, which shamed him a little. But he was not primarily concerned, at the moment, with weaknesses of the flesh. Even his own.

His concern was centered on the library of São Rafael. He considered it a dangerous place, a repository of too much knowledge. Fr Jerónimo belonged to an organisation known as *Verbum Dei,* the Word of God, which did not approve of the collection of occult texts. Or, indeed, of any other writings of which the Church would disapprove. Which, to his narrow asceticism, was a pretty wide compass. Heresy was a real and present danger to Fr Jerónimo. He would have been at home with auto-da-fé.

The young priest was also disturbed by the appearance of da Silva on the scene. Having come to the conclusion—from empirical evidence—that Fr Pereira had suffered a seizure in the library, he wanted to know how the captain had found him there. And that begged a lot of other questions. How had he known of the library in the first place? He did not look like a seeker after arcane knowledge. Although Fr Jerónimo was well aware that appearances could be deceptive. He played on his own lanky youthfulness enough.

Maybe more importantly, how had he found his way there? São Rafael's arcane defenses against prying eyes made him profoundly uneasy, not least because they barred his own unaccompanied passage to the library.

Nobody seemed to know very much about da Silva. He didn't attend Mass, though his wife did. Nor did he go to confession. Which should have been understandable, since as a ship's captain he was at sea much of the time. Fr Jerónimo chose to interpret it as sinister. This was mainly because the man had alarmed him at their last meeting. He did not know why. It made him uncomfortable. That it was simply due to the fact that other people he encountered bowed to his authority, despite his youth, did not occur to him. And having decided that there was something wrong about the captain, Fr Jerónimo's subconscious was already entrenched in the belief that he was somehow responsible for Fr Pereira's strange illness.

He arrived at da Silva's house in time to see him stoop to lift an unconscious boy from the street and carry him indoors.

* * *

I laid Felipe carefully down on Zé's bed, then met Emilia's gaze. She looked at me bleakly. "Zé, run for the doctor," I said, and for once he didn't argue.

"Mother of God, Luís, what have we done?" whispered Emilia. I put my arms round her, conscious of being sweaty and dishevelled and exhausted beyond measure. She leaned into me. She smelled of floral-scented soap.

"I'll get him back," I said. "And the others."

And then someone else knocked at the door. I sighed. Emilia patted my back.

"I can go," she assured me, starting to make her careful way downstairs. "You go and make yourself presentable." Presentable. Not a word that springs easily to the lips in describing me. Well, I could try.

Felipe had come to fetch me, evidently. I washed and changed my clothes hurriedly. Anxious both for him and to get back to *Isabella* to find out what required my presence. What could my officers not handle? Surely not more souls…Get a grip, da Silva. It won't be so soon. And what makes you so sure of that? I asked myself.

Assuming Emilia would have gotten rid of the caller, I was startled to find her sitting talking to the infant priest who was Fr Pereira's stand-in. He had the blazing eyes of a zealot, which made my heart sink. And he radiated hostility. Or so it seemed to me. Maybe I was sensitized by my encounter with the demon. I felt my face freeze into a scowl.

"This is Fr Jerónimo," Emilia said to me, her voice carefully neutral. I wondered what he could have said to annoy my easy-going wife so comprehensively. In such a short time, too. That takes real talent.

"Father," I said, pulling out a cheroot and lighting it. More to irritate him than anything else, since he looked like the sort of pinched ascetic who would disapprove on principle. Or, at least, looked as if he'd grow up to be one. "Any news about Fr Pereira?"

He looked startled, but recovered well. "There's no change in his condition," he said. "I came to speak to you, senhor capitão."

"I have an urgent errand," I told him, not wanting to sit there and be preached at when I was needed elsewhere. "If you can talk and walk, come along."

The priest shot Emilia a minatory glance—I'll have to ask her about that, later—and bounded to his feet. "Very well," he said.

I crossed to Emilia, kissed her hair, and said, "I won't be long." She squeezed my hand.

"Be as long as you have to," she said softly. "Take care."

Outside, the sun was traveling down the sky, but the heat was still fierce. A feeble ineffectual breeze blew eddies of small rubbish—torn paper, dried-up leaves—round my legs. It had no effect on the hovering ghosts, which were even less substantial. The priest's aura was stronger. He was sweating, and smelled like it.

"Well, Father?" I said peremptorily. "What can I do for you?"

"I came," he said, "to save your soul."

Hardly what I'd been expecting. But then I couldn't say what I *had* been expecting. I raised an eyebrow at him, but he was staring straight ahead. The cut on my wrist stung. I blew out smoke. "And what makes you think it needs to be saved?" I asked.

"When was the last time you confessed your sins?" he countered, evenly. "Or even attended Mass?"

A furious anger threatened to rise up my throat. I fought it down. I've got no intention of letting him bait me, I've got more important things to do. "Fr Pereira knows my reasons."

"I am not Fr Pereira," he said tartly.

"That's pretty obvious," I snapped back, stepping over an insistent cat that wanted to entwine my ankles. Five minutes in the sunlight, and I was feeling damp already. I slung the butt of my cheroot to one side, aiming it through a grandmotherly ghost with a phantom wart on the end of her nose.

He rounded on me, his face red and pinched. "You people never understand what you're doing!" he burst out. "Why can't you see the devil's works for what they are?"

I put a placatory hand on his arm, and he flinched away and made the sign of the cross at me. This irritated me immensely.

"What d'you mean by that?" I asked coldly.

Breathing heavily, he whispered, "I mean that infernal library! It should have been burnt to the ground long ago."

"If you start out burning books," I pointed out, scratching absently at my cheekbone, "you end up burning people."

"People whose souls will burn in hell anyway," he retorted. A sad-eyed ghost drifted through him, insubstantial as a mist.

"Fr Jerónimo," I said, stepping in front of him and lighting up another cheroot, "what exactly are you accusing me of?"

"Heresy. Blasphemy," he spat. "Apostasy."

Well, I couldn't really argue with him there. "Then why bother?" I asked impatiently.

"You stink of evil," he replied, low-voiced and intense. "But you can still repent of your sins. God will forgive you. Renounce the devil—" I'd had enough of this. I took hold of his arm again, this time in a grip he couldn't break, and spoke in his ear.

"You don't know what you're talking about," I said. "I've fought what you call the devil in more ways than you can possibly imagine. You know who a demon would devour, Fr Jerónimo?" I went on, savagely. "Given a choice between you on your knees praying your head off and a sinner with the will to fight back? Try it some day. You'll find out there's not much cause to have faith in the power of prayer." I flung him aside and marched off, through a dense cluster of drifting ghosts thronged where a roof had fallen in on them more than a century and a half before.

Which, of course, he couldn't see at all.

Harris met me at a limping run. "We got trouble, skipper," he said.

Still irritated by the recent priest, I said grimly, "Tell me something I don't know." He stopped in his tracks and stared at me until I wanted to ask him whether I'd grown an extra head.

"Another," he said at last. "He's taken another."

"I know. It was Felipe." And it was my fault. But I'd had no option, and I'd do the same again. I make decisions. It's part of my job. I don't expect everything to be easy—hell, I don't expect *anything* to be easy—or every decision to be easy to live with. Right now I'm in the midst of a war, and that means sacrifices have to be made. Right. Lecture over, da Silva. At least Felipe, like my father, like Ortigão, like Fr Pereira, like Verdinho, stand a chance. If, of course, I can find out how to release them. Which I have to do.

"Goddamnit," Harris said, "And that ain't all." Still watching me carefully. I scratched my cheekbone in annoyance.

"Harris, unless my hair is on fire, d'you mind not staring at me like that?"

He shook himself and looked away. I searched for a cheroot. The humidity under my eye-patch stood at around ninety per cent.

"We got your bookseller friend on board," Harris said.

I raised my eyebrows. "Pierce?" So that's where he ended up.

"Yeah. Seems he paid a call on this Batista fellow." I stopped with a cheroot halfway to my mouth.

"He did what?" Yes, I can ask stupid questions just as well as the next man.

"You better ask him yourself," said Harris, gesturing towards *Isabella* where I could see a Pierce-shaped figure hunched unhappily at the rail. "Chucking up like a sick baby," he added, with that mystified superiority sailors feel towards people prone to *mereado*. "We're in harbor, for Godsakes."

Lighting the belated cheroot, I went on board, saying "Carry on, Mister Ashley" hastily to the First, who seemed to be winding himself up towards a fully-fledged ceremonial of some kind. He really ought to be in the navy. My informality irks his regimental soul.

"Da Silva, thank God you're here," Pierce exclaimed, shaking my hand in a limply relieved sort of way. His palm felt unpleasantly moist, like a small frog. "Did your Mister Harris tell you about my follower?" There was a sheen of sweat on his brow, but I didn't know whether it was from heat or seasickness.

"No, he didn't," I said. "He did say you went to see Batista, though." You must be mad. "What happened?"

"He's got the book, I'm sure of it," Pierce said. He was looking distinctly green about the gills. I tried to direct my smoke away from him, but the wind blew it straight back again. And isn't *that* a metaphor for life, I thought, sourly.

"He didn't tell you so, did he?" The antiquarian shuddered.

"Oh no," he said. "They were playing games."

"They?" Of course. He would know who the woman was. I kicked myself for not asking him before. Wake up, da Silva!

Pierce punctuated the conversation by turning abruptly, leaning over the rail, and adding his own contribution to the garbage in the water. A moment later, he wiped his mouth on a crusty handkerchief and continued.

"Batista and that mad daughter of his." Daughter, I thought, nodding. So now I know. Much good it does me.

"Mad?" I repeated. Good God, I was in danger of sounding like an Englishman. Or at least like the feed to a vaudeville comedian.

"Oh, well, you don't know, do you? I keep forgetting I'm not in Rio. God. Her name's Teresa. Teresa Graça Batista. She's as crazy as he is. Bit too fond of swordfighting."

I finished my cheroot and flung the butt over the side. "You mean she—?"

"Fences," Pierce supplied, with a croak of a laugh. "With a saber. You don't...insult her. Oh no. Or you find yourself in a field at dawn."

"Mother of God," I said, thinking about the tall woman. The armored figure slipped into my mind. What if they were one and the same? But how could that be? "What were you saying about being followed?"

"He sent something after me. I don't know what it was but it scared me half to death." The antiquarian swept his gaze along the quayside again. I realized he had been doing this all through our conversation. Scanning the shore nervously, unceasingly. Except when he had turned aside to throw up, of course. "It's out there, I can still feel it. I'm safe here, though, I think. I don't believe it can cross water."

Sanctuary, I thought. Pierce must be pretty scared if he was braving seasickness for a feeling of security. "Are you sure?" I asked.

"No," said Pierce, "but I still feel safe here."

With a sigh, I realized I wouldn't be able to get home any time soon. Nor get to see John Yeoh, which I'd intended to do today. And by tomorrow night Batista might have six out of the seven souls—I *have* to see Yeoh. He's got to get that bloody book out of the House of the Four Winds tonight. I pulled out my watch and looked at the time, although I could tell just as well from the sky. It was something for my hands to do. Yes, Harris could go— *and* get back safely. Yeoh would recognize him in his human shape.

"Wait here," I said to Pierce. "Will you be all right for ten minutes?"

He managed a shaky smile. "The Captain is aboard—the ship is whole. I'll be all right." That sounded a bit metaphysical, but I didn't have time to go into it.

"Angelotti," I called, seeing him nearby, "find Signor Harris and ask him to join me in my cabin. Then ask Signor Ashley to break out a glass of brandy for Signor Pierce here." Pierce looked round at his name: I had been speaking *veneziano*, impenetrable even to most Italians. I'm not quite sure why. Angelotti speaks perfectly serviceable English. Bizarre, but serviceable.

When I got to my cabin, which even after just a couple of days smelt musty, salt-tainted. I poured myself a brandy as well. Harris came in after a minute, and I pointed to the decanter. He shook his head. He doesn't drink much. If at all. I suppose a drunken werewolf is not the most desirable thing to have around.

"You look like hell, skipper," he said without any preamble, "and you've been awful close to one of them demons."

Close. Yes, you could say that. Now I understood why he had been staring at me. He knew I'd crossed the line. Damn it. I thought briefly of just sticking to the topic of Felipe. But I owed Harris more than that. Honesty, da

Silva.

I scratched my eyebrow and said, "That's because I summoned one."

"Christ up a tree!" he exclaimed. "What the hell for?"

"To protect Zé," I said, rubbing the back of my neck. Damp hair. Get it cut. "And Caterina. The soul of a child…The last one took my father."

Harris blinked, and his eyes looked lupine for a second. "Jesus. I didn't know, skipper. He's really gunning for you, ain't he, this Batista fellow? But why'd he wait so long?"

That was my biggest question, as well. "I don't know," I said, shrugging my shoulders. "Maybe he wasn't skilful enough before. Or not powerful enough."

"I guess." He didn't sound convinced. But I couldn't think of any other explanation. At the moment, however, it wasn't my most pressing concern.

"Harris, you remember what John Yeoh said last night?"

"John Yeoh, that'll be the Chinaman?"

Oh yes. They hadn't exactly been introduced. "You think there's more than one?"

He paused. Took out his cigarettes and lit one, absently. "Huh," he said. "Far as I can recall, he offered to do a bit of burglarizing for you."

"I need you to go and take him up on that," I said.

"Right, skipper. How do I find him?" Direct action. I like that. Harris doesn't beat about the bush. Although I don't know whether it's because he's a werewolf or because he's an American. I gave him the address of Yeoh's shop.

"Go with him, if you want."

Harris shot me a sardonic look. "Uh-huh, silver bullets and all?"

"You'll heal," I said, raising an eyebrow.

"Wasn't you got shot in the butt," he pointed out, a trifle acidly. True. I lit a cheroot and pointed it at him.

"You mind your…butt, then," I said, and he barked one of his unsmiling laughs.

"I'm on my way," he said, getting to his feet with an exaggerated limp. "Skipper?"

"Yes?" I asked, expelling smoke.

"What is it with this Yeoh fellow? That old ghost said he was living in the shadows…like me. What's he turn into?"

"I don't think he turns into anything." Although a cat-burglar would be useful. "He's just been around a hell of a long time. He'll tell you about it if he feels like it, I suppose. Now bugger off, or you won't get back."

He turned at the door. "You going to look after your tame bookseller?" I nodded. "Right, see you later." Delegation. Like I said.

As soon as he had gone, I got rid of the eye-patch. The cabin was hot and stuffy, as if the bulkheads had sucked up the day's accumulated heat. There was, also, a sense of oppression in the air. It was almost, but not quite, like thunder. I wondered whether it was a loitering sense of Pierce's pursuer. Or just a hot day in Lisbon.

It's easier to think on the water. The gentle motion of the ship was soothing. Except to people like Pierce, of course, I thought. I finished my brandy, considered pouring another, and decided against it. At least for the moment. Put my feet on the desk. The chair creaked. Every muscle I had, and some I didn't know I had, ached slightly, and the cut on my wrist felt sore. I peered at the bandage somewhat suspiciously, but there didn't seem to be anything wrong with it. Da Silva, medical expert.

If Yeoh could get hold of the *Book of Souls*, I wondered, would it stop Batista in his tracks? Or did he have all the spells memorized? Hell and damnation. Wish I hadn't thought of that. Have to hope for the former. It's about time things started going my way. But at least I've taken the initiative from him just this once. Even if it's only temporary. I do regret poor Felipe, of course. But I'm selfish enough to be glad it wasn't Zé. Or Caterina.

The task was still depressing, though. Even if the *Book of Souls* told me what I needed to know I still had to find the amulets before the souls could be released. I wondered whether Paciência's spell of finding could help. If she had been able to use the mutilated *Mappa Mundi* to locate the book's missing pages, perhaps she could use an unconscious person to discover where his stolen soul might be. Does she have enough power to do that? Finding souls has to be in a different league to searching for misplaced earrings.

And then there was the question of overcoming the guardians. Even supposing John Yeoh agreed to help with Verdinho, Isaiah with Fr Pereira, the other instructions in the spell were just as specific. Against a guardian, only a specific person could stand. And only that person, presumably, could release the imprisoned soul.

A venturer who was invulnerable. A dead scholar. A lover...I couldn't remember the lover's guardian. What else was there? I pulled the *Mappa Mundi* from my pocket and opened it.

"*The soul of a lover shall be gathered by the demon Bitru and stored in an amulet of beryl. And the guardian of that soul shall be the castrator. And the soul of a lover may only be released by a lover. Against the castrator, only one who cannot be unmanned may stand.*"

The castrator. There's a word that makes you cross your legs. Então, I don't know any eunuchs, so that rules that out. Damned thing's as cryptic as the answers Paciência's finding spell turned up. Where am I going to find all these people? And how persuade them to help? I stared at the book, perhaps hoping that the answers would materialise there.

They didn't, of course. But then the thought struck me. *"One who cannot be unmanned"* could equally mean a woman. A woman who—Meu Deus. Paciência's own daughter was Ortigão's lover. Could she do it? Could any woman? I drew in a breath. Found my cheroot had burned out, so lit another. Returned to the book.

"The soul of an artist shall be gathered by the demon Belphegor and stored in an amulet of jasper. And the guardian of that soul shall be the destroyer. And the soul of an artist may only be released by an artist. Against the destroyer, only a creator may stand."

Emilia. Emilia could save my father.

If I could contemplate asking Paciência's daughter, I couldn't avoid asking my wife. Especially as she's the only other artist I know.

"The soul of a child shall be gathered by the demon Gaziel and stored in an amulet of malachite. And the guardian of that soul shall be the corruptor. And the soul of a child may only be released by a child. Against the corruptor, only the innocent may stand."

The innocent. Well, that depends on how innocent Zé is. I don't think I was particularly innocent at his age. But then I'd had to grow up more quickly.

And if not Zé, Caterina. My eight-year-old daughter.

* * *

Harris was a hunter—maybe not so much in human form, but certainly in his soul. So, although he didn't know Lisbon very well and had never, despite da Silva's best efforts, got to grips with Portuguese, he found John Yeoh's shop without much difficulty.

Yeoh was sitting outside, apparently reading a book. *Son of a bitch ain't reading. He's watching me. Knows who I am, right enough.* Harris recognized him neither by sight, which was negligible when he was wolf, nor by smell, which was of little significance to his human shape. He knew him by that other sense which those whom Isaiah had identified as "of the shadows" develop. Likewise, he supposed, Yeoh did him.

"You Mister Yeoh?" he asked casually, looking at clocks disinterestedly. "Name's Harris. 'Spect you remember me."

"Oh, yes, Mister Wolf," said Yeoh without raising his head. "Where is your captain?"

"Busy," replied Harris, laconically. "Sent me to ask you for that favor."
Yeoh looked up, his eyes shadowed, and then returned his gaze to his book.

"And what would that be?"

"Fetching a book, I guess."

"Somehow you seem to be more suited to the word 'fetch' than I ," said
the other sharply. Harris winced.

Whoa, back off! What'd I say? He eyed Yeoh warily, then offered him a
placatory cigarette, which the Chinaman accepted silently and offered a
match.

"Need it tonight," Harris told him. "The old bastard's gathering souls
like they was going outa fashion."

With a silent sigh, Yeoh closed his book, saving his place with a silken
marker. "Very well," he said. "What is the name of this volume?"

"The *Book of Souls*," said Harris. He eyed the other curiously. "Mind
telling me how you're gonna manage it? 'Cause that place is sealed up
tighter'n a...uh, seems pretty well defended against the likes of—"

"Of us?" Yeoh supplied pleasantly. "Us being people with a half-
life?"

You said it, not me. "I guess." Harris sighed, then shrugged his shoulders.
"Just curious, y'know." *Jesus, he's prickly. How does the skipper find these people,
anyhow? Well, he found me...* Harris didn't really like thinking about the past
very much.

"I don't think I'm going to share that information with you, Mister
Wolf," said Yeoh. "Tell your captain he will have the book in the morning."

Harris knew a dismissal when he heard it. "Right," he said, hiding his
annoyance, and slouched off crossly down the street.

When he was out of sight, John Yeoh put him out of his mind— although
he was well aware that Harris was loitering not far off— and turned his
attention back to the book in his lap. He opened it at the marker and read
Ch'ien-Tuen-Ti's words, *"My bed is so empty that I keep on waking up: as the cold
increases, the night wind begins to blow. It rustles those curtains, making a noise
like the sea: O that those were waves which could carry me back to you."* His eyes
grew distant with memory. The past lapped over the present, and deep
down inside him a tiny spark of hope began to sputter faintly.

* * *

I resumed my eye-patch with a sigh. There's no avoiding the damn thing.
Emilia did try and interest me in getting a glass eye when it first happened.
But really that was a lost cause from the outset. It's bad enough sometimes

people fixating on the patch (you can tell by the glazed stare) without displaying what's underneath it. If that's vanity, well, too bad, it's vanity. Least of my worries, at this moment.

Someone had found Pierce a box to sit on, and he was leaning back against the rail with such a beatific expression that I wondered just how much brandy Ashley had given him. His face wasn't relaxed, however, even though he had his eyes closed.

Our paths'd first crossed twenty years before. I, at forty-four, am very well aware that I'm a different person now. Although I still *feel*, if not twenty-four, at least no more than thirty-four. Pierce's age is difficult to tell. He's probably ten years older than me, but the blond hair and beard, as I said, don't show the grey so much. Although he's grown a lot more lines on his face. Haven't we all? But for all I knew, his life had been so uneventful that he'd hardly changed at all inside. One thing was certain. He hadn't had a demon rip open his eye and leave him with every ghost that ever met an untimely death as his companions.

"Pierce," I said quietly. He opened his eyes and gave me a tipsy smile. I raised an eyebrow. "How are you feeling?"

"Better," he replied. "It's still out there. It can't get to me. And this aguardente is marvellous for sea-sickness."

I will shoot Ashley, I thought, if he's given him the good stuff. Not that you can expect an Englishman to know the difference. Pierce possibly doesn't count on that score, being sort of an honorary *brasileiro*. Ah well. Shouldn't begrudge it, I suppose. Except that when you run out in Ceylon or wherever and have to replace it with palm toddy, you really regret squandering the stuff. Still, at home I can stock up, so that's all right. I shook myself, irritated at expending thought on something so trivial, and lit up.

It was getting dark. I wondered where Harris was. Although I hadn't expected him back. He wouldn't be able to resist finding out what exactly Yeoh was going to do.

Pierce had closed his eyes again. I felt momentarily sorry for him, thrown into a maelstrom of intrigue outside anything he'd ever experienced.

Because of what I was going to do next.

"You want to get rid of this thing, I imagine?" I said to him. He opened his eyes and gave me a puzzled look. Partly from brandy, I suppose. "You can't stay here forever." The English and their siege mentality.

"No, I suppose not," he said after a pause. "What are you going to do?"

"We have to draw it out," I told him. "Which means you'll have to go ashore."

Panic rushed across his face, palpable as seasickness. "But I came here to be safe!"

"You'll be safer after we get rid of it," I pointed out, trying for reassurance. Yes, well. I didn't know what Batista might have sent after him. I was only guessing I could dispose of it. Hoping. Confidence, da Silva. Inspire the man with confidence.

Fat chance.

"I'm sorry—" Pierce choked. Another English trait, apologizing for no reason. I felt like slapping him. Restrained myself. Not the way to inspire trust. Scratched my eyebrow instead.

"Listen, Pierce," I said. "I've dealt with this sort of thing before." Batista hadn't sent anything so dire as a demon after the man, or Harris, for one, would've sensed it. So I guessed it would be something I could kill. They fight dirty, some of these lesser nasties. But at least they fight. And they die. "You'll be all right. All you need to do is stand on the quay until it shows up, then get back on board as fast as you can and leave it to me."

He looked a little happier at this. Not much. But a little. I saw his Adam's apple move as he swallowed. "Very well," he said, pushing himself to his feet. "Shall we do it now?" So he did have courage, of a sort. I respected that. He may have been scared spitless, but he was willing to act as bait.

I slung the remains of my cheroot into the water. "Why not?"

"Let's go, then," said Pierce, and walked towards the gangplank. He was a trifle unsteady on his feet. That might have been lack of sea legs or excess of brandy. He looked round to make sure I was following, and I gave him what I hoped was a reassuring grin. My grins don't always come out as I expect, though. Still, if it looked menacing, he could interpret it as menacing to his pursuer. *Oxalá.*

As soon as he set foot on shore, though, he began to shake. I put a hand on his shoulder. I could hardly say "don't worry," but "It'll be all right," sounded confident enough. So I said that instead. He nodded, obviously not trusting himself enough to speak.

Whatever it was that pursued him, only Pierce could sense it. I hoped, suddenly, that it wouldn't turn out that only he could *see* it, or I would be up the creek without a paddle.

I needn't have worried. As the sun dipped below the horizon, I saw the drifting ghosts begin to mill around as if something had disturbed them. My scalp prickled. I unsheathed my knife. I thought it was only the demons that could panic them. Could I be wrong about Pierce's pursuer? Could Harris have missed it?

And then there was no more time to think.

It came from above, and I nearly missed it, jumping to one side just in time.

The twilight made it difficult to see. Or maybe it was half-made of shadows anyway. Essentially, I suppose it was a jaguar, although it seemed to be shaped like a man. It stood upright, but moved like a big cat, graceful and predatory. I saw claws as long as my thumb flex in and out from its stubby fingers.

Having missed its spring, it went down into a half-crouch and growled. The growl was subterranean, echoing in my bones and my brain with the urge to flee. It ran a shiver down my back in the hot evening air.

I advanced towards it, knife extended. The blade felt very light in my hand after the weight of the gladius. My palm was slippery with sweat. Pierce's pursuer went on growling. Then it opened its mouth and roared.

And sprang, launching itself from powerful thighs. I thrust the knife straight up into its path, raking a long furrow down its chest. The clawing hands—paws?—missed me, but its falling weight nearly wrenched the blade out of my hand. I gave with the momentum, clutching the knife desperately, following the jaguar-thing, but I was completely wrong-footed and my next wild slash missed it by a mile.

It twisted round, impossibly fast, and its hand/paw caught me a glancing blow on the side of the head that made my teeth rattle. I actually saw stars for a second, and pivoted instinctively, unsighted, to dodge any follow-through. It was so close I felt the moving air of its passage as it sprang by me. I stuck out one foot to trip it up, and it crashed to the ground, only to roll immediately and bounce back upright to face me. In hot pursuit, I was too close to back off in time—I smelt its fetid breath as I drew back the knife and punched the blade upwards under its ribcage, straight into the heart. If it had one.

Or if it hadn't been so inhumanly fast that the blade only got to penetrate a couple of inches before it sprang back with a yowl of pain. Well, at least it could be hurt. I felt blood running down my face. The left side, fortunately.

Panting, the jaguar-thing circled me. I wasn't having any of that. I was out of breath, too, and damn nearly exhausted, mentally as well as physically. I jabbed the knife at it, and it backed a pace, then turned and leapt in Pierce's direction.

Who, I now saw, had not retreated back on board, but was loitering on the gangplank, watching the proceedings.

I charged in pursuit and cut the creature off not ten feet from Pierce, so it would have to go through me to get to its quarry. And I wasn't moving. It jumped straight for us and we crashed to the ground together with an impact that drove all the breath out of my lungs, but I had managed to get my knee between us as we fell and levered it off me. Rolled over on top of it and severed its windpipe. Breath and blood fountained out, its last gasp a dying whistle, and its arms flopped loose to the ground by its sides, claws convulsing in and out like a dying wasp's sting. I knelt beside it, trying to get my own breath back. I was pretty sure it was dead. But you can't always tell with these things.

Pierce came hurrying towards me, his face gleaming white. "Are you all right?"

"Stay back," I said breathlessly, but he was staring at the body.

"My God," he exclaimed, "it's Eduardo." I turned my head to find that the jaguar-thing had changed into the body of a dark man in his thirties. With his throat open to the bone. *Merda*. I stood up slowly, disregarding the new ghost boiling up out of the corpse.

"Eduardo?" I repeated.

"He's one of Batista's servants."

Was one of Batista's servants, I amended. And now there's a very dead and extremely inconvenient corpse lying on the quayside. One who had, apparently, been murdered. A lot of supernatural creatures dissolve when they're dead. Or turn to dust. Werewolves aren't among their number. Neither, it seemed, are were-jaguars. If that's what the late Eduardo had been. But I wasn't sure. He hadn't been a true cat, not in the way that Harris was a wolf. He'd merely given the impression of being one. Possession, more likely. It all comes back to possession. To slavery, in one form or another. I hate that. Loathe the very idea.

I'm damned if I'm going to waste any more time on him. I said irritably, "Well, I wish he'd bloody well go back to Batista."

And the body vanished. I felt my jaw drop open, and hastily closed it again.

"How did you do that?" Pierce exclaimed.

"I haven't the remotest idea," I replied. My head throbbed, reminding me I needed to break out the holy water. "Come on, let's get out of here." Not being one to look gift horses in the mouth. Or jaguar-creatures, for that matter. Nothing if not pragmatic, da Silva.

I was already light-headed when I got back to my cabin, so though Pierce was prattling away I didn't hear a single word. Sight was coming in waves, hearing a fragmentary thing. I found my shaving mirror and sat down at my desk. Or rather, fell into my chair.

"Don't you have a doctor on board?" I heard Pierce ask, from somewhere in the Indies. Ha, I thought vaguely. I'm not fool enough to let

O'Rourke anywhere near me when I need any doctoring doing.

"'S all right," I said, slurring a little. There was only a small cut above my eyebrow, though it had bled a lot. As such things always do. It was already swollen and beginning to suppurate, but the holy water would get rid of the infection. I located the flask in my desk drawer and soaked a handkerchief in the stuff before attempting to clean the cut. I didn't trust my hands not to shake and tip the whole lot down my neck. The holy water burned briefly, and then the cut was clean. The blurriness in my head cleared quickly, although the ache didn't.

The Englishman watched this with the slightly disbelieving air of a man at a conjuring show. Right now, I didn't feel like explaining. Or sawing a woman in half, either. I pressed the bridge of my nose briefly, trying to ease the pounding in my head. It didn't work. I found a cheroot instead and lit it. I inhaled gratefully. If the smoke made Pierce ill, that was too bad.

"What just happened?" he asked finally, in plaintive tones.

Finding a second glass, I poured brandy for both of us. "Holy water," I said. "Better than carbolic. At least in cases like these."

"But that…thing only just cut you," he said.

"Yes, well, that's what happens." I blew smoke out. "We can't endure their touch. Just as silver will kill them. Only we can clean up with holy water." So that's an advantage. One of the few. Nice to know there's one thing I can rely on. "Anyway, Pierce, it's gone now. You should be safe." For now.

He took a large gulp of brandy. I thought he had the right idea there, so followed suit. "But what if he sends something else?" he objected.

"Quite frankly," I said. "I shouldn't think he'd bother. No offence, but he probably thinks you're beneath his notice." I really didn't know why he'd taken the trouble in the first place. Unless the late Eduardo was indulging in a little freelance stalking. And in that case, why—how—had his body vanished?

"But you killed it." Thank you, Pierce, I had noticed. I scratched my cheekbone. "Don't you think that might…annoy him?"

If sticking a sword in a bull annoys it, sure. I exhaled through my teeth. "You can stay on board, if that's what you want," I said. God knows, we've enough room. And getting emptier by the minute.

"I'd feel safer," he said, looking relieved. Though why he had this conviction that Batista's sendings couldn't cross water, I didn't know. It hadn't ever stopped anything else from coming aboard uninvited. Though that wasn't quite true, was it? Now I came to think about it, there'd always been a reason for past incidents. The box Arkright brought on board, for instance. Perhaps they did need an invitation, or a bridge of some sort. I ran a hand through my damp hair.

"Take the 'prentices' cabin for tonight," I said. I could work out what to do next when morning came. At the moment I was too tired to think straight.

"Thank you," Pierce said. "And thank you for...what you did." I smiled wearily. I was also too tired to say *"nada"*. It wasn't true, anyway.

* * *

John Yeoh closed the book of poetry and put it in his pocket. Then he got up out of his chair and walked to the corner of the street, where an even narrower alley dog-legged away out of sight, and called softly, "Mister Wolf?"

A moment later, an abashed-looking Harris emerged and grumbled, "How'd you know I was there?"

Yeoh smiled. "I felt you," he replied. "Also, I knew you wouldn't go away."

"Huh," said Harris, and stuck his hands in his pockets like a schoolboy caught in the act. And despite himself, he looked up nervously at the sky.

"You will no doubt be more comfortable indoors," Yeoh suggested. "You are quite welcome to use my shop to...change." He gestured at the open door.

"Well, that's mighty civil of you." Harris looked at the other man curiously. "You change your mind, then?"

"About what?" Yeoh asked, picking up his chair and heading indoors. Harris padded after him.

"Letting me tag along."

"I cannot stop you tagging along," said Yeoh. "But you will not be able to follow me once I reach the house." He shut the door and pulled a blind down to cover the glass, then turned the key in the lock.

"Why?" inquired Harris, mulishly. The other gave him a long steady look.

"Because I am going to fly, Mister Wolf."

Harris scowled. It was unanswerable. Since *he* couldn't fly. After a moment, he said, "D'you mind not calling me that? Name's Harris."

"Ah, but your soul is wolf-shaped," said Yeoh.

As if to underline that, a familiar pain lanced through Harris, and he screwed his eyes shut in reaction. Yeoh, watching, saw his face seem to shift momentarily into something that was not yet wolf, no longer human, and then back again. Beads of sweat popped out on the American's forehead. He opened his eyes on a shuddering breath.

"Jesus, that was a bad one," he muttered.

5

I AM CAUGHT IN THREE PIECES, THOUGHT JOHN YEOH AS HE WATCHED THE WEREWOLF CHANGE. One piece was the John Yeoh who had been waiting in his long self-induced half-life for a death that never came; another, the lost young man whose soul died when a ship went down off Ceylon two years before Lisbon's great earthquake. The third, newborn, had been brought into being by da Silva's visit, and now, strange to tell, it was one he found he didn't want to relinquish.

For now, he was fascinated enough to concentrate on watching. He was not doing this overtly, since he did not want to embarrass Harris, but all the glass-fronted cabinets and mirrors in his shop had been placed just so for a purpose.

The American's metamorphosis, to him, was literally that: the changing into a true form, as caterpillar becomes moth. Harris's body was adapting to fit his soul. That he had to change back again when the moon ceased its pull at his tides struck Yeoh as inefficient.

He had learned to see people's souls—their true selves—only gradually, as long time went by, as the years turned without respite or solace. Those of most people he met were small. Mouse-souls, bird-souls, rabbit-souls. Servants, happy in servitude, usually had dog-souls. The year of birth had some influence, but the shape of the souls remained the same.

As a man more conscious than most of time, since he was its prisoner, Yeoh was interested to note that Harris's metamorphosis lasted less than five minutes. And the after-effects of the pain were apparently gone in under sixty seconds.

To walk more stealthily in shadows, Yeoh had dressed in the black pajama suit which some older Chinese still favored. His sleight-of-body would aid him in this too, for there are many ways to manipulate time even if, in the end, the ultimate manipulation proves impossible.

Out of politeness, he waited until Harris-wolf was ready, then set off via his own secret ways. Only the fact that Harris actually knew where he was headed kept the wolf on his trail.

Once, he would have done this playfully: stolen a kiss from a pretty girl, tweaked a mandarin's nose as he passed by unseen. But those days were long gone. Now he moved single-mindedly, purposefully, his only concern to reach his goal.

A quarter of a mile from the House of the Four Winds, he felt disturbed air. It was like a broken ant-hill, but instead of ants, the particles of the air itself were milling round in confusion. He smiled to himself. That could only be to his advantage.

Reaching the house, he found that the airstorm was, indeed, centered on it, and paused, wondering what had caused it. But it made no difference. He slipped back down the street, and Harris saw him start to sprint; gaining momentum, he was suddenly airborne, running still, but four, seven, ten feet above the pavement. A moment later, he landed lightly on top of the wall, then leapt from there to a first-floor balcony.

He paused, listening at the shutters for a second, and then disappeared.

If Harris had been in human form, his jaw would have dropped open. As wolf he did not feel the need to show astonishment, but Yeoh vanished from his perceptions all the same. A moment later he became conscious of the man again, and knew he was now inside the house. He put thoughts of Yeoh aside. His hackles were bristling with the knowledge that this was the place he'd been hurt the previous night, and the healing wound throbbed to remind him.

Crouched in the shadows, he let his senses expand to give him a detailed picture of his surroundings. Dogs had passed recently, humans a short while before. He could tell many things about them by their scent. One of the dogs had been lame, one of the humans pregnant. And one of them had been dead.

And he was now walking.

Harris-wolf caught the scent, and it was unmistakable. The man who had shot him the night before, who smelled of peppery cordite and the particular chill silver scent of the bullet the wolf had taken, had left the house this morning alive and returned to it dead. He could smell the still blood going stale in his body, so different from the rich odor of the living. Taste the necrosis of the tissues that made eating anything but newly-dead meat so unpleasant. Smell the lack of breath, the faint stench of rot that was coming out of the mouth. And he could hear the man moving about stealthily. He growled faintly with disgust at the taste of the animate corpse.

Now he was aware of the man, he slipped further back into the shadows. It may have thought, if it could still think, that it was hunting him, but it was not. The next moment, his senses presented his quarry to him.

Though sight was only a small part of the wolf's awareness, he had a distinct picture of the man, and the picture was not properly man-shaped. It was distorted. The head hung wrongly on the shoulders, drooping to one side. More scents came to the watching wolf. A taint of cat, which he didn't understand. And a scent he knew very well: the captain's knife. He smelled the silver chattering coldly against the steel in the alloy.

The walking corpse was carrying a rifle, and Harris knew without question that the bullet that had injured him had come from it. His lips went back from his teeth in a snarl. This man had been trying to kill him, so he would return the favor, even if the captain had already done it once. He crouched, waiting for it to come into range.

As soon as it passed the end of the alley, the wolf sprang onto its back. The dead man crashed to the pavement, lacking the reflexes to break its fall. Harris heard bones snap. He wrenched the rifle out of the corpse's hand with his teeth and flung it away. The man thrashed feebly under his weight. He worried at its coat-collar, reluctant to sink his teeth into the dead flesh. Eventually he stepped off the body and turned it over. Dead eyes rolled in the sockets, whites already occluded. The wolf went for its throat, to find it already laid open to the spine.

Nonetheless, he worried at it, ripping and tearing, until the corpse lay quite still.

Yeoh slid briefly into a time when the shutters and window were open, passed through, then came back to the present inside the dark room beyond, all in the blink of an eye. Up here, the house was quiet, though the strange airstorm still whirled all around. But that cast no sound.

He found himself in a bedroom, a man's: a tidy man's. Someone who liked to be in control. Yeoh smiled to himself and let his perceptions move through the recent past. There was no book used in here. The man slept in the room, no more.

Moving delicately, he went to the door and turned the handle slowly. The catch gave the faintest of clicks, and he pushed the door open a crack. It gave onto an unlighted passage, and Yeoh passed through, very light on his feet. No floorboards groaned under his tread, but the house was old, and he respected its age.

The next door opened into a woman's room, but also austere, also neat. This time he frowned slightly, finding the orderliness of both people a little disturbing. He passed on to another door: bathroom. And a third, and knew at once that this room held what he sought. The door was locked, but that was no barrier.

Once inside, he stood still for a few moments, both to orient himself and plan an escape if anyone came in. He could only slip out of time for a second or so, but that should be enough to gain the window. But the window would have to be open, or he would lose the advantage. He padded across and unlatched it, and the shutter as well. The shutter creaked, and he froze, but after long seconds he heard no noise and resumed his scanning of the room. It reeked of magic. Only great power resonated through time like that. Things had been summoned here that he was glad to perceive only briefly, and only as memories held in the room.

As he had suspected, the volume he had come in search of was under lock and key. He could not remove it from its cabinet by slipping out of time; he could only move himself in and out, not carry objects from one moment to another. But he had more mundane skills, and also a set of lock-picks on a chain round his neck. The lock soon yielded to his persuasion, and he opened the door to reveal the *Book of Souls*.

He did not want to pick it up. Whether a spell of protection had been placed on it, or whether it was its own inherent power that induced the revulsion he felt, he couldn't tell, and didn't much care. As an observer of souls, he could see that the book possessed a soul of sorts, and it was evil, corrupt, rotten.

Thankful that his gloves meant he didn't actually have to touch the thing, he lifted the book carefully out of the cabinet and placed it in his knapsack. As he shouldered it back on, the door to the room burst open.

In the first blink of an eye Yeoh saw a tall woman, her face distorted by fury, and then she changed. Not as the wolf had done, into the true shape of her soul; she mutated. Became armored, but the armor was not so much something worn as something *of* the figure, intrinsic to it, as an insect's carapace is to the creature it protects. Shining breastplate, barred helmet, mailed limbs, all seemed grown in place. In its iron fist it held a mace, a morningstar, and it swung this at Yeoh with an inarticulate cry of fury.

Panicking, Yeoh time-skipped to avoid the crashing blow, and raced for the window. The armored figure chased after him, and the mace smashed into the windowframe inches from his head. He dived through with no thought of safety, rolled himself into a ball in the air, and came to earth awkwardly in a courtyard under a lemon tree.

His pursuer launched itself out of the window, landing with a clang of metal but absorbing the impact easily, and Yeoh ran for his life. Gained the air a few steps from the high wall, scrabbled out of the way of another blow that could have broken his ankle, grabbed the top of the wall and hoisted himself up. The armored figure hurled the mace at him, and it whirled through the air too fast for him to think.

And passed straight through him. He sprinted along the top of the wall, taking advantage of his antagonist's momentary confusion, and leapt lightly off to run down the air into the street, where he kept on running the instant he hit the pavement.

He knew what had happened. He had time-slipped involuntarily. Instinctively, without thinking. The blow had passed through a space where he was not. That was something he had never done before. He marvelled as he ran. A skill like that would make him invulnerable.

Harris looked up from the corpse to see Yeoh float off the wall, light as thistledown, and scampered after him. A moment later he was aware of pursuit, but he and Yeoh were both fleeter of foot than any follower and cleverer at passing unseen.

The night swallowed them.

* * *

I'm turning into my father. I'd fallen asleep in my chair. Oh, God, I thought, waking with a crick in my neck, retire me now. Da Silva's past it. I felt about a hundred and two.

What had roused me, it turned out, was someone at the door. I pulled out my watch. At this time of night? I heard Emilia's voice, but couldn't make out what she was saying. Better put the eye-patch back on. Couldn't do anything about the creeping decrepitude. I pushed myself to my feet, feeling as though I'd spent the day hauling ropes or stowing heavy cargo in the hold, and wishing she'd woken me. I found a cheroot and lit it.

"Sr Yeoh," she said, opening the door. My heart thumped. Had something gone wrong? Where was Harris? Oh, pull yourself together, da Silva. He's out wolfing somewhere. I took Emilia's arm and handed her back to her chair.

"Senhor capitão," said Yeoh formally, with a little bow. He looked used up. His face was hollow, not hiding the skull beneath.

"What is it?" I asked.

"I have the book," he replied, taking a satchel from his shoulder and extracting a newspaper-wrapped package. "But it is an extremely unpleasant thing. And I have no doubt that its owner will very soon be wanting to get it back."

"That's for sure," I said. My brain was still fuzzy from sleep. I took a long drag at my cheroot. "Any suggestions? Can you get your friend Isaiah to look after it?"

"He couldn't hide it." Yeoh grimaced. "It…resonates too much. It needs to be somewhere protected."

I thought of the library of São Rafael. Not tonight! Haven't I done enough for one day? "Were you followed?"

Yeoh shook his head. "It'll be safe for a day, perhaps. No more. He set a guardian outside, but your wolf took care of that." Now he was doing it.

"He's not my wolf," I said. Yeoh just smiled, but then sobered instantly. "What?"

"There was another guardian. One I didn't understand." He swayed on his feet, covering a yawn.

"Sit down before you fall down," I said. Yeoh nodded, and complied. "Another guardian?"

"Yes. When I had put the book in my bag, a woman came in. At least it was a woman, at first. Then she changed into some armored creature and attacked me."

Armored, I thought. "What did it look like?"

"Tall," he said. "Helmet, breastplate. Shiny but dull. Chain-mail on the arms, hands, fingers, and legs. But light on its feet."

"Did it have a sword?" I asked.

"No, a mace—a morningstar." Yes, because I had its sword, of course. "You know this creature?"

"Yes," I said. "I think it's the guardian of the first soul. The armored one." The one I'd wanted to ask him to tackle. Too late now. Damn it. *"Against the armored one, only the invulnerable may stand,"* I quoted, somewhat bitterly.

John Yeoh's face had gone ash-pale, and then color flooded into it. He looked thunderstruck. Anyone who wants to call the Chinese face inscrutable, take a look at this man. "Invulnerable?" he whispered. I nodded. "What?"

"Senhor capitão," said John Yeoh, "it couldn't harm me. The mace went through my leg. It should have broken a bone. But it went through…a time when I wasn't there. I went out of phase with it when it tried to hurt me." He leaned back and closed his eyes, then opened them again. "I think, even if I had not decided to help you, I would now be obliged to."

Obligation. I understand that well enough. It's pretty much the same as a geas. On the sliding scale of slavery, though, it's pretty low. Since you do it because you should and not because you must. Although sometimes you have no choice.

Well, I only said I understood it. Not that it makes sense.

Yeoh, who had been sitting with the book on his lap, held it out to me. I stubbed out my cheroot in the ashtray and took the package, half-expecting to feel some sense of leashed power or latent evil. But the newspaper wrapping must have insulated it. Or me.

"Don't—" Emilia blurted out. I looked at her, surprised. She bit her lower lip (as I suddenly wanted to do). "Don't open it now."

I nodded. "All right." Who am I to deny the power of intuition? I do things by instinct often enough. Yeoh bowed his head to her. He had folded his hands in his lap, and looked suddenly very mandarin-like.

"You are a very sensible lady, *senhora joalheira*," he observed, with a small smile. "We should all get some sleep." He got to his feet. "I will bid you good night." I stood up too, expecting to hear myself creak.

"I'll see you to the door," I said.

"Good night, Sr Yeoh," said Emilia.

At the door, he turned to me. The street was deserted, except for a black-and-white cat strolling purposefully past. The moonlight was so strong it cast shadows. "If you can, put some protection on the book. It may be safe from its owner for now, but it shines like a beacon to anyone with the will to use it."

"Yes," I agreed. "And…thank you." I suppose.

He grimaced. "Thanks are not really appropriate, as I'm sure you agree."

"Good night, then."

Well, the joke's on me. Making fun of poor old Arkright for his pentagram. And I end up doing the same. It would either work, or not. I was certainly more inclined to believe in this ritual stuff after seeing how it confined something as overreaching as Gaziel. Ha. Next thing, I'll be believing in prayer.

"Luís?" said Emilia from behind me. I turned round, saw her silhouetted in the doorway. She was leaning to the side, which meant that her leg was bothering her. "Are you done?"

"As much as I can," I said. I wasn't going to worry about it. Like Yeoh said, we all needed some rest. And if the last few days were anything to go by, tomorrow wouldn't break the trend by being any easier. I yawned, then pushed the eye-patch up onto my brow and laid my finger along the scar. It still feels strange to touch, even after all this time.

"Come to bed then."

Finally, I slept like a stone. Not like the dead. At least, not like any of them I ever encounter.

    * * *

You can't always solve a problem by sleeping on it. These days it seems I can't even cure exhaustion by sleeping on it. Well, not the mental kind, anyway. Which is why I had the *Book of Souls* over my shoulder in a duffel bag at nine o'clock in the morning. Not something I enjoyed, but my tired brain couldn't come up with any better solution. I wanted to get it to the library of São Rafael as soon as possible. But I also wanted to get Pierce to the library, and Pierce had spent the night aboard *Isabella*.

So, since I didn't trust the book. and certainly wasn't going to leave it anywhere near my family, it went with me. Little as I liked the idea. John Yeoh, I thought, was being over-optimistic. I reckoned I could expect some kind of envoy from Batista pretty soon. Of what sort remained to be seen. Ready for it, da Silva? Not really.

Being Portuguese, João, *Isabella*'s cook, can make coffee strong enough for me. That, of course, is one of the reasons I employ a Portuguese cook. Pierce, having spent most of his adult life in Rio, drank it with enjoyment, but Harris, the barbarian, puts milk and sugar in it. He looked none the worse for his night, except for his usual morning-after-wolf headache. But I'll have to wait till later to hear about that. I thought Pierce had gone through enough yesterday without being confronted by a large and hung-over werewolf when I wake up. You see, I can be sensitive to people's feelings, after all. Altruism, my middle name.

The pair of them looked at me expectantly. As if, I thought irritably, I suddenly had all the answers. Well, I've got one. I hope. I put the *Book of Souls* on the desk, still in its newspaper overcoat. My own coat was on the back of my chair. It was another hot morning. I had to wipe sweat out of my eyebrows already.

Lighting a cheroot, I said, "There it is, gentlemen. According to Sr Yeoh, we have a bit of time before Batista sends someone to look for it...but I don't think I'd like to rely on one person's opinion."

Harris eyed the parcel with distaste, as if he thought it might explode. And, I thought sourly, it might, at that. "What're you gonna do, skipper?"

"Take it somewhere I think it'll be safe. And I want you, Pierce, to come with me." Pierce had started to look alarmed again when I mentioned Batista sending someone after the book.

"Are you sure it'll be safe?"

No, was the short answer to that. I wasn't. But equally, I wasn't going to tell him that. Or repeat Yeoh's remark about it shining like a beacon. I scratched my cheekbone. "As safe as anywhere." Spoken like a politician. Meaningless as a manifesto.

"What if he does manage to get it back?" Harris asked, dourly. "We'll be right back where we started."

He doesn't usually play devil's advocate unless he has an idea. "What're you thinking, Harris?" I enquired.

"You suppose we could photograph the pages we need?" It *was* an idea. I nodded slowly, liking the thought. He went on, "And then I reckon we oughta burn the goddamn thing. Stop him getting his mitts on it again."

I thought about Fr Jerónimo. And what I'd said to him. I didn't like the prospect, even with this book. Could burning a book ever be the right thing to do? Destroying knowledge? Could knowledge really be destroyed? Surely, once someone knows a thing, it's never gone from the world. Getting a bit metaphysical here, da Silva. Back to the matter in hand.

"Pierce?" I said, blowing out smoke. He looked down at his hands.

"I don't like the idea of burning any book," he said, echoing my thought. "But I think Mr Harris's photography idea is a good one. We couldn't *copy* the spell safely, but I imagine a photographic plate is quite... inert. Magically speaking, I mean."

"Do you know anything about photography?" I asked. He nodded eagerly.

"A little," he admitted, his eyes shining. The idea, obviously, interested him. Good. Give him something to do. Something else to do.

"We'll sort that out later," I said. "Right now, we need to make a move."

"Ain't you going to open it?" Harris asked.

I looked at the parcel, rubbing my eyebrow thoughtfully. Somehow I'd almost forgotten that unwrapping it was even possible. And part of me didn't want to unwrap it at all. Superstition, I thought. It's a book. Not a box of snakes. I reached my hand out, picked up my pocket-knife from the desk, and slit the string. The newspaper, several sheets of it, slowly unfolded. Revealed just a glimpse of a dark leather cover.

Harris sneezed suddenly, and I caught a trace of what had caused it. Not a smell, precisely. Not a taste. A taint. Something that made the back of my neck prickle. The cabin seemed airless all of a sudden, oppressive. Pierce, wide-eyed, looked round quickly, as if he'd heard a sound, and crossed himself. I was distantly surprised, for some reason. There are plenty of English Catholics, after all, even in England.

And I understood what John Yeoh had meant. Something had peeped out of the wrapping and called "I'm here!" Something very nasty indeed. I refolded the paper swiftly with the point of the small knife and held it shut.

"On second thoughts, I believe I won't open it right now," I said, keeping my voice level with an effort. I found another piece of string and tied it securely round the parcel. I felt as if I'd opened a door a crack to find a tiger in the room beyond and only just shut it again in time. I found I was sweating.

"*Porra*," muttered Pierce. I didn't think antiquarians knew words like that.

Putting the re-wrapped book back in the duffel, I stood up, stubbed out my cheroot, and retrieved my coat. I would bake. But you have to conform. "Let's go," I said. "Harris, you stay on board. Pierce, you're with me."

"Any special instructions, skipper?" Harris asked. I gave him a deadpan stare.

"Yes. Watch your butt," I told him.

"Where are we going?" Pierce wanted to know. Before I could answer, there was a knock at the door.

"Come in," I said. The door opened, revealing Joaquim Grego, senior 'prentice until Zé had joined *Isabella*. With Felipe…missing and Zé on shore leave—which I hadn't had the heart to cancel—he was temporarily the lowest of the low again. He wasn't pleased at this development and came in looking sullen. Something he does rather well.

"There's a gentleman to see you, captain," he said, scowling and contriving to look put-upon. "Wouldn't give his name."

I exchanged a glance with Harris, who raised his eyebrows. "What does this gentleman look like?" I asked.

Grego grimaced. "Like a bleeding aristocrat, sir," he said. "If you'll pardon the expression." I stifled a laugh. He may pretend to be a republican, but his family's blood is bluer than my mother's had been.

"Batista?" Harris speculated. Pierce looked thoroughly alarmed.

"Let's go and see," I said. "Where is he, Grego?"

"On the quay," he replied. "Bit miffed, I think. Sr Costa won't let him on board." I should think not, too. But you don't argue with Costa. Not unless you have a death-wish. He has muscles like a gorilla. Even his muscles have muscles.

"Come on then, Harris." I shrugged into my coat and did the buttons up, then clapped my cap on my head. Better look as official as I can, never mind the heat. I feel more apprehensive about the prospect of seeing Batista than I had about summoning a demon. Well, I thought grimly, the demon had nothing against me personally. Nor should Batista, damn it. Only a madman holds a grudge for twenty years.

This madman, as Grego had said, was on the quayside. Surrounded by floating ghosts and glowering at the square form of Costa barring his way. I stared at him for a second before he saw me. Cold eyes, oddly red lips. His hair and beard had gone white, his face grown deep lines. Otherwise he was unchanged. I found I was suddenly furiously angry, and clenched my fists momentarily. My heart was pounding. Sweat trickled down the side of my face, and I wiped it away. Batista looked up. His lips thinned into a sneer.

"You," he said, and there was satisfaction as well as murder in his chilly voice. I stayed where I was, breathing heavily.

"What can I do for you, Sr Batista?"

He pointed his cane at me rudely. "Still taking things that don't belong to you, da Silva," he observed. "You have something of mine. I want it back."

For something to do with my hands, I lit a cheroot. Stared at him coldly. Finally I said, "I don't think so."

"Do you deny that you employed someone to steal a book from my home last night?" He was angry, too. I could see a vein throbbing in his temple. Somehow it made me feel better. I stopped myself from smiling with an effort.

"Of course I do," I said. Moreover, it was true. Since I hadn't employed Yeoh. At least, not in the sense of paying him to do a job.

"Then you'll ask your thug to stand aside so I can come aboard and see for myself," he suggested. I laughed. Though I was damn sure Costa objected to being called a thug. The wide back of his neck had gone red.

"I'll do no such thing." Evil can't come on board unless invited. As I had belatedly realized. And Batista was evil. I had no doubt about that now. He wasn't just vindictive. There was more to it than that. "And I'll thank you to be civil to my officers."

"I might have expected you to skulk on board your wretched boat like a coward," he sneered. "Since you can't hide behind your employer any more."

It didn't make me angry, as he wanted. Since I was already way past furious. It had, strangely, the opposite effect. I stepped onto the gangplank. Harris, recognizing tone if not words, put a hand on my arm.

"Don't let him rile you, skipper."

"It's all right," I said. "I know what he's up to." And *he* doesn't know what *I'm* up to. I hope. Harris eyed me dubiously. I raised an eyebrow at him, then walked towards shore. "Thank you," I said to Costa, "I'll deal with him." He turned from Batista to me and gave me an unfathomable look, then he nodded and stumped off. He has entirely too much imagination, but at least he knows when to keep his mouth shut. Unlike some people I could mention.

I continued walking until I stood in front of Batista. He hadn't expected that, I think. A strange sour smell came off him. It was almost palpable. I wondered if it was the odor of black magic. But I had met sorcerers before, although perhaps none had meddled with things as dark as he did. Not even the Venetian. He looked down his nose at me, disdainfully.

"I should have killed you then and been done with it," he said.

"And how would you have occupied your time since then, if you had?" I asked, blowing smoke at him. "Brewing up love-potions?" His eyes narrowed.

"I *could* kill you now."

"We both know you won't do that," I said, then lowered my voice. "On the other hand, Batista, you can't be sure I won't kill *you*."

He looked around at the dockside bustle. "You can't kill me here."

"Maybe not," I agreed. "But I never said I would. Here."

"Are you threatening me, da Silva?"

Dropping the butt of my cheroot, I ground it under my boot. "Why would I do that?" I asked, most of my anger gone now. Now I was, I admit, enjoying myself.

Batista gave me a disgusted look. "I didn't come here to bandy words with you."

"No," I said, putting my hands in my pockets. "I don't suppose you did." And I turned my back on him and walked back to my ship. With a broad grin on my face.

"*Cabrão*," I heard him say, *bastard*.

"Skipper!" shouted Harris at the same moment. I swiveled instantly, ducking under his swinging cane. It whistled harmlessly over my head. I grabbed his wrist and twisted it until the cane clattered to the ground. He struggled, but I kept hold of him.

"Don't," I said, looking at his other hand. Which was clenched into a fist. "Try it. I don't want to have to hit a man old enough to be my father." Even though he has stolen my father's soul. "Where are the amulets?" I asked. He turned his head away.

Fine. I hadn't expected him to tell me. Just as he can't have expected me to admit I had the *Book of Souls*. I let go of his wrist and walked back to *Isabella* without turning.

"What the hell was all that about?" Harris demanded. "Jesus, makes me wish I'da paid more attention when you was trying to teach me your lingo."

"Power," I said. "It was about power."

"Reckon you won that round, then," he said, baring his teeth.

"Reckon I did." And about time, too. I knew one thing, though. I couldn't let him win. There was something very old and sickening about

Batista. Something that made me think Pierce's apocalypse theory might be right, after all.

Are you on a crusade, Mohan Das had asked me. And it was only then that I realized that yes, I was. I hadn't made a conscious decision to hunt down evil. But that's what I found myself doing. Except that I didn't need to hunt for it. It came and found me of its own accord.

Da Silva, front line of attack. And last line of defense. What a pleasant thought.

* * *

There was a demon at large in the city. Baulked of its prey, for the vessel was as hermetically sealed to it as an alchemist's bottle, it cast around for mischief to occupy it in the meantime.

Some demons might consider small acts of malice beneath them, and disdain a purpose twisted, a quarrel begun. But all are deceivers, and misdirection comes naturally.

And all are drawn to people who are most receptive to malign suggestion.

* * *

Fr Jerónimo strode up and down, black flapping round his legs, head thrust forward, hands behind his back. He looked like a stick-insect in a soutane. Where was that damned library? Which alley led to it?

It did not occur to him that both his purposefulness and his motives prevented him from finding it. But he did realize that the best course of action was to find someone headed there and try to tag along behind.

Unfortunately, the only other person he knew who had access was da Silva.

Deep in thought, he almost bumped into a small man with a mulberry-colored birthmark on his face.

"Oh! I beg your pardon!" he exclaimed.

"De nada...de nada," the other replied. His voice was harsh, like a crow's; it grated on the ear. It held an accent Fr Jerónimo couldn't identify. "You seem deep in thought, Father."

The young priest colored. "I was...miles away," he admitted, apologetically. "Are you from around here, my son?" It would be a long time before he knew everyone by sight. Although the stranger's accent suggested he was not a local.

"No," said the disfigured man with a strangely sweet smile. "I'm visiting. I was looking for a library. I believe there's a famous one somewhere round here?"

"It's not exactly famous," said Fr Jerónimo dubiously, since he had thought the exact opposite.

"Among scholars, Father," the other chided gently. "Among scholars."

"I see." Although he didn't. "I'm afraid I can't tell you where it is, except that I know it's around here somewhere." He looked narrowly at the man. Behind the port-wine mark his face was smooth and unlined, like a child's. And as guileless. "I'm afraid I'm not allowed in."

"That seems unfair," said the small man. "Allow me to introduce myself. Jean Malfamé...at your service." Due to his accent, Fr Jerónimo heard the sound of *Alfama*, but not knowing any French, might not have understood the joke anyway.

"At my service?" he repeated.

"Well, I am a scholar, of sorts," said the man who had called himself Jean Malfamé. He sighed. "Although I have little love for the arts that some call learning."

Fr Jerónimo pricked up his ears. "Some books were better left unwritten," he agreed.

"Ah, you are a sensible man," exclaimed Malfamé. "There is much knowledge too dangerous for common men to have access to, indeed."

"Yes," said the priest. "And that damned library is full of it."

The small man lifted one arm to his face, and a small pointed nose poked out of his sleeve, startling Fr Jerónimo badly until he realized it was only a mouse. Malfamé made kissing noises at the rodent.

"You would not be distressed, then," he suggested, "if someone were careless with a lamp, perhaps."

"It has electrical lights," Fr Jerónimo pointed out, somewhat annoyed. He thought that a needless extravagance, too.

"So you have been there?"

"Yes, accompanied," said the priest, bitterly.

Malfamé stroked his tiny pet's head and asked casually, "Who by?"

Guiltily remembering Fr Pereira's unfortunate illness, Fr Jerónimo replied, "A poor soul who can no longer visit the place."

"What a shame," observed the other. "And you know no one else who could take you? No one at all?"

"Well, yes, I do, but he wouldn't take me—I mean, he knows that I, that Verbum Dei, think the books should be destroyed."

Verbum Dei! thought the demon in great amusement. What presumptuous names these humans coin.

"I know a way around that," said Malfamé softly, apparently to his mouse.

Hopelessly trapped, the young priest leaned forward eagerly. "What?"

"My little friend will show you the way." He held out his hand. The mouse hopped onto it. "Take him."

Despite himself, Fr Jerónimo held out his own hand to receive the mouse. Its feet tickled his palm. It weighed nothing. But for its tiny warmth, and the dainty touch of its feet, he would not have known it was there.

"What do I do with him?" he asked.

"When you see this man going to the library," Malfamé said, "slip Mouffi into his pocket. When he returns to you, he will be able to guide you there."

"Why are you doing this?"

Jean Malfamé smiled his sweet smile. "For love," he said, then turned away, moving swiftly into the crowds. Fr Jerónimo started after him but found his way blocked by milling people and soon lost sight of the small man.

In the palm of his hand, the mouse groomed its whiskers.

* * *

I must confess I'm not a hundred per cent sure I could find the library again. Hell, I'm not even seventy per cent sure. And I can certainly do without running into Fr Jerónimo again. If I didn't want to hit an old man, I certainly didn't want to end up thumping a priest. And it might well have come to that. Bloody young fool. All right, I know you're supposed to get more tolerant as you get older. Tolerance wasn't designed for bigots.

Pierce didn't find me much of a conversationalist as we walked, but then he didn't show any signs of wanting to talk either. I was inclined to think rather better of him for bearding Batista in his den now I'd renewed my acquaintance with the man. He was still skittish and nervous, looking over his shoulder every two minutes, mopping his face with a yellow silk handkerchief. Which irritated me. I was sweating just as much as he was. I dearly wished I could take my coat off, and my eye-patch, come to that. But I didn't want to attract attention. And walking through the streets of Lisbon in shirt-sleeves, I'd stand out like a whore at a wedding. Oh, and not to mention the fact that I had a fourteen-inch knife in a sheath down my back. Blend in, da Silva.

This is all supposed to take my mind off the book I was carrying. I was acutely aware of it. It felt as if everyone was staring at me anyway. As if I had a boa constrictor looped over my shoulder. My shirt felt damp and unpleasant. And I had smoked so much my mouth felt like the inside of my duffel bag.

Passing the church, I kept a suspicious eye open for the priest, but there was no sign of him. Which was a relief. I tried to make my mind blank and receptive, and slowed my pace. Pierce, perhaps sensing he shouldn't distract me, dropped back.

And then I saw Isaiah's ghost. I had forgotten all about him. I looked at the shade curiously, wondering again if these faint images were aware at all. Whether it had any real connection to the rather more substantial spectre I'd met. If you can use the word substantial to describe a ghost. But it simply hovered there, my personal signpost to São Rafael.

"Down here, Pierce," I said, then turned into the cool darkness. Feeling immense relief. The scholarly ghosts I had seen before wavered and drifted. I turned to make sure Pierce was following, and found him staring at the strip of blue sky above the rooftops and mopping his forehead again. I dragged my hand over my own face and lifted the eye-patch a fraction to let some air in. Never works. Don't know why I try.

"My God, it's hot today," he remarked.

"Not as hot as Rio," I said.

"I don't go rushing round town like a headless chicken when I'm in Rio," he said. I laughed. Got more sense, I suppose.

There was a feeling of timelessness in the small square that fronted the library. A bit like Isaiah's workroom in the walls, I realized. The same sense of peace. And I wondered whether São Rafael was similarly out of time. That might be one of the reasons it was difficult to find. I saw the big black cat basking luxuriously in a patch of sunlight, obviously not as sensitive to the heat as Pierce. Cat wasn't doing any rushing around in the midday sun, though. Only people who associate with me seem to have to do that.

I looked up at the library, presenting its shuttered windows like closed eyes. It looked asleep. We negotiated the flowerpot shoals, and I put my hand on the ancient door. The wood was warm from the sun and smelt like the deck on a hot day. A powerful desire to be back at sea overwhelmed me. No chance of that, da Silva. I pushed it open, and Pierce followed me over the threshold, then stopped dead in his tracks. Remembering my own reaction, I smiled.

"This is amazing," I heard him say, in awe. "This is just the most astonishing thing I've ever seen. Look at the *books!*" He walked to the nearest shelves and started to do just that. Exclaiming in wonder, muttering titles. Running his hand tenderly over their spines.

"Pierce," I reminded him. "We're here for a reason."

"Oh yes," he said distractedly. "How long has this place been here?"

"Centuries, as far as I know."

I took my coat and cap off—might as well be comfortable—and put my duffel on the big table. A flash of memory: finding Fr Pereira slumped there. I grimaced and took out the *Book of Souls*. Wondered whether this would work. Untied the string and let the newspaper wrapping part slightly.

Something sly peered out, but this time it didn't bellow its whereabouts to the world. It was, if you can say this about a book, wary. But then I already knew that this was no ordinary book. Ha. You probably couldn't burn it if you wanted to. It might bite your hand off. The image of its having teeth was unpleasant but not, unfortunately, fanciful enough to dismiss. I knew I didn't want to touch it. I looked at Pierce, but he was still rapt at the bookshelves. Ah well. If you want anything doing, da Silva, do it yourself.

With the point of my pocket-knife, I pushed the wrapping back completely. The book that had caused all the trouble was bound in leather so ancient it had cracked like an old pair of boots, though Batista or someone had tried to salvage it with neat's-foot oil. It smelled of the oil and of mildew, in fairly equal proportions. Still using the knife, I opened the cover carefully. Nothing happened. No teeth. None showing, anyway.

It was a mighty thin volume for what it contained, I thought. And for something worth two and a half thousand dollars American. A lot of the pages were loose, and all of them were brown and disintegrating at the edges. There were no helpful bookmarks inserted between them. Salt-stains added to the illegibility. I couldn't read it at all. Damn it. I called to Pierce, and he turned reluctantly, an open book in his hands.

"What?" he said.

"Come on, Pierce, I need you to decipher this thing."

"Oh. Right." He replaced the volume reluctantly on the shelf and came over to look at the *Book of Souls*, wrinkling his nose with distaste. I turned pages with the point of my knife, and he looked over my shoulder. Scanning for the spell we wanted. But I was the one who spotted a name I recognized.

Mastiphal, it said. I pointed to it.

"That's one of 'em. One of the demons." Pierce drew in a deep breath.

"The first soul," he translated slowly, *"shall be the soul of a venturer. It shall be gathered by the demon Mastiphal and stored in an amulet of agate.* Good God!" I looked up at him. He seemed to have had some kind of revelation.

"What?" I asked.

"An amulet of agate," he repeated. "Batista's daughter was wearing an agate. A banded one. Round her neck."

"She's the guardian," I said, sure of it at last. Pierce frowned. I pointed the knife at the text. "Read the next bit."

He looked back to the page. *"And the guardian of that soul shall be the armored one. And the soul of a venturer may only be released by a venturer. Against the armored one, only the invulnerable may stand."*

"Teresa Batista is the guardian," I repeated.

"I don't understand."

Neither had I, until now. But knowing that Batista's daughter was wearing the agate, I now thought I knew how it worked. It explained why the armored figure had attacked me. Why it had been able to come from the church. Why she had transformed on seeing Yeoh. She, or it, was reacting to threats. To the amulet, and by association, to the entire spell.

"Whoever wears the amulet turns into the guardian when it's threatened," I said. Which meant that simply finding the stones wouldn't be enough. The guardians would have to be overcome, somehow. All of them. Well, you knew it really, da Silva. No use hoping for someone to wave a magic wand and make everything easy all of a sudden.

Pierce shook his head. Not in disagreement. "Why?" he asked plaintively. "Why would Batista go to all this trouble?"

"Because he's not sane, Pierce. You met him. Couldn't you feel it?" Or smell it, I thought suddenly. Maybe the strange sour smell he gave off was the odor of madness. Although I can't help feeling sanity is relative. Before I found myself seeing ghosts I might have thought that anyone who claimed to be able to do that was pretty much off his rocker. If I'd never seen anything odd in my life, that is. Or if I hadn't been working for a damn sorcerer.

"Here," said Pierce suddenly. *"Of the binding of souls, and their release."*

I peered at the densely-written, time-darkened vellum where he was pointing, but even when I knew the translation I couldn't decipher the script. Which is more or less what Emilia says about my handwriting.

"Do you really think we can photograph this?" I asked dubiously. It all seemed pretty dark and illegible.

"I think so, yes," he said. "Give me a moment here, da Silva. It's—is there something to write with?"

Given that we were in a library, I would've been mighty surprised if there wasn't. I got up and searched for a pencil. Pierce sat down in the chair I'd vacated and found a sheaf of scrap paper left by some previous occupant.

"Didn't you say copying the spell might be dangerous?"

"The spell itself, yes," Pierce replied. "Not the, uh, peripheral stuff."

"Pencil," I said, finding one. Watched him write. His handwriting was almost as bad as the monk's. But who am I to throw stones?

"The souls must be preserved apart until the moment of coming together," he wrote. It was so quiet I heard the sound of the pencil on the page. *"The souls may be released when they number one. The souls may be released when they number two."*

"Ditto, ditto," he muttered, scribbling, *"...three, four, five, six. The souls may not be released when they number seven. No soul can be released without the release of all the others. The souls may be released by the crushing of the amulet by its antithesis. All those collected must be broken before the souls may return to their vessels."* He crossed this out and wrote *"bodies"*. Then he went back to reading. I badly needed a smoke. I scratched my scar instead.

"Well?" I asked, when an inordinate amount of time had gone by.

"Nothing else," said Pierce. He closed the cover of the *Book of Souls* carefully, using the pencil. "We'll have to look somewhere else for the stones." The stones? I thought, frowning. He explained. "The antitheses of the amulets, they must be gemstones as well. Do you suppose this place has a catalog?"

I laughed humorlessly and told him about Fr Pereira's method. Pierce looked thoughtfully around. "Everything's so weird at the moment it might just work," he remarked. He put his hands on the table in front of him and closed his eyes, muttering, "Stones, stones." I watched him for a second, then sat down in one of the other chairs, surprised by a yawn. Oh, God, I thought, let the ancient mariner have a seat. Stretched my arms over my head. Wished myself back at sea, with no concerns save navigation and wind and weather. Not for the first time. Not for the last, either. I'm sure of that.

Pierce pushed himself to his feet with a grunt, then walked to one of the ladders. He can bloody well climb that himself, I thought. Which he proceeded to do. Right up to the top story. I saw him swing himself off it and head off to his right. Obviously Fr Pereira's method had worked for him. Amazing. Or perhaps not, at that.

He picked a book off the shelf and opened it, then nodded, tucked it under his arm, and descended. A triumphant grin on his face.

"I take it it worked," I said drily. He held out the book, open so I could read the title. It was in English: *Amulets, Talismans, and Magic Stones.* How neat. How convenient. I looked suspiciously in the direction of the *Book of Souls.* Pierce followed the direction of my glance and gave me an anxious one of his own.

"D'you think we should wrap that thing up again?" he asked.

"Yes," I said shortly, and did so. It had told us what we wanted to know, but I didn't trust it. Not one bit. I tied off the string and sighed.

"What?" said Pierce, as if he thought I'd said something else. I looked up to find him staring oddly at me, and shrugged my shoulders.

"I didn't say anything."

"No." His voice sounded preoccupied. He shook his head, frowning. "I was just thinking that I know how you found your way here so easily."

I was about to say, you call that easy? when I realized that yes, this time it had been easy. "What do you mean?" I asked. He doesn't know I see ghosts.

"You seem—it's difficult to explain—more real than I do here. I feel sort of insubstantial. I can't describe it any better than that. But you're not out of place at all."

My place, if I have one, is on board *Isabella*. On the open sea. Not cooped up with thousands of books I can't even read. "More your kind of place, I would have thought."

"Oh, believe me, da Silva, if I felt this was my place I'd never leave," he said with a regretful laugh. "But I'm the interloper here." He returned his gaze to the book he'd fetched down from the top story. I suddenly felt as if ants were tramping all over me. Ants, a form that witches like to take. Or so they say.

"Pierce—" I said. "I don't think you should look any further in that." I couldn't say why. Except that I have a nasty suspicious nature, perhaps. But as soon as I'd re-wrapped the *Book of Souls*, the other volume looked much less like a book than something masquerading as one. What, I had no idea.

Obviously he felt uncomfortable too. "I'll take it outside, shall I ? Can I do that with these books?"

"You can, yes." If it was a book at all.

"Then that's what I'll do." I followed him to the door. As he opened it, I saw a mouse skitter past him and run out into the sunlit square. It struck me as an uncharacteristic thing for a mouse to do. Come on, da Silva, Pierce has a book in his hand, and that's a mouse. Don't go reading omens and portents into everything. That's Dona Paciência's job.

Sunlight struck through the open door onto the volume Pierce held, and it burst into flames. With a startled yelp, he flung it out into the courtyard. It went off in mid-air like an explosive charge, and I ducked instinctively. Pierce, nearer, staggered with the force of it. At the same time, I was aware that the big black cat had caught the mouse.

Green shadows danced in my vision as I hurried to make sure Pierce was all right. He seemed a little dazed, but nothing more.

"That was quick thinking," I said to him, scratching my eyebrow and wishing for a smoke. Pierce rubbed a scorched hand.

"It was reflex," he said ruefully.

"Never mind what it was," I said, looking at shattered pots and earth and scattered scarlet petals as bright as blood, "it worked."

Pierce closed the door again and growled, "But now we're no nearer finding out about the stones."

I wasn't so sure. "Maybe," I said. "I think that was a real book. In the sense that there is a book called *Amulets and Talismans and Magic Stones*, or whatever its name was, somewhere in here." The trick being to find it.

"How, though?" asked Pierce. And that, of course, was the question.

Although I already had an idea where I could find the answer.

"This is probably a silly thing to say, Pierce, but will you be all right if I leave you here for a while?"

A beatific smile crept across his face. "You're absolutely right," he said dreamily. I raised my eyebrow at him. He smiled. "It's an extremely silly thing to say."

Outside, the sun was beating down like a furnace. It was not long after noon—I still occasionally find myself listening for the ship's bell when I'm ashore. And am always surprised when I hear the great brazen clangor of church bells, like explosions in a foundry. I'd cooled off in the pleasant interior of the library, but instantly began to sweat again. Crossed quickly to the shade of the alley and lit a much-needed cheroot. São Rafael's high ceiling was browned by smoke. But I thought it was probably the legacy of centuries of candlelight, and had no wish to be a fire hazard. Not when the books were, it seemed, perfectly capable of doing it on their own.

Isaiah's shade, at the alley mouth, ignored me as usual. It would have been nice if this faint echo of his death could tell me his name. But at least I knew where to go to raise his ghost once I found that out. The mob had burned his body, he had said, in the Rossio. Though how I was going to find a quiet spot there to raise him was another matter entirely.

But I was getting ahead of myself. Assuming John Yeoh knew Isaiah's real name. And his real name didn't mean one he might have assumed when they forced him to convert. You can often tell whose forebears did that. Names like Coelho and Pereira are a dead giveaway. Nowadays you don't think twice on meeting Mr. Rabbit or Miss Pear-tree. But back in the sixteenth century they usually only meant one thing.

The whole topic of names is one I find puzzling. Speaking the name of a ghost—and, I now know, a demon—not only calls it, but binds it. Thank God. you can't bind the living that way. We enslave each other by ways that are either far more brutal or infinitely more subtle. Perhaps the flesh protects the soul. In that case, how had Batista's demons stolen the souls of five people? I'd probably have to read the *Book of Souls* to find the answer to that one. And I didn't want to know it that badly.

By the time I came to John Yeoh's shop I felt like a limp rag. You could have rooted tropical ferns under my eye-patch. Everyone sensible was indoors, and I wished I was too. Sensible as well as indoors, in fact. But the words sensible and da Silva don't seem natural bedfellows.

John Yeoh wasn't indoors, either. He was in his usual chair in the shade outside his shop. Calmly reading, and apparently not sweating. Bred to Hong Kong's fierce humidity, perhaps. But then, maybe he just didn't sweat any more. Grown out of it.

Seeing me, he closed his book and waited patiently for me to speak.

"I need to find Isaiah," I said. He didn't reply. Just looked at me out of his dark eyes. "Can you tell me his name?"

Yeoh shook his head. "I do not know his real name. And I don't think it would be mine to tell, even if I did. I only know how to find his dwelling in the walls."

"Can you tell me how to find it?" Or should I have asked, Will you? He looked at me speculatively for a very long time. Eventually he reached a decision. Of sorts.

"I think you will find it," he said judiciously. "You are a mortal who can see the world of shadows. Just as I am a shadow living in the mortal world. You will find your own way."

I didn't like the implications of that.

"You knocked at the door," I pointed out. "It sounded like a pattern?"

"Oh, I can teach you that," he said. "But you have to find the door for yourself. You remember how to get to it?" I nodded.

"Rua dos Santos da Purificação." A grand name for a tiny street. I could picture it quite clearly. Creepers trailing over the wall. Leaves like little hands stroking the surface. Whispering against the brickwork. Hiding a door into time. Or was that out of time? I'd have to take care, so close to Batista's house. Well, that makes a change.

"Then knock like this." He made a fist with his right hand and beat the rhythm on the palm of the left. I copied him, or rather mirrored him. He stopped me. "You have to knock with your right hand. I don't know why. It's part of the magic."

"How did you find it in the first place?" I asked curiously, when I had the pattern of the knock memorised.

"I had need of him," said Yeoh. "Much as your wolf did. If I had not been with you, the old man might have come to his aid anyway." A sort of Good Samaritan for the shadows, I thought.

"I need his aid," I said.

"But he doesn't trust you."

"Can't he tell if people's intentions are good or bad?" Yeoh looked at me expressionlessly, then nodded his head.

"He can. But the best intentions can go awry. As I'm sure you know."

Thinking of poor Felipe, I had to agree with him.

6

SINCE THIS TIME I DIDN'T HAVE A WEREWOLF WITH ME, I saved some sweat by taking a tram. They're all electrified now, of course. Very modern. Though I didn't save very much sweat in this weather. The tram-car was as crowded as a train in India. Except that there weren't any people riding on the roof. And only a couple of chickens among the passengers. But unwashed humanity smells much the same the world over. Especially when confined in a small space on a hot day. And you're not contributing to it, da Silva?

I prefer it to the rank feral stench of the demon any day. Or Batista's spoilt-milk reek. It's a human smell. Uncomplicated. Alive. And other words evoking normal lives. Not that you could call most of the life I've lived normal, even before I started seeing ghosts.

Along with the rest of the passengers, I got off and exchanged a small enclosed oven for a large open-air one. Unlike most of them, though, I didn't scurry for shade at once, much as I would've liked to. Instead I stood aside, avoiding a pile of horseshit, lit up, and considered my route. After a moment I had it clear in my mind. Avoiding the House of the Four Winds entirely would be a good plan. I set off. A hot wind had got up, but all it did was stir dust off the streets. Of course it blew grit into my eye, and I had to stop again to fiddle around getting it out.

Coming into the little street, barely twenty yards in length, from the opposite direction—not to mention in daylight—I only recognized it by the creeper-draped wall on the left. It had a shallow niche about half-way along, housing a rather flattened statue of the Virgin. Once she had been painted in gaudy colors, but her robe had faded to pale blue and was flaking away in places. Still, someone had tucked a wilting bunch of flowers in the bend of her elbow.

Isaiah's door, I recalled, had been just to the left of the little shrine. There was no sign of it. I sighed. Well. I hadn't expected this to be easy.

Trying to attain the same disinterested frame of mind that had directed me to São Rafael, I paced the cobbles slowly. Hands behind my back—too hot for pockets. Staring at my scuffed boots. Trying to ignore the sweat trickling down my face. I failed at that one. Too annoying. A cat slunk across in front of me, skinny and feral.

The ghosts of two small children distracted me. Unlike the cat, in life they'd been too well-fed for waifs, too clean for beggars, and I found myself wondering how they died.

Looked up to find Isaiah's door staring me in the face.

In sudden panic that it would vanish again before I could knock, I rapped Yeoh's rhythm on it. Waited two heartbeats. Then it swung open. But I hesitated on the threshold, unsure of my welcome. Or lack of it.

"Master Isaiah," I said, after some searching for an appropriate title.

"Captain da Silva," he replied, with a chill in his voice. "Why have you come?"

Don't beat about the bush, I thought. "I came to ask for your help."

"And what makes you think I will give it?" the ghost enquired coldly.

This surly old person was the Good Samaritan? I took a deep breath. "Because the souls who need it can't get here," I said.

He nodded, as if finding this, at least, satisfactory. "Ask your question," he said, carefully neutral still. Not, apparently, finding a da Silva satisfactory yet.

"How well do you know the library of São Rafael?" I asked, rubbing my cheekbone. Wondering vaguely what kind of spectacle I presented to a passer-by, if there had been one to see. A sweaty man with an eyepatch in a sea-captain's coat, talking to a wall. Yes, the picture of sanity.

"How well do I know it?" he repeated. "I know it as it was when I died. I have not been able to visit it since, as you may have noticed."

So he was restricted to this strange little room outside time. I wonder how that works. But that's a question for another time. A time when other concerns aren't so pressing.

"I could take you there, if you let me summon your ghost," I said.

He looked at me with distaste. "And how would you do that?" he enquired. "With your blood, that you have tainted by binding a demon?"

I was not surprised at his knowledge. Resigned to it, more like. "I released it," I said. The ghost laughed. It sounded like pebbles clashing together. There was no humor in it. None at all.

"You think you can release them, just so, senhor capitão?" he said. "Have you ever heard the word hubris?"

A shiver went down my back. "What do you mean?" I asked.

"You bound it to your blood," he said again, implacable. "It is yours to call. You have a demon as your slave. You reek of it. Why should I help you?"

"No," I said involuntarily. Put my hands over my face. Not this. I met his implacable gaze and begged him. "Help me release it."

"That was not what you came to ask me."

"No, it wasn't." I felt hollow inside. Sick to my heart. "But can you help me?" He must have heard some of the despair in my voice, because he relented. Gave a deep sigh, or a good imitation of one for someone with no lungs.

"I will," he said resignedly, and stood to one side to let me pass. "You may come in." I stepped inside and heard the door shut softly behind me. The close—closed—atmosphere, familiar after one visit, settled over me. "Ah, look at me now," the ghost observed. "Agreeing to help a Christian, when they put me in the flames."

"I'm not sure I am," I said candidly, feeling my face flush as he looked back at me. "Too many problems with its rules. And its... practitioners."

Isaiah made no comment. "If I aid you in this, and agree to the other matter, how do you intend to summon me for your other task?" I'd given some thought to it.

"With your name, and with holy water," I said. Water being the antithesis of fire. The ghost nodded slowly.

"It makes sense. You use this water, though, water blessed by a Christian priest, and you profess not to believe in the rituals of your faith? Your...erstwhile faith," he added with a trace of amusement.

"This particular priest," I said, "doesn't suffer from a narrow mind. And he's one of the people who needs your help."

"What is the man's name?" Isaiah asked.

"Pereira," I said. "Father Carlos Pereira." And the ghost did something I hadn't thought possible. He blanched. What did I say? I wondered.

"It's a common name," Isaiah muttered, more than half to himself. "A common name." The color, such as it was, crept back into his face. He stared at me, his eyes like pits. I rubbed my cheekbone.

"What's the matter?"

After a long pause, the ghost said softly, "It was the name I took. Pereira. I, and my daughter, and my son."

"There are no such things as coincidences," I said, feeling my scalp prickling. Still a cliché. Still true.

"Not where such matters are concerned," he agreed, and appeared to come to a decision. "My name as a 'New Christian' was Pereira, but my real name is Isaac Zacuto."

Like the explorers' astronomer, I thought remotely. Relief made me sag slightly where I stood. *Merda*. I hadn't realized I was so tense. I let out a breath, and I hadn't known I was holding that, either. "You trust me, then."

"I trust your intentions, I think," he said tartly. "Your methods leave more than a little to be desired."

"I'm working in the dark," I said, a little defensive.

"You are likely to end up working *for* the dark, if you don't take more care," the ghost retorted. "You walk a very narrow path, Luís da Silva, and you have stepped the wrong side of it more than once. However much you may think you are on the side of the angels." He looked at me narrowly. Or maybe looked *through* me would be a better description. At any rate it made me feel extremely uncomfortable. But anything I say now would be superfluous. "Seeing ghosts does not make you judge and jury and executioner."

"Then what does it make me?" I asked irritably.

A slight smile curved his mouth. "A man with a skill." He shook his head. "I don't deny that you have done admirable things. But you of all people, with your wolf, should know that not all the shadow-dwellers you meet are evil. You misuse your talent sometimes, senhor capitão, and that makes you a murderer."

"The man I killed in Venice—" I began. He cut me off.

"I'm not talking about that. Maybe that was justified, if you didn't simply want the woman for yourself—"

"Now wait just a minute!" I shouted. That was too much.

Isaiah—Zacuto—held up his hand. "All right. I apologize. But you did not need to kill yesterday. The man was possessed, and not with his consent. I would expect you to understand that, too."

"He would have killed Pierce."

"Would he?" Zacuto asked. "Your friend was safe on board your ship."

"Safe, maybe. But terrified. And I'd promised to protect him." And I needed him off the ship. The ghost frowned at me.

"You are arguing like a lawyer. The fact remains, had you given the matter any thought, you could have freed the man from that which possessed him and killed that instead. Now the man is dead, but the evil remains."

I *had* known it. Even at the time I'd thought the creature wasn't a true were-beast. But nobody likes to hear unpleasant truths. I met Zacuto's black gaze squarely.

"You're right," I said. "But you're missing something. You may have been murdered, Sr Zacuto, but I bet you never had to fight in earnest. Possessed or not, he was trying to kill me. So call me a lawyer if you like, but that makes it self-defense in my book."

He smiled thinly, but I don't think he conceded the point. "Be that as it may, you have asked for my help, and I have agreed to give it. First of all, the demon." I nodded.

"What do you want me to do?"

"I will need to know its name—no, don't speak it." As if I'd been going to. Give me credit for some sense. I bit my tongue on a sharp retort. Not that five centuries had made *him* any less irascible than a forty-four-year-old da Silva. But then, I suppose he was entitled. Being slaughtered by a mob and then thrown on a pyre must jaundice your world-view considerably.

After a moment's search, I found pen and ink on his desk and wrote *Gaziel* on a piece of paper. The pen scratched blottily, but then most do. It took me years to learn to write without dragging my cuff through the wet ink. This in open defiance of numerous teachers who tried to beat right-handedness into me.

Zacuto looked at what I had just written. "Hubris, as I said," he remarked. I raised an eyebrow at him. Decided I'd taken enough harsh words from that source. "Brought the earthquake, that one did."

Any retort I'd thought of died on my lips. My face went cold, and I wiped my hand over the moisture in an automatic gesture. I bound that? "Meu Deus," I whispered, involuntarily, and swallowed on sudden nausea.

"I never accused you of being without power, Captain da Silva," he said. "I just caution you not to abuse it."

Would I have attempted to bind that thing, if I'd known for sure? Yes, of course. To safeguard my family. Safe was a relative term, of course. I felt like a man halfway across a quicksand. Who has only just realized that it *is* a quicksand.

"Let's get on with it," I said hoarsely, cold with a mixture of apprehension and an appalled understanding of what I'd called.

The ghost nodded his head. "Understand, senhor capitão, the magics I use may seem unfamiliar to you, being based on rituals you are not familiar with. But releasing you—cleansing you—is merely a kind of exorcism, if you prefer to think of it that way."

Merely. Well, you brought it on yourself, da Silva. I took a deep breath to steady myself. "What do I do?" I asked again.

"Be still a moment," he said. "I need to gather a few things."

He busied himself at his desk, while I wondered if they were things of his world or of mine. Or, somehow, of both. As many things in this room seemed to be.

"Sr Zacuto—" I ventured after an indeterminate amount of time had gone by. Well, maybe a minute. If time could be said to pass here.

"Be still," he said, and a moment later, "Where is your soul, do you think?"

"I beg your pardon?"

"Where do you feel your soul resides? That which makes you Luís da Silva? One man will say in his brain, another in his heart. Which do you think?"

"In my heart, I suppose," I said after a pause.

"Then I will have to inscribe a figure over your heart."

How was he going to do that? I wondered. Scratched at my scar in puzzlement. "I thought you said you couldn't touch me."

"No more I can," he said sharply. "I told you, this is ceremonial magic. You will need to unfasten your shirt and remove any silver jewelry or...other items."

Other items. How delicately put. I took off my jacket, with the silver flask of holy water in the pocket. Unsheathed my knife with a slight smile and put the blade on the table. Zacuto's expression was unreadable. He didn't like it any more than Harris did. I curbed my momentary amusement. Don't poke the bear, da Silva. Finally I placed my watch beside the knife and unbuttoned my shirt.

"That's everything," I said, somewhat unnecessarily. Felt rather foolish with my shirt hanging loose.

"Very good," the ghost said. He had hung a medallion round his neck, I saw, but I couldn't make out the design. It seemed to evade my sight, to slide away from it and blur. "Now be so good as to fetch the ewer and fill the bowl on the table with water." I did as requested. "And now stand still," Zacuto instructed, peremptorily, and began to move his right hand slowly in a pattern, opening and closing his lips silently as he did so. Or maybe I just couldn't hear what he was saying. His hand left a faintly glowing trail as it traced through the air. I saw without much surprise that he was drawing a pentagram.

As he outlined the figure, I felt a cold burning sensation on my skin. Looked down to see the five-pointed magical star take shape as if inked over my heart. When that was done, he inscribed Hebrew letters at various points. I thought briefly of the Russian witch, who had used a qabbalistic spell to give life to her golem. But the memory was distanced by more than the bare three years since it happened. In this room in a wall, where there was no real space for a room to be, I was adrift on a sea of time. My scalp tightened at the realization.

When the diagram was complete, the ghost paused, then began to chant out loud. The design on his medallion suddenly pulsed intensely bright like liquid fire, and I saw the two were identical. At the same instant the surface of the water in the bowl started to quiver. A violent throbbing ache ran through me, starting from the cut at my wrist. I gasped and would have doubled over with it, but something held me upright. It was hard to breathe. I struggled to get enough air, strained against the pain. I thought I was going to suffocate.

The water in the bowl began to boil. My vision blurred with the excruciating agony streaking through my veins, my throat closed up. And then the bowl of water shattered, and I could breathe again. I drew in a huge whooping lungful of air. The pain disappeared, except for a throbbing in my head that rapidly died as well. On the table, there wasn't a trace of water round the shards of the bowl. It had all boiled away. The pieces formed a pattern I couldn't read.

"*Esta é a chave de Solomon,*" said Zacuto into the sudden silence. The key of Solomon. Whatever that was.

I put my hand to my head and dragged off the eye-patch. The ghost would hardly care. My hair was wringing wet, and so was the rest of me. But I felt so much *lighter* that it seemed I'd been deathly ill for some time, but was now cured. I didn't need to ask whether the spell had worked. Being human, I did anyway.

"I take it you were successful." My voice sounded hoarse, long-unused. I found I was trembling with weariness, so pulled a chair over so I could sit down. Yet the spell had left my mind energized. I felt again things I hadn't realized I'd lost, even if temporarily: pleasure in life, desire for Emilia. Hope, as well. Optimism.

Zacuto, though, looked pale and faded. Almost transparent at the edges. I looked at him in surprise. Should I be concerned? What if he disappeared altogether? The medallion he wore was dark, the design burned to ash.

"Aye, successful," he said tiredly. "But I tell you, that was almost beyond my powers. Had you left it another day, the corruption would have taken too deep a root. And," he turned on me, "then, eventually, the demon would have gone from being your slave to the other way round…and possessed you entirely." I shuddered.

"I'm in your debt," I said. "Thank you."

"Best you know it all," Zacuto went on. "It may serve as an object lesson to you about having truck with demons. Had I not cured you within these walls, your kith and kin had been long dead before the spell were done. Not for nothing is this place out of time." I stared at him, appalled. A tiny vestige of kindness came into his voice. "That was the reason I admitted you. I am not…entirely… implacable."

Hubris, he'd said. I hadn't known the half of it. I felt the ghost of a weight of years on me. The ghost of guilt at leaving my family. The ghost of loss as deep as John Yeoh's at losing Emilia. All ghosts I wouldn't need to see, now. But, meu Deus, it had been a narrow escape.

My watch lay on the table. I picked it up. It had stopped at half-past twelve. Or maybe not stopped, for all I knew.

If Zacuto was telling the truth—and I had no reason to doubt him—no time at all would have passed in the outside world since I had been here.

* * *

Harris, listening to the slap of the waves and the screeching of the seagulls, the creak of the rigging and the sounds of wood and wind, yawned hugely. He did not, however, relax his vigilance. His wolf's senses were still alert although his month's wolf-nights were done, his shipboard duties resumed, his watch underway. Ashley was gone to his mistress, Costa to his wife and seven, or was it eight? children. Most of the crew had shore leave; a few had been paid off and gone. At harbor, *Isabella* was quiescent. Her third mate was not.

There's another of those goddamn demons on the loose. Getting the book didn't stop that, then. *Huh, thought it was too easy. Wonder what poor bastard this one's come after?*

He leaned on the rail, smoking. His wound was almost healed. Since he'd joined *Isabella*, a little over two years before, he'd known that strange things happened around her captain. It was scarcely three years since a yellow-eyed wolf in Riga had eaten his throat out and made him what he was. Since then he'd hunted werewolf twice with da Silva. However it was only since he had become other than human that he had discovered a human who deserved his loyalty. He owed the captain, but that wasn't the only reason he had pledged himself to *Isabella*.

The other was that he fitted in. And that was something he'd never managed as a mortal man.

Wish I knew what the skipper's up to. Summoning demons. Harris didn't like the sound of that. *Don't like the feel of it, neither. Made him…different, somehow. But, hell. Ain't my place to try and second-guess him. He thought it was the right thing to do, Mrs Harris's little boy ain't arguing. Saved my hide, he did. Course I saved his too. But he didn't have to keep me on.*

His back was prickling. He shook himself. This close to the end of the moon's influence, he still felt more than half-lupine. He wanted to go and bite something. But he was human enough, or honest enough, to know that he was no match for any demon. The one that had taken the hapless Ortigão had left him paralyzed, unable to move. Not through fear, it hadn't been fear. His memories of what happened in wolf-shape were entirely sensory, and he was sure of that.

Face it, Harris. Reason you're fretting is, you want to be up and doing, and you can't right now. May be nothing happening on God's green earth, but it's your watch. Though what he could have been up and doing, he couldn't imagine. *About as much use as tits on a bull to that Chinaman.* He acknowledged he was grumpy because there wasn't anything he *could* do. *Wait for the skipper. Can't go nowhere, anyhow.*

Finishing his cigarette, he tossed the end into the stinking water that lapped sluggishly at the sides of the ship. He caught sight of Zé at a distance, scampering about his duties, and nodded to himself. The captain had, much to Zé's disgust, cancelled his son's shore leave because of Felipe's "illness". But the lad seemed to be taking it well enough, considering. If he knew that Felipe had taken his place, he showed no sign of it. But Harris doubted very much that the captain would have told him.

Feeling guilty, I guess. Shoulda known dealing with one of them things'd rebound on him. Yeah, Ed my boy, but would you've done any different, if'n it was your kid?

The unlikelihood of his ever having a son—*'less I already got one I don't know about,* he thought sardonically—made him even more morose than he had been before and sent his thoughts off in unprofitable directions. He shifted position uncomfortably, lit another cigarette, and dragged on it in irritation.

And it's too goddamn hot, as well.

"Sr Harris?" said Zé at his elbow, having come up more or less unnoticed. Harris turned to look at him.

"What's up?" he asked casually.

"Is there something wrong?"

Now what's gotten into him? Harris stalled. "Wrong?"

"Fil's sick, my grandfather's sick, my father's in a foul mood, and..." His voice trailed off, and he stared perplexedly at Harris. "Everything seems funny," he finished lamely, making a frustrated grimace at the inadequacy of words to express what he felt.

"Well, if your dad ain't told you anything," Harris began, and Zé interrupted with passionate irritation.

"He doesn't tell me anything. He thinks I'm a little kid. And it was *me* that made him that silver bullet, when you—" He looked round, alarmed, and put a hand over his mouth. A blush spread over his face.

"Don't worry, I don't think anybody heard you," said Harris gravely, commendably stifling a desire to laugh.

Zé stuck his hands in his pockets and hunched his shoulders, a mulish expression on his features. "Yes, well," he muttered. Harris wondered what to tell him.

"I mean it," he said, chickening out. "It's the skipper's business."

"Then there *is* something going on," exclaimed Zé, triumphantly.

"Look, Zé," said Harris. "Don't mess with this stuff, it's dangerous." The boy pulled a disgusted face.

"I thought *you'd* understand."

"I *do* understand." Harris was completely serious now. "But you don't. So take some good advice for once."

"It's not *fair*," objected Zé, taking refuge in the oldest complaint in the world.

"That it ain't," agreed *Isabella's* third mate, wholeheartedly.

* * *

Here we have now a much-chastened da Silva drinking a second glass of aguardente in a bar just off the Rossio. It'd take more than brandy to get me drunk right at this moment. I've been scared several degrees past sobriety. The alcohol wasn't even managing to warm the chill inside me. And with the mercury on eighty-five degrees, that's quite an achievement, or lack of one. Snap out of it, I told myself. Move on. As Zacuto said, I've had a powerful object lesson.

And I know something else now. That if I could bind a demon—something I certainly wasn't going to try again—I could also, probably, kill one. Which I might have to attempt before much time had passed. If Gaziel, for instance, decided to come back bent on revenge. Or even on simple malice, which I suppose they are pretty big on.

Or, on the other hand, if there were any loitering demons that needed to be disposed of. But, of course, I'd need Harris to sniff them out for me.

Draining my glass, I went back out into the brazen sunlight without waiting to finish the cheroot I was smoking. Everything seemed very sharp and clear, as if my sight had grown an extra dimension. *Óptimo.* I have enough dimensions to it already, thanks. Ghosts quivered in the strong brightness, distorting the wavy pattern of the paving like flawed glass. Even they looked slightly debilitated by the heat.

I wasn't entirely sure how I was going to proceed without either grave or exact idea of where Zacuto's body had been burnt. I started muttering his name under my breath. Perhaps I'd get some sort of insight. I didn't want to waste my dwindling stock of Fr Pereira's holy water. Don't think anything blessed by the unlovely Fr Jerónimo would cure much. Give it a good strong talking-to, maybe. Or convert it.

At the moment, my hip-flask was full, anyway. I took it out of my pocket and contemplated it, then uncorked it. Possibly with the vague idea that it might give off holy fumes, like alcohol, that a ghost could perceive.

As I thought that, I sensed fire. A burning other than the sun's pounding heat. A different source. Flames that were no longer here, but that had left an echo in time. Fires so fanned with hatred that they had their own malevolent soul. And had left ghosts as plain as the ghosts of the people who thronged the square. Living people had gone on those pyres, as well as the bodies of the dead. Well. Show me one country without something shameful in its past. Show me one man. I rubbed my eyebrow thoughtfully.

The elemental flames crackled silently, and I poured a little holy water into my hand. Flicked my fingers to spread it around, and spoke Zacuto's name out loud.

No sign of him. Well, there were other ghost-fires. I turned away and jumped, startled into a curse. There he was, solid as the living, taking in his surroundings with what looked like fascinated interest on his bearded face. In a crowd drawn from the four corners of the earth, he didn't stand out at all. His robes were no less outlandish than any given dozen passers-by. He looked the same as he had half an hour before. Although he seemed taller, somehow. The shades flitted by, taking no notice. But then they never do.

My hand went involuntarily to my chest, feeling for some trace of the sign he'd inscribed on it. There was none visible. I'd looked.

"Captain da Silva," Zacuto said. There was no trace of censoriousness on his features. No doubts, either. You wouldn't have known that not very long ago he'd been driving out demons. He gestured round. "It's been a long time. Lisbon has changed since I saw it last." And that's an understatement. Most of the city's been flattened since then. And rebuilt by the egregious Marquês de Pombal. What's more, man has managed to invent the motor-car, the electric tram and the omnibus. None of this appeared to surprise Zacuto.

A lot of years had gone by since he'd been alive. Which I didn't point out. It seemed more than superfluous. I just nodded. I was pretty sure Pierce had forgotten me entirely by now. But I found I was slightly uneasy to have left him in the library on his own. That was, after all, where Fr Pereira had been when he was taken. Not that I believed Pierce to be in that kind of danger, or I certainly wouldn't have left him there. Though how he would've reacted to ghosts in the walls, I had no idea.

Zacuto hadn't moved. He was still looking around him. Observing, perhaps, how the world had changed. Marveling, no. I wondered what the city would look like in another five hundred years, dismissed the thought as irrelevant, and lit a cheroot. "Shall we go?" I asked.

"To the library?" he said eagerly. I nodded. "Yes, let us go. What exactly is it you want me to do there, Captain da Silva?"

I sucked in smoke and said, "People who know the library seem to be able to find things in it. I need you to do that for me, if you can."

"There will be many more books than there were in my day," he pointed out.

"I'm sure there are," I said. "But you haven't said you can't."

"No," murmured Zacuto. "What book do want found, senhor capitão? What is so urgent that you need to call me?"

"There's a book called the Book of Souls," I began. He interrupted me.

"By one Estêvão Gonçalves. Yes. This is not a book you should want to find."

"I've already found it," I said. "I took it from a man who's been using it."

"Someone is attempting the Eidolon?" His voice was more scandalized than horrified.

"A man called Batista is gathering souls," I told him. "He's got five of the seven. The book says they can be freed by destroying the amulets they're stored in. But it doesn't tell us what stones will destroy them."

He nodded slowly. "I see. Do you know where the amulets are?"

"I know where one of them is."

"And the others?" I frowned, and blew out smoke in a long breath.

"I'll find them."

"If you will heed my advice, look for people who have need of those particular amulets. What are the stones?"

"Agate, beryl, jasper," I said. "I forget the others."

"Jasper is said to prevent fever, epilepsy and nightmares," Zacuto said slowly. "It strengthens the brain and promotes eloquence. Find a man who thinks he will benefit from these attributes, and I think you have your amulet of jasper."

"You know the properties of stones?"

"Some," he replied, looking at me sideways. "This is what the library is for, no?"

"Yes," I agreed. "Yes, you're absolutely right."

It's very strange, walking with ghosts. You'd think I'd be used to it, but this is nothing like the company of the shades I see day and night. Obviously I knew, or a part of me did, that my companion had been dead for five hundred years. But he *looked* as real and alive—apart from not sweating, of course—as the living crowds we walked through. Apart from a tendency to shy away from motor-cars, and he was hardly alone in that. And I don't suppose he needed to avoid stepping in horseshit. Plus, he was as visible to everyone else as he was to me. No one spared him a second glance. Yet he wouldn't even have been there if I hadn't summoned him.

But I had summoned him. And, how strange, I felt no guilt. He *wasn't*, I realized, bound to me. He remained his own man, or rather, ghost. Which was a great relief to me. Still haunted as I was by what I had unknowingly done.

At the entrance to the alley, Zacuto walked past his own shade without seeing it. Which was almost the strangest thing of all. Life is damned complicated enough for the living without bringing the dead into it as well.

We'd hardly turned the corner when I smelled smoke. For one disbelieving instant, I stood still. Swore. And then began to run.

The library door stood open, and smoke was billowing out into the little square. I had time to see, with gruesome clarity, that the big black cat was dead, its head a scorched mass of meat as if it had tried to eat a stick of dynamite. Then I rushed to the door, but had to stop on the threshold, coughing and cursing, moisture streaming from my eye.

I sensed, rather than saw, Zacuto come up behind me.

"Wait," he said urgently. He couldn't physically restrain me, but something in his voice gave me pause.

"For what!" I exclaimed.

"Use your brains, senhor capitão," he said. "There is malice here, as much as the ignorance that burns books—and men."

Fr Jerónimo? I thought. But how could he have got past the defenses?

"Pierce is in there," I said.

"So let me go in," said Zacuto. "This fire cannot harm me now."

Maybe not, but fire had consumed his physical body. Would the ghost of a drowned man plunge into the sea? But he vanished into the churning smoke, to emerge a moment later.

"Can you see anything?" I asked him.

"Your friend is alive. He lies just within the door," he said. "You can, I think, drag him out if you remain below the smoke."

"Right," I said, then dropped to all fours, my lately-bruised knee sending a twinge of pain up my leg. Thank you, armored guardian. I peered in through the doorway, acridity catching at my throat. Yes, I could see Pierce. Yes, I could breathe, just about. I ducked back outside and took the deepest breath I could. And then dived in again, under the worst of the smoke.

He'd made it almost to the door before collapsing, which meant I didn't have to add a slightly smoke-damaged antiquarian to my running total of people to carry. I pulled him out without too much trouble and knelt beside him, blinking rapidly and coughing. Zacuto plunged across the smoke-filled threshold again before I could ask what he was doing. And then the door closed.

Pierce began to cough, distracting my speculations. I turned him on his side as you do to rid a man of water in his lungs, and a moment later he opened his eyes and looked blankly at me. They were bloodshot from the smoke.

There was entirely too much to explain, so I hoped he'd remain incapable of asking questions until I knew what the answers were. He obliged. He scrambled to his feet, but occupied his time by coughing feebly into his handkerchief. A few moments later the library door opened again, releasing a burnt sour smell but no smoke. Then Zacuto emerged with a satisfied smile.

"Life needs air, and so does fire," he said. "But I am no longer alive, and I deprive the fire of what it needs. The books are unharmed. The malice that set the library afire could not touch them. Knowledge is truth, and truth can prevail."

"What happened?" Pierce asked plaintively, looking from me to the ghost and back again. I sighed. "You weren't gone very long," he added. As I'd suspected, he'd hardly noticed my absence. And from his point of view, of course, I'd not been gone very long. From my point of view — it could have been longer than I could bear.

Let it go, da Silva. However big a part blind luck and chance played, there's no point in worrying about what might have been. What nearly was.

I introduced Zacuto to him without mentioning that the old scholar was actually a ghost. He could work that out for himself, if he wanted to. The clues were all there for him. The pair of them were soon deep in conversation. I just hoped they wouldn't dig themselves so deep into esoterica that they lost sight of why I'd gone to the trouble of bringing them here.

Which was to discover what stones would destroy the amulets. I needn't have worried. Pierce was already discussing the properties of gems.

Would it be safe to leave them to it? Someone, whether Fr Jerónimo or not, had made one attempt to burn the library. The *Book of Souls* itself seemed to have some kind of defense mechanism. Maybe even Batista could have breached São Rafael's defenses. But somehow it didn't feel like his work.

Zacuto and Pierce went into the library. I didn't follow them at once, but went to take a look at the dead cat. The Venetian had sacrificed a cat to call the demon that took my eye, but this looked like a piece of pure malice. Someone, or something, playing with the beast as cats themselves do with mice.

I remembered the mouse that had run out of the library earlier. What better way to dispose of a guardian cat than with a mouse that wasn't a mouse at all? Which was something that hadn't just killed the cat, but had blown most of its head away.

But I was sidetracking myself. I followed Zacuto and Pierce into the library and looked at the damage. There wasn't much. Anyone curious about how the fire had started would blame that blackened electric light fitting. New-fangled stuff, not reliable, you know. Work of the devil. Yes. And naked flames are safer in a library. I needn't have worried about smoking, it seemed. Funnily enough, I didn't fancy a smoke at that moment. Now there's a surprise.

Below the burnt-out light, the table was charred almost all the way through. All the paper on its surface, including the newspaper wrapping round the *Book of Souls*, was burnt to a crisp. Its leather cover wasn't even scorched. I found an ancient piece of oilcloth and covered the volume, not wanting to leave it unprotected. Or perhaps that should be, not wanting to leave *us* unprotected from *it*. After a moment, Pierce pulled the package across the table and lifted the oilcloth. Zacuto eyed the book beneath with distaste, but said nothing.

The pencil Pierce had been using to turn the pages had turned to a stick of charcoal. Wordlessly, I handed him my pocket-knife, and he leafed through gingerly.

It's time to take back the initiative. More than time. Face it, da Silva, you've been blundering around with less sense of direction than a maiden auntie in the middle of the ocean. Make a plan of action.

First of all, I need to find out what Batista's done with the other amulets. And then I need to do something about them. Which problem I hoped these two scholars—one dead, one alive—would solve.

Pierce found the page he was looking for. "Agate, chrysophase, beryl, jasper and malachite, so far," he said. "Then, jacinth and sapphire." I raised my eyebrows.

"Too late if he gets as far as sapphire," I pointed out.

And, ultimately, I had to do something about Batista. My mind's full of euphemisms. Do something about…probably means kill. A man of Zacuto's day, I thought rather savagely, wouldn't be so squeamish at the idea. And yet he was the one who'd taken me to task for it. He knows entirely too much about me for comfort. Yes, and I called him. Ha. Not many men have a conscience so very large and solid-seeming.

Still, it was one dilemma I could defer to another day. Prevarication? Perhaps. But it was a problem I really couldn't solve at the moment.

I scratched thoughtfully at my cheekbone. If I'd been the sort of man Zacuto accused me of being, I would already have killed Batista. And no danger to my soul. Instead of which I'd nearly lost everything by messing with demons.

At that moment Zacuto looked up, and I was glad. These thoughts were going to give me nightmares, so daylight distractions were welcome.

"The properties of jasper, I already told you," he said. "Agate is a victory charm, and—I forget what else."

"I know where to find the agate," I said.

"Beryl used to be worn by women who wished to keep their husbands faithful," Zacuto went on. "And by witches, to give second sight. Malachite was used to preserve the cradles of infants from spells."

"And chrysophase?" Pierce asked.

"I believe it was supposed to be a charm against weak sight. But I may be mistaken. I never knew a great amount about hedge-witchery."

Hedge-witchery, I thought. Emilia had called Paciência a hedge-witch. Maybe the answer's been under my nose all along. It wouldn't surprise me. Haven't been noticeably observant up to now, have I?

"Will you be all right here if I leave you for a while?" I asked Pierce. But it was Zacuto who replied.

"If you are asking about safety, senhor capitão, your presence would not have prevented the fire being set. This place is both more and less vulnerable to arcane attack than others."

"What do you mean?"

"It is not a dwelling, and so the people who may be within its walls cannot always deny admission to evil. On the other hand, its own defenses— as you know—are sufficient to safeguard it against most forms of malice."

"Then who, or what, set the fire?" If I hadn't been so preoccupied with my own problems, that was a question I should've asked before.

Zacuto shook his head. "That I do not know. Although if I were inclined to make a wager, I would say a demon was probably involved."

Oh, wonderful. That makes it a perfect day.

"Where are you going?" Pierce asked. He sounded less than interested.

"To try and locate the other amulets," I said. Pierce nodded absently, then went back to the book he was looking through. But I noticed he still kept casting half-covetous glances at the *Book of Souls*. I suppose a price-tag of twenty-five hundred dollars would tempt the most upright citizen to slip it under his coat. Not a good idea. In its own way, it's as explosive as whatever had killed the cat. It wouldn't blow your head off. But it might do something similar to your soul.

I left them to it. Went back outside, tiredly. The sun was still beating down, and I was starving. That was easily remedied. I could pick something up almost anywhere. I also wanted a smoke, but my throat still felt raw. All right if you do it with your own smokes. Burning buildings are a different matter.

Someone was watching me. Someone, or something. I turned. Almost went back to fetch Zacuto, but decided against it. What could a ghost do, anyway?

Where the watcher was, I didn't know. But I was sure there was one. Nothing else gives you quite that particular prickle between the shoulderblades. The library's neighbor buildings were locked and shuttered as usual. If someone was looking out through a gap in a shutter, I wasn't likely to spot him. But I quickened my pace, remembering the night Harris was shot. Come on, da Silva, if he wanted to put a bullet in you he'd have done it by now.

Something scurried past me, and I jumped like a schoolgirl, cursing myself. Another mouse, out in the sun. Or the same one. Or, as you might say, a not-mouse. It scuttled into the alley and I lost it in the transition from sunlight to shadows. I rubbed my eyebrow and looked involuntarily back at the cat's corpse. Was there a whole flock of booby-trapped mice scampering around? Would you lose a hand if you picked one up? Don't intend to test that theory, thank you very much. And if there'd been a gold coin at my feet, I'd have let that lie, too. On the principle that if you offer a cat a deadly mouse as irresistible bait, what would a man be most likely to pick up? Money. Or, perhaps, a book of extraordinary value.

Absorbed in speculations about exploding mice, I didn't notice Fr Jerónimo until I bumped into him. Oh no...I thought, but it was too late to escape. He caught my sleeve, scowling. His baby-face made him look like a choirboy with constipation.

"Where have you been?" he demanded. I raised an eyebrow at his peremptory tone and stared at him without replying. At length he took his hand away, his face reddening. It was a good question, though. He would've been surprised by a full answer.

"Fr Jerónimo," I said irritably, "it's none of your business where I've been."

"Did it burn?" he whispered. He sounded feverish. "Your coat smells of smoke. Did the accursed library burn?"

"You set it alight? When you knew there were people in it?" He gave me an odd look, part-alarm, part-cunning. Then peered round like a man afraid of being overheard.

"I think Mouffi did," he said, conspiratorially. As if that helped. What was wrong with him? Was he possessed too? There was no scent on him. He smelled of sweat and carbolic soap. I wished Harris was around.

"São Rafael didn't burn," I told him in a low voice. "It's protected against the likes of you. Who's Mouffi?"

He spun on his heel and strode away, leaving me staring in complete mystification. I think I prefer the foaming bigot to the sly arsonist.

I was still wondering whether Paciência's finding spell would work when I got home. I wasn't expecting to find her sitting in Emilia's workroom. She seemed to be making a habit of it, I thought uncharitably. I'd been hoping for a little time with Emilia. But I gave our visitor a little bow, anyway. It doesn't hurt to be polite. Sometimes I forget that.

"Dona Paciência," I said. "Is something the matter?" She was still pale, and I realized with something of a shock that I could tell her where her husband's soul was imprisoned. Emilia shot me an odd look, as if to say of course there's something the matter. Then she blinked and widened her eyes slightly. What had she seen? It would have to wait. I looked away from her, when all I wanted to do was put my arms round her.

Paciência seemed unaware of this. "Nothing the matter," she said. "But I've heard there's a woman offering amulets. Sort of a ready-made charm service," she added, with a touch of haughtiness. That sort of thing being beneath her dignity. I was sure she was more powerful than she let on. Certainly she was more than the hedge-witch Emilia had named her.

"How did you hear about this woman?" I asked, my gaze drawn magnetically back to Emilia. "Witch's grapevine?"

"Something like that," she answered wanly. I turned back to her. "Anyway. The description I got should interest you."

"Let me guess. Tall. Dark. Haughty-looking."

"And wearing an amulet herself," said the witch. "A banded agate." Her fingers strayed to the stone round her own neck. There was a stricken look in her eyes. She already knew, but she looked to me for confirmation. I nodded.

"Do you know how to destroy them, Dona Paciência?" I asked. She closed her eyes wearily. Then opened them again. Shook her head.

"Even if I did, what about the guardians? Oh, how would you feel if you were in a storm at sea and all your skills deserted you?"

Involuntarily, I made the sign to avert ill-fortune. Then looked at my hand in mingled disbelief and amusement. Strange what instinct can wake. Haven't done that since I was a child. Out of the corner of my eye I saw Emilia hide a smile.

"There's always something you can do," she said to her friend.

"I know how to defeat the guardian," I said. Or at least I know someone who can. Paciência's eyes blazed all at once. Hope, I suppose. Revenge, perhaps. Well. I understood that. "And—soon—we'll know how to destroy the amulets."

She crossed the room and, to my surprise, took my hand. "God bless you," she said. I stared at her in astonishment. You would never call her a demonstrative woman. Normally, she didn't need to be. She doesn't have anything to prove.

"Can you find them?" I asked. "Jasper, chrysophase, beryl, malachite? Knowing what the amulets are for?"

"Yes," she replied. "Yes, I can find them. Or at least, I know how to start looking." She released my hand and looked up into my face. "Thank you."

Thank me when Henriques is back with you, I thought. But I knew she was thanking me for hope. It was nice to have some to spread around, for a change.

Emilia pushed herself to her feet. I moved to help her, surprising envy flitting across Paciência's face. Checked momentarily. Emilia slipped, I caught her. She steadied herself with a hand on my chest, and I felt the heat of her palm send a jolt through me. The air in the room suddenly felt charged like a thundercloud. I thought I could almost smell the ozone.

Her hand was resting where Zacuto had made his magical diagram. Over my heart. Her lips shaped the words, *what is it?*

"Later, love," I said softly, confused. And, louder, to hide it, "Let me get it for you, whatever you want."

"No, I need to open the cabinet," she said in her normal voice. "Paciência will need some more stones, won't you?"

"Yes, all of them, sapphire and jacinth too," said the witch, sounding a little breathless and staring at us curiously. I stood to one side to let Emilia lean on me, intensely aware of her. Of her reality as well as her presence. Not just of her as Emilia, a person, a woman, my wife. But of the space she occupied in the world. In time.

All I did, of course, was watch her. She knows where everything is. Not because she's obsessively neat (that was my mother). But because she never forgets anything.

She put the gemstones into my hand, naming them as she did so. Five polished ovals, all more or less the size of my thumbnail. And a smaller sapphire of intense blue. The touch of her fingers seemed exaggerated when they brushed my palm. I gave the stones to Paciência, who nodded her thanks and added to them the stone Emilia had given her, the banded agate.

"What are you going to do?" Emilia asked.

"Two things," the witch replied, taking the tip of her thumb between her front teeth. Obviously an aid to thought. "First," she went on slowly, "I need to…link the stones, so they have the same relationship to each other as the amulets. *Their* charm is incomplete, you see, but needs—you might almost say wants—to be made whole. Do you understand?"

"I think so," said Emilia, frowning. I nodded, distracted by that frown, the little wrinkle in her brow. I was with Paciência so far, but explaining how magic works must be a bit like trying to explain why a joke is funny.

"*My* charm, on the other hand," she continued, "is whole, but made to be broken. The conflict will create instability. Which has…resonance."

"Resonance?" Emilia asked.

"Echoes. Vibrations. Those are analogies, of course. It's difficult to describe. Something you can perceive, if you know how to look." She paused and looked not at Emilia, but at me. I couldn't fathom her expression, but it seemed faintly disapproving. Like a mother with a disobedient child, I thought. "Then I have to work with the individual stones and their attributes. And that, I hope, will lead us to the people who have the real amulets."

Under her gaze I was uncomfortable. "Is there anything else you need?" I asked.

"Yes, a bowl of water, since the stones aren't big enough to scry with. Thank you." I thought of the last bowl that had been used for magical purposes in this room, and a shiver ran down my back.

When I came back with the water, Emilia's face was tinged pink and she was trying not to laugh. Paciência, on the other hand, looked embarrassed. I put the bowl down and looked from one to the other of them.

"What?" I said, and Emilia started to cough. I turned to the witch in puzzlement.

"If you want to stay," she said finally, "please stand away from Emilia. The…energy between you two could interfere with the magic."

"In other words, Luís, go take a cold bath," said Emilia and dissolved into laughter.

That puts you in your place, da Silva. I couldn't escape from that with my dignity intact. So I didn't try. I gave an unrepentant grin. Kissed Emilia thoroughly as I'd been wanting to do all along. And said, "I'm going down to *Isabella*." There was no need to watch Paciência at work again. Too much watching, not enough doing. I want to talk to Harris.

* * *

Still wearing the form it called Jean Malfamé, the demon sought the docks again, drawn there although it knew its presence might alert the one it sought. But the task laid on it would not let it stay away. Which was intensely frustrating to it, as its absence might tempt the quarry into relaxing his guard, but it could not remain absent for any length of time.

Nobody took any notice of a small man with a wine-colored birthmark on his face, and the demon amused itself by causing a rope to break here, a man to slip into the smelly water there. But such petty diversions were hardly worth the name. If Jean Malfamé had been human, you would have said his heart wasn't in it.

The demon Malphas changed into a crow and flew spitefully into a flock of seagulls, causing great squawking and consternation.

* * *

It's mighty close.

Harris could sense its direction as a blind man can feel where the sun is. It gave off something not perceptible to the normal five senses, perhaps not even to the elusive sixth. Not an odor, not a sound, not heat, not cold.

He had to describe it as *evil*—a noun. It gave off an evil, and he could discern it. And although he couldn't smell it or hear it or touch it or even see it, it tainted all his other senses so that a sourness lingered in his throat, a sickness in his belly, and he kept wanting to rub his eyes. His skin shivered all over, a completely involuntary movement, like a frightened horse.

Examining the feeling, he still wasn't sure if it was fear. At least not fear as humans experienced it. Which he remembered very well from a night of intense cold and wolves, but it had been eaten out of him then. He was not afraid of death any more, and that was the root of most human fears. Or so he recalled.

After a while, the sensation receded. Harris relaxed slightly and lit a cigarette. He heard the ship's bell sound seven times and nodded to himself in confirmation: he could always tell what the time was, and that was a human talent, not a lupine one; as far as he could recall, he'd always had it.

Half an hour now and I can go scare up something to eat from João. Maybe he'll have some a that beefsteak left. Even before wolfhood, Harris had been an unrepentant carnivore, tucking into green meat that no one else would touch in preference to anything pulled from the ocean. And as for salting codfish, he didn't get the point of that at all. Why preserve the stuff when you could have it fresh any time you wanted?

He drew the line at tripe, though. Harris ate some things under protest. That wasn't one of them. It might come from a cow, but it was the one thing he couldn't stomach at all. The thought amused him. *My gut can't take stewed guts.*

As much as the sewery stink of the harbor could ever be said to clear, the air seemed cleaner as the demon retreated. He hardly noticed the everyday reek. Bilges were something you learned to live with quite quickly if you chose a life at sea.

Living in the moment, Harris pitched his dog-end overboard and leaned on the rail, about as content as he ever was.

* * *

I saw Harris before he saw me. He was leaning on *Isabella*'s rail, looking distant. Then he spotted me, and raised a hand. I nodded back.

"How's things?" he called.

"Promising," I said.

He was suffering from the heat, as usual. His face was beet-red, and his nose peeling. It always looks painful. Strange that growing fur every month doesn't seem to affect him. But then, I suppose a werewolf wouldn't get very far if it ended up being allergic to its own pelt. And this train of thought is useful in what way, da Silva?

"Skipper," he said when I drew near, and narrowed his eyes. I saw his nostrils widen and realized he was sniffing me. I felt vaguely affronted. "You've gotten rid of it."

"Yes," I replied, and did not elaborate at once. I took out a cheroot instead. Harris, in the course of lighting a cigarette, passed me his match, and I lit up, shielding it automatically against the freshening wind. "Thanks to a friend of yours."

"Of mine?" he said, eyebrows climbing.

"Someone who did a bit of fancy needlework on your...butt."

Harris blinked. "The old man in the walls." I nodded. "You go to him for that, or something else?"

"Now why do you say that?" I asked curiously, inhaling smoke. He shrugged and blew a smoke-ring. Just because he could. I can't.

"I dunno," he said. "Just popped into my head. He do anything else?"

"Such as?"

"You ain't seeing anything else besides ghosts, at all?"

"Harris, are you asking out of idle curiosity, or do you have a reason?"

Sniffing again, he said, "You don't got that demony smell no more, that's for sure. No, I don't think there's anything else. Just gave me the creeps when you did. You know there's another of 'em hovering around?"

My heart sank. We hadn't stopped Batista, then. I scratched my cheekbone. "No, I didn't," I said. "Can you tell where?"

"Yeah, kinda. It's been here on and off all day. Right now it's taken itself off again. I ain't seen nothing, mind. But I can feel it, like the sun in my face." He yawned enormously, a wolf's uninhibited yawn rather than a human's. Covered his mouth belatedly."Jesus, I'm tired. And I could eat a horse. Uh, figuratively." I hid a smile. I'm sure wolf-Harris would eat a horse. He's eaten rats, or so he's told me. But human-Harris thinks it's a bit barbaric, and does it under protest. Americans are a bit like Englishmen in respect of diet. "Anyhow—skipper. You said *promising* when I said *how's things*. What's been going on?"

"I think we can find the amulets," I said. "And I, ah, enlisted your friend in the walls to find out how to destroy them."

"Well, goddamn," said Harris, sounding pleased. "'Bout time we started kicking old Batista's ass for him."

"Yes," I agreed, leaning on the rail and looking out to sea. "Time to go hunting souls."

7

MY FATHER'S BOOKSHELVES, I'D DISCOVERED, WERE FULL OF ENGLISH MYSTERY NOVELS. He'd always enjoyed puzzles. Solving them, at any rate. Which was fine when they were happy to stay on the printed page. Real problems, though, as Harris memorably puts it, are likely to rear up and bite you in the ass.

It was a real problem I had to air now, and I didn't think my Third would like it any more than I did. I scratched my cheekbone thoughtfully. Come on, spit it out, da Silva.

"Harris," I said. He turned from his contemplation of the harbor. A view he ought to've been pretty sick of by this time. The cigarette in his hand had grown a long tail of ash. He flicked it overboard.

"Yeah, skipper?"

"Have you given any thought to who the sixth soul might be?" I asked him. "Since Batista's obviously sent a demon to get it."

Harris rubbed his chin. His beard made a rasping sound, and I grew a sympathetic itch. "Run it by me again," he said. Which meant he'd forgotten the litany.

"The soul of a hunter," I told him. He shook his head and took a drag on the cigarette he was holding. It made him cough, and he eyed it darkly.

"Sometimes I think I oughta give these things up," he said morosely. "Play hell with your wind. But then I think, what the hey, I can't drink to speak of, and I enjoy a smoke. Better'n those horrible things you use."

I took the cheroot out of my mouth and contemplated it. "You mean these? Rolled on virgins' thighs, these are."

"Believe you're thinking of Havanas there, skipper. Different beasts entirely."

Speaking of beasts. "I think it's you, Harris. You're the hunter."

He shook his head again and puffed out a cloud of smoke, saying judiciously, "Reckon you're wrong there."

"Mind telling me why?" I asked. "Seems the obvious choice to me."

"'Cause I don't got a soul no more, is why," said Harris, his voice deadly serious. "I ain't human, skipper, case you ain't noticed."

"Oh, and so what happened to Edward Harris's soul when he became a werewolf?" I had to be blunt about it.

There was pain on his face as he replied. Pain, and the closeness of wolf. "Captain, I died. My throat was et by a werewolf. And when I died, I guess my soul went wherever souls go when their bodies peg out. It didn't stick around waiting to see if'n I was gonna wake up. Had more sense, if y'ask me."

"I think you're wrong," I said. Harris shrugged. Obviously I'm not going to change his mind. And equally obviously, I can't stop him going ashore if he wanted to.

"You living in here?" Harris asked bleakly, thumping his chest with a fist. "You know what it feels like?" There was an awful intensity in his tone. I held up a hand in submission.

"Humor me, Harris," I said, "all right?" Perhaps he doesn't want to believe he's got a soul. Life's complicated enough being a werewolf without worrying about that sort of thing, I should imagine. But I think he's quite wrong. He'd been dead, or so he claimed. So what had brought him back to Harris-dom, if not his own soul? Certainly not some malevolent monster. I know very well that he's not typical. I don't know *why*. But I'm grateful for it.

This speculation isn't getting me anywhere. I came here to ask him whether a demon was around and found one was. And to warn him. To no avail, apparently. I threw the remains of my cheroot over the side.

"Yeah, all right," he said. "I'll be careful."

I suppose it's better than nothing.

"Where is it now?" I asked him. "Near, or far?"

"Gone off for now." He took a deep breath, something I would've hesitated about doing, given the stench from the harbor. "You want to try this?"

"Try it?" I repeated, slow on the uptake.

"Stake me out," he said.

"No! Harris, you've seen one of these things. You know they shouldn't be messed with." Yes, and you're a fine one to talk, da Silva.

He raised his eyebrows. "Right," was all he said. So I got off lightly. "What do I do, then, skipper? You want me to skulk here the rest of my life? 'Cause it ain't gonna quit, is it?"

Unfortunately, he was right. Even if I succeeded in freeing the captive souls, there'd still be a demon out there with Harris's name on it. Harris saw that knowledge on my face and gave me one of his grim humorless smiles.

Baring his teeth until even his human features looked like a wolf's. I sighed.

"If you do this—" I began. He interrupted me.

"Got two choices, way I see it. One, I'm right, and there's no soul to take. Two, hell, you got a good chance of killing it, don't you?"

It's not often I'm at a loss for words. But I honestly hadn't expected him to—well, to have such confidence in me. I stared at him for a moment, then pushed my eyepatch up. "That's what the last demon I fought did to me," I said.

"You're still here," he pointed out.

Yes, and so was that demon, somewhere. I hadn't killed it. I hadn't even killed the man it was possessing, because he was already dead when I cut his throat. But I hadn't known what I was doing then. Hell, I don't now. Like I said to Zacuto, most of the time I'm groping in the dark.

"Harris, I don't know whether I can kill it." I replaced my eyepatch.

"Then I guess I'd have to wait till you get a hold a those amulets." Still seems like a choice I didn't need to make.

"I could order you to stay on board."

"Yeah, reckon you could, at that," he said, staring at me. "But I purely don't want to hafta disobey an order."

I ran a hand through my hair in exasperation. Felt as if I was banging my head against a brick wall. As they say, it's nice when you stop. But stopping's not an option.

"Then I suppose we'd better figure out a way to beat it," I said.

"We should choose the place," suggested Harris, showing some grasp of tactics to make up for his lack of sense. "Guess you won't want it on board."

"Not on my ship," I said flatly.

"Castle?" I considered it. It had definite possibilities. High enough to see anything approaching. Ruined enough to make pursuit difficult, haunted enough to confuse even a demon. And even if none of that made a blind bit of difference, at least we would have chosen it. I nodded slowly. Took out another cheroot and lit it.

"Castle it is."

Eight bells went, surprising me. The sound was dragged out to sea by the wind. Costa appeared, shrugging into his jacket, to relieve Harris. He looked mildly surprised to see me. Not to say resigned. They're all used to having the Old Man breathing down their necks by now. I hijacked a passing Benjamin to fetch Zé before he disappeared. A moment later he materialized, eating a pastry. He brandished the remains at Harris.

"João's made cakes," he said indistinctly, spraying crumbs, and eyed me suspiciously.

"What?" I said.

"It's Jo's watch," Zé protested. "You *said* I could go home."

"You can go home. I want you to fetch something for me."

"All right." He stuffed the remains of the pastry into his mouth. "What?"

"Ask your mother for the gladius," I said.

Zé's eyes widened, and he shot Harris a triumphant glance. "I *knew* there was something going on!" He subsided under my look and added hastily, "It's all right, Sr Harris didn't tell me anything. But—"

"Zé!" I said. Otherwise he'll never shut up.

"Is it a real Roman sword?"

"No, otherwise it'd be rust and dust. Can you possibly do it without any more questions?"

He nodded, but his eyes were glinting. Which meant, having got nothing out of me, that he was going to grill Emilia. And that'll get him precisely nowhere, I thought with grim satisfaction. I do *not* want him messing round with this. It's bad enough thinking he might have to help recover Felipe's soul.

When he'd gone, Harris turned to me. "This the sword that guardian-thing had when it went for you?"

"Yes," I said, rubbing my chin and finding more stubble than I really wanted. "I can hardly give you something silver to fend it off, can I ? But the other demon didn't like cold iron. This one probably won't care for it, either."

"Bit of a gamble," Harris remarked.

"And who was it who upped the ante?" I asked, glaring at him.

"That would be me," he admitted.

"Then work with me," I said.

* * *

Emilia was still unsuccessfully trying to smother giggles as she watched Paciência carefully wiping the small collection of stones she had given the other woman. Paciência shot her an irritated glance.

"Virgin's fingers, the way you two carry on. You're like a couple of newlyweds. How long have you been married?"

"Nineteen years," replied Emilia. "But we've spent a lot of time apart. We haven't exactly had the chance to get fed up with each other."

The witch laid the stones down in a line, in sequence according to the spell. "I was a little afraid of your husband when I first met him, you know."

"Goodness, whatever for?"

"He always looked so grim. But I suppose I know why now. Henriques said he was a good man, anyway." She paused. "You're very brave."

"*I* am?" said Emilia in surprise. "I don't think so, not particularly." Paciência nodded, emphatically, in contradiction.

"You're vulnerable. So are your children. You could easily become a hostage, didn't you know that?"

She had thought of it, of course. But there was no point in worrying about the risk. What had happened to her father-in-law and nearly happened to Zé appalled her, but even that was no cause for fear.

"I believe in him," she said, realising it was a profound truth as she spoke the words. Paciência raised her black eyebrows and made no reply.

"You need to sit quietly now," she said instead. "I have to concentrate."

Nodding, Emilia shifted her leg so she could sit more comfortably. "All right," she said.

It was stuffy in her workroom, but she was used to it, mostly. Today, though, was really oppressive. Her blouse was damp under her arms, and she was glad of her light summer clothes. She was also glad that fashions had relaxed from the endless layers one had been obliged to put on when she was twenty. Although Venice didn't get as hot as Lisbon, and she didn't remember perspiring all that much. She banished the thought, mildly annoyed at its irrelevance.

Paciência, ignoring her completely, whispered a charm over the stones. It was made of chains and links, cords and connections, clasped hands and contracts. Binding things that could be broken. The air in the room seemed to change texture, taking on a thickness that didn't exactly make breathing difficult, although it felt as though it ought to. This sensation was familiar to Emilia now, and she tried to breathe deep and slowly as she watched. Paciência's face was rapt, her expression like a painted saint's in divine ecstasy, though Emilia had always thought the saints looked as though they were experiencing something a lot more down-to-earth than that. If they were painted well, that was. But most of them looked constipated to her.

She was letting her thoughts wander again. She returned her attention to Paciência. Around them, the room grew a little darker, but it was an underwater darkness rather than premature evening. A slight obscuring of vision, not shadows. When Paciência moved, extending her hand over the line of stones, the motion was slowed by this perceived density of the air.

Just as slowly, she lifted her hand into the air, and the line of stones rose from the workbench, agate at the top and the others as if suspended beneath it. They looked like an unclasped necklace, if you would ever make one out of such a bizarre mixture of gems. Emilia drew in a silent marveling breath. Paciência sealed the spell, and smiled. Not at Emilia, but a secret smile of her own, a fierce delighted expression.

"They are linked," she said, sounding slightly breathless, and there was pleasure in her voice and a line of moisture on her brow "Now for the scrying."

Putting the stones carefully back on the bench, she spoke a word Emilia couldn't make out, but she felt her ears pop. There was a sudden scent of roses, strong and warm, like a sun-heated garden.When the sorceress lifted the agate again, it came up without the rest of the stones. Holding it loosely in the palm of her right hand, she drew it slowly over the bowl of water in a complicated pattern.

Emilia, watching, saw the water begin to bubble, and a curl of steam rose from it. She half-expected it to form into some shape, but it was only water vapor. Paciência replaced the stone with the others, then stared into the water. Her eyes lost their focus, and she seemed to be looking at something very far away.

"Nike's triumph. The compass rose," she said quietly, her voice casting the slightest of echoes. Then: "The waters of Janus." And finally, "Penthesilea."

I need to write this down, Emilia realized, abruptly. She fumbled for pencil and paper, trying not to distract her friend. Paciência, oblivious, stirred the water once, anti-clockwise, with the third finger of her left hand. Emilia scribbled the witch's three utterances, while Paciência repeated the process with the second amulet stone, a chrysophase the barest green of new leaves.

"Polyphemus's fear; the dweller lately beneath the ram; the benevolent serpents; Tiresias." Emilia wrote it down dutifully, though it all seemed the purest nonsense, except—Janus, she thought suddenly, they named January after Janus, then that means Rio de Janeiro. And that was where the woman came from. So if that makes sense, maybe the rest of it will.

Meanwhile Paciência had picked up the beryl (also from Brazil, Emilia thought in passing) and was moving it over the bowl. Presently she said, "The beloved of Hera. A roof of stars. The red planet. Desdemona."

A jealous man's wife, said Emilia to herself as she wrote. Perhaps she was getting the hang of it, she thought as the witch stirred the water. But what did the rest of it mean? The red planet, Mars: a soldier? It was odd how it never boiled, otherwise Paciência's finger would be badly scalded by now. Emilia watched her repeat the ritual with the next stone in the sequence.

Jasper. That was her father-in-law.

"The gift of Neleus's son. The navigators' beacon. The caged bestower of the golden bough. Jove's valiant bird," intoned Paciência. Emilia managed to identify the Tower of Belém and the Cumaean Sibyl before wondering where on earth the latter came into it and losing her thread of thought entirely. She looked up to see Paciência already busy with the malachite. Perspiration was pouring down her face, and Emilia became belatedly and uncomfortably aware that she too was sweating more than before. The room had grown tropically hot and humid.

"The hope of Rhea Silvia," Paciência said. "The tower-builder's ladder. Eileithyia's scorn. The spouse of Bromios."

They were getting more obscure by the minute, Emilia thought. Practically Sibylline, in fact. Luís would have a fit. She smiled absently, not really aware of her expression. The tower-builder's ladder, though, must be the peculiar steam-powered elevator up to the Bairro Alto built by some crony of the Frenchman Eiffel. Paciência picked up the jacinth. All the stones had to be scryed, for the sake of the spell's completion, or so she had told Emilia.

This yielded "The downfall of Midas; the renown of the Moors; the nature of the dragon; Monçaide." Which made Emilia want to throw up her hands in despair. We are going to need signor Pierce, she thought. Our antiquarian on call, like a doctor. Sometimes you do get a useful prize in the raffle.

She looked back at the sorceress and saw her holding the final stone. The sapphire. For no reason at all, Emilia shivered, despite the heat. For the seventh time, Paciência passed her hand over the bowl. For the last time, she replaced the stone and stared into the quivering water.

"Achilles's bane. An English crown. The lamed son of Ombrios. Darkness at noon."

Emilia wrote it all down resignedly, without even trying to interpret the words. She didn't know how long she had been sitting in the breathless heavy heat, but she knew the passage of time was deceptive, not to say erratic, while magic was being worked. It felt as though she'd been there a long time. Her clothes were clammy, and her leg ached. Paciência's hair hung over her face in damp tendrils.

The sorceress took a small twist of paper from the pocket of her skirt. When she opened it, Emilia saw that it appeared to contain nothing more exciting than common salt. Which she remembered had powers of its own.

Paciência sprinkled it over the water in the bowl, and it coughed—there was no other word for it—explosively. The air in the room cleared instantly, and Paciência drew a long breath.

"All done," she said, weariness deep in her voice. "Let's see what we have."

* * *

If you gave me a choice of things to do on a warm evening in Lisbon, most of them would include my wife. Well, all of them, really. And the list would be short. It would *not* include traipsing up to the castle ruins with a jittery werewolf at my side and a demon lying in wait somewhere. Which was what I found myself doing.

I remembered chasing a ghost up here once before. Encountering not only her unpleasant guards but a god of *vaudun* as well. São Jorge has been a fortress a long time, and it has more ghosts that I could possibly count. In places they cluster so thick it's like walking through a fog.

Back then, I hadn't known what I was hunting. Tonight, I know all too well. The more you learn about something, the less you realize you know. And despite Harris's apparent optimism, I was apprehensive. How about being honest here, da Silva? I was scared sick. Not to mention tired and sore and furious at the whole damned situation.

Behind us, the westering sun had dragged ridiculously extravagant colors into the sky. Ahead, over the toothed ruins, night was already boiling up. I turned my back on the dark and watched the red and gold clouds of the sunset.

We were standing in a flat open space some twenty feet by fifty. The tenacious plants of occupation had softened the outlines of fallen battlements, ruined ramparts. There was an olive tree growing in one corner, legacy of someone's lunch long years ago. The remains of a rusty iron railing trailed along one edge. Ghosts drifted aimlessly around, like tendrils of mist. No one's died up here for a long time.

As a defensive position, it left something to be desired. But it had its points. It was strewn with stones and debris that we had the chance to map out in advance. And *we* had chosen it, not the demon.

"Skipper?" said Harris softly, sounding more tentative than I'd ever heard him. He'd been carrying the wrapped gladius under one arm, but now shook the covering from it and hefted it in his hand.

Warned by his voice, I drew my knife. A shaft of sunlight glinted momentarily along the flat of the blade. Turned it to molten silver for an instant.

"Is it—?" I asked.

"Coming," Harris said, grimly.

"Where?"

He looked momentarily puzzled and stared around wildly. "Can't tell. Nowhere. Everywhere. You ready?"

"As I'll ever be." I dragged my hand over my face, more out of reflex now the fierce heat of the day was gone. A small amount of sweat lingered in my eyebrows, but the breeze had cooled everything considerably.

"You ever wish for times when life was simple?" Harris asked, resignedly, and turned the gladius to look at the blade. His big hand dwarfed it.

"Life was never simple," I said. And then the demon came.

Or, rather, demons. Batista's sent the last two together. The one called Malphas, to gather Harris's soul. And the one called Alastor.

To gather mine. I knew that the instant I saw it. They burst out of the sky together, tearing it open with a noise like a hurricane. The air rushed and boiled as if it were a whirlpool, then disgorged a monstrous crow that came squawking and screeching down like an express train. Or not a crow, I saw in a horrified instant, something with a crow's head and wings but with taloned hands as well as feet and a dreadful knowing look in its flat black eyes. The beak was as long as my forearm, thick as a young tree. The corvid's stabbing beak. It stank of carrion.

At the same time, Alastor. Adamastor, more like, the ghastly Titan of the *Lusíadas*. It was huge, more than human-sized, frightful and earth-clotted, like something sprung from a grave. Lich-colored, hollow-eyed. Reeking of the tomb. Of death. The charnel thing drew its black lips back from yellow fangs and roared louder than a tornado. Its breath was a noxious fiery wind that made me gag. I took one look at the eyes and had to drop my gaze at what was in them. Just seeing it made me want to run away. Anywhere. I gripped my knife and stood my ground. And it was one of the most difficult things I've ever had to do in my life.

An old India hand will tell you that a tiger's roar works on some sound frequency that paralyses its prey. Demons do it just by their presence. I had a bleak moment to think, how can I do this? And then my brain began to work again, and I shouted their names out loud. My voice was lost in the maelstrom of noise.

And the demon Alastor laughed. It sounded like an avalanche. Like titanic boulders clashing together. And as stony.

"You cannot compel what has already been bound," it said, and its voice was appalling, like the screams of all the damned. And then there was no time to think at all.

They were on us like a storm. Like an army. The only advantage we had was that they hadn't come to kill us. Because they could have done that in a second. And so the only thing I could think of to do was something they didn't expect. I turned my back on Alastor and went for the crow, yelling incoherently.

It was skipping back from the sword Harris was poking at it, oddly dainty on its great taloned feet. I ducked under its stinking black wing, holding the knife in both hands, and swivelled, putting all my weight behind the blow. It should have cut the thing in half. Instead the blade bit in and stuck. Hot blood, more black than red, ran steaming from the wound. The thing beat and slashed at me as I struggled to free the knife from its body, and I dodged a wing only to feel one of its great talons rip along my back.

I wrenched the blade out through its guts and fell to my knees under the force of its bellow of agony. A pile of reeking intestines like boiling snakes cascaded to the ground, and I scrambled away from their slithering fall, narrowly avoiding the huge beak stabbing down at me. It stuck in the ground, letting me roll to one side. I got a hand down, grunting at the pain flaring through my back, and bounced to my feet again.

Right in front of Alastor.

Swearing in fright, I let my momentum carry the knife-blade straight into this demon's body too. Punched clean through it and out of its back. Knew the instant I did it that I'd made a mistake. I was too close to it. Then I saw Harris in mid-air, and he was in wolf-shape. How and when had that happened? I was glad it was aimed at the demon. It's not something you'd want launched at you. Two hundred-plus pounds of werewolf hit the demon amidships and sent it crashing to the ground, roaring in fury and pain, and wrenching the knife out of my hand.

In panic, I spun round to look for the gladius that Harris must have dropped when he went wolf. Saw it, to my relief, nearby, and scooped it up, grateful for its reassuring weight in my hand. At that moment the crow-thing freed itself from the ground and flapped feebly into the air, dragging its dangling guts beneath it. I dodged it easily, and then with a dying effort it hopped aloft again and landed on Harris's back, sinking its monstrous beak between his shoulder-blades. There was a frightful sucking noise, and the wolf's yellow gaze met mine in terror.

I swung the sword over my head, ignoring the pain in my back, and severed the crow's enormous head, knocking it to one side. It was like trying to fell a tree with a single stroke. Jarred my arms all the way to the shoulders. The wolf slumped as the other demon reared back to its feet, tossing him aside as if he weighed nothing at all, and came for me. My knife-hilt was protruding from its breast, and I could see little silver flames licking round the entry point. I backed away, breathing hard, sweat pouring down my face, blood down my back.

"You will suffer for this," said the demon in its awful voice, and the sound of it crawled across my skin like the touch of something vile. It charged at me with its mouth agape, and I jumped to one side, all too aware of my shaking legs. Something came coiling out of its maw and the shock nearly rooted me to the spot. I ducked in fright as a thing like an enormous python whipped past me, hissing ferociously, and slashed wildly with the gladius, connecting with it more than half by accident. Severed, it writhed on the ground for a moment before disappearing, and I almost let the demon reach me as I gawked at it.

Its fiery breath was on my face before I realized. I ran unsteadily towards the iron railings, I suppose with some vague idea of trying to impale it. Though having a knife shoved through its vitals didn't seem to be slowing it much. The demon came howling after me, and I rounded on it with the iron sword, which made it skip back. Watching its mouth for more snakes nearly got me spitted by a handful of needle-like talons which it launched from the ends of its fingers. They whistled past my face like bullets, and I clenched my eye shut in reflex, bloody stupid thing to do but I couldn't help it.

Swinging the sword in front of me in a long arc seemed to be the only thing that made it keep its distance, but that wasn't much use against its long-distance tricks. As long as it couldn't reach me, though, I was safe. Safe being a relative term, of course. But on the other hand, I couldn't reach it to do any more damage, either. So it was an impasse. At least, as long as I could stay on my feet. Which was going to be a problem. I could feel my back beginning to suppurate. And that was apart from the blood loss. One or the other was already making me light-headed.

I lunged forward with the point of the gladius and made the demon flinch back. I did it again. The next time I slashed instead of stabbing at it and was rewarded with three severed demonic fingers which fell to the ground and began to creep around blindly like earthworms in daylight. It shrieked in pain, waving its injured hand. Steaming blood flew through the air, and I had to dodge it. I decided to try another tack.

"For a demon," I panted, "you're not the smartest thing I ever met."

For answer it screamed and threw another cluster of nail-darts, but its aim was off. "How can you stand against me?" it bellowed. "Why won't you die?"

Fending it off with the sword, I said breathlessly, "You weren't sent to kill me."

"But I will," the demon roared. "I can gather your soul as you lie drowning in your blood, mortal." And it dropped flat to the ground on its belly and came surging up under the swing of the gladius and God only knows where the reflex came from that made me reverse my grip on the hilt and slam it straight downwards with my whole weight behind it. Pure luck—or something—brought the point down in the exact spot where my knife-blade protruded from its back. Cold iron met silver and steel. The combination was too much for demon-flesh to bear, I suppose. It exploded outwards in a burning stinking vapor. The force of the collision sent me flying backwards through the air to land ten feet from the writhing demon with an impact on my injured back that nearly made me pass out.

The demon turned into a pillar of fire, silver-white flames gradually overcoming the black greasy smoke that roared skywards until at last it was pure white light that flared so bright I had to turn my head away, and then vanished.

I lay flat on my back on the still-warm ground for a while, unable to move, until the pain got worse. Then I rolled over. Right, da Silva. You've disposed of a brace of demons. Now do something really difficult, like standing up. I took a deep breath. Got myself onto all fours. Staggered to my feet. Went to see if Harris was alive. Saw, out of the side of my eye, sword and knife lying hilt to point in a scorched circle of stone. No sign of either demon.

Harris was Harris, not wolf. I suppose it meant he hadn't really changed to fight the demons. I had seen his true self. His soul. There was no sign of a wound, or blood. No great puncture between his shoulders. He opened his eyes as I knelt beside him. They looked a little out of focus, but he was in there. That was a relief.

"Seen 'em off, skipper?" he asked faintly. I nodded. Unwise move. Nausea lurched in my gut. I swallowed. "Knew you would." He closed his eyes again. I put a hand on his arm.

"Are you...hurt?" I said. "Can you stand up?"

"I guess so." He shoved himself upright, awkwardly, looking as unsteady as I felt. I helped him sit up. "Jesus, I feel strange. Think I'm gonna hurl." His face was faintly green.

"Coming too bloody close to a demon does that to you," I said.

He took a few deep breaths and looked at me narrowly, his eyes more awake. "*You're* hurt. Smells like a lot a blood."

Thanks for reminding me. Everything was spinning in and out of focus. Well, focus is the wrong word when you only have one eye. Things were haloed. Blurred round the edges. Flaring. "Let's just get out of here, shall we?" I said.

"Uh, your lady wife okay with this kinda thing?"

After dealing with what the Venetian's demon did to me, I'd back Emilia every time. I wouldn't have made it through that first awful night without her.

"Yes," I said shortly. "You'll have to get yourself on your feet, Harris. I don't think I'm up to lifting you this time." Not sure I'm up to lifting myself. Nice irony: I had a flask of holy water in my pocket, which would have set me to rights in short order. But the flask was silver, and the werewolf couldn't touch it. Good choice, da Silva.

So we staggered home supporting each other like a pair of drunks. And if Harris's "don't-look-at-me" charm was in operation, it was worth it. Personally I'm not entirely sure how I did manage it. My memory's decidedly hazy after talking to Harris. The next thing I remember clearly is Emilia. I was lying face-down on the bed with my head turned to one side, and she was sitting next to me with her hand on my brow. It felt cool. My back hurt, but bearably. She had obviously just done the business with the holy water. There was a cold trickle down my side. I felt remarkably well, considering. Just deathly tired.

"Are you back in the land of the living?" she asked softly. I made an incoherent noise. "It's clean. It's not as bad as it looked. Your knife-sheath got in the way of whatever it was. But I think you need sewing up."

"Not O'Rourke," I said indistinctly, and Emilia sighed.

"I don't know why you employ him if you won't let him do his job."

"He's good enough at it, most of the time," I said. "I just don't want him involved in all this." I really don't want to get into an argument at this stage. "How's Harris?"

"Asleep," she said. "He seemed dazed. Not quite with us. He sort of told me what happened, but…what happened?"

"Too much," I muttered, memories of the demons making me shudder. "Can you patch me up, love?"

She stroked my forehead. "I suppose I could put a dressing on it, but you'll have to promise not to move for a while."

"I don't feel like moving at all, to be honest."

"Well, you'll have to sit up a bit so I can do the bandage."

"Yes, doctor." I pushed myself up on my left elbow. Now I was facing her. "That wasn't very clever, was it?" I said. "You need me to be the other way round."

"Luís—" She put her hand on my chest, where Zacuto's mark had been.

It had the same effect, a shock like a bolt of lightning. I drew in a deep startled breath. "What's this? I can't see it, but I can feel…something."

"*A chave de Solomon*," I said. "It's a long story." Longer than I could ever describe, in a way. "The old man, the one who called himself Isaiah. He said I needed to be exorcised. That's how he did it."

"Exorcised?" she repeated, and her face had gone pale. Her eyes looked enormous. "Was it the thing you called up?"

"Yes," I said. She traced the outline with her finger. The five-pointed star.

"The key of Solomon," she said. "And this evening, you were fighting more of them, Sr Harris said."

"Emilia, I—"

"I wish you—" she said at the same time, then sighed. "Wish it had all never started. But I suppose it was worth it."

I wish. Words about as useful as "if only". She was right, though. It was, all of it, a small price to pay for freedom.

* * *

The part of the demon Malphas that wore the shape of a mouse lay shivering in a corner of Father Jerónimo's austere bedroom, shocked by its own carelessness that had let its victim move against it and not even seen the danger from the other mortal. It was now all that remained of a being that had thought itself invincible, and though one day sometime in the future thoughts of revenge could be acted upon, right now it was almost as powerless as the creature whose form it had. In comparison to its former self, anyway. Even a mouse-demon has some power.

It was also the bearer, in a sense, of a soul, though too small to maintain control over it. Which meant that what it could deliver to its present master could only be imperfectly bound to the amulet prepared for it.

Given the nature of demons, one day it might grow back into full size and power. But for now it had to release its hold over the priest. Which was something it regretted, for corrupting those who possessed—or even just professed—virtue was always sweeter than taking those predisposed to evil. The geas laid on its greater being, though, took precedent over its own amusements.

Recovering from the shock of its death took a long time. If Father Jerónimo had noticed the mouse was distressed, though, offerings of cheese or water would not have helped. Some of his blood might have, but Mouffi was not strong enough for that yet.

At last it was able to move again, and struggled to its feet, feeling its small power returning. Whiskers quivering, it made its way to the door and slipped through the gap beneath it. It had a long way to go, but it was now capable of shape-changing once more. As a flea it could ride unseen, changing mounts whenever it needed, and even indulge its natural malice as it did so.

In this way it came at last, on the coat of a mangy dog, to the House of the Four Winds.

*   *   *

It's amazing how much you can manage while trying to keep your back still. And when you think you're too tired to move, as well. I must have more energy in reserve than I think. Or perhaps Zacuto's symbol helped shield me from the worst effects of demon-contact. Certainly I was still sufficiently awake an hour later, duly bandaged, to demolish enough *feijoada* to feed the entire crew. Not to mention the best part of a bottle of wine. And then to ask Emilia the outcome of Paciência's conjuring. Harris had woken up briefly, long enough to eat a little. But he still looked sick, so Doctor Emilia sent him back to bed.

I had just managed to get comfortable in a chair and was feeling, I admit, somewhat smug, when Pierce turned up on the doorstep. With a triumphant grin on his face and a book clutched in his hand.

"Had to come and show you this," he said. "It's a start, at least." He bowed courteously to Emilia. "Senhora."

"What do you mean, a start?" I asked, a trifle testily, gesturing him to a chair and carefully re-seating myself. "And what have you done with Zacuto?"

"Don't think you could prise him out of that library with a crowbar," Pierce replied, somewhat wistfully. "You know he can get books off those shelves without clambering up to get 'em?" I'd wondered how a ghost was going to manage. Should've known he'd have some tricks up his sleeve. "Look at the book, you'll see what I mean."

He had marked a page with a slip of paper. I lit a cheroot and opened the cracked binding carefully. Had to strain to read the cramped print. Nothing to do with my eyesight. Everything to do with tiny, blurred type. Mind you I'll look pretty funny if I ever have to resort to spectacles, or should that be spectacle? Can't see myself with a monocle like an English toff. I'd rather squint.

Pierce's book was in English. Unfortunately it was sixteenth- or seventeenth-century English, which is another animal entirely. Put it this way: I can read Camões without much trouble, but stick Shakespeare in front of me and I'll end up with a headache and *possibly* the gist of what the man's talking about. Well, I never claimed to be an academic. I learned to speak languages because you don't get very far in foreign countries without them. Doesn't help tremendously with reading odd spelling. I looked at the page.

Of the Construxioun of diuers Amuletts theyre Proppertyes and Disposicioun...

"Meu Deus, Pierce," I groaned, running a hand through my hair, "why didn't you English learn how to spell before the year eighteen-hundred?"

He leapt to the defense of his mother tongue. "Camões couldn't spell," he pointed out. "Nor could Mendes Pinto."

"I can read odd spelling in my own language," I said.

"It's all very logical if you know any linguistic history," Pierce protested. I don't want a lesson in philology, thanks.

"Spare me. Latin is logical. Portuguese is logical. And Spanish. And, God help us, French. German is so logical it hurts. English, most emphatically, is not."

"I'll read it, shall I?" Pierce suggested mildly and took the book back from me. Emilia hid a smile, and I met her gaze and raised an eyebrow. The antiquarian missed this exchange and bent to the book. "'*To every amulet there is an antithesis or antidote, just as every demon has an adversary angel...alas, it cannot be said that the anithesis is the same in every case. Though the stone called sardius is the antidote to onyx, amulet stones are not so simply countered*'—this is the important bit—'*To discover the antithesis of an amulet, one must consider its purpose. The ceraunius stone borne by a sailor to preserve him from drowning will require a different antithesis from that same stone given by a mother to her child to bring pleasant dreams. Whereas the cactomite or carnelian, worn by adversaries to ensure victory in battle, will quite logically have its antithesis in another of the same kind.*'"

The Englishman looked up from the book with a quizzical expression on his face. Half-rueful, half-curious. I didn't know what he expected.

"It makes a kind of sense," Emilia said into the silence. "Would you like something to drink, senhor Pierce?"

"I wouldn't mind some tea," he said apologetically, and smiled. "If you don't find it too much of a cliché." He knows as well as I did that it was the Portuguese who introduced the English to tea. Might have been a better idea to educate them in something that's actually drinkable. Like wine, for instance. There's something fundamentally wrong with the English palate. It must have something to do with all the damned rain they have to put up with. You might gather from this that I can't stand tea.

"Well, I'm going to have a glass of brandy," I said pointedly, and blew smoke at him. He took off his spectacles and polished them with his handkerchief. They had left marks on his nose. He replaced them carefully.

"What do you think?" he said, sounding a little tentative.

"Does Zacuto think he can come up with anything more definite?" I asked, scratching my eyebrow. The torrid zone under my eyepatch was heating up again. I'd had to put the thing back on hurriedly when Pierce showed up. Was irritated at that. Why do I think it matters?

"I should think so," he replied, stroking the book like a cat in his lap. "But this does help, doesn't it?"

"It might," I said, then turned to Emilia. "What did Paciência come up with? You were about to tell me when Pierce turned up."

Emilia took a sip from her wineglass. She looked tired, never mind me. Her eyes were shadowed. My fault, I suppose. "You remember what her finding spell did? A bit like that."

"Not more bloody riddles," I said disgustedly, and poured myself a drink. My back sent a sharp reminder of pain twinging through me. Next time, listen to the physician, da Silva.

"I'm afraid so," she said, laughing at my expression. She picked up a piece of paper covered in her neat handwriting from the table and handed it to me. "The bits in parentheses are what I think some of the answers are. I'm afraid I didn't get very far."

My heart sank as I read it. It was every bit as bad as I expected.

"*Agate: Nike's triumph* (Victory). *The compass rose. The waters of Janus* (Rio de Janeiro). *Penthesilea.*

"*Chrysophase: Polyphemus's fear. The dweller lately beneath the ram. The benevolent serpents. Tiresias.*

"*Beryl: The beloved of Hera. A roof of stars. The red planet* (Mars: A soldier?). *Desdemona* (A jealous man's wife).

"*Jasper: The gift of Neleus's son. The navigators' beacon* (Torre de Belém). *The caged bestower of the golden bough* (Cumaean Sibyl). *Jove's valiant bird.*

"*Malachite: The hope of Rhea Silvia. The tower-builder's ladder* (Elevador de Santa Justa). *Forsaken by Eileithyia. The spouse of Bromios.*

"*Jacinth: The downfall of Midas.* (Gold? Or greed?) *The renown of the Moors. The nature of the dragon* (Or does this mean greed?). *Monçaide.*

"*Sapphire: Achilles's bane. An English crown* (Parque Eduardo VII?). *The lamed son of Ombrios. Darkness at noon.*"

"Well, you've solved all the ones I could," I said. More, really. I wouldn't have come up with a sibyl in a hundred years. I ground the end of my cheroot savagely in the ashtray. I really hate this sort of thing. Who has the time? My father would've loved it. But we had to find the time. I took a mouthful of aguardente. Good stuff. "Except, *the compass rose* must be Batista's house. *Casa dos Quatro Ventos.* But we know the answer to the first one anyway."

"Oh, and I've just remembered, Penthesilea was Queen of the Amazons," said Emilia triumphantly.

"Batista's daughter?" asked Pierce, inhaling tea gratefully. "That's a pretty good description. Er, may I see?"

Well, he had the best chance of any of us. I handed over the paper gratefully. "It's all yours, Pierce."

"All right," he said after a moment. "Knowing the answer to the first riddle is good. It gives us what you might call a template." He might call it that. Pain in the backside is what I call it.

"Didn't Paciência have any ideas?" I asked Emilia. "After all, she worked the other one out straight away."

"She was exhausted, Luís. I sent her home. But she said most of them were a complete mystery to her." *She* was exhausted, I thought, what about you? And God knows what I looked like.

"You need a hell of a classical education for a lot of these," said Pierce, pushing his spectacles up his nose. "You knew about the Sibyl," he added with a nod to Emilia, who shrugged tiredly. She was rubbing delicately at the corners of her eyes.

"Just one of those silly things you remember. I don't remember anything at all about the golden bough, though."

"She, er, gave it to Aeneas to help him get to the underworld," Pierce told her helpfully. I interrupted this learned dialogue, somewhat impatiently.

"Can we interpret some we don't already know?" A yawn caught me unawares. Tonight I do think I have a reason for being tired. A couple of reasons.

"Do you want to do this in the morning?" said Pierce, smothering a yawn as well. Contagious, aren't they? Just reading the word can set you off. But I was acutely conscious of time passing. I shook my head. Scratched my cheekbone.

"What were you saying about a template?"

"Yes. A model. A paradigm." He looked at the paper. "*Nike's triumph,* as Dona Emilia notes, is victory. So perhaps we can assume that the first statement in each, er, clue tells us what the amulet is being used for. Which should help us find the antidote."

"But what if it isn't?" asked Emilia. Playing devil's advocate. She drained her wineglass, and I saw her close her eyes momentarily.

"We have to start somewhere," said Pierce. He had finished his tea and looked round for somewhere to put the cup. Finally he put it on the floor by his feet. "Now then. Next comes where she lives, followed by where she comes from. And finally a description of her. Quite comprehensive, in its way."

Emilia was nodding eagerly. "I see what you mean," she said. Meu Deus, she's enjoying this. "So, what was *Polyphemus's fear?* Didn't Odysseus kill him?"

"No," said Pierce and shot a glance at me. His spectacles had slipped down his nose again. "He put out his—er—blinded him. Polyphemus was a Cyclops."

"Then that could be his fear? Blindness?" Emilia suggested. "Write it down."

Pierce complied. "Now. *The dweller lately beneath the Ram.* The ram would be Capricorn, the Tropic of Capricorn. Someone who's lived in Africa, perhaps?"

"Or South America?" I put in, lighting another cheroot. "Or why not a sailor?" Emilia considered it and finally shook her head.

"No, because it says *dweller.* That implies, in one place." She poured herself a glass of water from the carafe.

"*Benevolent serpents,*" mused Pierce. "Are there any?"

I had an inspiration. "What about a doctor?"

"The caduceus, of course," he exclaimed. "Well spotted. So—er—a doctor who's been in Africa. And *Tiresias.*" I knew that one, too. Thanks to my father. And others. And no, I'm not a seer. Or a sibyl. I just see ghosts. Just. Yes, you keep telling yourself that, da Silva.

"The blind seer."

"Or, by analogy, someone with knowledge."

"Yes," said Emilia, nodding, "that makes sense with the amulet."

"So, a doctor," Pierce summarised, "who worked in—er—let's say Africa, and has either gone blind or is afraid of losing his sight?" Emilia suddenly clapped her hand to her mouth. We both stared at her.

"I know who it is," she said. "O senhor doutor Bosque. He lives near the cathedral...runs an orphanage. He has cataracts in both eyes. Wears those thick bottle spectacles." I exhaled smoke in a long breath.

"Mother of God," I said slowly. Hardly believing it. "We've got one."

"We've got two," Emilia pointed out. She was right, of course. We grinned at each other, conspiratorially.

Pierce coughed gently. "Do you think I might take a glass of your brandy?" he asked diffidently. "In the, ah, absence of champagne." He had taken his spectacles off and was massaging the bridge of his nose.

It's a breakthrough. Somehow it feels more of an achievement than killing demons. Ha. Figure that one out, da Silva.

I pushed the bottle towards Pierce. Waved towards the glasses. Couldn't be bothered to get up. "Help yourself," I said. "Can we do as well with the next one?" We? Well, I did make a contribution.

He paused in the act of uncorking the bottle. "We'll have to see," he said. Confident enough to smile, anyway.

"What does it say?" I asked Emilia. She was covering a yawn. "Are you all right?"

"A little tired," she admitted, uncharacteristically, and drank some water. "Let's see—*The beloved of Hera.*"

"She was Zeus's wife," said Pierce, putting his spectacles back on. He sounded a little doubtful. Emilia shook her head.

"No, we're looking for the amulet's purpose. What was she the goddess of, senhor Pierce? Marriage, wasn't it?"

"Marriage, childbirth, the home." He drank some brandy. Drew a sharp breath. Like I said, the good stuff.

"Yes!" exclaimed Emilia. "She's *Desdemona*, remember? A jealous man's wife. She might want to protect her marriage."

"And the roof of stars? Is she a gipsy, perhaps?" he hazarded. But I had a better answer.

"Convento do Carmo," I said. "She lives near the Carmelite church."

Emilia nodded. "And her jealous husband," she said, "like Othello, will be a soldier. We can find her."

We exchanged glances again. Surely this was too easy. Pierce sipped from his glass. I did the same. I'd nearly finished mine. The silence stretched.

"*The gift of Neleus's son,*" he read, breaking the tension. "That was Nestor, *the clear-voiced orator.*"

"An amulet to bring eloquence?" said Emilia, doubtfully. Pursed her lips. "I suppose it's possible."

"He lives in Belém," I said, "but who is he? What does the Sibyl have to do with anything?" She shrugged.

"That's what I could never figure out."

"Pierce?"

"Predictions?" he suggested. "Not a fortune-teller, that would be too straightforward." He was right about that.

"Who else foretells the future?" wondered Emilia. "Or plans for it?"

"And needs to be eloquent," I added, examining my cheroot. Another couple of drags left in that, at least.

"A politician," said Pierce.

That was a possibility. Paciência's scrying was rather more charitable about the breed than I would've been, though.

"An economist," said Emilia.

"Doesn't need the gift of the gab," Pierce objected. They stared at each other. Made me feel a little superfluous. All that academic thought floating around. Inferiority complex, da Silva? I stuck a finger surreptitiously under my eyepatch and tried to wipe the sweat away.

"Well," Emilia went on, "let's not get bogged down. We'll say a politician for now. Should be easy to find, anyway. What's the next clue?"

"*Jove's radiant bird,*" Pierce read. "Er— that'll be the eagle, I imagine."

"Description?" I asked, pouring myself another drink. Alcohol is supposed to be a stimulant. Though there have been times when I've been so stimulated, I've passed out. Long time ago. If I put away that much these days I'd sleep for a week. I offered one to the antiquarian, who nodded and held out his glass.

"Someone with a Roman profile," Emilia translated, more tactfully than my thought. "We'll find him. Let's move on."

Pierce put his glass down and rubbed his eyes. "*The hope of Rhea Silvia.* She was the mother of Romulus and Remus."

"A mother, then," said Emilia. "Hoping for—what? Her child's future?"

"That's not very specific," Pierce objected.

I laughed. Couldn't help it. Stubbed out my cheroot and took a drink. "You suddenly expect this to be specific?"

"Not really," Emilia admitted. "But that's what all mothers hope." She looked wistful. I reached out and squeezed her hand. Earned a tired smile.

"Then someone whose child is what, I don't know, ailing? At risk in some way?" said Pierce, fiddling with his spectacles.

"Yes, that makes sense. Lives near Santa Justa. What else?" She turned the paper. "*Forsaken by Eileithyia.* Who on earth was Eileithyia?"

"I think she was a goddess of parturition," said Pierce doubtfully, if delicately.

"Forsaken by her, then— can't have any more children? Has one child, and sickly? Or died?" Emilia hazarded. I looked at her. Wondering what she was thinking. Caterina is the second child the doctors said she couldn't have. She'd nearly died with Zé. I pushed the thought aside. Emilia's stronger than she looks. In more ways than one.

"They do make a sort of sense, when you work 'em out," I admitted grudgingly. But why make us go through all this performance? Well, there's the question. Nothing's ever simple. Magic least of all.

"*Spouse of Bromios*," Pierce went on. "That's another name for Dionysius." This prompted him to take another drink. I hid a smile at the power of suggestion.

"Then her husband's a—what?" I hazarded. "Publican, wine merchant, wine grower, something like that?"

"We'll find out," said Emilia reassuringly. "That's more than enough to go on."

I looked from one to the other of them. They were enjoying it. Pleased to be solving the puzzles. Had Pierce forgotten what he'd predicted if Batista managed to complete the spell? "Does anyone else think this is all too easy?" I asked over the rim of my glass.

"It wouldn't be easy at all without senhor Pierce," Emilia pointed out. Pierce flushed pink and raised his glass to her.

"Too kind," he said. Very English.

"But true," she smiled, and finished off her glass of water. Drew a deep breath. "Next clue? *The downfall of Midas.* I thought, gold, or possibly greed. But *the nature of the dragon* might also mean greed. I'll have some of that brandy now."

"We don't need this one," I said, pushing myself to my feet. Fully expecting to hear myself creak. Getting too old for late nights, da Silva? After fighting demons, yes. "He's only gathered five, remember."

Emilia shook her head. "I think we do need to solve them all. Remember what Paciência said about patterns and completeness?" I didn't, really, but it had a perverse logic. If only because it made things more difficult. Cynical, who, me? I handed her the glass of aguardente. Her fingers brushed against mine as she took it, and I smiled.

"What's *the renown of the Moors*, then?" wondered Pierce, with a frown. "I haven't a clue on that one." He took off his spectacles again to rub his eyes.

"And you call yourself an expert on linguistics," I said, resuming my seat. Careful of my back. Moving, I thought disgustedly, like an arthritic old man. "It's Alfama."

"Don't get it."

"Moorish occupation? Names beginning with 'Al-' ring any bells?"

"Oh, I see. And *fama*, fame. Very good. Now interpret *Monçaide*." Smugly.

"Something to do with da Gama," I answered promptly, earning a surprised snort. Well, I did go to school once. Did learn history, once. Long time ago, however. Only Portuguese in the room, here, so think, da Silva. Who the devil was Monçaide?

"So what was it?" persisted Pierce. And I finally got it.

"Not a what, a who. Fellow at the Zarmorin's court. Moor who spoke Portuguese." I took out a triumphant cheroot and lit up. How's that for a feat of memory?

"How literally are we supposed to take that?" asked Emilia. "We didn't just jump to the conclusion that our Desdemona's husband was a Moor. And how do you define it, anyway? A Mohammedan? An Arab?"

"Same thing," shrugged Pierce. He may be resident in Brazil but he's a xenophobic Englishman at heart.

"A greedy Arab, who lives in the Alfama," Emilia mused, with a sip at her glass. "There must be something else. Wait a moment, dragons hoard things, don't they? Perhaps he's a collector of... something or other." She frowned in thought.

"Do you know anyone like that?" I said. Gave my eyebrow a vigorous scratch.

She shook her head. "We may not need to find him, though."

"I thought you just said we did," Pierce grumbled, owlish without his spectacles.

"No, just that we need to solve all the riddles."

"Sounds like sophistry to me," he said. Then brightened. "But you know, if we can find the others, we can find him too." He drained his glass with a pleased smile.

"That's true." Emilia closed her eyes again. Looked ready to fall asleep in her chair.

I stifled another yawn. "What about the last one?" Which made my skin crawl. The sapphire. Prepared to imprison my soul. I thought of my father and gritted my teeth.

"*Achilles's bane*," Emilia said, staring into her glass. For inspiration, perhaps. "His heel? An amulet to protect against...sore feet? Lameness?"

"That doesn't sound very likely," objected Pierce. "His bane—er—well, he was killed by an arrow, wasn't he?"

"Don't tell me it's supposed to protect him from bows and arrows," I said, knocking ash off the end of my cheroot. "That's even less likely than a charm against bunions."

"What else can you remember about Achilles?" asked Emilia. Me? Nothing at all. But then, my academic education was, let's say, cut short. Replaced by a maritime one.

"Not much, offhand," Pierce said, resuming his spectacles and taking them back off immediately. Apparently they needed another polish. "Er— he was bad-tempered, that's about it. Let's put it to one side for a second. What else is there?"

"*An English crown—I* thought that might mean he lives near the park," said Emilia, taking a small sip of brandy. "But *the lame son of Ombrios?*"

"Ombrios is Zeus. So his lame son is Hephaestus." He picked up his own glass, found it empty. Put it back again.

"A blacksmith?" she wondered. "We should be able to find a blacksmith."

"Yes, follow the trail the horses leave," I said, finishing my own drink. And that was enough for me. "But it may not be a blacksmith. You work with metals—it might be a goldsmith."

"I think Hephaestus, er, implies a blacksmith," said Pierce. "What could *darkness at noon* be, though?"

"Depression," said Emilia, so positively I gave her a sharp look. "My father," she added, by way of explanation. Yes, he'd had black moods. Mostly when he saw me. He never understood why I worked for the most hated man in Venice. And I could never tell him.

"Then that explains the Achilles reference. Achilles's bane, his, er, ungovernable temper."

A hot-headed blacksmith. That wasn't something I wanted to pick a fight with. "Do you think all these people know about the souls in their amulets?" I asked. "Apart from Teresa Batista, of course."

"I'd guess not," Emilia said. "What would be the point?"

"They turn into the guardians when the amulets are threatened," I pointed out. "That might give the game away somewhat." She shook her head.

"I don't think they know, Luís," she said. "I really don't. No one sane would agree to that." But Batista wasn't sane. Although it was a little difficult to imagine him recruiting a band of lunatics to take charge of people's souls.

Since the bearers stood a good chance of dying for it when I came to free them.

8

AFTER A NIGHT OF TROUBLED DREAMS IN A BED TOO SMALL FOR HIM, Harris woke with a pounding headache. A fact that irritated him out of all proportion, since he hadn't drunk enough in three years to deserve a hangover. Not since he became— what he was, in fact. He also felt light-headed and seemed to be viewing everything through a reddish, orangey haze as if he were wearing spectacles with tinted lenses. His mouth felt as though something had crawled into it and died. And he had a strange urge to eat cheese.

"Ah, Jesus," he said out loud and closed his eyes again, hoping it would stop the room spinning. Everything hurt, not just his head. *If I stand up now I really am gonna puke. What the hell's going on? Those goddamn things shouldn't be able to make me sick. I'm more like them than I am human.* He knew this wasn't true. *Guess I do have a soul after all. Well, I'll be. Still ain't about to try the skipper's holy water. Can feel that burning even when it's in his pocket.* He tried to laugh, but even that hurt.

His memory of anything after the great dying crow had landed on his back were hazy. But he remembered vividly the feel of its talons digging into him, the hot reek of its dangling guts. The paralyzing disgust of its presence. His mind shied away from the memory of a monstrous beak plunging into his back, a killing stroke that left no wound. Or none visible. *The skipper cut off its head, I think. Then I was right outa things there for a while.*

He was none too clear about what had happened before that, either. *Don't understand how I could move this time. But sweet Jesus, I went for that thing. Goddamn!* But had he been wolf or human at the time? Somehow he remembered changing, but it hadn't been a wolf-night, and the change had seemed instantaneous. And it hadn't hurt. He snapped his teeth wolfishly, almost unaware he was doing it.

What he did remember were his dreams. Not that there was anything clear about them, just confused visions of black wings, a bird's eye the size of a whale's, jet-shiny and knowing. Rushing wind. Being carried through the air. Being carried, confusingly, close to the ground. A rodenty stink, meaty and feral. The memory of fire. The sense of being almost infinitesimally small. Nausea, like the first time you met a really big sea. And feeling trapped.

Trapped, he thought, *goddamn it. I know what happened. It got me. And the skipper killed it, so it couldn't finish the job.*

Shit and hellfire. Why, I only just realized I still got a soul, and now I ain't really got it no more, do I? Where in God's name is it at now? He ran a hand over his face. It felt the same as his human face usually did in the morning, not too bristly— which meant it *hadn't* been a true change last night— rumpled with sleep. I *gotta talk to the skipper.*

But first I gotta get on my feet. Goddamn it. He stared at the ceiling helplessly.

There was a knock on the door, and Zé came in, looking disgustingly awake as he usually did. This despite the fact that Harris was occupying his bed and he'd had to double up with his little sister. Who snored like a pig in its sty.

"Morning, Sr Harris," he said. "Do you want some coffee?"

"Coffee, yeah," croaked Harris. "Zé, I need to talk with your dad. Can you go get him? I, uh, I ain't sure I can get up right now." Zé nodded, his eyes alight with interest. *Jesus, don't he look like his ma?* Harris thought irrelevantly.

"What happened? They were up really late with the *senhor professor* Pierce."

So Pierce had showed, had he? Harris wondered whether that was good or bad, but felt too ill to pursue the thought.

"Get me coffee, son," he said. "Before I die." Zé's eyes widened. "I'm kidding." *I hope.* He started to cough. It jarred his head agonisingly, and he clutched at his temples, trying to make the pain recede.

"I'm outta here," he heard Zé say, in a passable imitation of his own accent.

He lay on the bed, looking at the little room through a sunset-colored glare and seeing only bars.

* * *

Once when Zé was about eleven or twelve, he burst in on Emilia and me without knocking. I've never known him forget since. This morning his mother was up, and I was somewhat creakily getting dressed. That's not quite true. I'd got as far as putting my pants on and was sitting on the bed smoking and looking out of the window. Watching a piebald cat on a narrow balcony. Thinking about the fate of the big black cat of São Rafael. And other things.

He knocked. Waited. "Come in," I called, coming back to the present. Heard his voice.

"Ouch," he said, feelingly. "What happened to you?" I didn't turn my head. He was on my blind side.

"It's only a cut," I said.

"But it's huge."

"It's not deep. What do you want, Zé?" It was, I confess, feeling a bit sore. Made me prickly. I shoot off quills like a porcupine when I'm like that. Not an excuse. Just a statement of fact.

"I wish you'd *tell* me things sometimes." The bed dipped as he sat on it. Without invitation. Cheeky brat. "It's not like I don't *know* stuff," he went on. "I made you that silver bullet in India. I'm *fourteen*." And two weeks. "I'll be *shaving* soon."

"Won't that be fun for you," I growled. And sighed. Perhaps I *was* being too hard on him. Turned round, then, so I could look at him. He was wearing his hurt expression. I tried not to smile. "Zé...what's going on. It's complicated. And I don't want to—" Put you at risk, I was about to say. But you already did that, didn't you? "—involve you," I substituted. He scowled. Turned away, hunching his shoulders. "But I may need your help."

The sulks were gone in an instant. He bounced on the bed. Which I admit I could've done without. "Anything!" The eagerness of youth. Meu Deus. Was I like that, at his age? I honestly can't remember. So the memory's going too, da Silva.

"Don't make promises until you know what they are," I advised. "Now tell me why you came barging in here."

"Sr Harris is sick," he said. "He wants to talk to you, but he says he's too ill to move. And I promised to get him some coffee."

Across the street, the black-and-white cat stretched itself. Looked like a good plan. I emulated it, a little stiffly. "When are you on?"

"Afternoon," he said. I checked the time. Twenty past nine.

"Go and fetch some coffee, then," I said. "You can get me a cup while you're at it. And after I've seen Harris, I might tell you how you can help."

"Right!" he exclaimed, springing up. I winced. Zé charged out of the room. I must've used up two days' worth of energy yesterday. And here he was rushing around like a steam-engine. When do we lose that limitless energy? I suppose around the time puberty hits. Or maybe it just gets redirected then.

I stubbed out my cheroot and went to have a shave. The face that stared back at me didn't look any different from usual. Either I always look this bad, or battling demons no longer has any effect on me. No, I must always look this bad. I sighed. Splashed my face with water in a last attempt to wake myself up enough not to cut my own throat. And started working up a lather.

Harris could put up with me in shirtsleeves, but I gave him the benefit of the eyepatch. As it happened I could've gone dressed up as the German Kaiser and I don't think he would've noticed. He looked terrible. Why mince words? He looked like a corpse. I had a vision of the crow-demon perched on his back, stabbing down with its beak. And felt a chill.

The smell of coffee announced Zé, and I stood to one side to let him come in. He handed me one cup. Put the other on the floor by the bed. Left, thankfully, without speaking, though he was obviously bursting with questions. Let him stew for a while. I've promised to talk to him later. Sort of. I shut the door, and Harris's eyelids snapped open.

"Harris?" I said. If he felt as bad as he looked, he was in trouble.

"Skipper," he answered weakly. "You killed that crow thing, right?" I nodded. "I think it got me first. Or it half-got me. Or something." He struggled to sit up. His face was the color of putty, and there was a thin sheen of sweat on his brow. I picked up the coffee from the floor. Handed it to him. He sipped at it. "Jesus, that tastes good." And drank the rest in one go.

"Talk to me, Harris," I said.

"It's hard to explain," he said. "I'm here but I ain't here. It's like I'm in two places. I can feel I'm sitting here talking to you. But my mind's…seeing something else as well."

"What, exactly?" I asked, sucking in caffeine.

He shrugged. "I dunno," he replied, running his hands over his face in a sort of scrubbing motion. "Kinda red haze, is all right now. Skipper, you sure's hell need to find them gemstones. 'Cause I ain't sure I can hang on."

"You can hang on," I told him. "You're about the stubbornest man I ever met." That earned me one of his barking humorless laughs.

"Me?" he said, raising his eyebrows to the hairline. "You ever hear an English saying about pots and kettles?"

I scratched my cheekbone. Wanted to reassure him a bit. But *don't worry* doesn't seem quite the right thing to say to someone half-imprisoned by a sorcerer who, apparently, wants to bring about Armageddon. I finished my coffee. Thought about lighting up. Looked at the color of Harris's face and decided against it.

"We'll find 'em," I said. "Got a good idea where to look, now."

"Yeah?" I nodded. Harris took a deep breath, then pushed the covers back. I raised an eyebrow at him.

"Maybe you ought to stay in bed."

"Maybe it'll catch me if I stay in bed," he said. "If I'm well enough to get my pants on, I'm well enough to get up."

"Is that Mrs. Harris talking?" I asked. He glared at me.

"Goddamn you too, and the horse you rode in on," he said mildly. And swung his legs shakily over the side of the bed. I left him to it. The skipper doesn't act as the werewolf's valet. Not in my own house, anyway.

To my not very great surprise, Zé was lurking outside. Trying, without much success, to look nonchalant. I paused to light a cheroot. Attempted to look at him objectively. It didn't work; he looks far too much like his mother.

"Come on then, you young villain," I said with resignation. He grinned unrepentantly and padded after me.

"Where are we going?"

"You'll see when we get there."

Narrow streets, cobblestones. Fado and fishwives. Canaries in cages. Ghosts ancient and modern. Laundry draped from balconies. I didn't grow up in this part of the city, but I'd explored it. Up and down, under and over. Zé spent the first ten years of *his* life in Venice, but he probably knows this labyrinth of alleys better than I do now. He called out to people we passed, and not just boys his age. Neighbors. I wasn't really conscious of having neighbors. Hadn't ever been at home long enough to get to know them. What's it like to live your entire life on land? I ran away from narrow minds as much as narrow horizons. Ha. Introspection. Not something I indulge in very often. Another sign of middle age, da Silva.

After a while Zé, who can't keep his mouth shut to save his life, asked, "What is it you want me to do?"

I considered what to say to him for a long time. Finally I said, "How much have you picked up?" What's the gossip, in other words. I was sure he had his ear to the ground. Or, in this case, the deck. His pink-tinged face confirmed that guess.

"Fil and grandfather and Don Giov—Pedro—" He broke off.

"All right, Zézinho, I know what they call him," I said. "Go on."

"They're all sick, but Sr Harris saw something suck out Pedro's brains and it came after Sr Pierce and you cut its head off," he finished all in a rush.

The power of rumor never ceases to amaze me. I scratched my cheekbone, wondering whether to laugh or just give in.

"Well," I began judiciously, but he interrupted me.

"Is that right? What are you smiling at?"

"It's almost completely wrong," I said, unable to keep a straight face.

"Oh." He looked momentarily crestfallen, then brightened. "But you're going to tell me what's *really* going on, aren't you?" Eagerly.

Momentarily distracted by the ghosts of two women who had probably died from exposure if that was really what they'd been wearing, I didn't reply at once. Zé did a little dance of impatience, and nearly tripped over a small yellow dog.

Gathering my thoughts and pretending not to notice, I said, "They're not ill, exactly. Their souls were stolen."

"Their *souls?*" he repeated, open-mouthed.

"Yes, theirs, and some other people." I took partial refuge in smoking. If you think this sort of thing looks easy, try it yourself. I'm not about to tell my fourteen-year-old son that the man who's behind all this is doing it because I slept with his sister-in-law twenty years ago.

"Who by?"

"A man called Batista. He's following a kind of magical recipe, and he needs particular people's souls."

Zé blinked at this preposterous-sounding statement, but seemed willing to accept it at face value. "Why?"

"Because it says so in his book of spells," I said.

"Is he a warlock?"

"I suppose so, yes. The book also gives very precise instructions for releasing the souls." I blew smoke at the ghost of an immensely fat man that was hovering close by. Sometimes it distracts them. Not this one. "And I might need you to help me release Felipe."

"Really?" said Zé. "Will he know?"

"I've no idea."

Now we came out of the shade of the alleys into the bright narrow square outside the church. Today there were clouds in the sky, small, puffy, frivolous-looking things. They tempered the heat a little. But as soon as the sun escaped them its brazen light struck down again. I felt sweat start to trickle.

By now I was confident of finding the library. I looked at my watch. Plenty of time to take Zé there before sending him back to *Isabella* for his afternoon watch.

* * *

Fr Jerónimo watched the two of them cross the square. He had been looking out for da Silva, but the man's son was an unexpected plus—and a much better idea.

The young priest looked little the worse for wear after his sleepless night. His ascetic leanings dictated that he live simply, and there was little comfort to be had in his hard narrow cot. Bad dreams woke him less frequently than the discomfort of his bed, the heat of the summer nights.

Curled by his hand that morning he had found the mouse cleaning its whiskers. It no more occurred to him to evict it than it would have to omit his morning prayers. He added a small prayer, though, for the destruction of the unholy books which niggled in his mind. That his prayers were heard by other agencies would have greatly surprised him, not to say shocked him considerably. Was he not an agent of Verbum Dei?

His equivalent of the hair shirt, the straitjacket of piety, buoyed him up like a lifebelt. He felt strong and justified. Now was not the time to confront da Silva, but that time would come. There were easier ways to confront Satan's legions.

Mouffi, the remnant of Mastiphal, released from Batista's geas to mischief of his own, crouched in the priest's pocket. He was well-satisfied. For a small being, he had managed to accomplish a great deal.

* * *

"Where are we going?" Zé asked me again.

"A library," I replied and grinned at his predictable reaction. Show him a book and he runs a mile.

"Why?"

"Because that's where I'm going," I said, "and you wanted to know what's going on. So you asked for it, didn't you?"

That shut him up. But not for long, that was for sure. *Chuva em Novembro, Natal em Dezembro.* The sun rises in the morning, the sea's wet, and Zé can't keep quiet for more than two minutes.

There was the alley mouth, there the drifting shade of Isaac Zacuto. I led Zé past it into the cool dimness beyond. Wondered if the mutilated cat's corpse was still there. Strange how that image kept returning more insistently than far more monstrous things. Demons, for instance. Probably because it was the Venetian's sacrificing a cat that led to the loss of my eye and started all this off in the first place.

But it was gone. Can't say I was particularly surprised. São Rafael's unseen caretakers, the ones who replaced electric light-bulbs and the like, wouldn't have left it to decay. They'd also cleared up the flowerpot shards and debris and replaced them with a wooden tub of geraniums. The sharp musky odor of the flowers was strong in the still hot air.

Zé looked round at the silent courtyard, the shuttered buildings. "Why's it so quiet?" he said, then flinched at how loud his voice sounded.

"I'm not sure," I said absently. "Come on."

Putting my hand on the sun-warmed wood of the ancient door already had its own set of memories. I pushed it open. Stepped over the threshold, Zé at my heels.

Found Pierce inside with Zacuto watching him in fascinated incomprehension. He was photographing the *Book of Souls*, which was propped upright on the table in front of the camera. I'd completely forgotten about that. Rather too much had happened since then. Either that, or my memory really is going.

Though it now dawned on me, with an unpleasant jolt, that this is more important than ever. No, the *most* important thing was to prevent Batista somehow getting the thing back. I'd disposed of the demon that he sent for me. But I'll bet he's got a substitute lined up. With luck, Batista hasn't been playing with the reserve team and can't complete the set without the book. He's stuck on five, or five and a half if you count Harris.

Pierce, busy with his camera, gave us a rather desultory "bom dia." Zacuto, however, turned with a glint in his eyes. I introduced Zé, who was staring up at the bookshelves with his eyes wide. The ghost seemed to approve.

"Listen," I said to him. "Did Pierce tell you what happened?" He nodded. I think he had a smile hidden somewhere in his beard. Though it was difficult to be sure amongst all those whiskers. The thought of beards made me scratch my chin in sympathy. Silly thing to do. He couldn't feel anything, having no skin to itch.

"It was very well done," he said. "A fitting atonement." I frowned slightly. Didn't consider I had anything to atone for, except perhaps using a sledgehammer to crack a nut. Então, we'll have to agree to differ on that point.

"Batista will still want a seventh soul for his—what was it you called it?"

"The Eidolon," Zacuto said. "Yes, that thought had occurred to me."

"Does the Book of Souls give any...understudy demons?" I asked.

He shot me a sardonic look. "Without reading further, I do not know. I would not read any more in that vile work without good reason—" He held up his hand. "—yes, senhor capitão, I do consider this a good reason, and I will address myself to the task with all despatch. But I believe I also have some good news for you concerning the counter-amulets."

I saw that Zé had wandered over to watch Pierce taking photographs. He was welcome to quiz the antiquarian if he wanted to, I decided. Pierce was too engrossed in what he was doing to give anything like a coherent answer.

"You've worked out what they are?" I said to Zacuto.

"Based on the information Sr Pierce gave me about their bearers, I believe so. May I make a suggestion?" Asking my permission? That was a first. Disposing of demons really was the way into his good books. Da Silva, sucking up to the teacher. I stuck my hands in my pockets. Imitating Zé, I think.

"Of course," I said.

"You should retrieve the amulets whose bearers you are certain of. Then even should this Batista discover a way to recover the Book of Souls, he will be further handicapped in his construction of the Eidolon."

"Is it true what Pierce told me about the spell?" I asked. "That it could upset the whole world's equilibrium?"

"Indeed," said Zacuto. "Yes, it could well have that effect."

Did Batista knew that? I don't think spells come with warnings attached, like a bottle of prussic acid. Hell, he probably wouldn't care if he did know. I shrugged mentally and looked across to Pierce and Zé.

"Well then—" I began, and at that instant Pierce fired off his flash powder. My eye snapped shut automatically, but a fraction too late, and I muttered a curse. Opened it, blinking, and rubbed the corner. After-images flared in my vision like thronging ghosts. Zacuto allowed himself to look faintly amused, having no sight to blind with explosions of magnesium and potash.

"The antitheses?" he said. "They are here." He gestured to the table. A sheet of paper lay there, covered with Pierce's loopy handwriting. I scanned it cursorily and put it in my pocket. "Captain da Silva?"

"Yes?"

"When I have completed the tasks for which you summoned me, I have a favor to ask. I would like to remain in this place for a while. There is much to learn."

"What about your room in the walls?" I asked.

"It still exists *in potentia* without my presence," he said. "When I do ask you to release me from this form, I shall return there."

I didn't even try to comprehend this. So I nodded. "There is one other thing I need you for," I said. He raised his bushy eyebrows.

"And that is?"

"To help release Fr Pereira." To go after the executioner-guardian. Against whom only the dead can stand.

"Ah," he said. "Who might be my many-times-great grandson. The world turns, but everything is still made up out of patterns."

Which was more or less what I'd thought when I first met the ghost of Isaac Zacuto.

* * *

Clocks ticked. In such numbers as they were, the sound became like the sussuration of the sea. Every quarter-hour some wound up a selection of pendulums, balances, mechanisms, in preparation for chiming, every half-hour a few more, and every hour the shop was filled with a demented clicking and whirring like a flock of mechanical birds until an orchestra of chimes, bells, avian whistles, bongs, gongs and percussion overtured the striking of the hour and marked the passage of mundane time.

John Yeoh, neat and immaculate, a dapper figure in the western clothes he has worn for longer than his true lifetime, smiled at the tall cruel-faced man who was looking down his long hooked nose at him, and read from the card he had been given.

"Sr Batista. How may I be of service?"

"I desire to see your collection of documents," said Batista imperiously. His tone made it an order, not a request.

Yeoh allowed his face to become blank, the picture of polite incomprehension, the inscrutability westerners accused his compatriots of having. Inwardly, though, he was shuddering at the shape of his visitor's soul.

Most men's were tempered by humanity, even when they were wolves. But there was very little, if anything at all, human left in the man who stood in front of him. His soul had no real shape at all: it wavered and changed. It was fanged, maybe, horned, maybe. Not a thinking thing. Not held in check by even a thin veneer of humanity.

If he had not discovered his own new talent, he would have been afraid. But whatever this Batista was, one thing was certain. He was mortal, anchored in time. His lifespan remained that of a man. He could not move as Yeoh could.

As far as Yeoh knew, no one could.

He brought his attention back to his customer, aware of a dangerous lapse in concentration.

"I fear you must be mistaken," he said blandly, gesturing round the shop. "As you see, I am merely a humble horologist."

Batista ignored this. "A book was stolen from me. I am anxious to replace it." The man had a strange, sour smell, Yeoh noted, that seemed to be intensely personal to him. He had not detected anything like it when he'd been in the House of the Four Winds.

"Suppose I did possess a few manuscripts," Yeoh said carefully, "I assure you there would be no books among them." He was tempted to add "have you tried the public library?" but could see that this would be a bad idea. He did *not* want to incur this man's wrath. If man he still was.

"I do not need the entire book," said Batista, "although that would, of course, be preferable. Just certain of its pages."

"And if I were able to find those pages, or even the book itself?"

The other man gave him a level stare. Yeoh was quite sure he was seriously considering possibilities other than actually handing over money, and thought of the revolver in his drawer. But finally Batista said, "I can pay you well."

"What book…what pages are you looking for?" Yeoh asked.

After another pause, Batista said, "It is called the *Book of Souls.*"

"I have heard of it," murmured Yeoh, with perfect truth. "Unfortunately, I regret to say that I do not have any part of it in my possession."

"But you might—" the other man said silkily.

"—for a consideration. Yes."

All around them, the clocks ticked. Yeoh felt his heart pounding, and part of him was remotely surprised, as always, that it still beat at all.

"May I ask," said Batista conversationally, "how you intend to go about finding this book, since I am unable to do so?"

"I am a collector," Yeoh pointed out, "as you seem to have heard, Sr Batista. Others know this, too. And I in turn know many like-minded people." He smiled. "In addition, this modern age has given us a number of useful inventions, among them the telephone and the wireless telegraph. And thus like-minded people can communicate, instantly and over long distances." *Instantly* was pushing it a bit, given the parlous state of the local telephone exchange's competence, but Yeoh thought it was permissible as rhetoric.

"I should like to impress the urgency of the situation upon you," Batista said, and named a sum of money that had Yeoh's eyebrows climbing up his forehead in shock.

"Indeed," he agreed, keeping his composure with an effort, "I will make every effort to accommodate you, Sr Batista."

"Then I shall await your call, Sr Yeoh. Please send someone round as soon as you have any news. Unlike you, I do not wholly subscribe to the wonders of the modern age, and I do not possess a telephone."

"Once the box of progress is opened," observed Yeoh, "it can never be closed."

"We shall see about that," Batista said, and the reptilian expression on his face made the other man quail. But he tipped his hat politely enough and took his leave.

As if drawing a collective deep breath of relief, all the clocks began to click and whirr in preparation to strike the hour.

Now I need to speak to Captain da Silva, Yeoh thought, and began to shut up his shop amidst a symphony of percussion and woodwind.

*   *   *

For once when I arrived, Yeoh wasn't seated outside his shop with his book of poetry. But the door was open, so I stuck my head inside and called his name. A moment later he emerged from behind one of the cabinets of his clock-maze.

"Ah, senhor capitão," he said. "I wanted to speak with you. I confess I didn't expect you to materialize quite so promptly." Before I could respond, he went on, "I have just had a visitor." He shook himself like a dog, looked annoyed at his own reaction, and explained, "Sr Batista came to call."

Did he, by God. "What did he want?" Not to get a clock repaired, I'm damn sure.

Yeoh smiled. "He wanted me to locate his missing book. Or, shall we say, a reasonable facsimile thereof."

I felt a wolfish grin break out on my own face, and rubbed at my cheekbone. "Now isn't that interesting."

"I thought you would think so," said Yeoh. "So if you know of someone who can make simulacra, I can enter his house quite legitimately to retrieve the amulet."

Paciência could probably do it. "We have to plan a little more carefully than that," I pointed out, taking out a cheroot. Yeoh shot me an amused glance, and I shut up. *Your English heritage is showing, da Silva.*

"Believe it or not, senhor capitão, I have given the matter some thought," he said, then took out a cigarette.

"Go ahead." I struck a match to light the cheroot I was holding. It snapped in two, the flaring head falling to the floor. I stepped on it quickly, and tried again. Handed him the match so he could light his cigarette.

"The amulet *transforms* its bearer into the appropriate guardian if threatened, is that correct?" I nodded. "So, we must make sure that it does not perceive the threat which I pose."

Well, I think I could've figured that out for myself. "And how do we do that?"

"By distracting the bearer," he said. "What single thing would engage all the attention of both Sr Batista and his warlike daughter?"

Damn it. I knew where he was going. Didn't like it a bit. I raised an eyebrow. "You want me to go and knock on his door?"

"Yes, Captain da Silva, just after they've let me in."

Don't people always say, if you want anything done, do it yourself? I sighed. I suppose I should've known something like this would happen. After all, it has every other time. At least this time there's one novel element. This time it's not my idea.

Expelling smoke, I said mildly, "Yes, I suppose it would distract Batista." If he didn't decide it was all too much trouble and just shoot me, that is. But I didn't think he would. I was pretty sure he was going to play out his elaborate plan to the bitter end. Whatever that turned out to be.

Yeoh smiled, thinly. "I shan't contact him until later this afternoon," he said. "I don't want him to get suspicious if I get in touch too soon."

"And we don't actually have a fake book yet," I reminded him.

He inclined his head in one of his mandarinish nods. "Yes, there is that. Do you know a witch who can make a simulacrum?"

"I know a witch," I said. "I'll have to ask her whether she can."

"Most witches can do it," he said dismissively. Then it was almost certain that Paciência would be able to.

I inhaled smoke thoughtfully. "There's just one thing."

"What?"

"Are you sure it's not a trap?" I asked. I had no desire to walk into the lion's den if the lion knew I was coming.

"You think he might have recognized me from the other night?" He considered it. "It's possible," he conceded at last. "He is a powerful sorcerer, after all. But I don't think so."

"Why not?"

"Two reasons. Firstly, I think he is too obsessed, too wound up in his own web, to do anything but pursue the obvious course."

It was a good point. I found myself nodding in agreement. "And the other reason?"

He gave me a long calculating look. "His soul."

"His soul," I repeated. "Explain."

"Senhor capitão, you see ghosts." Now how does he know that? I don't think I told him. "I see people's souls. What shape they are. Their nature. Your senhor Harris, for example. As you might imagine, his soul is shaped like a wolf, yet it remains a human soul." Now that's interesting. In an academic sort of way at this moment, admittedly. Since we'd already proved that he did have one— almost too late. "But this Batista, his soul has no shape. Whatever it is, is no longer human. I think it is excessive congress with demons which does this. What I am trying to say, is just as a wild beast has no guile, he has lost the capacity for subtlety."

"Let's hope you're right." I rubbed my cheekbone, not wholly convinced. Wondered what shape he saw my soul as. Had no intention of asking.

"Then perhaps you could get in touch with your witch and ask her." I nodded, and an idea struck me.

"Do you have a telephone?" Personally I dislike the things. I prefer to talk to someone face-to-face. But there's no denying they have their uses. Like now, for instance.

"Indeed," he said, looking amused. "Despite what you may think, I do run a real business from this shop. Your witch also has a telephone?"

I realized I didn't know her number, so I called Emilia. After the usual wait for the operator to wake up, followed by clicks and assorted sound effects, her voice came echoing down the wire.

"*Estou.*"

"Emilia, it's me," I said. I always feel faintly foolish talking into these things. Also I have a tendency to shout.

"Hang out the flags," she said, laughing, then sobered. "Luís, whatever's happened? Are you all right?" I nodded. Then realized she couldn't see me.

"Yes, I'm fine. Can you hear me?" Stupid question. "I need you to ask Dona Paciência something."

"You can telephone her yourself," she pointed out, which was of course true. I scowled. She couldn't see that, either.

"I don't have her number. That's why I called you."

"I can," she said, "give you her number. Where are you calling from?"

"Sr Yeoh's shop," I replied.

"Oh, well, I suppose we shouldn't run up his telephone bill. What do you want me to ask?" I glanced at Yeoh, but he was leafing through some paperwork. To show me he had a business to run, I imagine. I changed hands. The instrument was slippery with sweat.

"If she can make a 'simulacrum' of the *Book of Souls,*" I told her.

"I'll ask her. Did you get what you went for?" The list of amulets. I'd almost forgotten I had it. Stupid as that sounds. Memory's definitely going, da Silva. I took it out of my pocket and stared at it. "Luís, are you still there?"

"Yes," I said. "Yes, I've got the list. Do you want me to read it out?"

"Let me get a pencil. Yes. Go ahead."

"Agate: agate, for victory," I read. Yes, because Pierce's book had said they would cancel each other out. "Chrysophase: onyx. For the eyes. Am I going too fast?"

"No, carry on," she said.

"Beryl: jet, to dispel illusions. Jasper: amethyst, against confusion. Malachite: crystal, for bad dreams. Jacinth: heliotrope, against the poison of greed. Sapphire: opal, to dispel sadness."

"...dispel sadness," she echoed. "Got them. I'll tell Paciência when she gets here."

"How's Harris?" I asked.

"Dozing in a chair. Still with us, I think."

"Good," I said. "I'll see you in a while."

"All right. Hang up, Luís, or I can't call Paciência."

"Yes, I know how these things work," I said testily. She laughed. The sound echoed strangely in my ear. *"Até logo."*

Yeoh, still busy with his papers, looked up briefly. "In your witch's hands, then, Captain da Silva. Here," he held out a business card, "telephone me when you have any news." I took the card from him.

"I'll do that," I said resignedly.

* * *

It was late. He would have to run. And it was too hot to run. Zé parted from his father at the entrance to the alley which led to the library of São Rafael and felt the sun hit like a hammer. The minute-hand of the church clock lurched onto the half-hour, and he muttered a word that would have had his ears boxed for him if his mother had heard it, fourteen years old or not.

He was just about to break into a trot when he felt his shoulder seized from behind and looked round to find he'd been annexed by a tall thin young priest with an Adam's apple that looked as if he was swallowing a hard-boiled egg.

Oh, not now, he thought. "Excuse me, Father, I'm late for my watch," he said. The priest squeezed his shoulder with a benevolent smile, but Zé felt the steel in his grip. *Uh-oh, I'm in hot water,* he said to himself, and his heart sank. He focused on an angry pimple at the side of the man's nose, wondering why he hadn't popped it.

"My son, it won't take long. Will you do me a favor?" the priest said, still smiling. "Can you spare a moment for God's business?"

Zé, who privately agreed with his father about religion—and especially the undue influence of priests—but wasn't stupid enough to say so, said doubtfully, "I suppose."

"Then you can show me the way to the library, my son."

"Don't you know where it is, sir?" Zé asked, surprised, and not quite understanding. Although he felt, deep inside, that something was wrong. Nothing he could identify, though.

"No, I'm a stranger to it." The priest stared at him, his eyes shadowed, but Zé was used to staring people down and refused to drop his gaze. After a moment he shrugged, too conscious of the passage of time, and turned.

"It's down there—" He broke off, mouth dropping open. Where had the alleyway gone? He'd only just come out of it.

"Where, my son?" asked the priest, insistently. Zé shut his mouth with a snap and stared up at him in confusion.

"I—I don't know," he faltered. "I *thought* it was just over there." He looked around, puzzled and annoyed. "I'm sorry, I don't think I can help."

The priest seemed to sag. He released his grip on Zé's shoulder and turned away, infinite weariness evident in his stance. Zé rubbed his shoulder—it felt as if he'd get a bruise—and watched him go in some astonishment. *Well I wonder what all that was about,* he thought. *And where...* He looked around and saw, plain as day, the entrance to the alley.

His eyes narrowed, and he scratched his cheek in an unconscious imitation of his father. He glanced rather nervously at the church clock, and grimaced. Then he took to his heels and ran back to São Rafael, down the alley, across the silent, sundrenched square redolent with flowers, and pushed the door open.

Pierce looked up from his camera as he came back in, automatically pushing his descending spectacles up his nose. "You'll be late for your watch, young man," he said sternly, and Zé almost giggled. His father was always complaining about Englishmen's penchant for stating the bloody obvious.

"I know, sir," he said, somewhat breathlessly, "but I think it's important. There's this priest. There's something *funny* about him."

Zacuto turned to him, who had reason enough to be suspicious of priests. Not that Zé knew that, of course. "What has happened?" the ghost asked in his dusty voice.

"Well, he wanted to know the way here," said Zé, "and I thought *that* was weird to start with. And then I couldn't see the alleyway, and I'd only *just* come out of it! So I said I didn't know, and he went away, and I looked round and there it *was* again. So I thought, there must be some kind of *protection* round the library that keeps...bad people out."

"That's very astute of you," Pierce murmured. Zacuto frowned at him and made shushing gestures. Zé didn't miss a beat.

"And if it keeps him out, it means *he's* up to no good, I suppose," he finished, "so you ought to watch out for him." He looked from one to the other of them.

"You did the right thing, coming back," Zacuto said, reassuringly. Zé gave a rueful grin and hunched his shoulders.

"I'm going to catch it from Sr Costa, though," he said.

"Shall I come with you to the ship and explain it was something—er—important?" Pierce offered.

"Oh, no, thanks, Sr Pierce," Zé said, sounding a little horrified at the prospect. "I'll be all right. But honestly, I have to go now. That priest, he's tall and thin, I mean *really* tall, you can't miss him."

The antiquarian nodded. "Well, thank you for the warning. Er—see you later, I suppose." He turned back to his camera.

"Yes, right," said Zé, looking in Zacuto's direction. He tried to think of something else to say, but drew a blank. Finally he just gave a sort of salute that he had copied from Harris, and set off *Isabella*-wards as fast as he could run.

* * *

Now I have a problem. Which, given my life recently, is nothing unusual. My current dilemma is whether to bring the witch to the book or the other way around. I wasn't totally confident that São Rafael would let Paciência in. But on the other hand, removing the *Book of Souls* from its protection would be asking for trouble. The thought of calling on Batista was bad enough without inviting him to home in on a beacon.

I decided on the first alternative. It was less risky. And, as it happened, I needn't have worried. Obviously the library's wards were subtle enough to separate intention from surface. Though I thought it had been suspicious of me at first.

"Gentlemen, Sra Verdinho," I said, resisting the temptation to call her *senhora bruxa*. I'm not completely convinced she has a sense of humor. Good thought, da Silva. When in doubt, don't get up the witch's nose. "*Os senhores* Zacuto," I indicated the ghost, "and Pierce."

Zacuto bowed gravely. Pierce, who had finished his photography, actually kissed her hand. Dona Paciência seemed torn between amusement, embarrassment and accepting it as her due. Finally settled on an indulgent smile.

"Senhor professor," she said to Pierce, then turned her dark gaze to

Zacuto. Given her looks, I wondered whether he was speculating about her forefathers. "*Senhor fantasma.*" The ghost startled me with a deep growl of laughter.

"Very perceptive, senhora *bruxa*," he said. Having, evidently, less delicacy than me. Or less to lose by getting into the sorceress's bad books.

She smiled thinly, unamused. Maybe she had to put up with this it all the time. "Where is the volume?" Speaking of bad books. Pierce indicated it, once more wrapped safely in oilcloth. "Would you uncover it for me, please?"

The antiquarian finished polishing his spectacles and replaced them. Picked up a pencil from the table. He still approached the book gingerly, I saw. I scratched my eyebrow reflexively, wishing I could have a smoke. Watched him insert the pencil under the oilcloth and push the wrapping open carefully.

Dona Paciência drew in a sharp breath and crossed herself, regarding the book with distaste. "A very…nasty volume," she said. "You should seriously consider destroying it."

"None of us likes the idea of destroying any book, senhora," said Pierce. "No matter how much we disapprove of it. '*When books are burned, sooner or later, men will also be burned.*'" I saw Zacuto's nostrils flare at that.

"That is very true," he said, looking in my direction. "Captain da Silva, you should know that your son came back here after you had gone, with some disquieting news."

Zé came back? I turned to him, surprised. "What news?" I asked.

"Apparently he was accosted by a priest who wanted directions to this place. He was unable to locate the route at that time, but had no difficulty once the man had gone. This aroused his suspicions, so he returned to warn us."

That was smart of him. "Fr Jerónimo," I said resignedly. "Yes, he's a real pain in the…neck. He wants all this devil's knowledge destroyed."

"Was it he who set the fire?" Zacuto asked.

"He said not," I replied. "And I think I believed him. He said someone called—" I ran a hand through my hair. What was the name? Oh yes. "— Mouffi did." The scholar's ghost went very still. "What is it?"

"That name," he replied, frowning. "I seem to recognize it. No, nothing comes. Perhaps I will remember later." Well, I hope so. Since it's bound to be important. No such things as coincidences. As I keep on saying.

Meanwhile Paciência had taken out a small mirror. She placed it on the table with something of a flourish.

"The speculum," she said, apparently to Pierce. Then she turned to include me and, presumably, Zacuto. Though I got the odd impression, somehow, that she thought him of little consequence. Being a ghost. "This is a very simple spell," she explained. I tried to look intelligent. "Do you have any objections, senhor Pierce, if I take a small piece from the cover of the book and another from one of the pages?"

"Sra Verdinho," he said, spreading his hands, "please do. I didn't mean to cast any aspersions on you, or your Art." What did I miss? She was speaking to him, but looking at me. I fingered the scar on my cheekbone self-consciously.

"Now, I will also need a clean sheet of paper," she said, finally turning away. From her bag she took a small pair of scissors. Without touching the *Book of Souls*, she snipped the cover and a random page. These fragments she placed with great precision on the paper Pierce slid towards her. Then she picked up the mirror and positioned it carefully. Suddenly an image of the book was projected onto the paper, like a magic-lantern slide. Not an ordinary mirror, then.

The witch drew a deep breath and closed her eyes. Her face grew red, sweat bursting out on her brow. She spread her hands above the tiny pieces of leather and paper, or parchment, or whatever it was. Vellum. I don't know. Not quite touching them. I could feel the heat radiating off her, even where I stood. She was as hot as an open fire. Her lips moved, forming inaudible words. Very slowly, she began to raise her hands.

Under them the semblance of a book rose from the surface of the paper. At first semi-transparent, but solidifying as I watched. It glowed faintly. I could hear her breathing now, harsh and ragged. Felt a trickle of sweat run down my own face, and wiped it away with my hand.

Her palms steady a good foot above the simulacrum, she said, "*Sic fiat, amen.*" There was a pop like pressure releasing from your ears. The illusory heat vanished, leaving the perfectly ordinary heat of the afternoon. For an instant the book glowed as bright as Pierce's flash-powder, then faded. The sorceress removed her hands and opened her eyes. Let out a long breath, and mopped her face delicately with a handkerchief.

"Your simulacrum, gentlemen," she said. Zacuto was the first to move, advancing to the table to examine it more closely.

"A remarkable illusion, senhora," he said. Real admiration in his voice. "But will the other senses be so easily deceived?"

Pierce moved to wrap the real *Book of Souls* in its oilcloth covering once more. Leaving me to approach the table and touch the witch's handiwork. As I'd never touched the real book—and didn't intend to—I couldn't say whether it felt the same. But my fingertips felt old perished leather, and it smelled the same as the real thing. Mildew and mustiness and neat's-foot oil. I looked up at her.

"Thank you," I said. "One step closer to freeing your husband." She nodded, a genuine smile on her face.

I wrapped the false book in a second piece of oilcloth and set off again for John Yeoh's shop. Well, it was nearly as close as going home. Why telephone when you can call in person?

* * *

And now here I am again outside the House of the Four Winds. Has to rank among the most foolhardy things I've ever done. Although the rest of today has been like a vacation compared to the last few. No armored guardians. No demons. No were-jaguars. Not even a pestiferous priest. Well, all that was about to change. You've had your rest, da Silva. Time to make life interesting again. Ha. I'd rather poke a sleeping tiger with a short stick. This had better work.

Yeoh raised his eyebrows at me and rang the doorbell. I stood to one side, out of sight of the front door. Heard a woman's voice, soprano. Presumably not the Amazon. They must have a maid. I wondered what had become of the late Eduardo. The door closed behind Yeoh. My hands were sweating. I rubbed them on my pants. Looked at my watch. Then poked about under my eyepatch to try and air it a bit. Nervous, da Silva? Who, me? But I felt in the pocket of my jacket for the reassuring weight of my revolver. Hoped I wouldn't need it. Wasn't taking any chances, though.

I took a deep breath and stepped up to the front door. It was painted the same shade of blue as my father's. I pulled the bell. Heard solemn chimes from far-off. A moment later a stunningly pretty fairhaired girl in a maid's uniform that fitted her in all the right places opened the door and looked enquiringly at me.

"Luís da Silva," I said, not too apprehensive to admire the view. "He'll see me."

She stood to one side to let me pass. Her dress had a high neck. What a pity. Blonde, where did he find a blonde girl? "Sr Batista has someone with him at the moment, sir."

"I know," I said. "I'm with him." She gestured to the left.

"In there, sir."

"Obrigado," I said politely, and went in. My right hand on the gun in my coat pocket. It's impossible to sight the thing if I hold it in my left hand, so I had to learn to shoot right-handed. Besides, I had something in my other hand.

In other circumstances I might've enjoyed the expression on Batista's face. A brief tableau met my eye as I went through the door. Yeoh, smiling blandly. Batista, apoplectically turning purple. Another young woman, tall, with the agate suspended on a gold chain round her long neck. Features distorted in a scowl. Teresa. On the desk, the false book, a vase of flowers, a fencing saber. Then all hell broke loose.

"What in the devil's name are you doing here?" bellowed Batista, advancing towards me. "How dare you come into my house!" And Teresa changed as I watched. Armor grew over her. A carapace slid round her body. The helmet rose from her shoulders until it covered her head. Mail slithered over her arms, her hands, outlined her legs. All in the blink of an eye. Which is, of course, all I can blink.

I held up the sapphire Emilia had given me. "It's dead, Batista," I said. "Alastor. I killed it. Yesterday."

His eyes bulged. "Where did you get that?" To the armored guardian that had been his child: "Wait—wait."

I raised an eyebrow and gave him a humorless grin. "Same place your daughter did," I said. He smiled nastily. Red lips curling back from yellow teeth. I caught a breath of that strange sour odor again.

"It won't help you, da Silva." He picked up the false book triumphantly from the desk where it lay. "I can send another. Because I have the *Book of Souls.*"

"I don't think so, Batista," I said, then spoke the word Paciência had taught me.

The book exploded in his hands in a dazzling flash and a spectacular shower of bursting sparks like a firework. There was no substance to it. It won't do him any lasting harm. But it made a hell of a show. Hell, it made *me* jump, and I was expecting it. Batista staggered back, flinging his hands to his face. It should blind him for long enough.

"*Filho da puta!*" he screamed. The guardian that had been Teresa advanced with a wordless roar of fury. My hand curled round the butt of the revolver.

And Yeoh blurred. One second he was by the window. The same instant he was in front of the armored figure, barring its way. It raised one mailed fist over its head and brought it down with crunching force, but Yeoh was no longer there. The fist smashed into the desk, splintering a great dent in its surface. Then Yeoh was in front of it again. He seized the agate in one fist and pulled. Its chain snapped. Yeoh fuzzed again, dodging a final furious stroke. And suddenly Teresa was there once more. She faltered for a heartbeat, scooped up the saber from the desk and came straight for me.

Yeoh stuck out his foot, and she fell headlong with a curse.

"Run!" he shouted. I didn't need telling twice. In the hallway, I got a brief impression of the pretty blonde maidservant's startled face as I thundered past her and wrenched the blue door open, Yeoh close behind me.

Out of the cool house into the baking sunlight. Suddenly breathless as the heat hit me, I kept on running. Didn't look back. If Teresa pursued, we outran her.

The pair of us came to a panting halt about five minutes later and looked at each other. Yeoh held up the amulet in triumph.

"We got it," he said, unnecessarily.

"Yes, we did," I replied, equally superfluous. Meu Deus, we did. I felt a stupid grin plastered on my face. Saw the same expression on Yeoh's.

He took out his cigarette-case and offered it to me. I shook my head and found a cheroot instead. Now all I needed was a long drink.

"And now what?" he asked, holding out the lit match for me. "Can the prisoner in this stone be freed?"

"Not until we have all the amulets," I said, gradually getting my breath back. "Or so the book says."

We fell into step, though he was a few inches shorter. Two colleagues walking purposefully to their next meeting, perhaps. Except that I was wringing with sweat and even Yeoh looked a little damp. I ran a hand through my wet hair. There was far too much of it round the back of my head for weather like this.

"What progress have you made?" he asked, and it was only then that it struck me. Oh, God, wake up, da Silva! Yeoh had been in the city longer than anyone. Anyone living, that is. He was the obvious person to ask.

"We know who one of the others is," I said, blowing out smoke. "You might be able to help us find the rest."

"I might?" he said. "I don't know. Try me."

"How about—" the only one I could recall offhand "—an Arab, a collector of some kind, lives in Alfama. A greedy man."

"Not a man, a woman," replied Yeoh promptly. "Fatima al-Ghuri." I took the cheroot out of my mouth and gaped at him like a codfish. Hadn't expected him to come up with the goods that quickly.

"I'll be damned," I said. "Can you spare half an hour to look at the other clues?"

"Of course." He smiled. "What, senhor capitão, did you think I could just walk away now? Your quest has interested me more than anything in the last hundred years."

Obscurely pleased, I took a drag on my cheroot. We walked in silence for a while. Took advantage of the shade under an avenue of trees. Came back out into the sweltering sun, which showed no sign of cooling down. Its light bounced off windows. buildings, the pavements. The day descended towards evening as we descended to the Baixo. I felt deeply satisfied, not to say smug. We had faced down the bogeyman and emerged unscathed with what we went for. Retrieving the other amulets would be child's play in comparison.

The executioner, the castrator, the night-hag. Dire names. But I knew how to defeat them. Who could defeat them.

And complacency nearly killed me.

There was a sort of short-cut that I remembered from my childhood. It led straight down between two high walls, trees behind one side. They had grown considerably. Hardly surprising, in thirty years. I say a sort of short-cut because it was so steep you had to take it slowly, leaning backwards. In rainy weather or a rare frost, you'd be descending on your backside. Halfway down on the left-hand side was a door. I'd never known what was behind it. Had never even seen it open.

Today it was open. But on my blind side. And behind it was Teresa Graça Batista.

The first I knew of it was Yeoh suddenly pushing me so hard I almost lost my footing. I crashed against the opposite wall, which set my back protesting. At the same time I heard a gunshot, and Yeoh shouted "Get down!" Brick-shards sparked out of the wall an inch from my face. I ducked, pulling my own gun from my pocket.

Teresa's next shot was aimed at Yeoh, who blurred for an instant to avoid it. It whined away harmlessly. I had her in my sights now, and began to squeeze the trigger.

Then Yeoh kicked the revolver out of my hand, pivoted quick as a snake, and his foot shot out again to connect with her jaw. It cracked almost as loud as a gunshot, and she fell to the ground, stunned.

I retrieved my gun and gave Yeoh a reproachful glance. He picked up Teresa's weapon and stowed it in his own pocket.

"You didn't really want to shoot her, did you, senhor capitão?" he said mildly. I swallowed, as the implications of it hit me, and shook my head.

"No," I agreed, scratching my cheekbone vigorously. "No, I didn't."

"And perhaps she wanted you to. She is devious, this one. More subtle than her father." He paused for a heartbeat. "More human, still."

The woman stirred and groaned. Her eyes snapped open, and she scrambled to her feet. Ready to fight again. You had to give her credit for that. Her hair was falling in her eyes, her face pale, and Yeoh's foot had left a swelling bruise on her jaw. She clenched her fists and spat in my direction. I stepped back smartly.

"*Cabrão,*" she snarled, tossing her head to indicate the gun in my hand. "Go on, then, shoot me."

"Do you want me to?" I asked mildly, putting it back in my pocket. She glared at me. "You were the one who started the shooting." Sure, I was just walking along minding my own business.

"I missed."

Apart from agreeing with her, how do you answer that? "Your father wouldn't have been too pleased with you."

"You ruined his life, you know that?"

"No," I retorted. "I didn't. He ruined his own life. Mother of God, girl, it's been twenty years. Tell him to let go. If you have any influence over him at all." Though that seemed unlikely.

"You seduced his brother's wife."

I gave a bark of laughter. Couldn't help it. But really. "Is that what he told you?" I said incredulously. Though it made a kind of mad sense.

She surged forward in fury. I was conscious of Yeoh at my side putting out a restraining hand. I waved him back. "How you can *laugh—*"

"Listen," I interrupted. "She was forty years old. I was twenty-four. Who do you think did the seducing?"

Fire surged into her face. "I—I—*what?*"

"Elvira knew what she was doing," I said. Not that that really excuses me, of course. But pardon me if I want to hang on to the moral upper ground while I can.

"Twenty-four," Batista's daughter repeated. "You—*gigolo.*"

That burst the dam. I started to laugh, and then couldn't stop. "Gigolo?" I hooted, doubling over.

"I'm not hearing this." She turned abruptly and started to stride away. I stifled the laughter and took a step after her.

"Teresa," I said. She whirled round again. Apparently more scandalized that I'd used her Christian name than that I'd told her a truth she didn't want to know.

"What?"

"Think about it." I took out a cheroot. "Don't waste your life as well."

Her eyes narrowed, and she shot a minatory glance at Yeoh. "I should've recognized you, but I didn't. But I know you now." She turned back to me and said, "Next time, you might not have a watchdog."

"If there's a next time," I said, striking a match, "I won't need one."

"If there's a next time," she flashed back, "I'll bloody well castrate you."

And she stalked off. I decided to let her have the last word. It was better than carrying out the threat.

The funniest thing of all was not remotely funny. I liked her. Damn. Figure that one out.

9

THE NARROW BARE ROOM WAS STUFFY, THOUGH THE LATE SUN HAD NO DIRECT ENTRY, and dim with afternoon shadows. It was furnished only with a hard bed—cot would be a better description—and a small, unostentatious crucifix hanging on the wall. The only real evidence of human habitation was a half-empty glass of dusty water on the windowsill. Both the small window and its shutters stood open, but there was no breeze to stir the air, either outside or inside.

Outside, Lisbon baked in the summer heatwave under a sky of that particular luminous blue, azure, that evokes, all on its own, sky, sea, space, and summer. The deep blue air, showing nothing, being nowhere, being endless. Inside, Fr Jerónimo, kneeling on the bare boards, was used to discomfort. Welcomed it, in fact. Right now, it was an appropriate mortification of the flesh to accompany his prayers.

As he was not unintelligent, and far from insensitive, he was well aware that his failure to reach São Rafael was due to his desire to see the devil's work it harbored consigned to the flames of oblivion. However, he overlooked the fact that it was a branch of that very art which prevented him from entering the library. The fault, he concluded, was in himself. In his motives. They must be less than altruistic, somehow. In some way he didn't know.

So he prayed.

Holy Father, forgive me. I only wish to do your work. It is the works of Satan, the impure knowledge, no others, that we wish to expunge. I have no doubt the library also houses hundreds of good and worthy volumes of lore. We have no desire to rid the world of them. If there is a way to preserve such books for scholars whilst destroying the grimoires, the books of spells, the witches' manuals, all the knowledge of Hell, I pray for it most fervently. Let me only be admitted to São Rafael and all I will do is your work.

Resting his forehead on his hands, he wondered whether these words would be sufficient. Surely such intentions were for the greater good as well as being indisputably God's work. He sighed: he was not used to harboring doubts.

Unseen by him, a mouse crept back into the room, skirting the angle of the bare wall. And, somehow, his uncertainty went away.

In mouse-shape, the tiny remnant of the demon Mastiphal watched Fr Jerónimo. Intensely frustrated that what was once so great was now so small, it considered its options. Eventually, given the right conditions, it could resume its erstwhile size and power. But there was no short-cut. Growing back would take a long time, even as a demon might measure time.

There was, however, an alternative.

Even a fragment of a demon has certain powers. Unseen by the priest, Mouffi levitated to the window-sill and scuttled along until it came to the glass which stood there. It was a heavy tumbler, and an ordinary mouse might have had trouble, but one good shove from Mouffi and it crashed to the floor with sufficient force to shatter into a dozen pieces.

Startled, Fr Jerónimo's head jerked up. He blinked at the broken glass and made a pout of annoyance, then got to his feet and crossed the room.

The demon was counting on human nature. No one who breaks a glass ever fetches the brush first, and the priest was no exception. Squatting down, he started to pick up the larger bits of glass. Although he was being careful, he didn't know of Mouffi's purpose.

So when the mouse scuttled over his foot, his hand jerked and the shard he was holding sliced into his fingers. He dropped it with an inarticulate cry of pain, and his blood dripped to the floor in round red drops that feathered into the wet boards as they hit.

If he had been watching, he would have seen the mouse fade into his foot like water soaking into a cloth, but he was not. Lightheaded with the sudden shock and the blood, as well as the inadequate diet of an ascetic, Fr Jerónimo fainted.

And the essence of Mouffi—germs, as one might say, of Mastiphal—ran through his veins to his not unreceptive brain, taking possession quickly of the unconscious man.

* * *

You would hardly call certain aspects of my life normal. But sometimes something so bizarre happens that you start looking at some aspect of life in a completely different way. As if you've suddenly been skewed at a forty-five degree angle to it.

Developing sympathy with someone who's just tried to kill me, for instance. It doesn't rank up there with having my sight surgically altered by a demon. But it was pretty disorienting, I have to confess.

For now, I kept it to myself. It was a bit too strange to share with Yeoh. I could tell Emilia later, when we were alone.

Who, having expressed astonishment that I'd arrived home without anything that needed bandaging, was eyeing the amulet with distaste. Well, it had Paciência's husband somewhere inside it. Henriques Verdinho. A man we both knew.

"What are we going to do with it?" she asked, frowning. "Where can we hide it, until we find the others?"

"I suppose I could take it to São Rafael," I suggested, a little doubtfully. I didn't know whether the library's protection would extend to anything other than books. It hadn't helped Fr Pereira much.

"Sr Zacuto's room in the walls would be better," Yeoh said. Yes. A place out of time. Only there was one objection to that. Well, two.

"He wants to stay in the library," I pointed out, lighting a cheroot. "And we need him for one of the guardians."

Yeoh looked down at his hands. "Ah, well," he said softly. "As to that, I believe I can…find the place."

Of course. He manipulated time. I've seen him do it. The way he shifted in and out of the moment to avoid both blows and bullets was queasy to watch. But also, somehow, strangely exhilarating. And then a thought struck me.

"Could you create others, do you think?" I asked him. "The book says the stones need to be kept separate."

He contemplated the suggestion seriously for a while. "And this is why you are the captain," he said at last, smiling faintly and taking out his cigarette-case. "I do not believe I would have thought of that. But yes, now you mention it, the possibility is there. I believe I could. Folds, pockets in time Sr Batista could never hope to locate, because time is infinite. He could spend forever looking and still be no nearer finding them."

I stretched my legs out and exhaled smoke, wishing I could get out of my damp clothes. Wishing I could shed, at least, the damned eyepatch. Emilia, as usual, looked cool and tidy (except for that one persistent escaping strand of hair) and desirable. Ah. Not a good direction to send your thoughts, then, da Silva.

"You wanted Sr Yeoh to look at the list we made," she reminded me, giving me an escape route. I nodded, forcibly bringing my thoughts back to more urgent matters. Shifted about in the chair a bit.

"Yes," I said. "Since he guessed the Arab collector straight off." I turned to Yeoh. "What did you say her name was?"

"Fatima al-Ghuri."

"What does she collect?" Emilia asked.

Yeoh shrugged. "Jewelry, artefacts, art, books, anything of value," he replied absently. "She's a collector; she collects."

Emilia passed him her notes, saying, "We know who the second one is. *O senhor doutor* Bosque, who runs the orphanage in São Rocque." Yeoh took the paper and read it carefully. I watched him, wilting slightly. Also smoking, and puzzling over Teresa Batista. Somewhere, a trapped fly buzzed against a window.

After a few moments, Yeoh looked up and pointed his cigarette at me. "I can understand your not knowing these others, Captain da Silva, but senhora, most of these people have been involved in quite well-publicized scandals recently."

"I'm not really interested in that sort of thing," Emilia said mildly.

"Gossip, he's been listening to gossip," I exclaimed. "Or Teresa has. That's how they knew who to give the amulets to. What were the scandals?"

He sipped his tea. I'm surrounded by tea-drinkers. Pierce. Even Harris, sometimes. Who was snoring gently in the next room. Or who was with someone called Fatima al-Ghuri, somehow. Or, impossibly, in both places.

"Let me see," he said. "The wife of a jealous soldier. Some two months ago a certain Major Martinho was acquitted of attempting to murder his wife, whom he'd been convinced was having an affair."

"Oh, I do remember it," Emilia broke in. The tip of her tongue came out, tantalisingly, touched the corner of her mouth. "He tried to smother her with a pillow, didn't he? Desdemona!" She smacked herself on the forehead. "I should've thought of that!"

"I don't know where they live," said Yeoh, "but it will be easy enough to find out." He wrote the name "Martinho" on Emilia's paper. His handwriting somehow managed to resemble Chinese calligraphy. "Now let's see. Your 'orator' is a newspaperman, António Prado. Quite a well-known man. If you had ever seen him you would understand the 'eagle' reference." Yeoh traced the outline of a colossal *beque* on his own profile.

He made it sound so easy. I would've been days finding all this out. Days we don't have. Three cheers for John Yeoh. "What scandal was he involved in?" I asked, carefully tapping ash off the end of my cheroot.

"Someone accused him of bending the truth to suit his own purposes," Yeoh said. "A rival writer, I imagine. I do not know the details." Not interesting enough, I suppose. Our Sr Yeoh obviously liked a juicy bit of gossip. I raised an eyebrow and exchanged a glance with Emilia, who was evidently thinking the same thing.

She hid a smile behind her fingers and asked, "And the...wine-merchant? Is he a wine-merchant?"

Yeoh, writing, said without looking up, "An Englishman named Williams." A name none of us could pronounce properly. He put the pencil down. "He is an exporter rather than a wine-merchant. His wife, whose name escapes me, apparently tried to kidnap a child from the park. The little one's nanny caught her at it, though. Sra Williams later attempted suicide. I believe she is still in hospital."

"What hospital?" I asked, scratching my cheekbone absently. Yeoh sucked on his cigarette. The room had grown rather smoky.

"Not an insane asylum, if that's what you're asking." He finished his tea. "But perhaps she has been released by now."

The door-handle rattled, and I turned to see Harris. Dark shadows under his eyes like smudges of charcoal. His eyes looked out of focus. He leaned against the door-frame.

"Thought I heard voices," he said hoarsely. "How's it going, skipper?"

"It's progressing," I replied. "How are you feeling?"

"Like an elephant stomped on my head. Hullo, Mister Yeoh." Yeoh inclined his head politely to him.

"Mister Wolf."

Harris closed his eyes, frowned, and opened them again. Shook his head. "Can't seem to get anything to come clear."

"Can we get you something?" Emilia asked. I stubbed out my cheroot. Frankly, hoped he didn't want anything.

"No, thanks," said Harris after a moment's thought. "Believe I'll go back and sit down again. Feeling pretty goddamn strange." He withdrew, shutting the door. Yeoh was staring after him, an odd intense expression on his face.

"What is it?" I asked.

"The shape of his soul," said Yeoh. "The shape is there, but it has no substance. And yet he walks and talks."

Emilia, with a small frown, pulled herself upright, waving her hand at me as I started to stand as well. "No, Luís, don't get up. I'm just going to make sure Sr Harris is all right." She was using her stick rather than the crutch, so her leg was having a good day. As she passed me, she laid her hand briefly along my cheek. I touched her fingers. Looked up at her. "Behave yourself," she said softly, then moved away.

Now Yeoh was looking at me strangely. I heard the door shut behind me. "I loved my wife too," he murmured. Then shook himself. Ground the end of his cigarette out ferociously in the ashtray. And picked up Emilia's notes again. "The next person on the list is the woman you asked me about, the widow Al-Ghuri."

I pulled my damp shirt away from my chest and flapped it. Wished I could do the same with the damned eye-patch. I looked at the paper upside-down. "Was she involved in a scandal? Was the doctor, what's his name, Bosque?"

"Yes, to both," said Yeoh, nodding his head. "The orphanage had some financial trouble a while back. There was some suggestion that the *senhor doutor* had been helping himself out of its funds. But he turned out to be incompetent rather than dishonest. They brought in an accountant to help, I believe." And I bet that brought mercy and compassion to the orphans.

"What about the senhora Al-Ghuri?" I asked. Yeoh laughed.

"The police have been after *her* for years, and her husband before that. Everyone in town knows half the stuff in her collection is stolen, but no one's ever managed to prove anything."

The sound of the door opening made me turn round again. Emilia came back in, holding a bottle of wine in her free hand.

"How's Harris?" I asked, getting up and taking it from her.

"The same," she said. "With us but not with us. I told him we'll get him back soon. We will, won't we?" I put my arm round her shoulders and gave them a brief squeeze.

"Of course. Where's the corkscrew?" Oh, there. I picked it up and began stripping the foil from the bottle.

Emilia lowered herself back into her chair. I know perfectly well she can manage on her own. She does it all the time while I'm not there. She's done it since she was nine years old. But I still want to help her in and out of her chair.

"So," she said to Yeoh, looking down at the paper, "who has the sapphire? Who was going to be the final guardian?"

"I believe he used to be a leading light in the goldsmiths' guild at one time. Alexandre Aveiro. He's famous for his bad temper."

"Oh, Holy Virgin," exclaimed Emilia in disgust. "I should've known that. I was too caught up with the idea of a blacksmith, me of all people."

The cork came out of the bottle with a satisfying pop. I poured three glasses before even thinking to wonder whether Yeoh would want some. But he took it from me with a nod of thanks. "What's the gossip about this Aveiro, then?" I asked.

It was Emilia who answered. "He's always getting into trouble," she said, taking a mouthful from her glass. "I shouldn't laugh. But he's the one who's always so snooty about women being jewelers. I think he gets arrested several times a year for getting into fights. At his age. He tried to challenge someone to a *duel* last year sometime."

"What interesting lives jewelers do lead," I observed over the rim of my own glass, raising an eyebrow at her. Emilia stuck her tongue out. Speaking of people acting their age. Which philosophy is greatly over-rated. Invented by some stuffy old priest with no sense of humor, if you ask me. Yes, I know that goes for most of them. Proves my point.

"Well, that's all of them," she said, sounding a little surprised. That had been astonishingly easy. But then, so had every other bit of the puzzle. Once we knew how to solve it. Or who to ask to solve it. That's the trick.

"And have you also worked out who can stand against all the other guardians?" Yeoh asked me. I nodded, suddenly reluctant to share my conclusions. I don't know why. I took out another cheroot, to put off the moment.

"The thing is," Emilia said, "do we have to get the stones in the right order? Or can we release poor Sr Harris first?"

I struck a match. "In order, I would think. This whole damned business seems to be about patterns."

"So we...you need to go to Dr Bosque next," she said thoughtfully.

"Do you know him?" I asked. "Or just *of* him?"

"I've met him. He seems a nice enough man."

"He'll still turn into something called the executioner," I pointed out. Teresa wasn't at all nice, and she transformed into an invincible warrior. Which was not alien to her nature. A doctor, though. A man who saves lives. Would he remember, afterwards? Or would being an unwitting guardian protect him?

"Against the executioner, only the dead may stand," quoted Emilia. "You're thinking of Sr Zacuto, then."

"Yes," I said, drinking wine.

"He can't retrieve the stone," Yeoh said, and I could've kicked myself. Of course he couldn't. He was a ghost. Damn it, da Silva, any other fundamental things you've missed?

"We'll have to get Sr Pierce to do that, then," Emilia said. "The spell doesn't say the person who stands against the guardian has to be the same as the one who frees the soul in the amulet, does it?" She was quite right, of course.

"I'll have to ask Pierce first." I sighed. Scratched my eyebrow. "Well, I'll have to go to São Rafael to fetch Zacuto, anyway."

Yeoh drained his glass and got to his feet. "If you'll excuse me, I think I should secrete this stone somewhere. It feels far too vulnerable in my pocket. Where any common thief could find it, let alone Sr Batista."

"Where are you going to put it?" I asked him, a little concerned. Don't want it ending up somewhere only he can find again. Not that I don't trust Yeoh. But invulnerable or not, something might happen to him. What, I don't know. But can you blame me for worrying?

"Oh, this one I will simply take to Sr Zacuto's space," he said. "Until I can work out exactly how to make a...temporal pocket." He smiled. "Don't worry, Captain da Silva, I know more or less how it should be done. I just need to spend some thought on the exact method. Were you intending to confront the next guardian today?"

What's left of today? I pulled out my watch. No, probably not a good idea. Although I really do want to get all this over with as soon as I can. I finished my wine. I inhaled smoke, then blew it out. The room was decidedly hazy now.

"No. Should I go with you?"

"There is no need," he replied, with a twisted smile. "Truly. I am, it really seems, invulnerable." Ha. There you are. He doesn't think anything can harm him. Which probably meant there was something out there that could.

"Don't let it make you complacent," I said sharply. Look where it got me. "As you said, someone could pick your pocket." Yeoh smiled gravely.

"Senhor capitão, if you think I need to be guarded against pickpockets, by all means accompany me."

Something was urgently demanding that I do just that. Call it a sixth sense. Call it what you like. Sometimes it just works. I sighed again. Apparently I wouldn't be getting a bath any time soon. Or out of these sweaty clothes. Or anything else.

"Emilia, don't let anyone in while I'm gone," I said. She looked up. "Close the office early for once."

"What is it?" she asked, seriously. I shook my head.

"Probably nothing. Just humor me, *querida.*"

"All right."

I stood up, kissed her on the forehead, and turned to Yeoh. "We'll go out the back way."

"You're the captain," he said.

"Let's get out of here, then."

Once out of the house, the sense of urgency persisted. At least I was confident that the danger, whatever it was, was away from Emilia now. But I still don't know what kind of danger it might be. Human, demonic, sorcerous. No idea.

"What was it you sensed, senhor capitão?" Yeoh asked quietly. I walked through a clutch of ghosts before replying. Probably earthquake victims. They usually are when they're in a bunch like that.

"I'm not sure," I said. "But I suddenly got the idea that it'd be a very good idea to leave extremely quickly."

He looked around, as if he thought he could detect what I felt. "This threat, do you still feel it?"

"Yes." But not so strongly. "I think keeping on the move is the answer." Though I couldn't have said why. I don't even know whether whatever it was I sensed was looking for the stone or for me. Not too keen on either.

"Let's catch a tram or something, then," Yeoh suggested. I stared at him, half-wanting to laugh. Why did I never think of that? Because you're an idiot, da Silva.

Tram and funicular took us pretty near Zacuto's secret haven. Also a bit too close to the House of the Four Winds for my liking. But you can't have everything.

"You're sure you can get in without Zacuto being there?" I asked, not for the first time.

"Yes," he said patiently. "I can. But you do understand you won't be able to come in with me?" I nodded. "You are…too corporeal. Too anchored in time to move easily out of it. Though I could move you, if necessary, the experience would be unpleasant."

Watching Yeoh locating the hidden door brought back my last visit rather too vividly. I flinched at the memory. Felt the invisible mark on my chest throb once. And a strong urge to look round to my right.

What I saw made me break out in sweat again. It looked like a whirling vortex in the air. Reminded me rather too strongly of what the sky over the castle had looked like before two demons came roaring out of it. I unsheathed my knife at once and stepped between it and Yeoh. Battle stations.

"Ah, now would be a good time to get inside," I said to him over my shoulder. He grunted in reply. Fat lot of help that was.

From the vortex, a tail of air began to extrude like a tornado in formation. And I felt a tug like a ferocious wind, sucking me towards it, but not physically. My body wasn't being pulled. Something inside me was. Zacuto's mark felt red-hot.

"Hold firm, captain," muttered Yeoh. Easy for him to say.

The tail became a spinning cone of wind. A tornado right there in the alley. It was all I could do just to stand there. I strained against it, resisting the irresistible. Heard the blood pounding in my head. The cone grew in size, became monstrous. Bent over us like a giant contemplating mice. The whirlwind seemed to be casting about for something. This way, that way. As if it knew what it was looking for. I was suddenly convinced that the mark Zacuto had given me was preventing it from actually finding us. It could tug all it liked, but I was protected, and so was Yeoh.

It bent right over me now, and I began to make out the shapes of people in the spinning vortex. Or rather, a limb here, a hand there, an anguished face there. Where had it sucked them from? How long had they been imprisoned in that frightful tornado?

"Hurry up," I said, breathlessly.

"Got it," exclaimed Yeoh, and I felt him disappear. A split second later he popped back into existence. Grabbed my coat-sleeve, and pulled me through the wall.

I understood that Zacuto, when he was there, was the door, but Yeoh had found his own way in. Now I was in complete darkness. Didn't know up from down. Couldn't tell whether I was on my head or my ass. Rushing watery noise in my ears, loud as a hundred-foot sea. Strange, damp, metallic smell in my nose and a taste like blood in my mouth. My teeth ached. A wave of nausea rattled through my gut. Nose tingled like a sneeze aborted. I got the odd but vivid impression that my brain was pressing against the inside of my skull.

All this lasted less than an instant. Or more than an eternity. And then I was standing in the alley by the little shrine to the Virgin, looking at Yeoh.

"What the hell was that?" I asked. Though I could guess. The experience would be unpleasant, he'd said. He hadn't been joking.

"I took you out of time for a moment," said Yeoh. Well, nice to be right. I thought about swallowing. Had second thoughts. Tried to spit the vile taste away. That didn't work. I decided only a brandy would have the desired effect. "It worked, didn't it?"

"Yes," I said. "It did." I'd almost rather have had the whirlwind. Well, not really. "The agate?"

"Safe."

"Good." I smiled grimly. "Thanks."

"Nada," he said. "You'll bring me another stone tomorrow?"

"With luck," I said, then turned to go. The remnants of a breeze blew up a little eddy of paper scraps round my ankles. But that was only the weather.

* * *

She had always hated it when her father raised demons. Hated their hot meaty brazen stench. The way their presence seemed to insult the air, to wound it somehow simply by being there. They made her skin shiver all over, made it feel tender and sensitive as if with a fever. They made her sick to her stomach.

Today she hated it even more. Every time, before now, she had been able to justify it. A means to an end. The greater good. A politician's excuses. Or the last resort of a soldier: I was only following orders. But now, carefully-constructed certainties were crumbling like buildings in an earthquake.

It's been twenty years...Don't waste your life as well... The words echoed insistently, irritating as pebbles shaken in her skull. Why are you listening to *him?* she raged at herself. But even the rage was false. She touched her sore jaw angrily.

Every other time she'd encountered Luís da Silva, she had transformed. She'd never actually seen him before: the guardianship left little, if any, of Teresa awake or aware. When it possessed her, only the task remained, to protect the amulet at all costs.

Becoming the guardian had shocked her to her core, far worse each time it happened. It made her feel unclean and disgusting and violated, as if her soul itself had been brutally raped. Yes, the crest and surge of the power it gave her, raw and intoxicating, had burst in ecstasy inside her, incredible, blindingly bright; now it was gone she wanted to scrub every organ and muscle and bone and inch of skin until it bled. The change was an an abomination: the shit of it was stuck to her; she was riddled with it. Her mouth and throat and gut burned with an acrid taste like rancid rot, her head hammered and throbbed, and all her muscles ached as if a fever was racing through her body. Rank sweat ran from every pore, even she could smell how foul it was.

Trying to shoot da Silva hadn't helped at all.

My father did this, she thought. Used her, abused her. She had vowed even before she was old enough to understand never to be a victim, only to have it creep into her all unknowing.

How had her father's obsession taken her over so entirely that she had no time, no room for anything else? She was honest enough to recognize that she had been living a lie since the age of six.

After all that, she thought, da Silva was only a man. Not some kind of terrible seducing predator. Just human. Her father had lied to her. And not just lied. She had trusted him, given him her loyalty, her love...and he had betrayed her.

That last transformation had been the worst of all. It still roared and wailed in her brain, no hope, no light, no love, no joy, just the tides and storms of pain and shame. She had a horrible suspicion that if she hadn't been wrenched out of it, she might have remained there forever, a flayed soul pinned like a moth to a bleak bare mountain, with the memory of Inácio a faint moon in the black, small and cool and flawed as a pearl, mocking her with might-have-beens.

Her father had consigned her to hell for the sake of his pitiless, putrid vengeance.

—*Why does he hate you so much?* she imagined asking that man, that ordinary, not a monster, just a human, man.

—*Because he's mad,* she knew he would reply. And she also knew it was true.

Now she saw the image she had in her mind of her father through a shimmer, like a heat-haze. Saw da Silva, and could not equate him with evil incarnate.

Saw, with brutal clarity and for the first time, the full extent of the lie that she had lived; and was bitterly ashamed.

And now what was her father doing?

Somewhere in this tall white tranquil house, with its high-ceilinged rooms that the four winds blew through, and that had been named for them, he was conjuring demons. Again. She could feel it as surely as she could feel the heat of the sun. Feel it in the vibrations of the floor, in the sense of deep noise—noise that was not only too deep in tone to hear, but subterranean as well. It resonated somewhere that did not even have a physical location.

Teresa's scalp prickled. All the little hairs on the back of her neck were standing up. She restrained herself from picking up her saber. She knew it would do her no good. But damn, it would make her feel better. So she picked it up anyway, paced the room. She didn't want to know what it was he was speaking to. Which one of all the dozens he'd called up over the years to ask questions, to bind to tasks. She didn't want to know what he was doing.

The sensible thing to do, this new sensible part of her knew, would be to leave now. Cut her losses and walk away from him and start living a life. But she was too strongly tied to him. Too intimately, too tightly. He was, after all, her father.

For the first time, she began to consider how she might stop him.

* * *

The electric tram is a wonderful invention. And so is the funicular. These fruits of mankind's ingenuity conveyed Yeoh back to his shop. Leaving me to indulge in the single most significant contribution to the sum of human happiness. Which also happened to be the only thing that could take away the taste in my mouth.

Simple pleasures. Sitting in a bar. Sipping a drink. Observing the world at its affairs. Things I miss when I'm in the middle of the ocean. And things which are anchors to reality amongst increasing strangeness.

When I first started seeing ghosts I suppose I thought I could carry on more or less as before. Just as soon as I learnt how to ignore the damn things. Then I found myself hunting ghouls and soul-eaters and werewolves, not to mention ending up with one as my third mate. And it eventually got through the thick da Silva skull that perhaps I'd been given this new talent for a reason. Well, thanks very much. I didn't ask for it.

Seemed there wasn't very much I could do about it, though. I drank off the aguardente and called for another. After which I felt a little more attached to the world. Instead of drifting rudderless in a sea far too damn big for me.

Então. All this isn't getting me very far. Tomorrow I can collect Pierce and Zacuto and set them on this Dr Bosque. But that's going to need careful timing. Don't want him changing in the middle of a roomful of children, for instance. I took a thoughtful drag at my cheroot. Maybe I should go on a little reconnoitre.

The more I thought about that, the more it seemed like a good idea. As long as the man didn't see me. Because then I'd have something called the executioner mad at me, and that sounded like a very bad idea.

I knew where the orphanage was, of course. You can hardly miss that many children in one place. Fr Pereira was its priest, though. Which meant that the objectionable and obsessed Fr Jerónimo was standing in for him. Damn. I'll just have to hope that he's not around right at this moment.

In the end, I went for the direct approach. I loitered in the vicinity until I saw a woman who might have been an assistant, a nurse or a stenographer leaving to go home. Walked up to her, touched my hat, and asked, "Excuse me, senhora, would you know where I might find the *senhor doutor* Bosque?"

"Oh, I don't think he'll see anyone so late," she said doubtfully. "But he's usually in his office from nine to eleven in the morning." Which was exactly what I wanted to know. I thanked her politely and turned to make my own way home.

Ran smack into Fr Jerónimo.

For a moment we were both too surprised to react. Then I said "Excuse me" and he seized my arm. I had a shocked moment to find out how inhumanly strong his grip had suddenly become before he let go abruptly. His breath hissed between his teeth as though I'd ground my cheroot into his hand, and he recoiled from me. What was wrong with his eyes?

And my memory flipped back to the room in Venice where I first saw the rat-demon looking out at me from a dead man's face. At that I stepped back, and my hand went to my knife.

Before I could unsheathe it, though, a pack of people came chattering round the corner. Fr Jerónimo turned on his heel and hurried off, using them as camouflage.

I swore. I couldn't let him go. Who knows how much harm a possessed priest could do? Yes, I know, even more than one who's not possessed. Had he had a demon in him all the time? I'm sure he didn't. That, I would've noticed. This is a new thing. And I don't think Fr Jerónimo's dead, either. At least, his body isn't. His soul's another matter entirely.

Pushing through the sudden press of people, I started to run after him. Ignored a couple of ghosts standing in my way. If Fr Jerónimo's a newcomer to the district, there's a chance. If he knows it anything like as well as Zé, I've had it. I saw the edge of a black skirt vanish round a corner, and gave chase.

His height gave me one advantage. Two-thirds of the women in Lisbon wear black. Not many of them are six foot four. In the more usual sense, though, it's to his benefit. He's got longer legs than me. So he can run faster.

He darted up a flight of steps. I charged after him, taking them two at a time, but he'd still vanished when I reached the top. Right or left? Right, said the mental coin, coming down heads. A moment later I spotted him again.

He's an idiot, I thought. Or his demon is. All he really has to do is keep on my left, my blind side, and sooner or later I'll miss him. But the demon obviously doesn't want to cede the helm back to him. And that's good. Isn't it?

So where's he going? Leading me on a wild-goose chase, perhaps. Decoying me away from something, who knew what. Or it could be a trap. On the other hand, I might just be reading too much into it and all he's doing is running away from me.

Which is probably the case, because now I've lost him. I came to a halt and looked around, breathing hard. But there was no sign of him.

Merda. That was a waste of time. Time to go home, da Silva.

* * *

He didn't miss the tropics, not really. He certainly didn't miss the ramshackle hospital-cum-orphanage-cum-school that he'd spent so many years trying to make sense of. But sometimes he missed the simplicity of life there.

Dr Inácio Bosque was troubled, and he didn't know why. His hands, as he lit a cigarette, were shaking slightly, and he could identify no cause. The back of his neck was prickling, for no apparent reason. He also had a stupendous headache.

You would have said his life was going well enough, apart from the long-standing concern about his deteriorating sight. Since he'd returned from Mozambique, apart from that little nastiness with the finances, things had been pretty much perfect. The orphanage's financial worries were under control. He was doing a job he was not only good at, but thoroughly enjoyed. And his personal life was more than satisfactory. Dr Bosque smiled at the thought of Lídia, and a faint blush colored his cheeks. He smiled at that, too. Blushing, at his age! He permitted his thoughts to linger on that topic for a moment: he had never been with a woman that much taller before. It was…interesting, to say the least, the way things fitted together.

With a sigh, he brought his mind back to the present. His eyesight was getting worse, but what forty-seven-year-old man's wasn't? Almost unconsciously, his hand crept to the lucky charm that hung on his watch-chain. It was strange how Lídia had known. Or maybe not so strange, he thought. After all, she only had to look at the thickness of his spectacle lenses.

He took them off and rubbed his eyes carefully. They felt gritty in the humidity of his office, which had only one small window. And try as he might, he hadn't succeeded in opening the wretched thing any further than about two inches above its dead-insect-strewn sill. The heat didn't really bother him—after sixteen years in Africa, Lisbon even in a heatwave felt almost cool. He told himself he was tired. Working too hard.

Working to get as much as possible done before his sight went altogether. The doctor sighed. Yes, it was true enough, but it was hardly a new concern. There was something else, here, now, this evening. Something which *was* new.

Premonitions now, is it? he said to himself, wryly. Well, he'd been superstitious enough to accept the charm, hadn't he? And, if he would only admit it to himself, he'd seen magic enough in Mozambique. Children miraculously cured of terrible diseases as well as people cursed to death. There *were* more things in heaven and earth than anybody knew, and maybe this leaf-green stone was one of them.

Thoughtfully, he got to his feet and walked into the next room, which was the pharmacy. There he unlocked a cabinet with a key he took from his pocket and removed a small vial from it and carefully relocked the door. The vial went back into his office with him.

Dr Bosque sat down again at his desk, opened a drawer, and took out a hypodermic syringe in a box. He inserted the needle carefully into the vial and drew up about half the liquid. Then he put the syringe in the narrow central drawer of the desk with his pens, pencils and rulers.

He did not even notice that he had performed this entire operation without his spectacles.

* * *

The ghosts are restless. That's a bad sign. I know all the shades in the streets round my home by sight. And every last one of them is agitated.

Oh, God, I thought. I told Emilia not to let anyone in. She wouldn't have, either. But there are other ways of entering a house, for human malefactors at least. And humans are just as capable of evil as any demon. Just, luckily, not as powerful. Most of the time.

Heart pounding suddenly, I broke into a run. People got in the way. I cannoned into a solid old woman who was too slow to take evasive action. Nearly tripped over a cat, then sent a pair of gossiping women flying. They shouted after me, *balalao*, moron, idiot. I ignored them. Careered round the corner and skidded to a halt.

I'd found Fr Jerónimo.

He was standing outside my front door. It was closed. Obviously he couldn't get in, which was good. He was holding Zé by the arm. Which wasn't.

"Zé, are you all right?" I asked, swallowing a rush of fright. His face was white as paper, but he nodded. Seemed to be trying to speak, but nothing came out. "What do you want?" I said to Fr Jerónimo. Or whatever was in him. He seemed to consider it, staring at me with yellow unhuman eyes. Then he smiled. It was not the sort of smile you expect to see on a priest's face.

"Such a very *large* question," it said, and its voice was vast and hollow and echoed as if in a huge empty cave. "I could say: your soul. Or this boy's. Or even, all the souls in this city. In this world."

"What you want and what you get are two different things," I said, reaching for my knife. The terrible smile grew wider.

"Oh, take out your weapon, do," it said. "You think to murder a priest in the street? How…interesting the consequences of *that* would be."

Damn it. He—it—was right. I took my hand away from the hilt and scratched my cheekbone. Took a deep breath. Felt sweat running down my face.

"Let my son go," I said. Zé flinched, though it had done nothing I could see.

"You don't understand, do you?" The demon sounded amused. As far as

I could tell. "You are in no position to make demands. This little priest thought you corrupt, Luís da Silva. He couldn't have been more wrong, could he?" I didn't reply. Just wiped sweat from my face. "How gratifying it would be to possess such as you."

Possession. Ah no. Not while I live. Not at any other time, either. I tried to gather my scattered wits. This thing was possessing the priest. Who had mentioned a name. What was it? For God's sake, this is not the time for old age to kick in, da Silva!

"I'm not even a Christian," I said, stalling for time.

"As if that matters," laughed the demon.

"You can go straight back to hell." I took hold of Zé's other arm, and a shockwave knocked me backwards. I staggered, keeping my feet with an effort. The expression on the priest's features never changed.

"A simple choice, Luís da Silva. I shall go from this place owning a soul. Will it be your son's? Or yours?"

I bared my teeth in a grin. "It won't be either," I said. "Go away, Mouffi."

The priest's hand sprang away from Zé's arm, and a horrible grimace distorted his features. For a split second his eyes looked human. And terrified. Then the sickly yellow color bled back into them. I gave Zé a push.

"Get inside now." He didn't need to be told twice.

"Who told you that name?" grated the demon.

"You're not very powerful, are you?" I said nastily. "Otherwise you'd know it was that poor silly priest you're inside."

It opened its mouth and hissed at me. "This isn't over yet, Luís da Silva." I shrugged. Took out a cheroot and lit up. The grand gesture, you see.

"You can say *my* name all you like," I remarked. "It doesn't give you any power over me. But I know your name, and you aren't strong enough to break that."

Fr Jerónimo's hand came up and scratched at his chin. Blood followed his nails. The demon's control was less than perfect, obviously. "Everything changes," it said, then walked away. I let it go. It posed no threat. Or not much of one. At least, not for now.

I opened the door and went in. Closed it behind me. Sagged against it, wearily. Don't make me open it again until tomorrow, I thought. I've had enough of ghosts and demons and whirlwinds and guardians and all the rest of it. All I want is a bath, and a meal, and a drink, and a bed with Emilia in it.

That went unanswered, of course. Because what I had was a Zé clamoring to know what the devil all that was about. He was still rattled, and jumped when I put my hand on his shoulder. If I'd been tempted to say "later", that changed my mind. I owe him that much. And besides, I still had to tell him what I wanted him to do to help retrieve the amulet that held Felipe prisoner. I put my arm around his shoulders, and he didn't shrug it off.

"What just happened?" he asked in an unsteady voice. "That priest—" He shuddered.

"It's all right now, Zé," I told him, trying for a reassuring tone.

"He—" Zé swallowed. "He caught me this morning, wanted to know where the library was."

"I know. Did he seem the same to you?"

"No, he didn't." So the demon had taken him after that. Did that information help at all? Not really. "What's the *matter* with him?"

"He's possessed," I said. Even the shape of the word feels unpleasant in the mouth. I sucked in some smoke.

"Possessed?" Zé repeated. "What, by a, a *demon?*" No, by the queen of the fairies, what the hell do you think. Sarcasm not appropriate here, da Silva. I nodded. Zé went on, "What if he comes after me again?"

That, I could help him with. "Just use its name. Say, go away, Mouffi."

"That's all?" He looked doubtful.

"That's all," I said, ruffling his hair. He scowled automatically and ducked away. All right, I'm teasing him. "Trust me on that."

"Ha," he said, cheering up somewhat. "You mean he'll do what I say if I use his name?"

I raised an eyebrow. Realized I could actually rid myself of the eyepatch now and dragged it over my head. My hair was sopping wet. I pointed my cheroot at Zé. "Don't go trying anything silly. Making him go away is quite enough, believe me."

"Sr Costa made me clean out the heads because I was late," he said, with apparent irrelevance. "'Cause of that stupid priest." He pulled a face.

Well, yes, Fr Jerónimo *was* a stupid priest. He'd let in the demon. Or at least opened a pathway for it. His obsession with São Rafael, I suppose.

"I'll sort him out," I promised, blowing out smoke. And so I will. Because it couldn't be left undone.

* * *

The morning was already sweltering at eight o'clock. No let-up to the heatwave, then. Unbroken blue skies again. Skies that I now tend to look at with suspicion. Considering what's come out of them recently. Not weather, but demons. Paranoiac— who, me?

Not for the first time, I found myself getting irritated at all the clothes we civilized folk have to wear. Wished for a breeze. Rain. Anything to break the monotony. Didn't get my wish, of course.

Early as it was when I got to São Rafael, Pierce was already seated at the table. No surprise there, then. Zacuto, of course, had never left.

"We got the first stone," I informed them.

"Well done!" Pierce exclaimed.

"Indeed," said Zacuto, more restrained. I looked at him and raised my eyebrows questioningly. He inclined his head. "I have some answers for you, yes. You will not like them, I fear." What a surprise.

"I don't like anything at all about this business, period," I said.

"Of course, senhor capitão," he agreed blandly. "I did not mean to imply that you did." I saw Pierce smirking, and grinned ruefully back at him. Zacuto went on. "First of all. The Eidolon is one of the so-called Great Spells of making and unmaking. Once a sorcerer sets out to construct one of these spells, it can only be terminated by his death. Otherwise it is self-perpetuating. It exerts such a hold over its initiator, too, that he literally cannot stop attempting its completion."

Wonderful. I scratched my eyebrow. Said, finally, "He was always going to have to be killed." A complicated mixture of tenses, that. Note the use of the passive voice. I'd had enough of Zacuto taking me to task. He knew it, too. Smiled with his eyes.

"If that task falls to you, Captain da Silva," he said, "I for one will attach no blame for it." Thanks a lot. He may not have a problem with it. But I do. Killing a man in cold blood would mean crossing a line I never meant to cross. Well. I'll go over that bridge when I come to it. I exhaled, explosively. If I can't smoke I can blow air.

"What else have you found out?" I asked.

Zacuto steepled his fingers like a schoolmaster. "Your killing of the demon sent to gather your soul will delay him for a while. He will need to reconfigure the spell to allow for the use of a substitute demon to gather you. You have a few days at most."

A few days. And then I'd have to make the decision. Come to terms with it, da Silva. It has to be done.

"In addition," Pierce went on, "he's going to gather new souls to replace the ones you manage to get back. Ah, there is one good thing about it. He won't know when you take them from their guardians. They have to be kept apart until the moment of joining, and that means he can't, ah, monitor them."

The two scholars, one alive, one dead, had identical expressions on their faces. A mixture of pride in their discoveries and distress at what they'd discovered.

"A few days," I said.

"Yes," replied Zacuto.

"Better get a move on, then," I said, feeling an old queasy urgency inside. "Sr Zacuto, did you remember anything to do with the name Mouffi?"

"Ye-es," he said slowly. "It was once a name for a witch's familiar in France. Rather an obscure one."

"It's a bit more than a familiar," I said dryly. "It's possessing Fr Jerónimo. Can you exorcise it?"

The ghost blinked. "Indeed. The same way I freed you of your burden."

"In the walls?" I asked bluntly.

"Of course. Or here. Which is removed from time in a different way."

I had to laugh. After all his machinations and effort had failed, I had to bring the wretched priest here anyway.

"Well, gentlemen," I said, getting to my feet, "I'm going to need both of you to retrieve an amulet this morning."

Pierce took off his spectacles and gaped at me. "From the executioner?"

"Against whom only the dead can stand," Zacuto finished. "My presence I understand. But Sr Pierce?"

"To take the stone from him, Sr Zacuto. Or have you thought of some way you could pick it up yourself?"

He stared at me. I'd actually taken the wind out of his sails. He hadn't thought of it either. I scratched my cheekbone to stop myself from smiling. Wasn't going to admit it had been John Yeoh who'd had to point it out to me. We all need to score points sometimes.

"No," he admitted. "I regret to say I have not."

"Do either of you have any idea what 'the executioner' will look like?" I asked them. "Judging by what happened to Teresa Batista it could be dramatic, and we don't really want anyone seeing it. Dr Bosque's usually in his office from nine to twelve. So the sooner we go the better."

Zacuto shook his head to my question. "Plenty of the books show us engravings of demons, but remember, this spell is both little-known and very old. We do not know how any of the guardians will manifest. The corruptor, the destroyer, the castrator. They could appear in any form."

At the word *castrator* I saw Pierce wince and shift in his chair. An

uncomfortable word for those of us who're alive. But he only had to confront
the executioner. I'm sure that was a great comfort to him.

"What's the plan, then?" he asked, taking a deep breath and pushing his
spectacles up.

"Can you look like a potential benefactor?" I asked him.

* * *

The House of the Four Winds was utterly silent. Teresa could hear not
only the sound of her breathing, but the steady pounding of her heart as
well, like one of those great elaborate engines men of the previous century
had loved to build, all pistons and cogs and gleaming brass. The Victorian
era, they called it, naming an epoch after the tiny English queen as if her
empire had spanned the entire world instead of only half of it. Nowadays,
things seem to be built on a smaller scale. Or was that just her?

It was very early. The air was still cool, or as cool as it got these days, but
it remembered the scent of jasmine. Teresa dressed quickly and quietly, in
pants and shirt, how scandalous! or so people would have said if anyone had
seen her, and took herself down to the fencing salle to exercise for an hour.

Her father had given her this, cultivated her strength and her will as if
she'd been his son rather than his daughter. And she still loved that he had
done that.

But she couldn't let him carry on. Anger gave her workout a cruel edge,
and she was soaked with perspiration when she was done.

When she left the house, rather more conventionally dressed, it was still
only half-past seven. By now, though, the day's breathless heat was beginning
to build as the sun rose up a clear and limpid sky.

She was far too early, even if she walked all the way, and slowly.
Fleetingly, she considered going to his apartment, but that was out of
character for Lídia in the morning. No, she would stick to her original plan
and call at his office. Killing time proved surprisingly easy, stopping for
coffee, looking in shop windows, mingling with the crowds hurrying to
work, clerks and stenographers and shop-girls at this hour, later would come
the bankers and the businessmen and the lawyers, treading the same streets
as their minions but in such a much loftier way.

At last she heard the massed brazen clangor of a myriad church clocks
marking the hour of nine— she was aware she didn't really hear so many,
but one evoked another, echoes rebounded down all the narrow alleyways,
the idea of bells resonated over the city, setting pigeons to flight from
squares and rooftops.

Teresa knocked at the door, and the sour-faced maidservant admitted her. Graça, she was called, Teresa's middle name. What a person to share it with, and so inappropriate too for someone so singularly graceless and evidently not born on a Tuesday if the rhyme was to be believed. She dropped her martial scowl, let her shoulders droop slightly, took smaller steps. Waved the woman away, who withdrew, bristling. The sound of children's voices echoed, a happy clamor all the more pleasant for being distant.

Inácio Bosque looked up as she came in, and the sun came out in his face. Of all the amulet-holders, she disliked deceiving this one the most, with his thick bull's-eye spectacles and his untidy hair and his mischievous smile. Naturally enough, because she hadn't shared a bed with any of the others. She still wasn't quite sure how that had happened. Perhaps he was just so unlike anyone else she'd ever met. Kind. Generous. No hidden agenda.

A dreadful, unrealistic thought came to her then. What if she were to abandon her father and his schemes for this man? Her whole body throbbed, not with desire (though that was incipient in the sensation) but with possibilities.

"Lídia," he said. "How lovely to see you," and kicked himself mentally for the banality of the statement.

She smiled, and anyone who knew her would have marveled at the shyness of that smile, that she was capable of dissembling so wonderfully well. You should be on the stage, Teresa.

How to tell him she wanted the stone back? There it lay, on his watch-chain. Innocent-seeming, yet that green gem held someone's soul. She didn't even know whose. Before, it hadn't mattered. Now, it seemed vaguely obscene.

He had taken her hands, still smiling. She was on the point of speaking when a knock came at the door and Graça came in, evidently heralding an envoy of some kind.

"Gentleman to see you, *senhor doutor*," she said sullenly.

"Did he give his name?" His tone was amused rather than censorious: Graça could give old Cerberus a run for his money, but everyone put up with her nonetheless as part of the furnishings and fittings.

"Sr Pierce." Teresa stiffened, her hands still enclosed in the doctor's, and he raised his eyebrows at her. She shook her head slightly and reclaimed her hands, smoothing the palms down her skirt.

"Don't go," he said. She had no intention of going, so she smiled and sat down on the settee rather than one of the visitors' chairs. She knew she could reach him fast enough from there. At least, she hoped so. Her own guardianship, disgusting though it still was to her, had enhanced her already formidable strength and speed. And Dr Bosque was a far more sedentary person than she was.

Graça showed Pierce in, the thin, slightly-stooped scholar she remembered. But who was that with him, this strangely-attired man? Teresa had no time to speculate about it. The doctor opened his desk drawer and took out a hypodermic.

She was moving before he could aim it, but the guardian was even faster than she'd expected and had lunged at Pierce's companion before she could grab his wrist. She seized it an instant later and wrenched the syringe out of his hand. It fell to the floor.

"Whichever's the scholar, take the amulet *now*," she snapped, holding the struggling guardian by both wrists, and stamped hard on the hypodermic. It shattered, and the smell of bitter almonds rose, pungent in the stuffy office. Pierce, startled into movement, stepped forward and pulled Dr Bosque's watch from his pocket.

Instantly, the doctor sagged, and Teresa caught him, dragging him to the settee. Only then did she realize that the other man was still standing, and yet she had seen the needle plunge into his chest—oh. "You're a ghost," she said. "The dead man."

Zacuto nodded. "And that, I presume," he indicated the remains of the syringe, "is the executioner's tool."

Pierce, meanwhile, had removed the stone from Dr Bosque's watch fob and replaced it with an identical one. He held out the watch to Teresa, his eyes wary.

"What are you up to?" he demanded.

Teresa sighed, unable to summon up her customary anger. She didn't reply at once, but put her hand to the doctor's forehead.

"I know you'll find it hard to believe, Sr Pierce," she said, "but you could say I've come to my senses. You should take the amulet and go, before he wakes up."

"Will he remember what happened?" asked Pierce, eyeing the unconscious man with suspicion and vaguely surprised at the tenderness of her gesture.

"No, not if I can get rid of that syringe," she replied. Pierce took off his spectacles and polished them nervously.

"I don't understand," he said. "What—"

"Sr Pierce," Teresa interrupted, "Take that stone, now, and hide it wherever you've planned. I promise I'll explain everything to you when I can."

The antiquarian gave her a long raking unforgiving stare and hurried out of the room, Zacuto at his heels.

* * *

I would've said that Pierce looked as if he'd seen a ghost when he and Zacuto emerged from the orphanage. Except, of course, that he'd gone in there with one in the first place. I took the cheroot out of my mouth.

"Did you get it?" I asked, concerned at his expression. Wondering how the hell the executioner had manifested to make him look like that.

"Yes," he said tightly. "Let's get it to your Sr Yeoh." I raised my eyebrows at this peremptory tone. He gave me a nervous smile.

"Come on, then," I said, and started walking. Zacuto fell into step beside me. He hadn't uttered a word. "Pierce, spit it out. What the devil happened in there?"

He took off his spectacles and polished them with the corner of his jacket. "Teresa Batista," he said. I stared at him. "She was in there with the doctor. He—" He moistened his lips with his tongue. "He came at us with a syringe of prussic acid."

"The twentieth-century executioner's tool," Zacuto observed sourly. "So much *neater* than the auto-da-fé." Pierce glared at him.

"Anyway," he went on, "She knocked it out of his hand and stamped on it, and told us to take the amulet and get out. So we did."

Well, that was a turn-up for the books. What was she up to? "Did she say anything else?" I asked him.

"She said she'd explain when she could," Pierce replied. I contemplated this. Gave my eyebrow a rub. An aid to thought. Couldn't fathom her change of heart. If that was what it was. Had she actually taken note of what I'd said? Seemed about as likely as her sprouting wings.

"Captain da Silva," Zacuto murmured in my ear, "something approaches." I turned quickly—he was on my left—but could see nothing except the usual ghosts.

"What?" I asked him quietly. Threw the butt-end of my cheroot away. Reached for my knife. But the ghost shook his head.

"I cannot tell. I feel...a disturbance. Like, perhaps, the air before a thunderstorm."

"Pierce, give me the amulet," I said. He took it out of his pocket and handed it to me without argument. "Take Sr Zacuto back to the library." If I had to fight something, I didn't want him getting in the way. Or, if I had to run, I was pretty sure he couldn't keep up. Me, I'm getting a lot of practice these days.

When they'd gone, I had a good look round in all directions. Still couldn't see anything but ghosts. Couldn't feel anything. But, after a moment, I heard something. The sound of footsteps, running fast. I had the knife out in a split second, but I was just as ready to take to my heels. I felt a drop of sweat run down my face. Felt my heart pounding. Whoever or whatever pursued me, it was very close now. I turned to face the new threat.

And Teresa Batista came charging round the corner, stopping short at the sight of me. Not even out of breath.

"I've been looking for you," she said.

10

I put the knife away cautiously, watching her all the time. It's not often that I find myself completely speechless. Usually can't stop myself from making some comment. Must be where Zé gets it from. The silence stretched between us until it seemed something was going to snap. At last I said, "Senhorita—"

"You may as well use my name," she remarked. "You did when I tried to shoot you." Her voice had lost the bitter ferocity of that last encounter. And her face, as well, was less stern. Younger-looking. Slightly exotic, in the way some *brasileiras* are. Still haughty and aristocratic, but that was inherited. She can't help that. I realized I was staring at her but what the hell, I think I'm allowed to stare at someone who's tried to kill me more than once. Anyway, she was staring, too.

Sidestepping the question of what to call her, I said neutrally, "Thank you for your help."

"You're not at all what I expected," she said. Then shook herself. "We have to get away from here. He'll send a seeker after the amulet. Do you have somewhere to hide it?"

"Yes," I replied, not eager to betray Yeoh. She must've read my thought.

"I don't want to know. He might read it from me. But I do know how to…neutralize the seeker." She looked around, biting her bottom lip. Her teeth were very white, I noticed irrelevantly. "We should go. You can confuse them by keeping on the move."

"Found that out last time," I agreed. Teresa looked at me with narrowed eyes.

"What did he send?"

I saw no harm in telling her. "A sort of whirlwind thing."

"A Hofftman vortex," she muttered, and added a very unladylike curse. I started walking in the general direction of Yeoh's shop. She kept pace easily. After a while she ventured, "I thought about what you said to me."

There was nothing at all I could say in reply to that, of course. Da Silva, tongue-tied twice in less than five minutes. I stuck my hands in my pockets and eventually came up with *"È verdade?"* Which was beyond pathetic, but I still wasn't quite sure whether she was going to shoot me or not.

This is surreal. I'm walking along with this tall imperious woman who's spent most of her life being taught to hate me, and *I'm* supposed to reassure *her?* Oh yes, and there's something called a seeker following us. Something inimical, I've no doubt at all.

"I've been thinking about my father, too." She stopped abruptly and turned to face me, reaching out with one hand. I tried not to flinch back, but she checked for a moment. Then touched the scar on my cheekbone. Her fingertip was very warm. I felt a drop of sweat trickle down the side of my face.

"What did this?" she asked.

"A demon," I replied. The slight pressure of her finger seemed curiously intimate. I heard her breathing, and it struck me as odd. Since she hadn't been out of breath at first. And then I suddenly realized that I was breathing faster, too. Nervous, who, me? "Come on, you were the one who said we should keep moving."

"Did you kill it?" She took her hand away and started walking again.

"No." I took a deep, rather ragged, breath and decided I needed a smoke. My hand trembled slightly as I struck the match.

"How long ago was that?" Teresa asked. "Don't look round."

"Five years." I took a drag on my cheroot. It steadied me a bit. But I still wanted to glance over my shoulder.

"My father didn't know what he was getting into," she remarked, absently. So she'd gotten to the point of making excuses for him, had she? "I don't mean that as an excuse."

Então, maybe not. "Listen, Teresa—" I began. She interrupted me.

"Keep talking about other things," she said in a low voice. "Sometimes it confuses them." I thought she'd said she knew how to deal with any pursuer.

"Them?" Making small talk while being stalked by something invisible isn't one of my strong points. Being told it's essential made me unable to think of anything to say. For the third time in a row.

"Nobody likes to think they've been used," she went on. I raised my eyebrows. "But he did, he used me. And that's worse than anything you…might have done. He betrayed me. I can't forgive him for that."

I made a non-committal noise and scratched my cheekbone. It still seemed to remember what her finger felt like. Looked sideways at her. Face flushed, lips slightly parted. I realized I wanted to kiss her.

Oh now, come on, da Silva. Of all the inappropriate reactions. Here you are, forty-four years of age, missing one eye. There she is, twenty years younger, and her father is your worst enemy. I don't think kissing is the most constructive thing you could be doing. Or even thinking about. I sucked in smoke instead, and wondered if she knew what I was thinking.

Apparently not, because the next thing she said was "They're very close."

"How can you tell?" I asked curiously.

"Because my father sent them." Well, that made sense.

"Do you know what they are?"

"Yes. That knife of yours, does it have silver in it?" I nodded, and she smiled grimly. "Then we may do better after all. Take it out, captain," she went on. "It won't do us any good hidden down your back."

She was right there. I did as I was told. "So, what are they?"

"I don't know what they're called. The important thing is, they're invisible." Oh, great. "But sprinkling salt water on them neutralizes them. They lose their power for a few moments. They also become visible. And they can be killed with silver."

"Good," I said.

"Be ready. You won't have much time." She took a bottle from her bag, and pulled the cork out. "And don't let them touch you." I had no intention of that, thank you very much. I've taken enough damage from Batista's various pals.

"Can you tell how many?"

"Two, just two. They hunt in pairs. *Now!*" She flung the brine in a wide arc, and suddenly two hunched, long-limbed figures splashed into view. Their skin was naked, grey and wrinkled. They had no eyes. But they lunged at us, gibbering. Obviously they could see perfectly well. Just not the way we do.

Teresa skipped back nimbly, and I slashed at the nearer creature. Which dodged back even more nimbly, moving like a spider, and snapped its teeth at me. They had long bony heads, rather like horses' skulls. But without the eyesockets. I caught it on the backswing, and the knife passed right through it. It disappeared, but the lack of resistance caught me off balance.

Which was just as well, as it turned out. Because it meant the other one, which had sprung at me, missed me altogether. It flashed alarmingly but harmlessly past my face, Teresa kicked out at it, and I stuck the knife in its back as it went by. Just like its companion, it vanished.

That was easy. I wasn't even out of breath. Though I was sweating.

Surprise, surprise.

"Is that—"

"Now you need to hurry," said Teresa. "He'll know you've killed them, but it'll take him a while to send more. And if you've hidden that stone by then, there'll be no point in his sending anything else."

Now I could think of a lot of things to say, but none of them was appropriate. Instead I just said again, "Thank you."

"Listen," she said, putting her hand on my arm, "I'd like to do more, but I won't be able to help you get any of the other amulets back. The stones will recognize me as a threat now. Unless you know a witch who can make a masking spell."

"I know a witch," I said. But could Paciência work with the woman who helped imprison her husband's soul? More importantly, would she?

Well, you know the answer to that one, da Silva. You'll just have to ask her.

"Go," said Teresa.

"Where will you be?" I asked.

She blinked, then said, "The church where— where we first met." Well, that was accurate enough, I suppose. Though "met" isn't quite how I'd describe it. I nodded, and set off at a trot.

* * *

"What kept you?" John Yeoh asked me. "Your senhor Pierce has been here some time."

I handed him the gemstone, and he folded his fingers round it. "A pair of seekers. And Teresa Batista. What's Pierce doing here?"

"Ask him, Captain da Silva. As you know, I have to hide this stone. And quickly."

Wiping sweat out of my eyebrows, I followed him into his shop. To be met by the ticking of a hundred clocks. I wondered how he could live with this constant reminder of how much time had passed. Or perhaps that was the point.

As Yeoh disappeared with the amulet, Pierce looked up distractedly and pushed his spectacles up to the bridge of his nose. On his lap was a venerable-looking tome. Trust him to find something like that to read. Not that he was reading it.

"What's up?" I asked him, leaning against the counter.

"It's the *Book of Souls.*" Oh God, what now? "Or rather, the translation. I think Zacuto would've told you earlier, but he was distracted by that amulet for some reason."

"He thinks the soul in it may be one of his descendants," I told him. Pierce looked baffled.

"But I thought it was a priest," he said, so I had to explain about Pereiras and Coelhos and the rest.

"Never mind that now. What about the book?"

He frowned "You know the bit about the soul of a lover."

"May only be released by a lover, yes," I said a little impatiently, taking out my cheroots. Only two left. Have to get some more. Ha. Least of my worries. I hunted for matches.

Pierce took off his spectacles. "Our friend Zacuto thinks the translation should be, *may only be released by* his *lover."*

Damn. Paciência really isn't going to like this. I stuck a finger under my eyepatch. As usual, no relief to the humidity. "Ah," I said intelligently, since he seemed to want some reaction.

"Why don't you take that wretched thing off?" asked Pierce, polishing his spectacles with no awareness of irony. "You're always fiddling with it." I laughed. Looked pointedly at his hands. He glanced down and gave a rueful smile. "Point taken," he said. Replaced the spectacles on his nose. "Do we know the young man's inamorata?"

One of them, anyway. "Sra Verdinho's daughter."

"Oh," said Pierce. "She won't be best pleased." He doesn't know the half of it. "Prickly woman, that." English has some wonderful images.

"Yes," I agreed, picturing a sort of porcupine-witch hybrid. Yeoh reappeared. He had a satisfied expression on his face. I raised an eyebrow at him, and he nodded.

"Safely stowed," he said.

"Where did you put it?" I asked curiously.

"Senhor capitão," he said, "should I be unable to retrieve the amulets when the time comes, you will find that Sr Zacuto has given you the key."

The key of Solomon. So that was what it was. But it had also seemed to give me some protection. Useful thing all round, then. I put my hand over it, but could still feel no sign of it. Yet Emilia could trace its outline…Thinking of Emilia tracing the outline isn't going to get me very far now. I put the image out of my mind and shifted position. Took a long drag on my cheroot for good measure.

"Do we move on to the next one now?" Pierce asked.

"Couple of people to see first," I said, grateful for the distraction.

"Yes, I suppose so," he nodded. "Sra Verdinho and—who?"

"Teresa Batista," I said.

John Yeoh broke in, a cigarette halfway to his mouth. "Captain da Silva, what is this woman up to? The last time I saw her she was trying to kill you. And now Sr Pierce tells me that she *helped* him retrieve the amulet I've just concealed. What is behind this change of heart?"

Maybe Yeoh, whose constancy had given him his strange immortality, couldn't understand changes of heart. Though I didn't wholly understand Teresa's myself. "I think you'll have to ask her that," I said. "May I borrow your telephone?"

"Of course," said Yeoh, gesturing towards it. I still don't like them. But they have their uses. Da Silva embraces modern technology. Is that a pig passing by the upstairs window?

I asked the voice that answered if Paciência was there. A long silence followed, noisy with mechanical sounds, broken at last by an imperious contralto. Evidently she thought you needed to shout down the wire as well. We could yell at each other, then. And perhaps wouldn't need the telephone at all.

"Who is this?"

"Dona Paciência, it's Luís da Silva. I'm afraid we need your help again. And also your daughter."

Outrage travelled down the wire. Isn't science wonderful? "Luzia? She's only nineteen. Can't she be left out of this?"

"I'm sorry," I said, "but no." And I told her what Pierce had told me.

"Damn the boy," she said, but without heat. I breathed a sigh of relief. The ash from the end of my cheroot fell to the floor at that point. I looked round at Yeoh, but he and Pierce were deep in conversation, so I spread the ash around surreptitiously with the toe of my shoe. "We'll come right away," she went on.

"Thank you," I said. The other news could wait. Right now I had to meet Teresa Batista again. She broke the connection, and I hung up slowly. Turned to Pierce. "What did you do with Zacuto?"

"Left him back at the library," he replied. What I'd expected.

"Oh, senhor capitão," Yeoh said, scribbling something on a piece of paper, "here's the address of Sra Martinho. She's staying with her sister." I took the paper and stuffed it in my pocket.

"Right," I said, disposing of the remains of my cheroot in an ashtray full of dog-ends, "I'm off to meet Teresa Batista again. Anyone want to come along?"

Pierce looked at me over his spectacles, a slight frown on his face. "Yes," he said. "I'm curious. I want to know why she suddenly decided to help us." I glanced questioningly at Yeoh, who shook his head.

"Much as I would like to," he said, "I have a case-clock that won't repair itself and customers for whom time is an urgent thing full of deadlines and impatience."

Pretty much sums up the human condition, that.

We left the shop. Stepped out into the oven of midday. I was going to have to go down to *Isabella* soon. I have perfect confidence in Ashley and Costa, of course, and all they have to do now is get the next cargo on board. But I think I might've mentioned that I can't stop trying to do everything myself.

"How'd you wind up a shipowner?" Pierce asked me. Apparently reading my mind. "Last time we met—"

"A lot can happen in twenty years," I said. Then relented. "The Venetian—"

"Della Quercia."

I never say the name. Call it superstition if you like. "That one."

"How did he die?" Well, I wasn't going to tell him that. I shrugged.

"He disappeared," I said. It was quite true. If you're being absolutely pedantic. Though it wasn't until much later that I realized why. He'd been possessed by the demon he summoned. Not just possessed, but physically somehow *riddled* with it. And that corrupted, or infected, his flesh so badly that when it left, his body just crumbled to dust. It's why I use holy water. Maybe if I'd thought to use it on my eye a bit earlier, I wouldn't now be seeing ghosts. Ah well. Not really worth expending thought on.

"And?" enquired Pierce. I came back to the present. Walked determinedly through a ghost that had decided not to move out of the way. Lit my second-last cheroot. Must remember to stop at the next tobacconist's. And one of these days, a barber.

"Left a mass of debts," I said. "So we bought *Isabella* for next to nothing." Simple as that. Pierce seemed to sense that I wouldn't be drawn any further on the topic and lapsed into silence.

By unspoken consent, we walked in the shade. Pierce pushed through ghosts he couldn't see. I wondered what his reaction would be if he knew they were there. Probably much the same as mine when I first started seeing the damn things. Spent most of my time trying to get out of their way. Until I realized that, one, they couldn't feel anything, and two, I was reeling about like one of those muttering old loons you cross the street to avoid. You know, the ones who always sit next to you on a tram.

"Teresa Batista," he said, after a while. "Amazing. She scares the living daylights out of every man in Rio."

And I'd wanted to kiss her. I examined this reaction. I felt guilty now. But it was just a reaction. Like recoiling from something repulsive. Well, quite the opposite, to be truthful. Are we being a mite defensive here, da Silva? Still, I don't normally go round wanting to kiss every woman I meet. I wouldn't dream of kissing Paciência, for instance. Meu Deus. Perish the thought. I've no wish to have a hex banged on me.

Teresa was in the church. There was no sign of Fr Jerónimo, though I looked for him. And I had to do something about him, too. Just had to hope the thing inside him wouldn't get up to anything before I got round to it. How badly was it damaging him? I had no way of telling. But I really can't spare the time for him right now.

"Gentlemen," she said to us in a low voice, and held out her hand to Pierce. He took it rather nervously and shook it. I contented myself with a little bow. "I...owe you an explanation. Please bear with me. It's not going to be easy. I'm...a little adrift."

I sat down next to her, on her left. After a moment Pierce took a seat on her other side. The church was dim and stuffy and cool, except where massed candles made stalactites of devotion. Teresa bowed her head as if in prayer, and Pierce and I leaned forward.

"I loved my father," she said softly. "All my life, he built Captain da Silva up into this kind of epitome of wickedness, until I believed it as sincerely as I believe in God." She crossed herself. Turned slightly to me. "And then I met you, and of course you're only human, after all. I couldn't see you as this terrible bogey-man, however hard I tried."

Teresa raised her eyes to the high altar. I thought suddenly: I denied my faith, or at least admitted it for the first time, and to a demon. Or whatever Mouffi was. She went on, still in that passionate quiet voice. "I loved my father, but he used me. I was a willing partner at first. Though I always hated it when he called demons. But now there weren't just souls in stones, there were innocent people guarding them. And when I became the armored guardian, it hurt me right down to my own soul. I felt...soiled. I was sick to my stomach every time I came back. When you came and took the amulet away, oh God, it was such a relief. And that's what we'd put on Inácio. I couldn't bear it if anything happened to him." Her face colored. "I think I might be falling in love with him."

Pierce made a small sound, perhaps thinking of hypodermics full of poison. "He didn't actually change," he said, gently.

"Not physically, no," she agreed. "But if he'd used that needle...I went to take the stone back, since I was the one who gave it to him in the first place."

"You wouldn't have succeeded," I said, rubbing my cheekbone.

"I know. I wasn't thinking straight. I suppose I thought I might be able to persuade him before the amulet realized what I was up to. And then Sr Pierce turned up with a ghost. It was a kind thing you did," she added, turning to him, "replacing the stone."

"Does he remember what happened?" Pierce asked. Teresa shook her head.

"I got rid of the pieces," she said, "and covered up the smell with smelling salts. Told him he'd fainted. Gave him a telling-off for working too hard." She sighed. "I didn't even tell him the truth about who I am. He thinks I'm this innocent young thing who works in a hotel. However—that's my problem. What I have to do now is stop my father."

The words hung in the quiet between us. Does she know he could only be stopped by killing him? It doesn't look like it. I contemplated not telling her. Just for a moment. But she'd been too honest with us not to give her the truth.

"Teresa," I said, and sensed Pierce's startled glance, "The spell can't be stopped. It's—" what had Zacuto said? Oh yes "—self-perpetuating. The only way is—"

"Your father's death," Pierce interrupted me, a little too loudly. I don't know why he did that. There was a sudden silence. Then Teresa gave a soft groan as if she was in pain.

"Oh, the fool," she said, almost too soft to hear. She put her hands on her knees and worked her shoulders in a stretch. "Then you must let me help. If he knows what failure would mean, he'll be replacing souls the minute he gets the spell remolded."

"How long will that take?" I asked, feeling sweat trickling down my face. A drop stung my eye, and I wiped it away.

"Three days," she said. "He summoned something last night to ask how to do it." The man seems to call up demons with less thought than I use the telephone.

"The witch I mentioned," I said, "she's coming to my house. You should know she's the wife of the man in the first amulet."

Teresa looked directly at me. Her face was bleak. "Will she work with me?"

"I don't know," I said. "Does she have a choice?"

"We all have choices," she replied, with dignity. "Not all of us make the right ones."

Since all this stems from a wrong-headed choice (well, nothing to do with my head) I'd made twenty years ago, I'm in no position to argue.

"We'd better go," I said, getting to my feet. Acutely aware that time was passing. And besides, I needed a smoke.

"Here, hang on a minute," said Pierce to me. "Have you told your lady wife who you're bringing home?"

I shook my head. "No."

"Well, don't you think you should?"

He was right. Of course. I'd been too caught up in the moment to stand back and think. Da Silva, prime idiot. Look, love, she followed me home, can we keep her? I must've looked as blank as I felt. It was Teresa who came to my rescue.

"I'll wait here," she said. "I think a bit more prayer can't do any harm."

* * *

Caught between sleep and waking as well as between captivity and freedom, Harris realized that the part of him that was in the amulet was also seeing out of it. In his half-dream, his viewpoint was between three and four feet from the ground. The jewel must be suspended around someone's neck, he deduced. The motion sickening him, it progressed down a corridor hung with paintings in great baroque frames. Apart from the red tinge laid over everything, the hallway was only dimly lit. He could make out nothing of the art. His bearer went through a door, and his viewpoint changed to an ornately moulded ceiling.

Harris lurched awake, nausea burning in his throat. The sun was high. *Hellfire, must be midday already.* He leaned over and retched into the bucket beside the bed, bringing nothing up, but the disinfectant smell brought on more heaves. After a moment he pushed the bucket away and lay back, hair damp on his forehead.

Now he was fully awake he felt slightly better, though he already knew it was transitory. He sat up carefully and reached for the robe draped over the chair. Both it and the unfamiliar nightshirt had been borrowed from a neighbor with more girth than the captain but unfortunately not much more height. Harris contemplated his bare legs, mind fairly blank save for a vague relief that he didn't feel like dog puke.

Got this far, now try standing up. He pushed himself slowly to his feet. The room remained still. Showed no signs of the dizzying spinning it was capable of. That was a plus. He walked to the window and rested his head against the glass. Zé's room looked out over a descending jumble of red rooftops, blind once-white walls, trees poking up in unexpected places, and strings of washing festooning every available space. *Don't they ever stop?*

Harris had hazy memories of his mother, wreathed in steam, bitching at the tyranny of the weekly washday, but these Portuguese ladies seemed to make it a full-time occupation. He turned and looked at the damp sheets on the bed. *Skipper's wife sends 'em out. Well, maybe that's where they end up.*

Wondering distantly why he was thinking about laundry, not a topic that generally engaged his interest, he made his way to the washstand and splashed his face with tepid water.

As he did so, the significance of what he'd seen in those last moments before waking came home to him, and he raised his dripping face to the mirror.

She took it off. He was sure the amulet-holder was a woman, and not just from the trappings of her bedroom. *She took it off, and I woke up. That's gotta help.* It did not occur to him to wonder why she had apparently gone to bed in the middle of the day. He was accustomed to the concept of the siesta.

His reflection in the mirror depressed him, and his hands were too shaky even to think about shaving, so he walked carefully to the door and turned the handle. Much to his relief, his insides remained placid. In fact, they had begun to demand food. His stomach gurgled. Beef tea, he thought hopefully. And toast. And *coffee.*

Harris went out onto the landing, the short nightwear flapping round his knees, and realized belatedly that he ought at least to put his pants on. He found them neatly folded on the chair. That accomplished, he began to descend the stairs slowly, holding the bannisters tightly in both hands. The extra rail installed for Emilia gave him a welcome sense of stability.

The house was quiet but not silent. Harris's wolf-sense told him Emilia was in the office. Other knowledge told him Caterina was in school, the housekeeper woman who cleaned and cooked had just gone out, and Zé probably had ship duty, though he was unclear on that one, not even being sure what day it was.

He had to pause halfway down the stairs, which irritated him no end. *Haven't been ill in three years, less'n you count catching werewolf.* He had sometimes wondered whether he'd be prone to catching doggy diseases like distemper or rabies or hardpad (whatever that was), but appeared to be immune to sickness. Which was why *this* was so relentlessly unpleasant.

Finally reaching the bottom of the stairs, he paused for a moment to orient himself. Though normally it wouldn't have worried him, the house followed no logical plan. As if it had grown organically. He could sense that parts of it were extremely old. The door to the small room that served as an office was ajar, though, and he could see Emilia's dark head bent over paperwork. *Doing the books. Jesus I'm glad I don't have to worry about that kinda stuff.* He rapped on the door, and she raised her eyes.

"Oh, Sr Harris," she said. Her English was slow but accurate, *and goddamnit, that accent's cute.* "How are you feeling? Come in, sit down."

Harris did as he was told, almost feeling well enough to be embarrassed at his dishevelled state. The exertion had brought him out in a sweat, and he dragged a hand over his face.

"Ma'am, I'm sorry to be so much trouble," he said, sinking down into the visitor's chair. It creaked protestingly.

"It's nothing," said Emilia with one of her captivating smiles. "Are you well enough to eat something? I think Joana is back by now."

"Uh, yeah, I guess," Harris said, swallowing. *Man, it's good not to feel like throwing.* "You expecting the skipper anytime soon? 'Cause I got something I oughta tell him."

"You can tell me," she suggested. "Did you know they have the second stone back now?"

"I keep missing stuff," he muttered irritably. *This rate, I'll miss my own liberation. I hope to hell the skipper gets around to it soon.*

* * *

The office was full of a hungover-looking Harris eating omelette when I got home. Which was a very uncarnivorous thing for him to be consuming. Normally, if it isn't bleeding, he won't eat it. Not like most Americans, and the English are even worse. They all like their meat cremated. Though in Harris's case I suppose being a werewolf may have something to do with it.

He was fairly engrossed in it, so I took the opportunity of giving Emilia a thorough kissing. Always a little silly with anyone else in the room. But we spend so much time apart that I can't resist it. And perhaps this time there's a bit of guilt there about Teresa. Well, no perhaps about it, to be perfectly honest.

She disengaged after a while and pushed me away with a grin on her face. "Mr Harris has something to tell you," she said in English. I perched on the edge of the desk. Looked down at Harris, who was staring fixedly at his empty plate.

"How are you feeling, Harris?"

"Better'n I was, but it won't last," he said gloomily. "Figured something out. I can see through the stone when I'm asleep."

"See through it," I repeated, raising an eyebrow. Attacked an itch on my left shin with the heel of my other shoe.

"Yeah." He waved a hand in the air. "She was wearing it round her neck, I guess—I tell you it's a woman?" I nodded. "I could see out of it as she was walking along. See there was pictures on the walls, that kinda stuff. Makes me goddamn sick, pardon me, ma'am. Anyhow she musta took it off, 'cause it stopped moving. Put it down, and I woke up just like that. Like it wasn't holding onto me so strongly, see? So I figure that if'n these folks take off the amulets, might also mean they won't turn into the guardians."

Taking out my cheroots, I found I'd forgotten to buy any more. Damn. Put them back. Probably wiser not to make Harris inhale smoke anyway. There was a conspicuous lack of cigarettes about him. I took my jacket off instead and draped it over the back of Emilia's chair.

"They must take them off to sleep," she said.

"You'd think so," I agreed, sticking my hands in my pockets. It was really too hot to do that sort of thing. I took them out again. Folded my arms instead. "So why's Harris awake now?"

"Figured she was taking a siesta," he said. I nodded. He closed his eyes for a moment, perhaps encouraged by the concept.

"Dona Paciência's on her way," I said to Emilia, then explained about Zacuto's revised translation.

"You mean you actually telephoned her direct?" She clapped a hand to her mouth in mock astonishment. I tugged her hair.

"Yes, I've finally embraced the twentieth century, put out the flags," I said, and she laughed. I took a deep breath. "There's another thing."

I must've sounded—or looked—particularly strange, because both Harris and Emilia stared at me in alarm.

"What's up?" Harris asked.

"Teresa Batista," I said. Emilia put her elbow on the desk and rested her chin on her fist. Looked up at me with concern. "It's all right, I think," I added, reassuringly. I think reassuringly. "She seems to've had a change of heart."

"She what?"

"She showed up at the orphanage and helped Pierce and Zacuto. And she's offered to help get the rest of the stones back."

Emilia frowned. "Don't trust her," she said.

"I don't know, love." I brushed that always-straying strand of hair off her forehead. "I think I believe her. And don't you appreciate the irony? I know I do."

"Well, don't let her near Paciência. She'll probably murder her."

And as that was what I thought too, there was the problem. I heard the doorbell ring. That would be the witch. Right on cue. I shook my head.

"They're going to have to work together."

Joana's voice, and then Paciência's, sounded indistinctly outside. Then the door opened, and the sorceress came in, followed by her daughter. Who takes after Henriques when it comes to height and Paciência when it comes to looks. Which I suppose is better than the other way round. The room, already crowded with Harris, became like a third-class railway carriage. He pushed himself to his feet, looking rather embarrassed.

"Think I'll get outa your way," he said, adding politely, "Pardon me, ma'am," to Paciência. Wasted on her, of course, since she doesn't speak English. But she got the sense of it and moved aside to let him out. I resumed the vertical and gave the ladies a polite bow before sitting back down on the desk once more.

The expression on the witch's face was not encouraging. Luzia merely looked apprehensive. This isn't going to be any fun at all, I thought, looking from one to the other.

But then Paciência smiled. It was a small and rather resigned smile. Still, it was an improvement. She sat down in the chair Harris had vacated and folded her hands in her lap.

"Your efforts are appreciated," she said to me. I smiled back, not entirely sure how I should be reacting. "I've told Luzia what she needs to know. Now how do you propose to get her to see this woman?"

Bite the bullet, da Silva. "I'm afraid you're not going to like it, Dona Paciência." She frowned at me.

"I already don't like it," she said, sharply. "What haven't you told me?" I glanced away. Rubbed my cheekbone. Took the plunge.

"The person who gave Sra Martinho the amulet," I said, wiping a trickle of sweat from my face. "Teresa Batista."

There was a sudden, explosive silence. Then she said, "I assume you haven't taken leave of your senses, so please explain."

I really couldn't do this without a smoke. I took out my last cheroot and lit it. "She wants to stop her father."

"Then she's up to something," said Paciência, with certainty. I looked at Emilia, who raised her eyebrows and shrugged. I returned my gaze to the witch once more.

"She helped get the chrysophase from its guardian," I told her. "And she says she can help us get the others, if you can do a masking spell."

Paciência pursed her lips. "Masking spells are very unstable. It helps if both parties have perfect trust in each other. And I—will—not—trust—that—woman."

"I think you have to," I said, exhaling smoke on a long breath.

The sorceress looked down at her hands. Her knuckles were white. Then raised her head again to meet my eye. She spoke between clenched teeth.

"You ask a lot." She sighed. "I'll meet her, speak with her. Then we'll see."

"Thank you," I said, relieved. Emilia put a hand on my knee.

"Is now a good time?" she asked.

"You don't beat about the bush, either," remarked the witch, with some asperity. "Very well. Where is she?"

"Waiting in church."

"She has a nerve," said Paciência.

* * *

As she had intended, Teresa prayed. But it all felt hollow and empty. Her words were going nowhere. She felt like a tower in an earthquake, foundations shuddering, everything in flux. Anger welled up in her like lava, and she didn't know whether it was at her father for his lifelong obsession or at Luís da Silva for not living up to it.

* * *

Well. I'm damned, I thought. Teresa really was praying. Or, at any rate, down on her knees. I really wish sometimes I could believe it works. Paciência crossed herself dutifully. Luzia hovered a little distance away, silent and unhappy. And I said quietly, "Teresa?"

She raised her head. I saw a mixture of emotions chase each other across her face. None of them was anything I wanted to pursue.

"This is your witch?" she asked in a low voice. Paciência bristled.

"Dona Paciência," I said hastily, forestalling any action on her part. "Senhorita—" reminding myself not to call her *menina* since she was Brazilian "—Teresa Batista."

She nodded coldly at the younger woman. Teresa got to her feet, saying haughtily, "I regret what happened, senhora, but please believe I'm trying to make amends."

"Hmm," commented Paciência, looking from her to me. She narrowed her eyes and said to me out of the side of her mouth, "And you should be ashamed of yourself." I blinked and fingered my eyepatch. How the hell had she known my thoughts? My earlier thoughts, I mean. Currently I had no desire at all to kiss Teresa.

"Has Captain da Silva asked you about the masking spell?" Apparently she hadn't heard Paciência's aside. Good. My life's complicated enough already.

"Yes, he has," the witch replied austerely. "And if you have knowledge of such things, you'll know how dangerous they can be."

"I know," Teresa said. "But it's the best chance you have to recover the stones. The amulet holders all know me." Not all like Dr Bosque, I hope. "Especially Sra Martinho. She's not feeling very trusting these days."

"I don't trust you, girl," retorted Paciência. "But I do trust Captain da Silva." Well, that's nice to know. She glanced at me. I stared expressionlessly back. Still stung by that earlier dig. As if it had been voluntary. Ha. Still protesting a bit much here, da Silva.

"You're not proposing working the spell on him, are you?" Teresa said. Rather as if I wasn't there.

"Excuse me, ladies," I interrupted, " aren't you forgetting something?" They both stopped and stared at me. The intensity of it almost made me flinch. "The nature of this guardian? I'd rather not go up against anything called the castrator. I'm rather attached to—" I broke off in confusion, realising who I was talking to. Cleared my throat and rubbed my chin to hide my embarrassment. Didn't work, of course.

"So is Emilia," Paciência said tartly, with a sharp glance at Teresa, who looked bemused. "But no, I wasn't proposing that. What I meant was that I trust his judgment. If he believes you're sincere, menina, then I'll work the spell on you."

Finally. Thank God for that. Bring on the bloody marching bands.

Teresa was nodding. "Thank you, senhora."

"Don't thank me," Paciência snapped. "It won't be pleasant."

"But it is necessary," Batista's daughter pointed out. "And I'm used to...unpleasant things," she added, looking at me. I had a brief vision of the armored guardian. She must be thinking of it, too. Sweat crawled in my hair.

"Come along then," said the sorceress briskly. "We have to do this out of doors, as I'm sure you know."

"Yes," Teresa replied. "How long can you make it hold?"

"Three days." She turned to me. "Will that be sufficient?"

I raised my eyebrows. Ran a hand over my damp hair. Still haven't managed to get it cut. "It'll have to be, won't it?" I said.

"Luzia, come here," Paciência ordered her daughter. The three of them walked out of the church together, like the Fates. Or some other threefold goddess. I trailed along behind, feeling superfluous. Did Paciência need me?

"Dona Paciência," I called softly. She turned. "What are you going to do?"

The candles gave her face strange shadows. "Work the spell," she replied. "And then send the pair of them to this Sra Martinho. Will you be the anchor for the spell?"

"Of course," I said. "What does it involve?" Said those two things in the wrong order, da Silva.

"Standing firm," answered the witch.

I can do that.

And out into the fierce sun again. Wishing for a breeze, at least. I wondered vaguely whether the heatwave had anything to do with Batista messing with the equilibrium, as Pierce had called it. Or just a by-product of too much traffic with demons.

In front of me, I noted that Luzia, in the middle, was exactly the same amount taller than her mother as Teresa was than Luzia. Distracted by symmetry, I missed Fr Jerónimo's sudden reappearance on my blind side.

He didn't attempt to touch me—the key of Solomon?—but hissed in my ear, "What an interesting sight. A witch, a warrior and a whore. And you."

Paciência whirled round, eyes wide and furious, as I said, "What do you want?" Put out a restraining hand to the witch.

"You know what I want," he said slyly, and the demon looked yellow out of his eyes. Paciência made the sign of the cross. He didn't even flinch.

"Dona Paciência, go," I said. "I'll deal with this."

"We need you," she protested.

"How touching," sneered the demon.

"I'll join you later," I told Paciência. "Tell me where you're going." She frowned in the priest's direction, and he bared his teeth at her. His breath was foul. He hadn't shaved. Perhaps the demon didn't know how.

"He's—" she began.

"Are you afraid, *bruxa?*" he asked, leering at her.

"*Vai para a puta que te pariu,*" she spat, and Luzia gasped, her face reddening. Even Teresa looked startled. Not that I've ever heard a lady say anything like that, either. The priest, to my surprise, flinched back. Perhaps it was more than a simple obscenity from a witch's lips.

"I know what he is," I said, stepping between them. "Don't worry."

She narrowed her eyes. "You're sure?" I nodded.

"Yes."

"Then we'll be at the castle." She turned on her heel and stalked off, followed by the two younger women.

The priest licked his lips slowly. It looked incongruously sensual. I wondered regretfully if there was anything human left inside to save.

"What odd company you do keep, captain," said the demon.

"Including you?" I asked, taking a step towards him. He moved back, scowling. "You don't like this sign, do you?" I remarked. "Why is that, I wonder—Mouffi?"

He snarled at the name. "You can't compel me," he said. "Not without binding me. And you won't do that, will you?"

"You don't know what I'm going to do," I said.

"And what might that be, then?" he asked.

What Fr Jerónimo had wanted all along. I lit a cheroot and replied, "I'm going to take you to São Rafael."

Glad I'd replenished my smokes. It made the grand gesture more effective. He stared at me, in disbelief, I think.

"What are you up to, Luís da Silva?"

I bared my teeth at him. "Come along, and you'll find out." I'm counting on your curiosity, Mouffi. Don't disappoint me. I turned my back on him and walked towards the alley. Which was letting me in. The library must know what I was up to, then. I turned past Zacuto's shade, into the cool darkness.

Heard his following footsteps. Good. I didn't look back until I emerged into the light-filled cauldron of the courtyard. The heat struck down, and the pungent scent of the geraniums arose, strong as the sun.

Fr Jerónimo came out into the light, blinking and bemused. He looked sallow and not quite substantial. Less so than Zacuto's ghost. "Why have you brought me here?"

"Perhaps so you can see what you wanted when you were human," I said, blowing smoke at him. "What do you think?" He waved the smoke away viciously.

"I think you're a very irritating man," he replied in a savage voice, "and when I can, I intend to kill you."

With a smile, I said, "But you can't, can you, Mouffi? You can't even touch me."

"I grow in strength every day," said the demon. "You won't know when I come for you until I do. And I will. I shall take great pleasure in your death."

"Empty threats," I said dismissively. Pointed the cheroot at him. "You could take a hundred years to grow that strong."

He opened his mouth and roared. His lips gaped wider than a man should be able to open his jaws. His foul breath was a stinking gale. "You may be able to stand against me now, Luís da Silva, but your son cannot— nor your daughter—nor your wife!" His tongue lolled out of his open maw. There was no mistaking the lasciviousness of it this time.

I stepped up to him. Drew back my left fist and hit him as hard as I could in the jaw. His head snapped back and he dropped like a stone.

"I've been wanting to do that for days," I told his unconscious form, rubbing my knuckles and grinning. Sometimes physical violence is extremely satisfying.

The door of the library opened and Pierce peered out. Looked at the prone priest, then up at me. "Good God," he exclaimed. "Is he dead?"

Well, that's nice. I raised an eyebrow at him and said mildly, "No, he isn't." Pierce glanced at my hands. Presumably got the message.

"How did he get here?"

"I brought him," I said. Took a drag on my cheroot. "Zacuto's going to exorcise him."

This was apparently too much for Pierce. He took off his spectacles and pinched the bridge of his nose. I felt sweat trickling down my side under my shirt.

"I feel more like *Alice Through the Looking-Glass* every day," he complained.

It was too damned hot in the full sun. And I didn't know how long Fr Jerónimo was going to stay hors de combat. I walked up to Pierce and clapped him on the shoulder as I passed.

"Never mind, Pierce," I said cheerfully. "It all goes to make life more interesting." Part of life's rich pattern, as my father used to say.

"Life's a bit *too* damned interesting around you," he retorted.

"Sr Zacuto," I called. The scholar's ghost looked up.

"Captain da Silva," he said with grave surprise, as if he'd been expecting someone else. Though God only knows who. He bowed his head politely.

"I've brought Fr Jerónimo," I said, after a quick glance over my shoulder to make sure he was still out for the count.

Zacuto came out into the bright sunlight. The illusion of life was still complete, even on a bright day. Except that he didn't cast a shadow.

"You need to bring him inside, senhor capitão." I nodded. Dropped the remains of my cheroot and ground it under my shoe.

"Can I help?" asked Pierce, replacing his spectacles. The cleanest pair in Lisbon, by now.

"Take his feet." I've had enough of toting people around. This priest didn't have much weight in his long skinny body. But I never turn down help if it's offered. I don't have anything to prove. Hell, I'd have *told* him to help if he hadn't offered.

"What if he wakes up?"

"Then I'll hit him again," I said.

We propped him in a chair. He flopped, threatening to slide out of it. I contemplated him, fiddling idly with my eyepatch. Caught myself at it, and stopped.

"What happens when he does wake up?" Pierce asked. I looked in

Zacuto's direction.

"He will be restrained by the spell," the ghost replied. "If I am able to exorcise him, he will be too weak to move afterwards. Now I must ask you both to leave."

"But I was in the middle of—" the antiquarian protested.

"It'll be here when you come back," I told him. "Now come along, I need you to go to Yeoh's shop and fetch him."

Pierce squinted as the brilliant sunlight caught him full in the face. Shaded his eyes with his hand. "Have you got another stone already?"

"No," I said, "but Batista keeps sending things after them." And I'm a little fed up with having to deal with them. "If Yeoh's on hand to hide them it might put a stop to it."

"Fine," said Pierce, fanning himself with his hat. He was always open to reason, I'll say that for him. "Where are you going?"

"Apparently Dona Paciência needs my help for her spell." He pulled a face.

"Rather you than me. Where shall I bring the estimable Sr Yeoh?"

I wiped a trickle of sweat from my face. "Tell him to meet us at Sra Martinho's, the address he gave me."

"Right you are, er, skipper," he said. Sketched a salute, and headed off down the alley. Bloody comedian. I looked at the blank shuttered exterior of the library for a long moment. Remembering. Then I shook myself, lit a cheroot, and followed Pierce.

*　*　*

Some things never get better, and some wounds never heal.

Sofia Martinho had not set foot out of her sister's house since her husband's acquittal. Nor had she ever spoken a word to Beatriz about his attempt to kill her. She even vocalized the word in her mind with great reluctance.

At the window, but seeing nothing through it, her embroidery untouched in her lap, she sat swathed in memory. Cocooned in nostalgia, wrapped in remembrance. If asked what day it was, she would have had to think about it and, likely, got it wrong.

What do you want, Beatriz kept on asking her, Sofia, what is it you want?

For things to be as they were. For her untroubled marriage, her attentive husband. For Mário to be the man she married and not—what he had since become.

The room was stuffy and overfurnished, smelling of beeswax and lavender. Sofia's face gleamed with perspiration, and her clothes clung damply to her. From time to time, she stroked the smooth surface of her amulet. The stone hung on a gold chain bracelet around her right wrist. A bracelet Mário had given her. In all the room, only her fingers moved.

Beryl strengthens married love, she thought. If only I'd had this jewel before. Before, just that word, she shied away from narrative as she did from the word kill. Her life was divided like the life of the world, or at least the Christian part of it, by a momentous event. BC and AD. For Sofia, her miracle had not been the birth of faith, but its death.

A tear trickled down her face, moisture on moisture. You would not think her red puffy eyes had any more tears in reserve: she had already cried oceans, rivers, lakes. Cried herself to a standstill, a vacuum. Nothing left inside. Exhaustion. Her swollen eyelids drooped, and she dozed. Though if she had known she was going to sleep she would have tried to resist it, for fear of the dreams that came every night.

Dreams of Mário trying to suffocate her.

Beatriz turned the door-handle softly and peered into the dim room, relieved to see Sofia asleep. She was sick and tired of her sister moping round the place like some operatic heroine. But of course she couldn't say so, one doesn't say, Come on, for heaven's sake snap out of it, get over it, life goes on. It would be like speaking ill of the dead, and of course poor Sofia was suffering a bereavement. Though Beatriz had never observed her sister's marriage as being the wonderful stainless thing Sofia obviously viewed it as. In Beatriz's view, Mário had always been obsessive about Sofia. Possessive, and in the way most people were about valued things, a horse, a painting, a holy relic. Not your spouse.

And anyway, Sofia wouldn't have dreamed of cheating on him. Beatriz closed the door quietly and went back to her own affairs.

In Sofia's dream, she fought for breath under a relentless soft pressing weight that she had not the remotest chance of throwing off. Unable to breathe, unable to scream.

Unable to stop having this nightmare, even in broad daylight.

* * *

Over the years of my exile, the map of Lisbon imprinted on the inside of my head that I'd had as a child became overwritten by other things. Now it's being redrawn, but all the associations of the places are different. Ten-year-old Luís da Silva thought the castle ruins an exciting place. The forty-four-year-old version has a rather more jaundiced view. A place of ghosts and demons. And, now, witches.

The three women were waiting for me. The Fates, I'd thought. Or something equally implacable. But, of course, they were only Paciência, Luzia, and Teresa Batista. People I know. To one degree or another. And they were on my side. Though that might be a mixed blessing.

It was Paciência who stepped forward, her dark face worried. "Is everything all right?"

I raised my eyebrows. In the current climate it was a damn silly question. In terms of Fr Jerónimo, though, which was what she was asking, the answer would be yes. So I nodded.

"Are you ready to do this spell?" I asked her.

"We are," she said. "Come."

"What do you want me to do?"

She didn't reply at once, but pursed her lips and stared at me for a moment. I rubbed my cheekbone. Then she said, "The masking spell, in essence, hides the soul. It harnesses dangerous energies. Do you know anything about electricity?"

"Not really." Don't have much need to. Turn the switch, and the light comes on. A piece of modern technology I approve of. Wish we had some at home.

Paciência took a deep breath. Let it out again. "Well," she said, "I was going to draw the analogy that an electrical device has to be earthed. I need you to perform that function for the purpose of this spell."

Concealing Teresa's soul? I wondered whether John Yeoh would be able to see it. Well, I could always ask him, I suppose.

I looked out across the city. Down there, ghosts drifted, beggars importuned, politicians lied and thousands of ordinary people lived out their lives. But the noise they made was almost inaudible, high as we were. Up here, out of that sky, demons had exploded. That deep, steady, cloudless blue had ruptured. From it now only the sun beat down, merciless. Pigeons wandered round the ruins, pecking aimlessly. Taking to the air in mindless rattling panic from time to time. I shook myself. This is no time to be wool-gathering, da Silva.

"At your service, Dona Paciência."

"Take my right hand," she instructed. "You, girl, hold my left." I did as I was told. The witch's palm was damp, her fingers thin but surprisingly strong. Teresa's hand was warm but dry. Smaller than I expected. She held on lightly. I glanced at her face. It was completely expressionless. "Now, Luzia."

Paciência's daughter walked round us, drizzling a stream of fine white powder in a circle to enclose the three of us.

"What's she doing?" I asked. It was Teresa who replied.

"Enclosing the energy," she explained. "And hiding us from anyone who might be watching." She was her mother's apprentice, then. It made sense. I felt a little strange to realize they all knew more about this business than I did. Not a situation I find myself in too often. Inferiority complex, who, me?

"What's the powder?"

"Mainly salt," said Paciência. "Now, everyone, be silent."

Luzia finished her work, and stepped back. Around us, the circle she'd made rose in a core of shimmering air like a heat-haze. I could still see her through it, but only vaguely, as if through thick flawed glass. Her, and the broken walls, and the blue sky. And the pigeons. Inside the barrier, the air seemed cooler, but somehow stuffy. There was a faint smell of ozone, and an almost inaudible rushing right on the edge of hearing. No other sound at all. I found my nose was itching. Dealing with that would have to wait.

The witch closed her eyes, and her lips began to move. After a moment, I felt a tentative prickling from her hand, a bit like pins and needles. It traveled up my arm to the shoulder. Teresa's eyes widened, so I guessed she was feeling the same thing. Or maybe something completely different. What the hell did I know? The tingling hesitated, then spread all through me in an instant. A bright sharp pain throbbed from Zacuto's mark. Coupled with a murderous stab of agony along the scar on my face. I clenched my teeth and squeezed my eye shut. But a pulse later it was gone.

Opening my eye again, I saw Paciência outlined in a kind of pearly glow. A nimbus of sparks. Now it felt as if every single hair on my body was standing on end. The witch's eyelids snapped open, and silver light blazed suddenly from her eyes. It was so bright I had to turn my head away from her.

Teresa's face was contorted in pain or ecstasy. I couldn't tell which. Then from her hand I felt the same tingling prickle as I had from Paciência's a minute ago. It travelled the same route. I braced myself against expected pain, but it still made me gasp. A second later, Teresa's eyes burned with the same white fire. And the light in the witch's eyes went out.

Paciência blinked, rapidly, several times. Teresa's hand clutched mine in a fierce spasm, then relaxed. The fire in her eyes faded, and she drew in a sharp breath. I felt the power drain into the ground through the soles of my feet. My mouth was dry as dust. I swallowed a couple of times. Trying to moisten it.

"It's done," Paciência said, and released our hands. I let go of Teresa's.

Scratched the itch on my nose. Saw Luzia's blurred figure come back to the
barrier enclosing us. She raised one arm, made some kind of pass. And the
air cleared with a sudden incongruous smell of roses. Letting in the heat of
the day once more, and the faint sounds of the city below.

I looked back at Teresa. Her face was strained. She managed a small smile
for Paciência. "It feels complete," she said. "Thank you, senhora."

The witch nodded. If Teresa seemed tired, she looked grey as death. The
bones of her skull pushed at her skin. Even her flesh seemed to have sunk
away. I took a pace towards her in alarm, offering my hand. But she waved
me away.

"No need," she whispered, hoarsely. Luzia stepped to her side and
handed her a small flask. After several small sips, some color returned to her
face. "Ah, that's a hard one." She closed her eyes and sucked in a deep
breath. Which reminded me. I pulled out a cheroot and lit it, drawing in the
smoke gratefully. My clothes felt damp. A normal state of affairs, these days.

"Dona Paciência, are you all right?" I asked.

"Oh yes," she replied. Her voice was almost back to normal. "Thank you.
For your support, I mean."

"Nada," I said. "Shall we go to collect another stone?"

11

ALL HER LIFE, HER MOTHER HAD SIMULTANEOUSLY PUT HER DOWN AND TOLD HER THAT SHE MUST BE BETTER THAN ANYONE ELSE. Attend to your lessons, or you'll end up like that man sweeping the streets. No, you can't have a parrot, puppy, insert object of desire here, you're not responsible enough. How could you not be top of the class, you're much cleverer than those stupid children. Don't speak to that servant, beggar, girl, boy, one doesn't make conversation with one's inferiors. Why can't you master the piano, I was so good at it when I was your age…And so on, and on, and on.

Why don't you have any friends, Luzia? Because my mother never taught me how.

And now, even now, when she'd finally admitted there was something that only Luzia could do, she brought in a stranger to help. A foreigner. A *brasileira*. Leaving Luzia to do the menial work. Great-aunt Fernanda could make an exclusion ring. Next door's *cat* could make an exclusion ring. Luzia seethed with resentment.

If it weren't for Pedro's sake, she would have thought seriously about sabotaging this errand. She swallowed nervously and fiddled with her earring. The word *lover* had been bandied about with an ominous lack of expression that held unpleasant forebodings—And that was something else her mother had tried to deny her.

Luzia stole a glance at the strange tall young woman beside her. About whom her mother had told her precisely nothing. But Teresa Batista's face was unreadable. With a frustrated sigh, Luzia wiped a bead of perspiration from her brow.

See if you can get her to take off the amulet first, Captain da Silva had said. It might make things easier. But he hadn't said how.

How could she even start to do this if they kept her in the dark?

"What are we going to do?" she blurted out at last, unable to keep silent any longer.

"I don't know for sure," admitted Teresa. "We'll have to play it by ear."

She doesn't *know!* Luzia could have screamed in frustration.

The building they had just entered was a tall ornate structure with baroque balcony railings and florid stonework. Their shoes clicked and clattered on a complicated pattern of black and white tiles that made her tread carefully for fear of slipping. It housed, apparently, seven apartments, just one to each floor. Luzia eyed the lift-cage warily. She didn't like using such contraptions. But it appeared that she was not required to submit to its torture: Teresa rang the bell of the ground-floor apartment, and Luzia breathed a sigh of relief.

A very small, very stout maid answered the door and peered up at them, perhaps bemused at being confronted by two women so very tall. Teresa, at her most imperious, presented a visiting card and asked for the senhora Martinho. Luzia envied her confidence, and tried surreptitiously to square her own shoulders. She had studiously ignored her deportment lessons for years to spite her mother and had only recently come to regret this.

Now the maid ushered them in and asked them, in a startling baritone, to wait. Presently a plump matron not a great deal taller than the maidservant emerged from one of the closed doors, an enquiring expression on her face that cleared when she saw Teresa.

"Oh, it's you," she said. "I'm sorry, I didn't recognize the name." She squinted at the card in her hand, holding it at arm's length the way Luzia's father did when he couldn't find his spectacles. "Sra Pedreira." Luzia blinked at the nom de guerre, for it meant *stoneworker*, but said nothing. "I expect my sister will be pleased to see you."

"I was concerned about her," Teresa explained. It proved to be sufficient to gain them admittance. Luzia's heart gave a nervous little jump.

"At least she talked to you. She won't to me."

Sra Martinho, seated by the window, had a strong family resemblance to her sister, though she was voluptuous where the older woman was plump, and there was no grey in her shining black hair. But her face was drawn and sad, and her eyelids puffed up from crying. She blinked at Teresa, and then her gaze fell on Luzia. Her eyes widened, and at the same moment Teresa moved like lightning to seize her wrists.

"Get the bracelet off her," she snapped.

Luzia, who had been staring at the woman's face, saw with horrified clarity that the hands which had been folded in her lap had transformed into a pair of bony serrated pincers. Teresa, holding her arms, was struggling to keep them from her face.

Part of her wanted to run. Part of her wanted to scream. She did neither. A tiny, breathless sound escaped her lips, and she stood rooted to the spot in terror and revulsion.

The guardian wrenched one snapping claw from Teresa's grip, forcing her to duck under it. She swivelled round, twisting the arm she still held up behind the transformed woman's back, and Luzia saw what had been Sra Martinho wince.

"*Puta!*" spat the guardian, in a sort of whispered shout.

"Move, you stupid child," snarled Teresa at the same time, stinging Luzia into overcoming her funk. She ran forward, panic giving her speed, and snatched at the flailing arm. The side of the claw clipped her on the side of the head, making her gasp and see stars for a second as the pain took her breath away momentarily.

Teresa hooked a foot in front of the guardian's ankles, overbalancing her, and used her weight to wrestle her to the floor. She fell with a thud that seemed to reverberate through the whole apartment, and Luzia, suddenly terrified that the woman's sister would come to investigate, knelt firmly on her other arm and unfastened the gold bracelet.

As soon as it was off her wrist, Sofia Martinho went limp. The dreadful claws shrivelled down to bone, carpals and metacarpals, so that the hands of a skeleton protruded from her sleeves for a second. And then flesh and muscle and tendon and skin covered them swiftly, like a pair of gloves being pulled on.

Her own hands shaking severely, Luzia fumbled the stone off the chain and swapped it with the near-identical one she had in her pocket. Then she pushed herself to her feet and jammed her knuckles in her mouth. Whether she wanted to stop her teeth from chattering or her gorge from rising, she couldn't have said. She couldn't stop seeing the awful pincers in her mind, but the reverse metamorphosis was worse.

Meanwhile, Teresa had hauled the unconscious woman back into her chair. Collecting her wits, Luzia scooped up her fallen embroidery and replaced it in her lap, hands still trembling. Teresa nodded her thanks, and produced a bottle of smelling salts. Luzia wondered whether she could ask for some for herself and put her hand to her temple to wipe away the trickle of moisture she felt. She was astonished to find her fingers come away bloody and quickly searched for her handkerchief to mop it off.

Sofia Martinho came round, choking and coughing on the pungent fumes, and stared blankly at the two young women, one with her hair falling over her face and the other with a blood-spotted cloth pressed to her head.

"Are you all right?" Luzia asked, impulsively.

"Wh-who are you?" Her hand went to her lips and she gasped, "My

God, what happened to your head?"

Teresa stepped in smoothly and took her other hand, giving no sign that moments before she had been fending off its razor-sharp metamorphosis. "Sra Martinho, this is my friend Luzia. You fainted, I'm afraid, and she slipped and fell trying to catch you. We shouldn't tire you. Perhaps we'd better go."

Still looking confused, the older woman made only a token protest, fingers caressing the stone on her bracelet with no sign of noticing that it had been exchanged for another. Her sister came bustling in and dismissed the visitors.

Moved to sympathy, Luzia paused before they left the room and said, "I hope you feel better soon, senhora."

The front door shut behind them with a click, and Teresa turned to her with a fierce, if strained, smile. "Well done," she said, and Luzia's heart pounded with the unaccustomed praise. "Now let's get this stone to…" Her voice trailed off. Then she snapped, "Run!"

Thoroughly spooked, Luzia gathered up her skirts like a ten-year-old and bolted for the street door.

Behind her, she heard a sound like claws skittering on the tiles. Teresa shouted something incomprehensible as she wrenched the door open, her heart hammering. There was a flash so bright that her shadow suddenly lay black on the bright pavement before her and a sudden acrid smell like burnt feathers.

She shot out into the sunlit street, feeling the heat strike her face and aware to her relief that Teresa was close behind her, and turned.

"What—?" she began, slowing, but Teresa gave her a push in the back that sent her staggering forward.

"It won't hold it for very long, now hurry!"

People turned their heads to look at the two young women running down the street through the scorching afternoon heat as if all the fiends of hell were after them. Although of course that wasn't the case.

There was only the one.

* * *

As a child, the ruined Convento do Carmo always put me in mind of the ribs of a vast skeleton. A whale's, perhaps. Or one of those prehistoric monsters that people kept on digging up. These days its packed throng of ghosts just makes me think of the futility of prayer. And it's remarkably effective as a reminder of mortality. Not that I need reminding. I only have to look in the mirror for that. Although I don't *feel* old. At least not most of the time. I don't even feel middle-aged. And I've been used to seeing grey in my hair since I was twenty. Took after my father in that. But when the devil did all those lines appear?

The thought brought my father to mind. There's a photograph in his studio of him and me. It's nearly thirty years old, but it could be me and Zé a couple of years ago. Except that Zé looks like his mother and my father has both his eyes, of course. The next amulet we had to retrieve would be his. And that presented me with a dilemma. Nothing to do with him. It's this: *The soul of an artist may only be released by an artist. Against the destroyer, only a creator may stand.*

Emilia is the only creator I know. The only artist. She'd said "of course I will." But she has a withered leg. Needs to walk with a stick. How can she stand up to a guardian called the destroyer? How can I keep her safe?

"Where have they got to?" said Paciência irritably. I came abruptly back to the present. What an inappropriate name the woman has. She fanned herself with her hand in a fierce flapping movement that was certainly effective. Though the movement probably made her hotter than the breeze she made could cope with. Didn't she have some useful cooling spell she could use?

Pierce said in placatory tones, "They've only been gone a few minutes, senhora," and she rounded on him angrily.

"And who asked you?" she snapped. I rubbed my cheekbone and tried to fade into the background. Yeoh, smoking a cigarette, watched them impassively. Like a man at a play. I pulled out my watch and checked. They'd been gone fifteen minutes. Which was either enough time to retrieve an amulet. Or far too much.

I'm no good at this waiting lark. I wiped the back of one hand over my sweating upper lip and decided to copy Yeoh's example and have another smoke. I was just reaching inside my jacket for my cheroots and wondering if the weather would ever cool down when a voice shouted, or rather screamed, "Mother!"

It had more than an edge of panic in it, and the next moment, a wide-eyed Luzia came tearing round the corner, followed closely by Teresa Batista.

And following them, an impression of beating wings. Something monstrous and silent and unseen, but not invisible. It was an absence rather than a presence, a vacuum in the form of an enormous bird. A shape formed from the air but not of it, a bird-shaped heat-haze. Bigger than a man. The spread of its wings was huge. I whipped out my knife at once and stepped in front of Paciência and Pierce.

"Oh God, not another one," I heard his disgusted voice say behind me.

Luzia's fist was clenched round something. The stone, I hoped. Still running, she stretched her arm out in her mother's direction. I could feel the beating of great unseen wings. Then Luzia stumbled, and the stone flew out of her hand.

Everyone dived to catch it at once, like a comedy troupe. Except Yeoh. Who reached out one hand casually as the stone arced through the air, plucked it away from the impression of a plunging beak, and vanished.

Paciência threw a handful of powder in the air and shouted a word in no language I knew, but I felt the force of it in my mind. There was a sudden overpowering smell of ozone, and the bird-thing disappeared. Well, they hadn't needed me, then. What the hell. Let the witch deal with it, da Silva, you're evidently surplus to requirements. I ran my hand round the back of my neck, encountering wet hair and a damp collar. Uncomfortable.

Teresa helped Luzia to her feet. The girl was red-faced and panting with exertion. Even Teresa was breathing a little heavily, but her face was chalky white. Yeoh slid back into view, looking pleased with himself.

"It is safe," he said to my enquiring glance.

"Good," I said.

"Now, if you will excuse me, ladies and gentlemen…and I'd appreciate it, senhor capitão," he went on, "if you'd leave the next one until tomorrow."

I nodded. Realized I was still holding my knife. Resheathed it quickly, glad I hadn't needed to use it. Took out a delayed cheroot and struck a match.

"I haven't worked out how to approach this fellow," I said, with a glance at Teresa. Yeoh smiled smugly.

"Ah, I can help you there. By a strange coincidence," and he raised his eyebrows, "Sr António Prado is currently writing an article about the quarrelsome Alexandre Aveiro, so no doubt he will be interested in talking to your wife." And how did you arrange that? I wondered. "I expect your good lady will appreciate the irony," he added. Which she probably would. But I was hot and tired and I wanted to dehumidify under my eyepatch. I was not in the mood for bad-tempered silversmiths.

Yeoh inclined his head to me, then walked away. I sucked in a mouthful of smoke and blew it out thoughtfully.

"Three down, three to go," said Pierce cheerfully. He was fanning himself with his hat. Seems to be taking uncanny things in his stride now. Found his courage, apparently. But nothing since the late unfortunate Eduardo has had his name on it. It's better when they're not aimed at you. Not much. But better.

Teresa mopped her face. "That was too close for comfort." Her voice sounded strained and thinner than normal.

"What *was* that thing?" gasped Luzia, glancing at her mother.

"Garuda, I think," said Teresa automatically, and Paciência gave her a narrow look and pursed her lips.

"You seem to know a good deal about these matters, menina," she remarked. Teresa shrugged her shoulders.

"I'm a *mandingueiro's* daughter, senhora. What can I say?"

Paciência seemed on the point of making a sharp retort when a spasm of agony crossed Teresa's face and she doubled over with a gasp. Luzia seized her arm.

"What is it? What's the matter?" she asked. Teresa shook her head, apparently unable to speak for a moment.

"The masking spell," Paciência said austerely, staring at her daughter. "Do you still wish you'd been its recipient?"

Luzia ignored her. Squatted down in front of Teresa and grasped her hand. I saw Teresa's knuckles whiten as she took hold, then she relaxed her grip. And straightened, bringing Luzia up with her. The girl still looked anxious. A trickle of blood had crept from Teresa's nostril.

"Your mother's right," she said with an effort. "It's just a side-effect of the spell." She wiped the blood with her finger. Put the finger to her mouth and licked it off.

"Come along, Luzia," said the witch briskly, taking her daughter's elbow in a firm grip. "It's time we were going." The girl scowled.

"Are you sure you're all right?" she asked Teresa.

"Yes, of course," replied Teresa. Her voice sounded almost normal, now. But her face was still shockingly white. "Better do as your mother says."

And doesn't that make my memory do a flip-flop? Mind you, whose heart doesn't feel a chill at those words? Ranks right up there with *Because I say so* for parental ominous-ness. If there is such a word.

* * *

—*You have made this man into the keystone,* the demon had said to him. *Therefore he is the* raison d'être *of the spell. Everything you do is linked to him. But to succeed, you must be more powerful than he is. You must take back the initiative. Gain a hold over him, a lever. Only then can the drawing of the Eidolon be completed.*

—*How?* he had asked, his mind bruised by the demon's occupancy. Though he didn't know that. As far as he was concerned, it was confined by the magical diagram he had drawn. But it was a very long time since any

demon he summoned had been constrained by his figures. He had opened
his mind to them years and years before. They knew the pathways of his
brain, the nuances of his soul. Knew it for their own.

There could never be a chance of exorcism for him. He was too riddled with
their essence to survive it.

—*Just think of your own single weakness and you will know where your enemy
is vulnerable,* the demon had replied. He needed no further explanation.
Teresa's face came into his mind. Beloved child.

"Go and fetch the boy," said Francisco Domingues Batista to
Eduardo.

* * *

"I can feel your mark...your key," said Emilia in my arms last night.
Preoccupied, I'd hardly heard her. "I can still feel it," she said, a little later. I
lifted myself up on one elbow. Saw, to my astonishment, an identical
pentagram drawn shadowy on her breast like a faded tattoo. As I watched, it
glowed brightly for a second, and then the image vanished.

She could feel mine, though there was nothing to be seen. So can I feel
her mark? I touched the place it had been with a fingertip and made out the
thinnest of raised lines. Emilia drew in a breath and copied the gesture. I
shivered.

We had one each. What that signified, I had no idea. I would have to ask
Zacuto. I need to find out about Fr Jerónimo, too. And first of all there's
António Prado to deal with. Not that I can do that, unfortunately.

Well, it could all wait till the morning.

* * *

I'd wondered how Emilia would react to Teresa Batista. Paciência was
immutable and implacable, but then she's an unforgiving woman. She's the
type who'll hold a grudge until is dies of old age. And then have it stuffed
and mounted.

Emilia, however, though she eyed her warily, shook her hand and said,
"Thank you for helping us."

Teresa bent her head politely. "Senhora," she murmured. Her face was
still very pale. She looked as if she'd not slept.

"You'd better make yourself scarce," Emilia said to me. "Sr Prado will be
here any moment." And where was John Yeoh when you needed him? He
was the one who'd arranged this in the first place. Oh God. I can't pretend
this isn't endangering Emilia. The thing's called the destroyer, for hell's sake.
But what else can I do? I took a deep breath to steady myself. Can't say it had

any noticeable effect.

There was only one thing I could do. I put my arms round her and said, "Be careful." Damn it, she feels so slender and fragile. Over her head I saw Teresa give me a very odd look. What was that about?

"I won't break, Luís," Emilia whispered.

"I know," I said. "But—"

"It'll be all right," she said. "Now go and pester Sr Zacuto or someone and let us get on with it."

I went to pester Harris instead. If he was awake. Which he was, sitting up in the small bed like a bear in a hammock.

"Morning, skipper," he said hoarsely. "Tell you what, this woman keeps goddamn funny hours. Ain't she never heard of having a beauty sleep?"

"You seeing anything at the moment?" I asked, sticking my hands in my pockets and leaning against the wall. He seemed to've stopped smoking, so I guessed the smell was still making him sick. So don't light up around him, da Silva.

Harris shook his head. "She took it off again, all I get is the ceiling. When you fixing to go get the thing?"

"Soon," I said. "We should have the fourth one this morning." I swallowed. She'll be all right. The spell says she can stand against it. And she has Teresa Batista on her side. Who can fight like a soldier.

"The fourth one?" echoed Harris. "When did you get the third?"

"Yesterday."

He ran his hands over his face and made a disgusted noise. "Hellfire, I hate this. I'm sick as a dog and I don't even get the goddamned news."

Trying not to smile, I said, "We'll get it written up in the *Diario*. How're you feeling today?" Which was a damn silly question really. But it's sort of automatic, isn't it. When someone's hors de combat. Harris looked at me sourly.

"Like I've been shoved through a mangle." He breathed out loudly. "Don't it ever cool down in this place?"

"It's not usually this hot," I said.

"I suppose that's down to messing with demons too," he grumbled. "'Least you know where you are with a werewolf."

Was that a joke? From Harris? Surely not. I didn't comment on it. "Demon weather," I said instead.

* * *

So that's Teresa Batista, Emilia thought. She's very striking-looking. At least I suppose she would be if she didn't look so ill. "Are you…well?" she asked the younger woman. "Would you like something to drink?"

"I'll have some tea, if it's not too much trouble," Teresa replied, touching her forehead as if she had a headache. "This masking spell, it's a—a strain."

Emilia rang the bell for Joana, then said, "Do we have any idea of what to expect? What the destroyer will look like?"

"No," Teresa said, shaking her head. "They don't seem to follow any kind of a pattern. I think they adapt to circumstances." She looked at Emilia's walking-stick. "Can you—I mean, are you mobile?"

"I have one good leg. And my arms are very strong." Her heart was beating fast. She felt a little apprehensive, but wouldn't have described it as fear. "Can we make a plan, then?"

"We can, in outline," said Teresa, watching Emilia's face intently. "You're not Portuguese, are you?" she added irrelevantly.

"No, I'm from Venice." Joana came in, and Emilia asked her for the requested tea. "What do you suggest?"

Teresa glanced down at her hands. "As soon as he sees you, his amulet will know it's in danger, and he'll change. The guardians are fast, senhora, unbelievably fast. So I'll wait by the door here. Hopefully I can keep him under control long enough for you to swap the stones. He's wearing it on his watch-chain." She stopped, and Emilia observed a faint hint of red in her cheeks. "Do you think you can do that?"

Relieved, Emilia nodded. "It doesn't sound as if my part of it is very difficult. But what about you?"

"Well," said Teresa with a tight smile, "we'll just have to hope I can manage to sit on him, won't we?"

She looked so tired and strained that Emilia couldn't even summon up any resentment for her part in her father's spell. I wonder what she's thinking? she said to herself.

The mark that had appeared over her heart earlier throbbed suddenly, and she gave a tiny gasp which Teresa apparently missed: her eyes were closed, anyway. A wash of emotions tangled with images rushed through Emilia's mind like a wave rinsing over the sand, and she knew without any room for doubt at all that it came from Teresa. Tiredness, regret, hope, frustration, anger. Faces she knew: Luzia, Paciência, Dr Bosque, Luís. One she didn't, but who had to be the girl's father. All so fleeting that she hardly had time to recognize them. If she'd been standing, she would have staggered back with the force of it, and then it was gone.

Astonished and shocked, she pressed her fingers to the mark, but could feel nothing at all through her clothes.

Then Joana came in carrying a tray. "Here's your tea," Emilia blurted, and Teresa opened her eyes.

At least she no longer doubted the younger woman's sincerity.

As Joana left the room, she heard the doorbell, and glanced at the clock.

"Is it him?" Teresa asked, as if she thought Emilia could see through walls. No, not through walls, Emilia thought. But apparently into people's hearts.

"He's early, if it is," she said, so calmly it amazed her. "However, I expect it's actually Sr Yeoh."

Teresa sipped her tea, and Emilia contemplated her new talent. There are no such things as coincidences, Luís was fond of saying. So why had she been given this ability? Or was it just a side-effect of having the mark? Why had she been given something called the key of Solomon? And leaving aside the why for the moment—what about how? Her mark was identical to the one Luís had, as far as she could tell, and not a mirror-image as her first daft thought had been, as if its imprint had been left on her body by his. Her hand crept towards it again, and she forced it back to her knee. Stop that, she told herself sternly, you can't feel it. For some reason we can touch each other's marks, but not our own.

The door opened, and John Yeoh put his head round it.

"Senhora," he said with his usual politeness, though he must be irritated at having to rush all over the city at the drop of a hat to hide this amulet here, that one there. Emilia shied away from finding out, thinking, This could prove awkward. "Where would you like me to wait?" he went on. "I do not think I should be in the offing when our friend arrives."

"Oh—in the parlor, I think, Sr Yeoh, if you would," said Emilia, a little flustered. "Joana, do you mind?"

"You should come and sit this side of the desk," suggested Teresa after he was gone, half-rising from her chair.

"Yes, of course," agreed Emilia. Her mouth was dry now, but she found that the palms of her hands were sweating. She felt short of breath, and her heart was hammering away nineteen to the dozen.

Now I'm afraid, she thought.

The sound of the doorbell made them both jump. Emilia pushed herself to her feet with a strained smile, picking up her walking-stick automatically. Teresa stood up and walked over to the door, positioning herself to one side of it. Instead of sitting in the chair she'd just vacated, Emilia leaned against the front of the desk.

When Joana, no doubt grumbling at the number of times she'd had to answer the door (so many people, so early in the morning!), showed the journalist António Prado into the office, Emilia had time to think, *Dio mio*, the eagle reference was an understatement. His nose was heroic, a Cyrano of a beak. It defined him. You could no more separate the nose from what he was than remove part of his character. And António Prado had time to recognize Teresa: Emilia could almost read his thoughts, never mind feel them. *Why, that's the woman who sells the charms. She must buy her stones from Sra da Silva here. What a coincidence.*

And then he turned to Emilia, and the stone took him over.

Teresa was already moving and didn't see the change clearly. Emilia, right in front of the guardian, saw all the intelligence drain out of the journalist's dark eyes, and the humanity with it. Saw his mouth slacken and fall open, and a thread of saliva trail from the corner.

Saw his fist backhand Teresa casually, sending her crashing into the metal filing cabinet behind her.

"You pig," shouted Emilia at the drooling mindless thing, the destroyer-guardian, and brought her walking-stick down on its head as hard as she could. Wishing she had at hand the heavier crutch she used on the days her leg was bad. Reaching out quickly, she jerked on the watch-chain adorning his vest and was rewarded with a heavy half-hunter with a piece of jasper dangling from its fob.

The instant it left his body he collapsed bonelessly to the floor. Emilia, her heart pounding, replaced the stone with trembling fingers and limped over to check on Teresa.

Who, to her relief, was stirring. Her eyelids snapped open, and she struggled to get up. Emilia restrained her. Her wrists and arms, and her shoulders, were strong from over thirty years of helping support her weight, and Teresa sank back against the wall.

"What happened?" she asked in bewilderment, feeling the back of her head gingerly where it had slammed into the filing cabinet.

"He caught you by surprise, I think," replied Emilia, unable to help feeling a little smug. "And I hit him with my walking-stick."

Teresa laughed ruefully, wincing. "So much for me holding him down."

"Take the stone to Sr Yeoh," said Emilia, putting it in Teresa's hand and closing her fingers over it. "Best if Sr Prado forgets you were here."

They both glanced at the unconscious man. Teresa seemed about to speak, then thought better of it. She scrambled inelegantly to her feet, then held out her hand for Emilia, who took it without hesitation.

"You trust me," exclaimed Teresa in surprise.

"Yes," said Emilia, simply. "Now get that stone to Sr Yeoh, fast as you can."

Left to herself, she rang for Joana, then overturned the visitor's chair and scattered a few papers on the floor. I feel like Tosca doing this, she thought with a smile, and lowered herself carefully to replace the journalist's watch in his pocket.

His eyes flickered open, and he put a hand to his temple.

"Holy Virgin, what happened?" he asked, looking up at Emilia.

"You...passed out," she replied, after a brief semantic debate deciding that was preferable to *fainted* with its overtones of swooning delicate women. "Has it happened before?"

"Sweet Jesus, no," he said, struggling to his feet. Emilia, using stick and desk, did the same. "Did I hit my head?"

"Yes, sit down." She indicated the chair.

Some minutes later, the journalist supplied with restorative tea and Emilia with coffee, he sat back in the chair and said, "I wanted to ask you about amulets, senhora." He indicated the jasper, and a puzzled frown flitted over his face. Then he shook his head slightly. Evidently, whatever he was trying to remember eluded him. "I wear this, for instance. And Sr Aveiro lent me this."

António Prado delved in his pocket and brought out the sapphire Emilia had sold to Teresa Batista.

* * *

He felt as if his insides had been reamed out with a strigil, and light as though he could ascend to heaven on a puff of wind. There was no such buoyant air to be felt, however, only a still and musty smell of permanence, with a faint trace of mildew.

Opening his eyes, he found he was lying on the floor on top of a thin threadbare blanket. Somewhat incongruously, a bright electric light shone in his eyes. Bookshelves rose all around him, and rose and rose astonishingly, to almost dizzying heights. There was an intense aura of peace pervading the entire place.

Fr Jerónimo knew where he was, of course. The library of São Rafael. The place to which he had been seeking admittance so diligently. Although just for the moment, he couldn't remember why. Turning his head, he saw a carafe of water and a glass on the floor beside him. Water seemed like a good idea, but he wasn't entirely sure whether he could actually lift the carafe, and wondered whether he had been ill. His jaw felt bruised, too.

With some effort, he managed to sit up, but the movement left him lightheaded and trembling. He rested his head on his knees and tried to breathe slowly.

At some stage, by some sense, the one which allows us to know that we are observed, he became aware that someone had come to stand beside him. He raised his head. An elderly man wearing a curiously old-fashioned robe looked down at him speculatively out of dark eyes he didn't know how to read. Fr Jerónimo couldn't say how he knew that this was a ghost, because there was nothing in the man's appearance to suggest it, in fact the old fellow looked remarkably robust, but the certainty made him raise his hand weakly and make the sign of the cross.

The ghost merely looked amused, though it was difficult to tell under his bushy, even luxuriant, beard.

"What—who are you?" croaked Fr Jerónimo. His throat felt like sandpaper. The ghost raised bushy eyebrows.

"Are you so free with *your* name?" he asked. "You may call me Isaiah, if you need a label for me."

"You don't look like a demon," the priest complained, trying very hard to feel fear or dread or even self-righteousness, but failing on all three counts. He fumbled for his rosary.

"That is because I am not one," said the ghost. "Although I am, as you seem to have surmised, dead." He smiled, teeth showing white amidst the beard. "Nor will your holy symbol have any effect on me."

"*Ego te exor—*" began Fr Jerónimo. The ghost interrupted him.

"You cannot exorcise me either," he said austerely, "and the fact that you make the attempt to do so is an irony you do not yet appreciate. Now I am sure you would benefit from drinking some of that water."

"Who are you?" the priest asked again. "What are you doing here?" He didn't touch the water, although he was ragingly thirsty, like a man who has been toiling in the sun all day. And the sun these days would dry such a laborer out in no time.

"You ask the wrong questions," the ghost said, sounding much like a schoolmaster. Since Fr Jerónimo was feeling a bit like a schoolboy at the moment, he accepted the rebuke. He struggled to his feet, with the aid of a chair.

"What should I be asking, then?" he enquired, for much of his customary certainty had disappeared. The ghost shook his head, but not in a reproving way, or so Fr Jerónimo thought. He picked up a book from the table and opened it and was somewhat disconcerted to find its pages covered in meaningless squiggles. "Am I dead?" he asked, an old legend coming to his mind, or was it just a story someone had written, that ghosts cannot read, it is the first thing they lose.

"No, young man, you are not dead," said the ghost, peremptorily, and Fr

Jerónimo would normally have demanded the respect or at least the title due him, but today he found it seemed unimportant. "You were, however, possessed, and I drove out what had possessed you. It was not a demon, but something of prodigious malice nonetheless. Its occupancy will have damaged you somewhat, but your memory should return in time. Meanwhile, please drink the water. You need to replace fluid."

Fr Jerónimo stared at the ghost. His mind latched onto a single word from this explanation. He made the sign of the cross automatically, finding it strangely uncomforting. "Possessed?" he repeated.

"Just so."

A frenzy of thoughts chased through his head, most of them frightening and all of them confusing. He bent down, vision blurring for a second, picked up the water carafe a trifle shakily and poured some into the tumbler, glass clinking against glass with his trembling. A little slopped over the edge onto his hand. He raised the glass to his lips, thinking he could smell its contents, which was very strange, since water has no smell unless the careless housemaid has left the jug uncovered and dust has therefore settled on its surface.

"How did I get here?"

"You were brought," replied the ghost, "so that I could perform the exorcism." Fr Jerónimo took a mouthful of water. It was cooler than he thought it would be, but had no taste, so he must have been imagining things.

"By whom?" he asked. The ghost paused, as if considering whether or not to answer. Finally he nodded.

"Captain da Silva brought you."

And that was the strangest thing of all. Although to tell the truth, he couldn't remember what the grudge was that he had against this man.

* * *

Zé, having come at last to the end of his duty on the morning watch, which he hated, contemplated skipping *Isabella* breakfast. It was more than a little depressing being on board at the moment, and he missed Felipe. He could have as good a breakfast at home. He squinted at the morning sky, which was as bright and unclouded as it had been for days, and scratched an itch on the end of his nose.

But in the end he decided to eat now, partly because João was a good cook, and partly because he could have a second breakfast when he got home. He wondered when his father would ask him to help set Fil free, and what the delay was, and whether Sr Harris was any better so that he could have his room back. Having Caterina snoring in the next bed was much worse than sharing with Fil, who hardly ever made a sound.

He hurried homewards, therefore, but warily, in case of a lurking Fr Jerónimo. He was still cross with himself over letting himself be caught like that. It wasn't as if he didn't know about such things. He'd been stalked by a werewolf in India, and on another occasion something unseen had thrown him off the rigging. Zé was pretty sure that other things had happened to his father, too, and he itched to know about them.

Dime novels and shilling shockers had come his way via Dr O'Rourke: they were the only things he really enjoyed reading. Mostly, now, to try and work out what the authors and artists had gotten wrong, since none of the latter had ever managed to draw a werewolf that looked remotely like Sr Harris. As a result, Zé, with the confident expertise of a little knowledge, now sniffed at all the illustrations.

As he trotted into one of the narrow dark alleys that led him home by the shortest route, though, he smelt something else. Something like spoiled meat. He wrinkled his nose. Someone had chucked the rubbish out into the street, he supposed. A dog or a cat would enjoy that. They were less fussy than humans. He heard a soft footstep and whirled round, his heart thumping for no reason. A tiny elderly woman all in black padded along behind him for a moment, then disappeared through a doorway.

Rounding a corner, he slowed to climb the steep flight of steps he knew was there, but not very much. He was, after all, fourteen. He went up them two at a time. Halfway up, a bone-thin orange cat shot out in front of him, nearly tripping him up. Zé said, in English, "Bugger," a curse he liked the sound of, and checked behind him guiltily to make sure no one had heard him. It would be just his luck if some sniffy English-speaker came up and boxed his ears.

The stench of rot was still with him. He was fed up with it now. Even cleaning the bilges came to an end at last. It didn't follow you around.

Follow you around. His back prickled, and he realized he'd been spooked for some time, that was why he was so jumpy. Zé wished he had a knife like his father's—or, even better, that interesting Roman sword.

At the top of the steps he found out what was causing the stink.

Its head lolled forward unsupported by muscles or tendons, because most of its throat had been eaten. It had also been dead several days in near hundred-degree heat, and the soft tissue was beginning to putrefy. But the spell that animated the late Eduardo took no account of the weakness of the flesh. Nor of the stresses and strains the speeds it was forced to move at put on bone and sinew, enough to cause living ones to snap and fracture. One arm, indeed, seemed to have two elbows, but this didn't appear to impede its movement.

The corpse grabbed Zé before his yell of fright made it past his lips and clamped a clammy fetid hand over his mouth. Zé struggled against dead meat given sorcerous strength, choking on the stink, revulsion and panic reinforcing his efforts, but none of it was enough.

He didn't pass out from terror, but chloroform did the trick.

* * *

"D'you mind quitting, skipper?" said Harris. "You're making me giddy, and I can do without that right now."

In deference to his delicate state I'd decided not to subject him to my cheroots. It was driving me berserk. Pacing helped, but apparently it was having the same effect as smoke. Oh well. The parlor isn't really big enough to pace in, anyway.

"Sorry," I said. Sat down in the chair I'd just got up from. He leant back and closed his eyes. I glared at him. Couldn't make him dizzy if he wasn't looking at me. I crossed my legs, then uncrossed them again. The room's too hot. Don't know what I'm worrying about. The stone's safe. Emilia's talking to a perfectly mundane journalist who isn't going to transform into anything any more, about the perfectly mundane business of being a jeweler.

She just seems to be taking a hell of a long time about it.

We've now got four stones. Deployed by Yeoh in various locations. Where Batista doesn't have a hope of finding them. However, as soon as we take them out of their hiding-places to destroy them, he'll know. I've no idea what we'd do then. But I've got Zacuto and Pierce working on it.

At last I heard voices outside, and the sound of the front door closing.

I found Emilia in her workroom. Tidying things away with a thoughtful look on her face. She looked up as I came in and gave me a strange feverish smile. What was wrong?

"What is it?" I asked. Crossed the room in three steps and put my arms round her. She rested her head on my shoulder. "Was it the guardian?" Teresa had told me what had happened, of course. Resourceful, Emilia. I should never have doubted she could do it.

"The mark," she said. "The key of Solomon." Her whole body was tense. Nice as it was holding her, I moved back and gave her shoulders a rub.

"Relax," I instructed her. She smiled. "There must be a reason for it."

"I saw into Teresa's...mind. Heart," she whispered. "Something. I felt her emotions. Sort of knew what she was thinking." And how do I react to that? "I could...read you, now, if I wanted to. I don't need to, though," she added. "I always know what you're thinking."

She put the palm of her hand against my chest, where the mark was. It made me draw my breath in sharply. I touched her face. "How do you know it was the mark?"

"I know." She took my other hand, placed over her own mark, and shivered. "I felt it." Her heart was beating rapidly. "What's happening to me?" I knew the feeling. She wanted to be normal again.

"Listen," I said, stroking her face. "Do you remember when I first started to see ghosts?" Or couldn't un-see them, might be a better way of putting it.

"Of course." She closed her eyes for a second. Her fingers moved, tracing the mark under my shirt.

"I didn't want it," I said softly, touching her comfortingly, telling her things she knew. "But I had to learn to live with it."

"I know you're right," she replied. "But why has this happened to me, why now?"

Questions I couldn't answer. I touched her lips, and she kissed my fingers. "We'll have to ask Zacuto," I said.

"Will he know?" She looked so forlorn I pulled her to me and kissed her. Actually that's not quite true. It implies only one person was doing the kissing. This was definitely a joint effort.

A moment later, I said into her mouth, "You're a wanton woman."

"Yes, I know," whispered Emilia.

* * *

Society frowns on public displays of affection. Even on contact. It's embarrassed by its own humanity. Straight-laced. Narrow-minded. Hidebound. Well, damn convention, I say. At least when I walk with Emilia my arm round her can be viewed as a support. Like her walking-stick. And if people choose to find that shocking, it's their problem. Double standards here, da Silva? Why not take off the eyepatch, then?

Sometimes I find myself as amusing as other people. And for that matter, why should I be excluded?

So we walked slowly to São Rafael, Emilia with a support on each side. Not that she's not perfectly capable of getting around on her own, of course. And it was really too damn hot to have my arm around her. But we're together too seldom to waste an opportunity.

"So," I said to her, "how did you get Sr Prado to part with the sapphire?"

"I told him the truth," she said simply. "Well, part of it."

I looked down at her to see her smiling. She was enjoying this. I smiled back. "Go on."

"I said to him, if it really was all superstition, we should swap Sr Aveiro's stone with another one without telling him and see whether he noticed any difference. He thought it was a fine idea, so that was what we did."

Meu Deus, she's clever. I laughed out loud and tightened my arm round her. "Did I ever tell you, you're brilliant?"

It was her first visit to the library. I was a little surprised to realize that. But I got the feeling she'd become a regular visitor. She was as entranced as Pierce had been. Who was already ensconced, not to my great surprise. He stood up politely when he saw Emilia, spectacles glinting in the electric light.

"What an unexpected surprise," he said. "How nice to see you, senhora."

Zacuto bowed to her and announced, "A pleasure to make your acquaintance, dear lady." Which if you think about it is an odd thing for a ghost to say. But then he's an odd sort of ghost. "To what do we owe the pleasure, senhor capitão?"

"Something strange happened," Emilia put in before I could say anything, taking the ghost in her stride without any effort at all. "I seem to have...acquired a key of Solomon."

I'd thought nothing could ruffle Zacuto's composure. But that did. He blinked, his equivalent of having hysterics. Or a hissy fit, as Harris would say. Looked from one to the other of us in a very knowing way.

"What?" I demanded.

"How unusual," he said, urbanely. "I have heard that such a thing is possible, however." He paused. I scratched my eyebrow. "Did the senhora bruxa happen to involve you in her masking spell, by any chance?"

"Yes," I replied, "for grounding, she said."

He nodded, as if pleased to have something confirmed. "Then you were left with some residual magic, enough to pass on the mark during...intimate contact."

Emilia's face turned pink, and she put a hand over her mouth. I could see she was hiding a smile. Pierce was conspicuously absorbed in his books. And I can't say I'm entirely comfortable discussing such things with a ghost. Or anyone, for that matter. Weren't people in Zacuto's day a bit more coy about it, anyway? So maybe I do have a touch of the conventional about me, after all. Must be the effect of middle-age, da Silva.

I glared at him. "We—" I began, but Zacuto went on, appearing not to notice.

"And of course salt has certain magical qualities."

"Salt?" enquired Emilia.

"Sweat," the ghost explained, who couldn't perspire. "And saliva."

"All right, well, we are married," I said defensively, rubbing my cheekbone and wishing for a smoke.

"If I thought it would embarrass you, senhor capitão," he said gravely, "I would have tried to express myself more, ah, delicately. But the point is this. You could not have passed the mark on without being in...complete harmony with your wife, or without her trusting you completely. That it happened shows that you have a remarkable bond with her." Emilia and I exchanged glances, then we both looked back at the old scholar's ghost.

"But what does it mean?" she asked him. Zacuto stared gravely at her.

"Such things never happen at random," he said. Which is just another way of saying there are no such things as coincidences. "Although I cannot think why you have been given the key, senhora. However, it suggests a solution to a current problem."

"Which is?" I enquired.

"*Against the succubus, only the faithful may stand,*" he quoted.

"I thought I'd ask John Yeoh," I said. Zacuto shook his head.

"Sr Yeoh has retrieved one stone already; it precludes him from doing so again. But you can do it, Captain da Silva. Your passing of the key to your wife is proof of that."

"And what about the fact that it lets me see what people are feeling?" asked Emilia, apparently forgetting she hadn't mentioned this before.

"It does?" said Zacuto, raising his eyebrows. Surprised him again. Ha. Twice in ten minutes. Getting one back on him, anyway. Emilia nodded. Zacuto thought about it for a while. But all he could come up with was, "Then that may be a talent of your own which the key has woken, or amplified."

We all fell quiet for a moment. The library's calm intensified the silence. Then Pierce piped up, "Skipper, have you noticed our, er, guest?"

Maybe he was changing the subject a bit too obviously. But I couldn't have found a better reason if I'd tried.

Fr Jerónimo was sound asleep at one of the small work-tables under the shuttered windows. He looked pretty peaceful for a man who'd been possessed, but Mouffi's occupation had neglected him. The priest was filthy as a beggar, with dried blood crusted on his face.

"He survived, then," I said sourly, raising an eyebrow.

"Physically, yes," nodded Zacuto. "But he has lost a lot of his memory, including his reasons for wanting to find the library, *and* whatever cause he had for disliking you, senhor capitão." I shivered, for no obvious reason. It certainly wasn't due to a draught.

"He's also lost the ability to read," said Pierce, shoving his spectacles up.

I laughed. I couldn't help it. That was irony, if you like. Or poetic justice. Maybe God does have a sense of humor, after all.

* * *

The consciousness that was Mouffi, that had once been great Malphas and was now dwindled to a spark in a huge writhing darkness, spun and whirled like chaff on the wind, flung now this way, now that. It had no senses as humans understand them, but it perceived analogues of noise, buffeting forces, motion, and even motion sickness.

A kind of anxiety, too, even fear, as it sought for an anchor, a lifeline, a buoy, anything to catch hold of, any willing soul.

Mouffi had been ripped out of the body it had been inhabiting like a violent abortion and hurled into this limbo, a maelstrom not of time and space but beyond those things. It had no form, nothing; Mouffi had no form within it.

But the demon-remnant did have a will, and that kept it buoyant in the airs of this tempest raging outside time. And gradually it became aware of direction, because there was, in all that confusion, a fixed point. Not even a soul, not yet, but the potential of one.

Fixing its will on that inchoateness, Mouffi travelled towards it, plunging in a direction that became *down* as it was recognized, straight as an arrow to its target.

Out of the blue cloudless sky over the city of Lisbon the demon-remnant exploded, shattering the surface of the air like some leviathan's plunge into the ocean, always supposing such a beast could leap out of the waves in the first place. If anyone was looking up at that moment, as people sometimes do for no apparent reason, he would have seen a flash so bright it would leave greenish shadows in his eyes, but heard no accompanying explosion.

Still bodiless, but relishing the absence of storm, Mouffi floated on the calm air, and if it had owned a body, it would have salivated. Down there was a soul honeycombed with the tracks of his kind, richly rotten with their essence, riddled through with uncounted demon-presences. Like a dog sniffing a lamp-post, he could identify them all by the smells they left behind. This soul was as open to him as any whore.

He had only to wait until this man opened a channel, which he would surely do before long, because he obviously craved it like an opium-smoker his poppy juice— and Mouffi would have a body once more.

* * *

Zé wasn't home.

He'd left *Isabella* after his watch ended. Well, apparently he'd loitered around, eating as much as he could scrounge, and gossiping. A ship's crew is worse than a ladies' sewing circle for gossip. Though presumably they talk about different things. And I may even be maligning the ladies' sewing circle here.

"It might not mean anything," I ventured. Not believing it for a moment. It was Batista. Had to be. The inside of my head felt as if it was prickling.

Emilia wasn't fooled, either. "It's a trap," she said bleakly. "He wants you to go charging after Zé. And God knows what he has in mind."

Furiously aware that it was all, ultimately, my fault, I stubbed out my cheroot. Swallowed nausea. "He could've killed me any time he wanted," I pointed out.

"We both know this isn't about killing you," she said. "He's got something else in mind." Possession, neither of us said. But the word hung in the air like a bubble threatening to burst. A bubble filled with something unspeakable. I nodded unhappily and squeezed her hand. Urgency tugged at me, the urge to run straight to the House of the Four Winds and put a bullet through Batista's head, and damn the consequences.

"I'll get him back," I said again.

"I know," said Emilia. "But we have to get all the stones back first." She swallowed and then moistened her lips. "I can't bear to think of him there either. But that man won't harm him. He wants a hold over you."

"Oh, God, Emilia—" She squeezed my hand.

"And perhaps Teresa can help," she added. "But get those stones first."

"I need Zé." But I knew what she was going to say.

"We need Zé. But *you* need a *child,"* whispered my wife.

Caterina.

We clung together like two people in a storm.

* * *

Caterina Laura da Silva—a big name for a little girl—knows that her father sees ghosts, although she is only eight years old. Well, *nearly* nine, eight years and eleven months and two days is practically nine, and don't birthdays come round slowly?

She knows about the ghosts because she sees them too. They are her friends, although they never speak, never even notice her. She knows the fat old woman at the other end of the street, she calls her Senhora Porca because she looks a little like a pig. She knows the boy with the sad eyes near the school, and his name is Tristão, and sometimes she wonders why he can't play with the pretty girl she has christened Linda who loiters nearby, they seem to be about the same age. And more, many more.

At first she thought everyone could see them, that they were a part of the world as visible as cats and trees and trams and washing-lines. But she soon realized that her mother, and then her brother, and at last everyone but her father, walked these streets completely unaware of the transparent people who shared them.

There are other things in her mind, too, hiding behind those blue eyes. She remembers, hazily, a night more than five years ago when they still lived in Venice, although you would have to hypnotize her to get all the details. A nightmare had woken her, and she had been dozing on the couch, curled up in a nest of blankets like a puppy, half-awake or half-asleep, the two terms have slightly different meanings. Only the hypnotism would tell you that when her mother took away the bloody towel from her father's head, a single drop of blood fell on Caterina's face. It only took that much, for she was only a tiny person. If he had other children he might pass the gift on that way, or the curse, it depends on your point of view. But it seems unlikely, for Caterina herself was a miracle, or an accident, again, it depends on your point of view.

So she acquired the talent through blood, and perfect trust.

* * *

Caterina stared up at Teresa Batista and frowned. "You're too tall," she said reproachfully. As literal as the English, my daughter. Teresa looked helplessly at me. Then squatted down so they were more or less level.

"I just went on growing," she explained. Which struck me as a pretty good answer. I sucked in smoke, feeling apprehensive. I have Emilia's word, now, that Teresa sincerely wants to help. But she had no idea about Zé. He wasn't in the House of the Four Winds. So we'll have to call on Paciência's skills again. If she can find people as easily as she can find objects.

So here we are in the park. Where the grass has turned yellow and the trees have that dusty look they don't usually acquire until August. People strolling around taking the air, all in their summer clothes. Not that what we call summer clothes were designed to keep anyone cool. As far as I can tell they're the same as winter ones, but thinner and sometimes lighter in color. And by the way, who came up with the boater as a piece of fashionable headgear? Makes you look like a gondolier. And they're as big a bunch of bloody villains as you'll meet anywhere.

An oddly-assorted group, you'd probably think if you saw us. Especially amongst all these families enjoying the sunshine. One Chinaman, slight and sleek. One tall Brazilian woman with a haughty face. One rather rumpled, one-eyed Portuguese. And his small daughter. We hardly look like a family group.

However depressed the senhora Williams might be, the guardian would still recognize the threat we posed. Except for Teresa. Who was visibly suffering under the masking spell, hollow-eyed and pale, wiping blood from her nose with a handkerchief too often. If we retrieve the last two amulets today, I'll have to ask Paciência to remove the spell.

"That's her," said John Yeoh, interrupting my thoughts. I looked up to see a woman in blue walking slowly along, looking down at the ground. She was holding a parasol. A pace behind her was a tall bearded man who looked startlingly like the English King. The woman didn't appear to be wearing anything resembling an amulet. Malachite or otherwise.

"Has she got it?" I asked.

"I don't know," Yeoh said.

Teresa stood up wearily. "I'll go and see. She knows me." To Caterina, "Wait with your father, *pequena.*"

"Where are you going?" Caterina asked.

"Just to talk to the lady." Teresa smiled down at her. "I'll be back soon."

She walked towards the woman Yeoh had pointed out. I squashed the butt of my cheroot with my shoe and stared after her. Felt singularly useless. Being a spectator is a frustrating business. Caterina seized my hand and tugged at it.

"What is it, sweetheart?" I said.

"Is that lady a giant?"

"No, kitten." Teresa Batista might be a lot of things, but I'm sure that's not one of them.

"I like her," Cat announced. Well, good. That makes everything all right, then. I smiled and ruffled my daughter's messy hair. Thinking about Zé when he was that age. Not a very profitable thing to do, since it only made me fret and worry again.

The two women were much too far away to hear any conversation. Wish I could lip-read. But I can't even eavesdrop. Now the husband caught me looking at them, and I couldn't even watch. Caterina put her arms round my waist.

"I'm bored," she announced. I picked her up, drawing a disapproving look from a passing matron. But she looked so sour she'd disapprove of anything.

"Won't be long now," I said. Hoping I was telling the truth. Shouldn't tell lies to your children. The Da Silva Guide to parenthood.

12

"THEY'RE COMING THIS WAY," YEOH ANNOUNCED. I turned to look.

"Well, I hope she hasn't put it in her pocket," I said.

Caterina pulled my hair. Still haven't got round to visiting the barber. "Ugh, you're all wet." I made a face at her, and she giggled. "Put me down," she ordered. I did as I was told. Wisest thing with women, usually. Then had to smooth the wrinkles in her skirt. She's worse than I am for making clothes look lived-in. She'd also managed to find some mud. In this weather. I'm convinced she carries it around with her.

When I stood up, Teresa was six feet away. Caterina scampered to her and grabbed her hand. She'd made a hit with the youngest da Silva, anyway. Sra Williams approached, and my heart pounded. But she came right up to Caterina, looking at her with a wistful expression, and nothing happened. Harris was right, then. I breathed a sigh of relief.

Teresa made introductions in her best aristo manner. Yeoh had faded into the background somewhere. I raised my hat to the lady and shook hands with the husband. Not something you want to do much of in this heat. I had to restrain myself from wiping my palm down my pants. And wondered exactly what Teresa was up to.

Williams smiled rather tightly. His eyes kept flickering to his wife in concern. But he was perfectly civil. And his Portuguese was fluent, if bizarre. It sounded as though he was framing his thoughts in English and translating them literally.

"Captain, eh?" he said. "What ship?"

"*Isabella*," I told him. "She's a barque. I'm the owner as well as master."

He put his head on one side. "Really? How interesting." He actually sounded interested. "Fond of the jolly old sailing ships, don't you know. Being English. Drake and all that. But you chaps know all about exploring, of course."

"Of course," I agreed. "Da Gama and all that." Williams laughed.

"Absolutely," he said.

"I'm glad to see you out and about," Teresa said in kind tones to the woman. "Did the amulet help you at all?"

Sra Williams put her hand to her neck. "Oh, Edwin," she said in dismay.

"I forgot to put it on."

"What's that, m'dear?" he asked, still lost in maritime contemplation.

"My pendant, you know, the green stone that Sra Pedreira gave me." I had no time to contemplate this alias.

"Oh, that's all right, then," Williams said cheerfully. "Saw you'd left it on the dressing-table, so I popped it in my pocket."

And he put his hand in his jacket and drew it out.

There was a moment when the whole world seemed to hold its breath. Everyone stared at the thing for a split second.

Then Caterina piped up, "That's pretty. Please can I look?"

The Englishman held it out to her with a smile. "There, of course, m'dear. Now, be careful, won't you?" He spilled the chain into her cupped hands.

"May I see?" Teresa bent down in front of her, hiding her from the Williamses. Quickly exchanged the amulet with its understudy, neat as a music-hall conjurer. Slipped the live one into her own pocket and stood up.

"Thank you," said Caterina gravely, then handed the stone back to Williams. I realized I was still holding my breath and exhaled in relief and amazement. The Englishman fastened the chain around his wife's neck. Some of the tenseness seemed to drain out of her.

"Perhaps your mother can make you one like it, Caterina," Teresa suggested helpfully, keeping up the act.

"It's my birthday next month," Caterina said.

"How old will you be?" Sra Williams asked, managing a smile.

"Nine," she told her, proudly.

"Smoke?" Williams asked me, holding out a cigarette case. One of the unstuffiest Englishmen I've ever met. I took one from him. Didn't have the wit to say I preferred my own. I was still in a state of shock from Caterina and Teresa's inspired performance. And the closeness of disaster. Pull yourself together, da Silva, he's still talking. "Did I hear Sra Pedreira say your wife makes jewelry?"

"Yes," I said, hunting for matches and not finding any. Must've dropped them somewhere. I'm always doing that. Williams found his own after a short search, lit both the cigarettes and puffed contentedly.

"She's very good," Teresa observed. I shot her a startled glance.

"Top-hole," exclaimed Williams. I presumed that signified approval. Literal translation, like I said. "Captain da Silva, would you be interested if I put a shipment of wine your way? Idea of sending the stuff on a sailing ship appeals to me, don't you know."

"Certainly," I said. "I have an agent in England." All right, it's pushing it a bit to call Jorge Coelho *my* agent. But only slightly.

"Oh, very good. Toddle along to my office and we'll have a chat, let's say Monday at ten, that suit you?"

Still somewhat bemused, I nodded. "Good of you, Sr Williams."

"Not at all, m'dear chap. Delighted to make your acquaintance." He raised his hat. "Taken up too much of your time. And your delightful daughter. Good day to you all."

I watched them go. Took my own hat off and fanned my sweating face with it. Threw away the cigarette, which tasted of nothing, and took out a cheroot instead. Wished futilely for some cooling device to go under an eyepatch.

Yeoh came up silently and said, "That was very well done."

"Yes, it was," I agreed. "You're very clever, *gatinha*."

Catarina smirked, basking in the praise. She tugged at the hand she was holding. "Can we go home now? I'm hot."

"Of course you can, sweetie," said Teresa. "Why don't you go to your father now?"

"He's all hot and bristly." Some day I'll grow a beard again. See how she likes that. No, I won't. Not if the weather stays like this.

Teresa had grown very still and seemed to be listening. "What is it?" I asked. "Is something the matter?"

She shook her head. "No, quite the opposite. He's not sent anything after it. He doesn't know we have it."

"The guardian did not manifest," said Yeoh. "That must be what he senses." He held out his hand for the stone. Teresa fished it out of her pocket and handed it to him. "No doubt I will see you again very soon."

Does the sun rise in the morning?

* * *

In the library of São Rafael, time passed, but somewhat more irregularly than in the world outside. Many a scholar, if not many students, has wished for more hours in the day, but Montague Pierce was one of the few who achieved his wish, although he was not really aware of it. He searched, and Zacuto searched, and all they found were mysteries wrapped up in enigmas.

And by a shuttered window, Fr Jerónimo dozed, his head on his arms, lulled into slumber by the soft benign musty perfume of books, made up as it is of more than paper and ink and leather, glue and vellum, a book is always more than the sum of its parts.

Such a peaceful scene, but below its surface, what urgency. Both Pierce and Zacuto knew they were under a time constraint, though neither could have said what it was exactly. Just that a problem needed a solution, and soon. But no one can work non-stop, not even a ghost. Certainly not an antiquarian.

Suddenly weary, Pierce took off his spectacles and rubbed his eyes. "I'm going outside for a breath of air," he announced. Zacuto nodded without looking up. The antiquarian slipped his jacket on, more out of habit than anything, because he hardly needed it, and walked stiffly to the door. He glanced at Fr Jerónimo as he passed, but the priest was oblivious, snoring gently.

The heat struck him as he opened the door, like opening the door to a furnace. It was more like Rio in high summer than Lisbon in early June, he thought, not that he had visited this city before. He shaded his eyes and wished he'd thought to pick up a hat.

I could move here, he thought. The idea of leaving the library was almost painful. He imagined himself, years from now, his shop magically transported across the Atlantic, perfect in every detail. And then laughed at himself, something he was, like many Englishmen, able to do sometimes. We have to get through the next few days first.

Zacuto, inside the library, had levitated himself to the very top of the shelves—something he took care not to do while anyone was watching—and was standing on the uppermost story, deep in thought.

He was unaware that Fr Jerónimo had woken up. The priest, bemused anew by his surroundings, and still feeling pretty used up and wrung out from the exorcism, pushed himself to his feet and walked unsteadily to the central table, drawn by some unidentifiable force.

There was something unspeakable there. It was shaped like a book, but it seemed to cast hideous shadows in all directions. In all dimensions.

And a memory, or part of one, came back to Fr Jerónimo. He fumbled for the box of matches he'd found lying on the floor.

Pierce came back inside to see the fire begin to take hold of the *Book of Souls* in Fr Jerónimo's hands. For a moment he was rooted to the spot, then leapt forward with an inarticulate cry as the flames caught the priest's clothes and roared upwards as if caught in a draught.

Somehow Zacuto was in front of him. "Leave him!" the ghost shouted.

"But he's—" cried Pierce in alarm.

"It's too late. Believe me, I know."

Taller than the old scholar, Pierce watched in horror as Fr Jerónimo, the book clutched to his chest, turned into a pillar of white-hot fire. The heat forced him back, and the smell of burning cloth and hair and roasting meat turned his stomach, yet he found he couldn't look away.

Fr Jerónimo never moved, never screamed; he was long past that now. The flames billowed up, roaring, sending greasy smoke as high as the roof, but nothing around him burned. As Pierce watched, his body crisped, blackened, crumbled, within the fire, and then the flames were gone and there was only a pile of reeking ashes on the floor.

"God in heaven," muttered Pierce, and swallowed firmly. I will not be sick, he told himself. His face felt sunburned. He found he was shaking and made himself walk towards the smouldering cinders. The smell of burnt meat was making him salivate, and some part of his mind knew he should be disgusted by that, but he was too overwhelmed by the image of Fr Jerónimo's face melting off his bones to think straight. That would stay with him for a long time.

The whole thing had lasted only minutes. Zacuto, who of course had been unaffected by the heat, not to mention the smell, eyed the remains with a very strange expression on his face.

"And it was you Christians who invented the auto-da-fé," he said finally.

The words made Pierce feel guilty, as though he'd been personally responsible for the immolation of uncounted Jews, heretics and other misfits. When in fact, he thought indignantly a moment later, the English were historically quite reluctant to consign recidivists to the flames. They didn't even burn witches—they hanged them. He noticed distantly that he said *the English* to himself as if he wasn't one of them.

"I'm not responsible for the past," he said, a little stiffly, and took off his spectacles to polish them. This blurred his sight enough to miss Zacuto's indulgent gaze.

"Of course not," said the ghost. "Nor are you responsible for this." He gestured to the ashes. "But because of it, we will need to have recourse to the...images you made of the *Book of Souls*." Pierce had explained how photography worked to him, but wasn't sure if the old scholar had wholly understood.

Then the significance of Zacuto's words sank in, a moment late. He replaced his spectacles excitedly. "You've, er, figured something out?"

"Possibly," replied the ghost. "I believe the releasing of the souls must echo the original spell. Unbinding the Eidolon must mirror the binding. The key, in more ways than one, lies with Captain da Silva and his wife."

"Patterns," said Pierce slowly. His face cleared as understanding dawned. "Two equal, opposite forces—male and female—Did you do that on purpose?"

Zacuto began to pace. In many ways, Pierce thought, his reactions were just the same as a living man's. "No, it seems to have happened quite spontaneously...Nothing happens without a reason. If the captain holds the antitheses, then Sra da Silva will be able to gather the amulets without attracting the attention of the sorcerer. The power of the two keys will prevent him from discovering their whereabouts. There is only one problem."

"Only one?" the antiquarian echoed. Zacuto nodded.

"Yes. The stones must be brought together for the unmaking. But once they are, before the Eidolon can be unmade, its maker will have to be killed."

* * *

Déjà vu is what you call the feeling that says, I've been here before, but I don't remember when. I don't know if there's a word for repeatedly watching a witch cast spells.

Paciência was on her own this time, of course. We won't need Luzia until it's time to destroy the amulets. I felt sorry for the girl. I wouldn't like to be on the wrong side of her mother's temper. And Paciência'd certainly had an ominous look to her the last time I saw her.

Now, of course, she was being businesslike. If you can use that word about a sorceress. She flapped her hand as if to wave away smoke, giving my cheroot a dirty look. Which I ignored. My house. My smoke.

"Ideally I'd need a drop of his blood, but it's not usually feasible for finding missing people. So, hair's the next best thing."

I went in search of Zé's hairbrush. Came back with half a dozen and gave them to Paciência. She gave me a nod of thanks and a stern look.

"Yes, I know," I said, stubbing out the cheroot. "No talking, no smoking." Sat down next to Emilia and took her hand. She squeezed mine back and gave me a reassuring smile.

The witch put the hairs in a glass dish she'd brought with her. Then took out the pendant with the white stone that she'd used before. Finding a person, finding an umbrella, all in a day's work to a witch, I suppose. Maybe the spell she used this time was different from the one she'd used to find the missing pages from the *Mappa Mundi* book. But there was no way of knowing, since she rarely seems to speak a charm out loud.

It looked the same as before. She closed her eyes. Mouthed the words. And the pendulum began to rotate. I felt my scalp tingle. Raised my hand to scratch it, thought better of it. Rubbed my eyebrow instead.

"He has gone under the earth with the walking dead man," she said clearly. Emilia sucked in a shuddering breath and put her hand to her mouth. I gripped her other hand, feeling icy cold all over. It couldn't mean what it sounded like. Her answers were always obscure, right? "Not awake, not asleep."

"Oh, God—" Emilia whispered. So quiet I could barely hear her. Her hand was trembling in mine.

"Not lost, not found," Paciência went on. "Beneath the wind, in the minotaur's stronghold." The swinging pendant came to a standstill, but her lips were still moving soundlessly. The stone began to rotate. Below it in the dish, the hairs began to twine together, weaving themselves into a single strand, coiling into a circle. When they stopped moving, the pendant did as well. The sorceress opened her eyes.

"Please don't say he's dead," begged Emilia in a voice I'd never heard her use.

"Virgin's bones, no," said Paciência irritably. "Under the earth: a cellar, a sewer, a house with a roof-garden. You know how this works by now."

Emilia closed her eyes and sagged against me. I put an arm round her and glared at the sorceress, too angry to be tactful. Don't be such a bloody bitch, I almost said, but stopped myself just in time. "Go easy on her, damn it," I said. "It's Zé we're talking about."

"And it's Henriques's soul that's a prisoner," she snapped back. We glowered at each other for a moment. Then she sighed. "The walking dead man," she went on in her normal voice, "it might be a ghost, or someone with an incurable disease." Or even literally what it says, knowing Batista. "Beneath the wind, now—"

"I know what that is," I interrupted. "Batista's house, the House of the Four Winds."

"Then it must have a cellar."

"What about the Minotaur? A maze?" Emilia asked, sitting up straighter.

"Secret ways, sewers, underground passages. You know the stories, senhor capitão." Paciência shot me a wry glance. Animosity gone, I was relieved to note. Don't want the witch annoyed with me. I raised an eyebrow, and she pointed to the ring of hair. "Put that on your finger when you go to find him," she said. I reached out my hand. Paciência stopped me. "No, don't take it out of the dish until then. It will only work once."

There was nothing much I could say, so I made do with "Obrigado."

"They make it hard for you, I know," she said after a pause. I wasn't sure quite what they she meant. Didn't want to find out. I was saved, as the

English say, by the bell. The doorbell, in this case.

"Oh, what now?" exclaimed Emilia in exasperation.

I took out a cheroot and lit it. "Probably the king come home from England to ask me to raise his father's ghost," I said sourly. She gave a startled snort of laughter, and even Paciência smiled. A wintry sort of smile, but still a smile.

A moment later Joana ushered Pierce in. Who looked wild-eyed and more dishevelled than I am. He gave a visible wince on seeing Paciência. To which she responded by flaring her nostrils. But this non-verbal exchange was over in seconds.

"Skipper," he blurted out, "we've cracked it."

I still had Emilia's hand in mine. Felt her squeeze it convulsively.

"What?" I said, suddenly breathless.

"Everything," Pierce replied. "Everything."

* * *

Outwardly peaceful, the House of the Four Winds baked in the sultry heat. The sun reflected dazzlingly off white walls and azulejos, and baked the terracotta tiles and the blue window shutters. The bougainvillaea tumbling over its high walls like a party garland of improbable magenta luxuriated in the warmth, as did two basking cats, one ginger, one calico, which were the only signs of life in the street outside.

No normal person, looking at the house from the outside, would have been able to tell that a spirit of dreadful malice hovered over it.

Teresa Batista, lying in her shuttered room and nursing a foul headache which had defied all medication, knew, like Mouffi waiting above, that it wouldn't be long before her father summoned another demon. She also know that she ought to be doing something to find da Silva's son, but she couldn't summon the energy. I can't help anyone in this state, she thought with weak irritation. The spell was draining her like a vampire.

Her last thought before slipping into an exhausted doze was of Doctor Inácio Bosque.

Downstairs, deep below the house's wine-cellar and reached from it by a stair no one could find who didn't know it was there, was a lofty chamber. It could be accessed by other routes, however, secret ways forming a labyrinth under the city, parts far older than this house, parts of which, down the ages, had harbored fugitive Jews or made the lives of smugglers more profitable, and down which Eduardo had conveyed Zé some time before.

Who lay, now, in gloom lit by a single oil lamp whose light did not even penetrate to the walls of the sub-cellar, unable to move, listening to the distant furtive scurry of rats, held in stasis by a spell of immobility. Batista may have lacked the *Book of Souls,* but he had been a sorcerer for more than half a century and a spell like that hardly took any thought, though it did take a fair amount of energy to maintain.

Zé was disgusted with himself for letting himself be snatched. He'd let his father down. Should have fought, should have run, should have done anything, just not this. Zé knew that what had come for him had been stronger, and faster, and that he'd been no match for it. None of those things made him feel any better.

The chloroform had left him sick and woozy, and the smell in the chamber didn't help, a mixture of sewers and the putrid-meat stench of the late Eduardo, unanimated now Batista had no present use for him. Even such a powerful sorcerer could only work a limited number of spells at one time. While the spell that held Zé prisoner was active, he could animate Eduardo as well, but nothing else. And Batista needed to devote his energies to more important things.

Right now, that meant summoning a demon. Not to look for stolen amulets, or even a missing book. He had exhausted his own resources in trying to locate them, but the damned man had hidden them too well. However now he had the perfect bargaining tool. He smiled. He liked the irony of using the boy to force his father to give up the stones which would lead to his own enslavement. A very fitting revenge for Francisco Domingues Batista.

No, this particular demon would work a smaller and less subtle revenge on a man who had tricked Batista.

This demon had John Yeoh's name on it.

* * *

Timing. That's what it boils down to. A chronology as precise as the passage of hours.

"Old Zacuto says," said Pierce with a certain lack of respect, waving his spectacles in the air, "that you and your good lady have the keys. I mean, er, you have the keys, the marks, obviously, but what he meant—"

Emilia interrupted him. "I think we know what you mean." Pierce smiled in a flustered sort of way and started polishing the spectacles again. "How exactly does it work?"

That was what I wanted to know, too. But Zacuto's solution worried me.

"Well, er, the idea is that if the skipper has the antitheses, you, senhora, can collect the amulets without Batista knowing." Did I say worried? No. Appalled is a better word.

"Hold on a moment," I said, over a mouthful of smoke. "How sure is he about that?"

Pierce replaced his spectacles. Shrugged slightly. That is to say, like an Englishman. You know, a tiny twitch of the shoulders. "You've seen what he's like. Pretty, er, didactic. It all makes sense the way he says it, anyway."

"He's suggesting I ask Emilia to wander all over the bloody city collecting amulets on the off-chance that Batista won't notice?"

"I'm only saying what—" began Pierce.

"Don't I get any say?" asked Emilia at the same time. I scratched my cheekbone. Ha. Touch of the autocrats, there, da Silva.

"Sorry," I said to both of them. "It just seems—"

"Sr Yeoh would have to be with me," she pointed out. "I wouldn't be on my own."

I still didn't like the idea one bit. "I'm going with you too. Then I'll go after Zé."

"You can't," Pierce protested. "Go with her, I mean."

"Why not?"

"Er, Zacuto says that the amulets and the anitheses have to be kept apart until we're ready to unmake the spell."

Might've known there'd be something like that. And we still had one more stone to collect. Harris. I dragged one hand over my face. Damp and scratchy. Caterina was right.

Until I can find the time to get him back I need to put Zé out of my mind. That's not a difficult thing to do on board *Isabella*, which is hardly what you might call a risk-free environment—meu Deus, if I worried about, that I'd have put the boy on a leash five minutes after he joined the crew. Now, though, it's quite extraordinarily difficult.

So here we have the da Silva party on its way to pay a call on the widow Al-Ghuri. Or perhaps circus troupe would be a better description. With Teresa Batista as the white-faced mime. I'd say she was as pale as a ghost if we weren't surrounded by the damned things proving me wrong. John Yeoh, the Oriental magician. Emilia and I trailing behind. Me with so many stones in my pocket I'm rattling.

And I can't say I'm delighted at the prospect of meeting a succubus.

At least the afternoon was cooling down. Still bloody hot for early June, though. And still so humid everyone's expecting a storm to break it soon. But no sign of that. I could hear birds. Caged canaries singing. A pigeon somewhere. Or it might be a dove, what do I know. Seagulls, inevitably. Two chickens on the street, pecking in a lost sort of way.

Leaving Yeoh and Emilia ensconced fairly comfortably in a café, Teresa led me under an archway in a saltpeter-stained wall. It led into a small brick-paved courtyard. The bricks moved under my feet. A woman's ghost, probably less than twenty years dead, drifted aimlessly past us. By the door opposite, the shade of a man much more recently deceased. A man in Arab robes. And most like that in this city are a thousand years dead.

You can't tell how people died by looking at their ghosts. These phantoms are only echoes of their living selves. And you can't summon them and ask them how they died, either. Mostly, they're not allowed to tell you. Zacuto seems to make up his own rules. But the Arab by the door, who must be the late Sr Al-Ghuri, looked distinctly miffed.

Teresa stumbled. I caught her arm. "Are you all right?"

"I'll survive," she said grimly and wiped blood from her nose.

The widow's manservant had the haughty looks of a Castilian grandee. And the accent to go with it. He left us, disdainfully, in a room that resembled a small art gallery. I was confronted by a tortured São Sebastião. Blood pumping from his arrow-wounds. Mouth open in a scream of agony. And, next to him, a ferocious São Jorge with the signature S F da Silva. My father.

Staring at this picture, I didn't hear the widow come in. A low voice saying "Senhora" startled me. I turned, to see a dark woman in a dress that was rather startlingly low-cut for the afternoon. The amulet lay between her breasts.

"Boa tarde," Teresa began.

Then the woman saw me. She said, "And who is this?" And she changed.

It wasn't a change like Teresa's. No dramatic transformation. It just…emphasised things. And none too subtly, either. Teresa grabbed for the woman's arm with a startled curse, but I hardly heard her. The room shrank. The world went away. Suddenly I couldn't get my breath. Couldn't move. Felt my heart pounding.

Only the faithful can stand…

Shaking Teresa off, she advanced on me. Her lips were the color of blood. Emilia, help, I thought, reaching for the amulet. My hand was trembling. She seized me by the hair, pulling hard, and drew my head down.

"No," I said. But I couldn't break free. And I suddenly realized what being a succubus really meant. Not a seductress. That implies gentleness. But a rapist.

My fingers slipped against her slick flesh. I got them round the amulet and pulled. The chain held. Damn it.

"Captain da Silva," came Teresa's voice from a very long way away. "Luís."

"Teresa, undo the clasp," I gasped. A moment later the stone was loose in my hand, and I jerked it down, away from the succubus. She collapsed on the floor, and I nearly did too with the release of tension. Suddenly limp, I bent over and rested my palms on my thighs. Took deep breaths to steady myself. A lot of them.

* * *

Back in the small borrowed bedroom, Harris sat bolt upright, shocked out of sleep. Through the red mist he'd come to hate, he saw the foreshortened figure of da Silva, bent double and breathing heavily.

Skipper's done it, he thought jubilantly. *Goddamn but that's the best news since Garrulous Gertie got her tongue stuck in the mangle, as my ma used to say.*

His viewpoint swung wildly for a moment, and then the red-tinged vision vanished and he could see normally again. *Jesus it'll feel good not to want to throw all the time.*

He staggered out of bed and splashed his face with water from the washstand. The movement made his heart race, and he pulled a sour face at his reflection in the cloud-marked mirror. *Trying to run before you can walk. Take it easy, for Godsakes.*

Harris steadied himself with his hands and let his wolf-senses roam through the silent house, becoming aware only of Caterina, and the witch watching her placidly.

Go for it, skipper, he thought. *Gotta be on the home stretch now.* And managed, for the first time in days, a wolfish grin.

* * *

"Go," said Teresa, bending over the woman with the substitute stone in her hand. "I'll do this. I'm good for precious little else," she added disgustedly. There was another line of blood coming from her nostril.

"Here, take this," I said, fumbling in my pocket for the little bag I'd cajoled out of Paciência. *And if you think that was easy, you try it sometime.* "You open it to release the masking spell."

"Oh, God, thank you," she exclaimed. "Go on now, go."

I fled the house, relieved and ashamed. Paused in the courtyard long enough to light up. *Smoke is a great steadier for the nerves. Doctors ought to* prescribe it. But then all the sanitoria would be empty.

That really wasn't one of the more impressive episodes in da Silva history.

Pushing up the eyepatch to get some relief, I waited in the courtyard for Teresa. Couldn't feel any trace of seekers. But then I did have a pocket full of antidote stones. And the mysterious key of Solomon under my shirt. Or under my skin, I wasn't sure which. Harris's amulet—I couldn't think of it as anything else—didn't seem to be reacting to the antitheses. But what the hell do I know. You summoned Zacuto for this sort of advice, da Silva. So listen to the man. Ghost. Whatever.

She emerged a few minutes later, and I replaced the eyepatch hurriedly. I'd just looked at my watch for the third time. She'd used Paciência's charm-bag, that was obvious. There was color in her face, and she was moving like an athlete again.

"Thank you for thinking of that," she said.

"Nada," I replied absently. We walked the fifty yards to the café. I handed her the amulet. Teresa took it and hurried inside. She knew the need for speed as well as I did.

Watching from outside, I wished I was in there with Emilia. But now I couldn't be near her until the unmaking. Couldn't touch her, couldn't kiss her. Both things I very much wanted to do. I smoked another cheroot until an irritated waiter came out and asked me if I wanted anything.

"No," I said, staring at him. The da Silva stare has cowed more dangerous adversaries than a bad-tempered waiter. He went back inside, and Teresa came out. Like one of those elaborate clocks with all the figures.

"All clear," she said. I nodded. Looked past her at Emilia. Who gave me an encouraging smile. I smiled back, too much unsaid. Gave her a wave. And headed home to pick up a ring made of hair, then go in search of my son. Walking away from my wife to find my son.

* * *

The demon that Batista had confined in the ring was a feeble thing, a very minor minion of hell. But it was sufficient to dispose of a troublesome mortal, and it was sufficient to gain Mouffi admittance to the demon-riddled soul of its summoner.

This man is hell's whore, Mouffi thought, if we can impose subvocalisation upon a disembodied consciousness seeping through every atom of Batista's being. And the most delicious part of it was that the man didn't know it.

Squatting in the magical diagram, the demon, which had taken the form of a dog, or something that vaguely resembled a dog, absorbed its orders. It was not even as powerful as Mouffi and was easily bound. Not that binding was necessary, since destroying or enslaving mortals is one of a demon's purposes.

But it knew when Mouffi invaded its current master, and snapped to attention.

Mouffi decided, inasmuch as its limited consciousness could make a decision, that it had found the perfect host. Especially since it now knew every memory, every secret thought owned by Batista. And it knew of his plans for the man who had killed its greater self.

Da Silva thought Mouffi exiled. He would not suspect its presence a second time.

* * *

Emilia looked through the window, which had etched on it in fancy script the words *café, chá, vinhos,* and the names of various other beverages, at her husband. Seeing him objectively for a moment, as if for the last time (or the first), as if he were going away for ever, God forbid, she felt oddly omniscient. A man not tall, no longer young but not old, hair greying, she no longer noticed the scar, the eyepatch, hadn't done so for years. She smiled, giving no sign of her heart's sudden lurch, as if she stood now on the brink of a precipice. It was entirely too likely that she was seeing him for the last time, and that was an idea too dark to be borne.

Though to a certain extent that was true whenever he went away.

She turned to John Yeoh. "You can see souls," she murmured over the rim of her cup.

"Yes," he said guardedly.

"What's—what's my husband's? What shape?"

"Are you sure you want to know?" he asked. Emilia nodded. The amulet in her hand felt smooth, and she rubbed it with her thumb.

He looked at her for a long moment, his face quite expressionless. Then he said, "A paladin."

Storing the information to contemplate later, she finished her cooling coffee. "Well," she said. A statement, not a preface to a speech.

"Don't worry," Yeoh said reassuringly, crushing his cigarette out in an ashtray.

"Shall we get on with this, then?" she suggested, pushing herself to her feet and taking hold of her cane. He moved to help her, but she waved him away. "We'll do better if you try not to treat me like something breakable."

"I'm sorry," he said, bowing his head. "I do know very well, senhora, that you are not breakable." Emilia smiled.

"You might tell Luís that one day."

"Oh, I am quite sure he knows it too," Yeoh said.

It took them some time to get across the city to Zacuto's erstwhile haven, even using public transport, but Emilia, though she had many questions she wanted to ask, remained silent for most of the journey.

Only when they had disembarked from the funicular and were walking slowly over the cobbles through the slanting sunlight of late afternoon did she ask, "How does this work? Can you tell me?"

Yeoh turned his head to her. His black eyes looked flat and expressionless.

"To be perfectly honest," he said frankly, "I am not entirely sure. This key of Solomon, whatever it is, gives you the ability to see hidden things. It may be that I can show you how to find the amulets I concealed. This will be a good place for you to try, since it is more stable than a mere hidey-hole."

The street, narrow and silent, had filled with shadows, though the sky above was still the intense pellucid blue of the tropics. The only moving thing in view was a black-and-white cat. Emilia saw the little shrine, in the wall, the statue of the Virgin in its niche, someone had put a fresh garland about it, only wild flowers but it showed devotion. And then she saw a door where there had been none before.

"That—" she exclaimed, startled into speech, but cut herself off in annoyance.

"Is only another way of seeing," Yeoh said. "Try to keep this frame of mind; don't look too hard at the door, because it is not really a door, and you may begin to see a pattern."

"A pattern?" she echoed.

"The warp and weft of time," said John Yeoh.

She stared at the door, trying to keep her eyes unfocused, finding it surprisingly difficult, and at last understanding came. It was, as he had said, just another way of seeing. There were layers, like an infinite number of palimpsests, layers of time. The wall had them inherent in it all the years since it had been a wall, and all the time before that, and the room behind it had once belonged to a house. When she looked at Yeoh she could see many different versions of him, from infant to the rather more unwavering appearance he presented now, and knew that was fixed because he had remained unchanged for so many years.

"I see," she said wonderingly, and the invisible mark on her breast tingled as if Luís's fingers were upon it. Emilia drew in a deep shaky breath.

Yeoh nodded, smiling like a teacher pleased with his pupil, and opened the door.

And then the blue sky exploded.

Emilia never had a chance to see it properly, since Yeoh grabbed her arm instantly and pushed her through the door, but it was something like a dog. Or dog-shaped, though it didn't quite fit any space in her mind, mastiff, alsatian, doberman, well enough to convince her. She was left with a confused impression. Jaws, it had. Fangs, certainly. Red eyes, hot breath. And then she was inside the room in the wall, and Yeoh, wild-eyed and less composed than she'd ever seen him, was examining a pants-leg ripped open to the knee.

"Did it bite you?" she asked urgently, being well-accustomed to the uses of holy water. Yeoh shook his head, apparently not trusting himself to speak. "What was it?" half-expecting the answer, Cerberus, but what Yeoh actually said was worse.

"A demon. That man sent a demon after me." He sounded out of breath.

"How do you know?" whispered Emilia, who was feeling more than a little breathless herself. "That it was after you?"

He looked up. "Oh, you know," he said. "You always know," and there was something in his voice that made Emilia go cold all over, in a way that seeing the hell-hound had not.

She stared around the room, marveling not only at its existence but also at the fact that she was inside it. Out of time.

"Are we safe here?" she asked, than winced as a fierce ache ran down her leg, from hip to knee. Yeoh apparently missed this.

"You are safe from it, senhora, wherever you are. I am safe as long as I stay in here. But if I go out, that thing will kill me." He grimaced. "Unlike the senhor capitão, I cannot stand against these things. My…invulnerability does not profit me against things which do not occupy a place in time. Which leaves us with a problem."

With a sigh, Emilia pushed a stray lock of hair from her forehead and said, "Can I collect the stones on my own? You showed me how to look."

For answer, he asked, "Can you find the one I hid in this room?"

The chamber was dimly lit, although she could see no light source. There was an oil lamp on the table, but it was cold. But she needed no light. She relaxed her sight and her mind, finding it easier the second time around, and then the mark over her heart burned for a split second and she saw a pulsing glow in the center of the room.

"There," she said, pointing to it.

"Very good," Yeoh applauded. "Now to retrieve it, simply do the same with your hand as you are doing with your mind." It sounded like nonsense, but she knew exactly what he meant, so she reached across and took the glow in her hand, feeling her fingers close upon the stone. Something prompted her to give her hand a certain *twist* as she withdrew it, and there in her palm was the banded agate she'd sold to Teresa Batista.

"Mother of God," she exclaimed. John Yeoh smiled at her encouragingly.

"You can do this," he said.

Emilia wrapped the stone in one of the pieces of soft wool that Paciência had given her and slipped it into a drawstring bag, also provided by the sorceress. Which already held a jacinth and a sapphire, similarly shielded from the influence of the other amulets which were to join them. While she was doing this, Yeoh fumbled in his pocket and drew out a jingling keyring, from which he detached one key and held it out to her.

"The key to my shop," he replied to her questioning look. "The chrysophase stone is there. The beryl, in the Convento do Carmo. The jasper, in your workroom, senhora. And the malachite, in the Eduardo VII park. I am afraid it will be a long circuit of the city for you." She nodded ruefully. No matter, she thought. If my leg gets tired, I can rest it when this is all over. Although she knew from long experience that there'd be more to it than that, and groaned inwardly at the thought of the inevitable backache. "You may be able to save some time and effort," he said. "Since the stones are shielded now, and not with their physical guardians, you could collect them out of order."

"We are anyway," she pointed out, taking the key from Yeoh. "But I want to go home first, leave a message for Luís. Will you be all right?"

"For as long as it takes," he said wryly. "But I'd appreciate your husband's help, if he can spare the time to come and dispose of this demon for me."

"Of course," Emilia said. Drew a deep breath. And stepped out into the world once more, Yeoh's "Good luck" echoing in her ears.

There was no sign of the hell-hound. She placed her hand briefly over her heart, feeling the warmth of her own palm through her blouse. It gave her confidence.

Later, sitting on a tram with a stout sweating matron clad in rusty black wedged against her, Emilia wondered if John Yeoh's neighbors were as nosy as hers. What would they think of this lone woman who walked with a stick, this stranger, entering his shop? It's all right, she pictured herself saying, whether to man or woman her imagination didn't tell her, I have his permission, see, here's the key, I just came to pick something up. And what might that be, asks the hypothetical neighbor, to which the answer was properly, None of your business.

But aside from the unwiseness of annoying a busybody who might well summon the police, Emilia was far too polite to make such a retort to a complete stranger, and so if the question was asked, she would be quite at a loss.

And since she was also too much Emilia to take herself seriously all the time, she smiled, amused for spending time thinking of something so trivial, when she knew perfectly well that she was only doing it to distract herself from thinking of other things.

* * *

Teresa Batista, feeling better than she had for some time, let herself into the House of the Four Winds with her key after repeated ringing on the doorbell failed to elicit any response. She frowned. Where was Ana?

The sound of someone weeping came to her as she stepped into the hall, and her eyes narrowed. She picked a swordstick out of the rack by the door and drew the blade with a thin *snick*. Then she followed the sound of weeping into the library.

She swore out loud. She'd found Ana. But the sobbing girl huddled in the corner was almost unrecognisable as the pretty blonde who was their maidservant, her face puffed with bruises and tears, one eye swollen shut, her flesh darkening, her lip split. Blood on her disordered uniform. Blood on her thighs where her skirt had ridden up.

What the hell's going on? she thought, and crossed herself, thinking of demons. Incubi. Then she shook herself. She'd be able to feel something like that. Teresa squatted down beside Ana and laid her blade on the floor, reaching out a hand to the girl's shoulder.

Ana flinched at her touch, then fell against her, sobs fiercening. Teresa's blouse grew a damp patch from the girl's tears, and the slow fury that had been building in her since she saw Ana's beaten face thundered into her heart and turned it into something implacable.

"Who did this, Ana?" she asked, stroking the disordered blonde hair, and if Ana noticed, in her distraught state, the iron in her voice, it was only to be distantly glad that Teresa was apparently on her side.

"Sr Batista," she whispered thickly. "He's possessed. I swear it." And dissolved into weeping again.

The girl must have meant *possessed* metaphorically, since she could have no knowledge of such matters. But the chill in Teresa's heart, the fist that gripped it, told her that the maidservant, without knowing it, had told the literal truth.

Either that, or her father had completely taken leave of his senses.

She needs a doctor, Teresa thought angrily, but a sense of pressing time weighed down on her. She had to find her father.

It took too long to disentangle herself from the weeping girl, put arnica on her bruises, get her to bed with a sleeping-draught inside her. By that time Teresa's temper was throbbing like some large furious creature confined in a net too small for it.

Controlling it with an effort, fighting down the urge to smash her fist against the wall, she searched the house from top to bottom. Ended up in the cellar, which was the oldest part, she could tell from the brickwork.

What if there were a secret room? Teresa had, at best, a sketchy knowledge of the city's history, but there is no country which hasn't, at one stage or another, set one part of its citizens irrevocably against others, necessitating the provision of hiding-places. And she knew that much of Lisbon had been flattened by an earthquake in the mid-eighteenth century, which this house post-dated. So under this cellar, she reasoned, might well survive remnants of less tolerant times. Not that she was finding the twentieth century particularly tolerant of women who refused to know their place. Not that she cared very much about that, as several variously punctured men in Rio could testify.

Some bits of the brickwork looked newer than the rest, had obviously been restored. She tapped them with the handle of her swordstick, but without success. Her gaze roved the walls, seeking for clues to a hidden door.

Sighing, she resigned herself to a long task ahead and pushed the sleeves of her blouse above her elbows.

* * *

The minute I picked up the ring of hair, I felt a powerful tug from it. Well, I'm damned, I thought. Though why I should be surprised at something so small, I don't know. Ha. After all that's happened I shouldn't be surprised to find a dragon sitting smoking in the Rossio.

It led me down a rather noisome alley and a flight of narrow steps into a blind passage full of rubbish. At the end, a small opening that had once been sealed off with a rusty grille. But the grille lay on the ground in front of it.

Since Paciência's "under the earth" had made me expect something like this, I'd come equipped. The stench made me wish I'd brought a cloth to tie over my nose, too. I stared grimly into the narrow hole. Oddly reluctant to go down. Get on with it, da Silva. It's not as if it's the mouth of hell. Although it might well have been. It's not as if I don't want to get to Zé, either. Even though I found myself blaming him for getting kidnapped. How mad is that?

I squeezed through the opening and dropped to the ground. Lit the lantern, since the aperture I'd come through was precious little use as a window. Mice skittered nervously out of the light. And, from the larger noises of unseen creatures, rats as well. I'm not fond of rats. Even if it wasn't for the memory of the Venetian's rat-demon. No sailor likes them.

You do get used to foul smells, though. I think your nose shuts down eventually. But until it does, you just have to put up with it.

The tunnel was wider and higher than I expected. I couldn't imagine what it had been built for. Or, for that matter, why it smelt so foul. Since it evidently wasn't a sewer. The bricks that lined it looked ancient. Water ran down the walls and lay in puddles on the ground. It was stiflingly hot and intensely humid, and sweat was pouring off me. I pushed the eyepatch up on my forehead. No one to see down here. Wondered whether to take out my knife. Decided against it. Met nothing but rats, so far. And if I wanted to kill rats, I'd rather shoot 'em.

Zé's ring led me steadily onward, going fairly straight. Which was a relief since I'd had visions of getting lost in a maze of tunnels once the ring stopped working. Once I'd found Zé.

There were ghosts down here, too. Some old enough, in parts of the tunnels that were stone rather than brick, to be Zacuto's contemporaries. Which meant that some of these tunnels had survived the earthquake without collapsing.

Strange, being down here beneath the city. All those people, trams, dogs, what have you, going about their business. Oblivious to what was under their feet. I was also rather uncomfortably conscious of all that stone and earth over my head. Since I was down deeper than the foundations of most of the buildings. Under the earth indeed. Paciência hadn't been joking. Always supposing such a thing was likely. Or even possible.

I could really have done with a smoke, but I had vague schoolday memories of exploding underground gases. Firedamp. Methane. Or God knows what, given the stench. Which showed no sign of abating, so I was wrong about getting used to it. Unfortunately, breathing shallowly isn't an option. Just have to grin and bear it.

How long have I been down here? Feels like forever. I looked at my watch. Forty minutes. Is that all? How much further? The ring's steady pull went on. I went on following it. From time to time a faint breeze came out of a side tunnel, but nothing like enough for relief. Now and again I heard noises other than water and furtive scurrying. Voices, always too faint to make out any words. A dog barking, a long way off. Someone playing a piano. The coughing roar of motor-cars. Horses' hooves on cobbles. Even a snatch of fado from somewhere, though it was still daylight outside. Wouldn't've known it down here.

The ground underfoot changed again. I'd walked on earth and stone and brick. Slithered down muddy slopes and climbed flights of worn steps. Waded through streams, splashed through puddles, skirted stagnant water. My sea-boots may not be any good for running, but there's been no call for it. Yet. What they are good for is keeping my feet dry. Well, comparatively. Since I'm completely drenched in sweat.

At last I came to the end of a long curving brick wall to find a spiral stair. The ring was pulling me up. I noticed that the walls were drier here. The air fresher. Perhaps I'm near the end. I dragged my left sleeve over my face. Replaced my eyepatch. Wiped my palms, futilely, on my thighs. Drew my knife and started up the staircase.

After a hundred and forty steps I lost count. My legs felt like lead. I had to stop and rest, get my breath, let my heart slow. Sweat streaming down my face, stinging my eye. The ring tugged urgently. All right, damn it. I'm on my way.

I staggered up the last few steps, hardly able to lift my legs, and emerged into a wide high chamber. It must've been fifty feet across. The light didn't even reach the far edges, but I sensed several exits. There was a strong taint of spoiled meat in here, and I noted in passing that there was a body lying not far away. But I ignored it. Good move, da Silva.

My heart did a somersault. Propped against the wall nearest me was Zé. Thank God. Thank all the gods. His eyes were wide open, but he seemed unable to move. What the hell had that bloody man done to him? I started towards him, but my legs nearly gave way. Damn it. Getting older is a bastard.

As I stood there gasping and trying to get my breath back, Batista stepped out of the shadows. I raised my knife. He stopped.

"Da Silva," he said. "I've been waiting for you."

The light threw odd shadows up on his face. He looked urbane, suave, and pleased with himself. I was tired, bedraggled, angry, dripping with sweat. And fed up to the back teeth with the old swine.

"What the hell do you *want*, Batista?" I asked, wearily. "Don't you know what this spell of yours is going to do?"

"Oh yes." His lips stretched back from his teeth. "I know. What do I want? The stones, of course."

"Not even if hell freezes over," I said.

"Oh, what a pity," he smiled. "Wrong answer." And his eyes went yellow. Demon-light. He was possessed, I realized with a shock. Surprised he'd allowed himself to give up control. Oh *merda*. I could kill him, but I couldn't kill the demon inside. Hadn't been able to do it with the Venetian. Seems like you have to have the demon itself, in its own form, in front of you before you can kill it. Well, no thanks. Deal with bloody Batista first. Worry about the demon later.

He made a gesture, and the decaying corpse on the floor lurched to its feet. I whirled round to face it. I couldn't imagine how it was holding together. And it was so far gone I didn't recognize it at once for Pierce's pursuer down on the waterfront. Who I'd already killed once. It advanced on me, and I drew back my knife. Then I heard Zé gasp and jerked my head round to see that Batista had grabbed his arm. There was a gun in his hand.

I threw the knife at him in the same instant that Zé yelled, "It's Mouffi," heard Batista swear, and then the cadaver was on me in a wave of putrescence. I backhanded it furiously on the side of its head, a blow with all my weight and anger behind it. The spine snapped, the lolling head flew off, landing with a repulsive wet thunk and rolling away. I flung the body to one side and went for Batista, who was still clutching a struggling Zé. But his gun was nowhere to be seen, and his right hand was gashed to the bone.

"The stones, or the boy dies," he snarled. I clenched my fists and advanced on him, almost too angry to think.

"You can't harm him, if that's Mouffi in there," I snapped.

"Can't harm his soul, no," agreed Batista casually, with a nasty smile. "Can kill the mortal body." And then his yellow inhuman eyes widened, and he choked and looked down.

At about two feet of razor-sharp steel protruding from his chest. He stared at it in disbelief, releasing Zé. Blood gushed from his mouth.

Behind him, Teresa Batista, his daughter, withdrew the blade she'd stabbed him with. The demon bled out of his eyes, and he crumpled slowly to his knees, then to the ground.

Zé, fourteen he may have been, grabbed hold of me, skinny arms wrapped tightly round my back. I hugged him in relief. Teresa, who hadn't taken her eyes off me since she'd killed her father, bent and wiped the blade clean on his jacket. Then Batista's body collapsed in on itself, lost definition, liquefied, and ran away down the cracks in the floor.

Holding my son, I said, "Teresa?" Her eyes were staring. White all round the pupils. Not a good sign.

"Luís," she said tightly. "I killed him."

"You had to," I said. "If you hadn't, I would've done."

She drew a great shuddering breath and dropped the sword. It was the blade from a swordstick, I thought. Remembering, remotely, the Venetian's brother bent on rape and murder.

Teresa nodded, folded her arms tightly across her chest, hugging herself. Her armor. "He...raped...Ana."

"He did what?" I exclaimed.

"Ana, our maid." The blonde girl. God. "Beat her half to death."

"He was possessed," I said. "The demon did it. Not your father." I knew that for a fact. Not sure what I could *do* with the fact. Where was Mouffi now? Disturbing thought. Well, never mind that now, da Silva, you've more pressing things to worry about.

"I never liked him summoning demons," Teresa remarked absently. Her face was very pale. For a second I thought she was going to faint on me. But she set her jaw, took a few deep calming breaths, and shook it off with a visible effort. That's my Teresa. "All right," she said. "What do we do now?"

"We get the hell out of here," I said. "Come on, Zé."

* * *

The tram took her nearer Yeoh's shop than home, so she went to retrieve the beryl amulet first. No inquisitive neighbors stopped her, and she smiled to herself as she unlocked the door. As she went in, all the clocks were chiming the half-hour, as if she needed to be reminded that time was passing, a symphony of carrilons. A chime of clocks, she thought, that ought to be the word for a collection. The English had delightful words for that sort of thing.

She relocked the door behind her, in case someone thought she was opening the shop. Without its owner, the shop seemed emptier than the lack of one single person should have made it, as if Yeoh defined the space, as if it could not exist without him.

Now she had done it once, Emilia found the stone with no difficulty at all, its warm glow illuminating nothing but itself, and reached into the fold, or pocket, or cyst, in time, giving that particular twist to draw it out. The ticking of the clocks, far from giving her a sense of urgency, which she had already, thank you very much, proved a gentle soporific in the warm close dim interior of the shop. It took a conscious effort to shake it off.

Emilia emerged back into the street yawning, carefully locked the door behind her, and headed slowly for home. Her leg was aching a little, and she wanted to exchange stick for crutch, even though it was an awkward uncomfortable thing to use.

Loitering in the street outside, pacing up and down with febrile energy, she found Luzia Verdinho, too nervous to ring the doorbell, a mixture of apprehension and defiance on her face and a small suitcase in her hand.

"What on earth are you doing here?" she exclaimed.

"I've left home," said Luzia, sticking her chin out. A shaky smile came to her face. "Run away. *Tia* Emilia, may I stay with you?"

Oh for heaven's sake, thought Emilia in exasperation, I don't need this right now. And then she realized Luzia might actually be useful. She was, after all. Paciência's daughter. Paciênca's apprentice.

"We'll talk about that later," Emilia said sternly to the girl. "Right now, I need you to come with me."

13

THE DOCTOR MINISTERING TO ANA WAS TERESA'S LOVER. There was a bit of gossip for John Yeoh. He also had, on his watch-chain, a green stone. Which was harmless and inert. Unoccupied. But that one had never been a prison.

I took a drag of my cheroot, and a mouthful of Batista's best aguardente. Bit different from the last time I was in this house. I can hardly believe he's dead. And part of me was annoyed that I hadn't, after all, been the one to kill him. When I'd been agonizing over it for days. Figure that one out, da Silva.

Teresa had given me a clean shirt. One of her father's. Too big for me, of course. But the one I'd been wearing was in the trash. Admittedly it had been an old one. However the revolting stain on the left sleeve, left by the late Eduardo, would never come out. Putrid wasn't the word for it. Zé, of course, we could do nothing about. A shirt of Batista's would look like a tent on him. Though he seemed happy just to be free again. And Eduardo hadn't been quite as putrescent when he'd snatched Zé. Right now my son was munching some day-old bread that Teresa'd found for him. I was fiddling with the cuffs of the shirt when the doorbell rang.

"I'll go," said Teresa. Who had also resorted to the brandy. It had brought some color back to her cheeks. She pushed herself out of the chair, and presently I heard voices I recognized. A moment later she led Pierce and Zacuto into the room.

What the devil were they doing here? How did they know it was safe to knock on Batista's door? There wasn't any doubt that they *did* know. Pierce wasn't even looking apprehensive. Although he was eyeing Teresa with suspicion.

"Thought we'd find you here, skipper," said Pierce. Zacuto glared at him. He shoved his spectacles back into place with an apologetic smile. "Well, er, to be truthful, Sr Zacuto knew where you were. That key of yours." I wasn't sure I liked that idea.

"What's up?" I asked, giving my cheekbone an absent scratch. Zacuto stared at me gravely.

"Sr Batista may be dead—"

"How the hell did you know that?" I demanded.

"A spell such as the Eidolon casts many echoes, disturbances in what is sometimes called the ether, although that is an inexact, layman's term. When its maker dies, the ether resonates like the tolling of a bell. The Great Spell itself remains inchoate until it can be unmade, which I hope to be able to do shortly. However, Sr Batista, before he died, summoned a minor demon to perform a task for him—"

Teresa Batista, who had been listening carefully, interrupted him. "You can tell all this from the ether?"

Zacuto turned to her politely. "As I said, an inexact term. But yes. In this case, Captain da Silva, I am also aware that it appears to be guarding my...former haunt, if you will pardon the expression. Which leads me to suspect that someone may be trapped in there."

Oh God, here we go again. Another one. I finished my cheroot. Drained the glass. Got wearily to my feet.

"All right," I said. "I'm on my way." And then it dawned on me. Slow on the uptake again, da Silva.

John Yeoh must've taken Emilia there.

All my tiredness vanished. I grabbed my knife, in its sheath, from the table and took off at a run. Vaguely surprised I could manage it. The damned boots didn't help. Perhaps I should've borrowed a pair of Batista's shoes along with the shirt. Though they'd probably be too big, as well. Shut up, shut up. *Emilia.*

As soon as I turned the corner, there it was. I skidded to a halt and whipped out the knife, dropping the sheath to the ground. The thing was vaguely doglike. Well, dog is the nearest I can come up with. Describing things is difficult without a reference point. Your mind doesn't accept them. You have to make comparisons with familiar things. Like: It was the size of a calf. And its mouth was too big for its head and full of jagged teeth like a shark's. They were snapping open and shut, open and shut, like something mechanical. Its eyes were the fierce hot crimson of fire. And it stank of carrion.

Hackles were up on its powerful shoulders. I could see the muscles bunching under its black coat. It was growling, a low subterranean murmur that I could feel through the soles of my boots. But even so, I knew why Zacuto had called it a minor demon. It wasn't that powerful. Nasty, but no match for Mastiphal. And guess what, demon? I killed Mastiphal.

"Come on, you bastard," I said spitefully. "I've got better things to do than mess with pathetic creatures like you."

The demon advanced, stiff-legged and wary of my knife. I waited. Let it come to me. My boots weren't made for fancy footwork.

Even though I was ready for it, it nearly had me. That's what happens when you get complacent, da Silva. I wasn't expecting it to leap straight up in the air like that. With a startled curse, I dodged out of the way. Or tried to. I tripped over my own damned stupid feet and fell backwards hard, jarring my elbows agonizingly as I attempted to break the fall. The knife skittered out of my hand, quick pain shooting up my arm, and it was on me at once, snarling.

It was too fast. All I could do was seize it round the throat and try to throttle it, try to keep its razor-sharp fangs from my neck. But it was a bloody big throat, larger around than someone's waist. Stinking saliva dripped on my face, burning like acid. I wrestled the thing's head away from mine. It was tremendously heavy, like lead, weight out of all proportion to its size. My arms were already beginning to tremble with the effort of holding it off.

I had to get its snapping jaws away from my face. I turned my head to keep my eye safe. It meant I couldn't see the thing any more but then I hardly needed to. And didn't want to. Still gripping its throat, I rolled to my right.

It was too heavy. I needed more momentum. I rocked back to the left as hard as I could, grunting with the effort, then completely over and banged its head on the cobbles. At least that was the intention. It wrenched out of my grip and snapped at me, missing me by inches. I scuttled crabwise away from it. Scooped up my knife from where it had landed. My face was burning from the thing's drool.

The hellhound pounced again as I scrambled to my feet, and I kicked out. My foot connected solidly but didn't make much difference. Felt like kicking a stone wall, but I didn't have any breath left to swear. It bounced back and landed right in front of me, snarling. I took one quick step backwards, shifted my weight, and drove the knife into its chest. Into its heart, if it had one.

It screamed, a high shrill shriek in startling contrast to its menacing growl. Silvery flames played around the wound as I dragged the knife out, and boiling black blood spilled from it. Pints of the stuff. The demon snapped at my hand and then keeled over. Jaws still moving as it died. There was a brief explosion of white flame, and the body crumbled into dust.

Breath coming in ragged gasps, I went to my knees. That'll teach you, da Silva. I was, I found, shaking all over. Managed to fumble my dwindling supply of holy water out of my pocket and soak my handkerchief in it. Wiped my face. I stayed kneeling until I steadied, then used the wall to climb shakily to my feet.

Finding the door quickly, I gave the knock Yeoh had taught me. How long ago was that? Felt like months. Days, only. He answered it himself, peering out into the alley.

"Captain da Silva?" he said. He could see it was me. I pushed past him. My heart was pounding painfully.

"Where's Emilia?"

"Safe, she's safe. It wasn't sent for her—it's dead, I assume?"

"Yes, it's dead," I replied impatiently, wiping my face again.

"She's quite safe," he repeated. "She's gone to collect the stones." I stared at him, and he flinched back.

"On her own?"

Yeoh raised his eyebrows and said tartly, "She also told me to remind you, senhor capitão, that she is not breakable."

And so she isn't. "I...know. Yes," I said, deflated. That took the wind out of your sails, da Silva, didn't it?

I turned and left the room. Heard Yeoh following me. We emerged back into the empty alley. Empty but for ghosts.

"Thank you, anyway," Yeoh went on, "for dispensing of that piece of malice. Now I imagine—" He looked at the sky. I'd forgotten he'd been a sailor. "—that your wife will finish up at the park, if she has used the most sensible route."

"You can count on that," I said, lighting a cheroot.

"Yes, I thought so."

From behind me, Zacuto's voice said, "A park would be a suitable place to unmake the Eidolon. Therefore, shall we all proceed there?"

Oh óptimo. Circus troupe time again.

* * *

Harris, who had been dozing in a chair, woke with a start to find that the sun was low in the sky and that he'd been dribbling down his chin. He wiped the saliva away furtively, although there was no one to see him. *Jesus Christ in gumboots,* he thought in annoyance, *it's bad enough slobbering when I'm changed. Wonder how the skipper's getting on.*

Something new: there was a strange familiar eagerness in the pit of his stomach. *Better'n feeling sick all the time, I guess.*

A key rattled in the front door, quite loud in the silent house. *Emilia, and there's someone with her.* Harris called her by her Christian name in his mind, though he would never have dreamed of doing so out loud. But she was so kind to him, Sra da Silva sounded too cold and impersonal. *She's kind to everyone, dumbass. She's a nice person. Goddamn, I feel weird. And I want a smoke,* he discovered. *That's gotta be a good sign.*

Two sets of light footsteps approached. The tingling intensified inside Harris, became recognition, and at last he realized, *She musta brought the stone with her. Is she gonna come in here? Don't want to startle her.*

He heard her voice through the door. *"Espere aqui,* Luzia." *Goddamn, what's she saying.*

Outside in the hall, Emilia said, "Wait in here, Luzia, so your mother doesn't find out you're here."

"My *mother?"* squeaked Luzia.

"She's keeping an eye on Caterina for me, keep your voice down." She opened the door. "Oh! Sr Harris, how are you feeling?"

He pushed himself to his feet with an effort. "A whole lot better, thank you, ma'am," he said. "D'you have that stone with you?"

"Yes," said Emilia, chivvying the girl in. *"Appresse-te,* Luzia."

It was the girl he'd met the other day, the witch's daughter. *And Pedro's girlfriend, one of 'em, anyway. Lucky dog. Pretty little thing, not so little, neither.* He realized he was staring at her and looked down, embarrassed, saying, "Pardon me, miss."

She gave him a nervous smile and said in careful English, "You are the American, Mister'arris," this came out as one soft-syllabled word and lacking the H, "'Ow do you do."

This is not the time for being polite in the parlor, thought Emilia in exasperation, and interrupted. "Luzia, for heaven's sake be quiet, you know your mother has ears like a bat."

"I'll whisper," said Luzia, quietly and defiantly.

Emilia rolled her eyes to the ceiling. "Stay here, I'll be back in a minute." She switched back to English. "Mr Harris, we'll be going out again in a minute. If my husband comes back please tell him I'm collecting the stones and I'm quite all right. I know he worries."

"Surely, ma'am," said Harris.

Working things out as she went, Emilia climbed the stairs to see Caterina. Who was fast asleep. Paciência was sitting placidly by the window, reading in the fading light. She looked up as Emilia entered, and smiled austerely.

"Good as gold," she mouthed. Emilia nodded, smiling back, and whispered, "I'm sorry, I have to go out again. Joana'll bring you something to eat if you ask her."

"That's all right," the witch replied, just as quietly. "Take as long as you need."

My God, thought Emilia as she left, who did she catch politeness from? She liked Paciência—they had been friends for years—but was the first to acknowledge that the witch could be prickly. As a whole forest of cactus.

One more thing to do: collect the jasper amulet from her workroom. Her father-in-law. For the first time in days she thought about the portrait he was painting, with a pang of regret. He'll be fine, she told herself firmly. They all will. There was the now-familiar glow in the air. She extracted the stone, wrapped it, and put it with the others. Only two to go. Her heart thudded, and she took a deep breath and touched her breast where she knew the pentagram was.

Then she exchanged stick for crutch and went to collect Luzia.

* * *

Bodiless yet again, Mouffi had insinuated itself into brick and stone. It now inhabited the House of the Four Winds in much the same way as the souls of six people were imprisoned in amulets, though on a much larger scale. The difference being, of course, that Mouffi's tenancy was voluntary, the demon-fragment controlled it, and was able to leave whenever it wanted.

Indeed, Mouffi could have dwelt in an amulet, had that been its preference. But the house would suit its purposes as long as the girl Ana was within it.

It had been sheer malice alone that had led Mouffi to impel its bearer to rape her. The unexpected treachery of Teresa Batista having deprived it of a body, though, made Ana a very convenient vessel. When the tiny seed inside her grew big enough, it would make a fine home for a small demon.

In such incremental ways, Mouffi grew. It felt itself no longer fragment, but whole. Not Malphas any longer, but a new being. Child of Malphas, in every essential way.

A human child would make the ideal partner for it.

* * *

As the sky darkened towards evening, but the day's heat showed little sign of abating, Emilia became apprehensive. The city was no more dangerous to walk around than any other, probably safer than most, but unaccompanied women after dark would probably give the wrong impression, even if one of them was thirty-eight years old.

"Luzia," she said therefore, "do you know any 'don't look at me' spells?"

"Oh yes," replied the girl cheerfully. "Shall I do one?"

"I think it might be a good idea, don't you?"

Luzia thought it had been a good idea to come to Emilia's house. Happily, she constructed the spell, and because she was in a good mood she took extra care, with the result that they got to the ruined church without anyone noticing them and wondering what they were doing there at that time of day.

The gaping ruins towered overhead, stark against the turning sky. Emilia saw the gentle glow of the hidden gem at once, a soft effulgence that she was amazed only she could see. But then, the place was full of ghosts that only her husband could see. And everyone, she reflected, sees something different to everyone else, even if it is only beauty in a plain face.

She reached inside and withdrew the amulet, wrapping it quickly in its nest of wool. And then the two of them went in search of a tram.

* * *

This park, for some obscure reason, is named after the King of England. And it's not small. How the hell are we to find Emilia? Then of course I realized that she was more likely to find *us*. All six of us. Good God.

I admit apprehension. I admit a cold knot in the pit of my stomach. Batista's dead, but the spell remains. I admit to clammy palms and creeping dread and a hatred of waiting. And to smoking so much my mouth feels like the inside of a schoolboy's pocket. And where is Emilia? She'll be here, stop worrying.

In the end, as I might have known, it was the easiest thing in the world. There's Emilia, and with her Luzia, coming over the yellow grass. A kind of cloud about them. Luzia gestured with her hand, and the cloud vanished. I saw Emilia reach out *her* hand, give her wrist a smart twist, and then open her palm and wrap whatever she found in a piece of wool. The amulet that Yeoh had hidden here. He gave a small sound of satisfaction.

As they drew near, Emilia and I exchanged a glance as if we were alone. When in reality we couldn't even touch until the unmaking was done.

"Good," said Zacuto with satisfaction. "Everyone is here." And I looked at him, startled. Hadn't wondered until then what Luzia was doing with Emilia. Why she wasn't at home, nineteen miles away.

But of course it was true. My heart gave a jump as I realized it. The circle was complete. Seven amulets, seven people, seven antitheses. And if we weren't entirely the same people who'd retrieved the stones, we met the criteria.

"How does it work?" Emilia asked. She had the bag of amulets in her hand. I took a similar bag from my pocket. Inside, the antidote stones weren't wrapped in wool. They rattled together. Seven pebbles in a bag. Magic is a funny thing.

Zacuto drew a deep breath. Or didn't, really, because he couldn't. But it sounded authentic. "When the spell was made," he explained, "the sorcerer inscribed a diagram, an icon if you will, on each of the amulets, a symbol for the soul which it was intended to hold. These were drawn in ink mixed with the maker's own blood and certain other substances. To release the souls, each of you must take both the stone and its antithesis, and when I speak the portion of the spell which relates to that particular soul, bring them together. The antidote and the amulet will destroy each other, and the imprisoned souls be freed."

It all sounds a bit too easy. Easy. Listen to yourself, da Silva. After what we've been through I think we deserve something easy.

"I rather thought the amulets would have to be near the, er, bodies," said Pierce diffidently. He was polishing his spectacles. No surprise there then. I rubbed my eyebrow. The evening was sultry, and it was full of sweat. No surprise there either.

"Souls are very tenacious things," Zacuto said. "Once the constraints which bind them are destroyed, they will return to their bodies as iron is drawn to the magnet. And the men who have lain stricken by a mysterious sickness will be just as mysteriously cured."

John Yeoh asked, "Is there any particular time that is best for this operation?"

The ghost smiled, white teeth glinting in his beard. "Now," he said. "Remember, all of you, this will not be an easy thing. We will be dealing with immensely powerful forces, the forces which bind the world and the universe together. Forces which the sorcerer who attempted to construct the Eidolon has damaged, wounded if you will, and which may, like a wounded beast, snap at the hand that comes to help them. A crude analogy, but a true one." He looked round at us all. "Understand, without this unmaking, there is a danger that everything could unravel. But the unmaking itself could have the same effect."

Having effectively scared the hell out of everyone, he clapped his hands together. "Come, the amulets."

Without asking, Emilia held the sapphire out to Teresa. The dark blue looked black in the fading light. Now that I knew, I could see the symbol drawn on it, a sword. For the warrior. I handed her the antithesis, the opal, subtle colors glinting inside it. She held them loosely, one in each hand. Luzia took the beryl, inscribed with a lovers' knot, and its antithesis, the piece of jet, black as coal. Emilia gave Zé the malachite, and he looked wonderingly at it and the cradle drawn on the smooth surface even as I pressed the crystal into his other hand. Yeoh picked up the one agate with the outline of a ship and I handed him the other, which was blank.

My heart was pounding. Anticipation, I suppose. Pierce took the chrysophase —its symbol was an open book—from Emilia and its antidote, the onyx, from me. Which left only the two of us. We exchanged stones. I gave her the amethyst to counter my father's jasper, a stone with an artist's palette drawn on it, and in exchange she gave me a polished piece of heliotrope which would release Harris from the jacinth stone inscribed with a wolf's head. Our fingers were so close to touching you could hardly have passed a sheet of paper between them.

"It is time," said Zacuto. "Now, this must be done in reverse order. Sapphire, jacinth, malachite, jasper, beryl, chrysophase, agate. When I speak the stone's name, bring the two together." He looked around at all of us. "Let us begin."

He started to speak, very softly. So softly I couldn't have made out the words even if he'd been speaking in a language I knew. Around us the air, like the ring Luzia had made when Paciência had made the masking spell, formed into a wall. This barrier, though, was much clearer. Like purer glass. And around it, ghosts began to gather.

They drifted towards the circle from every side. Every direction. Each one had exactly the same expression on its face.

Fear. The shades of the dead, who have nothing to fear. Who are little more aware than a magic-lantern slide. They were afraid. I felt the back of my neck prickle, and sweat ran down my face. I mopped it away with my sleeve.

No one else could see the ghosts, of course. Not even Zacuto. But Zé's eyes were darting nervously from side to side, and Luzia was biting her lower lip so hard I could make out the indentations her teeth made. Pierce's mouth was slightly open, and he was rubbing his Adam's apple with the hand that held the onyx.

Zacuto's voice grew louder, and I felt the air tighten. As if the mother of all thunderstorms was on its way. Hell, maybe it was. Maybe this would break the demon weather.

Or break everything.

I realized belatedly that he'd switched to Latin, but I still couldn't make out any of the words. Of course when he'd been alive it hadn't been an entirely dead language. Not reserved for liturgy and secrecy. It had been the original lingua franca. Scholars had conversed in it. A savant from Germany could have a conversation with one from Portugal if neither spoke a word of the other's tongue. And so I should expect it to sound different from the unchanging chanting of priests. Who probably do it automatically. Thinking about what to eat for supper, how many Hail Marys to give the next idiot in the confessional. Or whatever priests think about. Burning books, in the late Father Jerónimo's case. I thought about Father Pereira. Wondered if he really was a descendant of Zacuto's. Stranger things have happened. And everything to do with this whole affair seems to slot together, somehow. You know what I'm going to say next. There are no such things as coincidences.

Your mind's wandering, da Silva. Pay attention.

Zacuto said suddenly, "Sapphire," and pointed at Teresa. Immediately, she brought her hands together, sapphire against opal. There was an intensely bright flash of blue fire. It outlined her for a split second, and then she staggered back. A powerful reek of ozone filled the circle, and everything blurred for an instant. Surely the destruction of the sapphire is the easiest. Since it didn't have a soul imprisoned inside it. Didn't have my soul imprisoned inside it. But if it had, we wouldn't be able to do this anyway. I shook my head and dragged my attention back to Zacuto, because it would be my turn next.

The stones in my palms began to vibrate. I clenched my sweating hands into fists around them, tensed the muscles in my arms. I still must've looked as if I had the palsy. Found I was gritting my teeth with the effort. Then Zacuto said, "Jacinth," and I hit the stones one against the other.

It felt like two mountains crashing together. The weight was immense. I groaned out loud with the strain, could feel myself weakening, my arms started to tremble, and then they burst apart, flinging my arms wide, stinging my palms viciously. The air itself rushed out and in like a leviathan taking a breath, Harris's startled face showed in front of me, very clear, for a heartbeat, and then it was all gone. I dropped to my knees on the dry grass, gasping like a landed fish.

Wished I could stay there, but it seemed important to get up. I pushed myself to my feet. My hands were still smarting. Realized only then that I'd not heard Zacuto's voice while all that was going on. God, I thought, I hope Emilia will be all right. And Zé—Zé will be next. But the stones might all behave differently, who can say.

"Malachite," said Zacuto, and I found out. Zé smashed the stones together, and they exploded into powder in his hands, flinging him backwards until he hit the barrier. He bounced off it as if it had been made of rubber and fell on his tailbone with a silent curse. What do you know. I can lip-read, after all. A huge column of white dust shot upwards, briefly formed an image of Felipe's face, and was gone.

I looked at Emilia. Our gazes met and locked. She smiled at me, such a sweet smile it always captivates me. And then Zacuto said "Jasper."

She brought her hands together gently. But there was nothing gentle about the way they jerked apart. What looked like a flock of black moths exploded outwards, their wings whirring like beetles', cannoning into the sides of the circle, ricocheting off it, frantic to escape, finally spiralling upwards and bursting like black fireworks.

Each one of them had borne a tiny facsimile of my father's face on its back, where the skull shows on a death's-head moth.

Emilia smiled again to show she was all right. Then we both looked in Luzia's direction. The witch's daughter clenched her fists in front of her collarbone. Stared intently at Zacuto. I saw her hands start to shake. Saw a bead of sweat trickle all the way from her hairline to her chin, then fall onto her dress. It hadn't been the first. "Beryl," Zacuto said.

Like Emilia, Luzia moved her hands together gently. As gently as a caress. Uncurled her fingers and united the stones. Drew in a huge shuddering gasp of air and closed her eyes as her hands, her breast, and then her entire body glowed red. So fiercely red I had to turn my head away. I could still sense the glow. Then it went dark, and Luzia screamed. I snapped my head around sharply, but she didn't seem to be hurt. She looked down at her open palms, and a red phantom of Pedro Ortigão's face pulsed there for a second, and then vanished.

Pierce glanced nervously at me and licked his lips. Almost as if he wanted to speak. Then back at Zacuto, who obligingly said "Chrysophase." He clapped his hands together like someone at a play and was rewarded by a melodious twang, like a monstrous guitar-string being plucked. I saw his eyebrows shoot up, and his mouth fell open in astonishment. He opened his hands slowly, and green light shone from them, arcing between them like a rainbow. The light forced his hands apart until he stood in a crucifixion pose, arms outstretched to his sides. Then everything went completely dark and a strange negative image of Father Pereira's face flashed into sight for the barest moment. The next instant, normal vision faded in again.

The air inside the ring was tremendously thick now. I hadn't really noticed, but pressure had been building since the first amulet had broken. I could hear the blood thundering in my head. It was getting difficult to breathe.

But there was only one left. Everyone looked at John Yeoh. His face looked ashen, his dark eyes like pits. When Zacuto said "Agate," a low thunderclap growled overhead and echoed hollowly around us.

Yeoh smacked the two agates together, and a vast cloud billowed up and surrounded him. I heard him gasp like a man in pain. The cloud was less like a thunderhead than the eruption of a volcano. Though lightning seemed to be flickering inside it. It boiled, elongated, flexed. Henriques's face looked out from one place, and then another, then a third, expression changing, alarmed, apprehensive, furious. Then it shot upwards and vanished, and Yeoh fell from about two yards in the air to land heavily at Zacuto's feet.

Who shouted into the sudden awful silence, "*Sic fiat,* amen!"

Everything *stopped*. The world held its breath. I held my breath. For all I know, the whole damn universe held its breath.

And let it out again. Zacuto closed his eyes. The ring of solid air around us vanished, and with it the oppression. We looked at each other like soldiers who've survived the battle to end all battles. As we had, I suppose.

I gathered Emilia into my arms and held her, feeling her heartbeat, breathing her, and that was all I wanted to do at that moment. Hell, it was all I was capable of doing.

* * *

When you've won a war, and I mean the sort with cannon and cavalry, broadsides and bullets, you generally come home to honor and glory. Parades, medals, cheering, that kind of thing.

But the one we've just fought and won, nobody else even knows about. And of course it's better that way. Couldn't be any other way, if you think about it. Just imagine trying to explain all that to the likes of Ashley or Costa. Who, incidentally, had spent his time in port getting himself a new job.

I gave him his papers quite happily, though *Isabella* will miss him. He and Ashley had managed perfectly well while I was otherwise occupied. And Harris was just otherwise. And then I took myself and my new haircut to visit Sr Williams. Came away with a contract. And went to tell Harris about his promotion. Nice to have some good news I can tell someone, for a change.

All Batista's victims had been restored, but most were in poor shape. Harris was the least affected, since at least he'd been able to eat during his imprisonment. Not much, but more than any of the others.

He was still lodging with us—much to Zé's disgust, who I think wanted a bit more appreciation for his part in the unmaking. I found him on the roof-terrace, smoking and looking thoughtful. I joined him in the smoking.

"You all right, Harris?" I asked.

"Guess so." He shrugged. "Wish I'd'a been more help to you, though." I suppressed a smile. Looked like he was more concerned at losing out on the action than nearly losing his soul. Which he seemed to view as a minor inconvenience.

"Never mind that now," I said. "What would you say to a second mate's ticket?"

For the first time since I'd met him, Harris actually smiled. "Well, that'd be mighty fine. Though I have to tell you, skipper, I'm gonna hold out for standard pay plus all the red meat I can eat."

And that was the second time he'd made a joke. I think.

Isabella will have to leave soon, I thought with regret. Ships don't sail themselves, so I have to go back to work. Back to work for a rest. But it grows more difficult each time to leave Emilia.

I found John Yeoh waiting for me in the office, with a sheaf of yellowing documents in his hand. "I heard, senhor capitão, that you are missing a third mate. May I apply for the position?"

His papers were all in order. If somewhat older than any I'd ever seen. I raised an eyebrow. Scratched my cheekbone. "What about your shop?"

Yeoh looked at me levelly. "It is thanks to you, Captain da Silva, that I am no longer a slave to time. The clocks have served their purpose." He glanced down at his hands. "I would ask only one thing."

"Go ahead," I said, lighting a cheroot.

"If *Isabella* ever sails to Ceylon," he said, "I shall ask you to summon Jing-Mei's ghost. And maybe I will be able to join her at last, and you will be missing a third mate. On the other hand, maybe after all these years she will be able to release me."

Well, there may have been stranger conditions to a contract of employment. But I doubt it. And since when did strangeness start to bother you, da Silva?

And finally. There is a low stretch of ruined wall up at the castle. I knew it as a child. And it was one of the first places I brought Emilia after I came home with her. It has the best view of all, better than any *miradouro*. This is where we're sitting now, Emilia and I. My arm around her shoulder, her head resting against me. In a moment, I'm going to kiss her. There's no one here to see. And if there were, I wouldn't care.

The weather is finally breaking. I look out to see, on the horizon, storm-clouds and a curtain of rain. There, where the sea ends and the sky begins.